"Terrific! Very Evelyn Waugh meets *The Sandbaggers*."
—John Chu, Hugo Award–winning author

"Powerfully seductive and wrenching."
—Fran Wilde, author of *Horizon*

"A glittering cabaret of a novel, with show-stopping language on every page."
—Lev AC Rosen, author of *Depth*

"Sexy and suspenseful, with characters who play for keeps . . . One that seduces before hitting you with an unforgettable kick."
—A. M. Dellamonica, LAMBDA Literary Award finalist

"Lust and betrayal, intrigue and treachery, feints within feints within feints—*Amberlough* will keep readers up late into the night."
—D. B. Jackson, author of the Thieftaker Chronicles

"Weirdly elegant, wholly engaging."
—Josh Lanyon, USA Book News Award for
GLBT Fiction and Eppie Award winner

"If you put David Bowie, China Miéville, and *Shakespeare in Love* into a blender, you might get something as rich and frothy as *Amberlough*."
—Cecilia Tan, author of the Struck by Lightning series

"Various rumors, rescues, and releases coincide toward the book's end— always believably, always unpredictably, and always in a superbly written, Art Deco–inspired atmosphere of louche extravagance."
—*The Seattle Review of Books*

"A sense of inevitable loss and futility permeates this rich drama."
—*Kirkus Reviews*

"A timely novel exploring the roots of hatred, nationalism, and fascism, while at the same time celebrating the diversity, love, romance, fashion, and joy the world is capable of producing, Donnelly's *Amberlough* is a thrill and a wonder from start to finish."
—*Book Riot*

ALSO BY LARA ELENA DONNELLY

Amberlough
Armistice

LARA ELENA DONNELLY

AMNESTY

A TOM DOHERTY ASSOCIATES BOOK · NEW YORK

AMNESTY

Copyright © 2019 by Lara Elena Donnelly

All rights reserved.

A Tor Book
Published by Tom Doherty Associates
175 Fifth Avenue
New York, NY 10010

www.tor-forge.com

Tor® is a registered trademark of Macmillan Publishing Group, LLC.

Library of Congress Cataloging-in-Publication Data

Names: Donnelly, Lara Elena, 1990– author.
Title: Amnesty / Lara Elena Donnelly.
Description: First Edition. | New York : Tor, 2019. | "A Tom Doherty
    Associates Book."
Identifiers: LCCN 2018047471 | ISBN 9781250173621 (trade pbk.) | ISBN
    9781250173614 (ebook)
Subjects: | GSAFD: Fantasy fiction.
Classification: LCC PS3604.O56326 A68 2019 | DDC 813/.6—dc23
LC record available at https://lccn.loc.gov/2018047471

Our books may be purchased in bulk for promotional, educational, or business use.
Please contact your local bookseller or the Macmillan Corporate and Premium
Sales Department at 1-800-221-7945, extension 5442, or by email at
MacmillanSpecialMarkets@macmillan.com.

First Edition: April 2019

Printed in the United States of America

0 9 8 7 6 5 4 3 2 1

TO EVERYONE WHO LENT A HAND ALONG THE WAY.

ACKNOWLEDGMENTS

Wow. Here we are. The last book in the Amberlough Dossier. We made it! And I do mean we. As always, this book is not just mine— it's the product of many people's love, support, and commiseration. Firstly, of course, my editor, Diana Pho, and my agent, Connor Goldsmith. Diana really whipped this book into shape so we'd end the trilogy strong, and Connor shone the light at the end of the tunnel so I had something to aim at as I trucked along. And all the gratitude to Desirae Friesen, publicist of publicists, who basically put this book in your hands.

The rest of this list is probably woefully incomplete. I know there are folks out there I've forgotten, and for that I truly apologize. Wherever you are, whoever you are: you have my undying gratitude!

My myriad communities of wonderful writer friends were indispensable as I closed out the trilogy. Special thanks go to Alpha student Zach Nash, who kick-started this plot with the two words "capitalist oligarchy." To all my friends in the Pub, of course, but most especially Jay Wolf, Andrea Tatjana, Jennifer Mace, Sarah Berner, and Marianne Kirby, who at various points solved particularly thorny problems for me. Also Nicasio Reed, who made me the dopest Amberlough playlist of all time and introduced me to Jidenna.

And Lex Beckett, Kelly Robson, Kellan Szpara, Sarah Pinsker, Jordan Sharpe, Debra Wilburn, and Alexandra Renwick: our Timberhouse retreat was exactly what this book needed in its second draft.

Shout-out to all the Clarion crew who have come on this journey, with special callouts for Patrick Ropp and Huw Evans, cheerleaders extraordinaire.

Kelsey Hercs, you are an inspiration and a joy to be around, not to mention a stellar playwright, and I am so pleased we stumbled into being friends. Eric Mersmann, thanks for being my due process consultant. I owe you some pickle flavored ice cream.

Thank you, of course, to my parents, who planted many words in my head as a small child by reading to me, and cared for the resultant carnivorous swamp plant. You're my biggest fans and probably have hand-sold enough copies of my books to put them into a second printing.

A world of thank-yous and apologies to the Routh family, who invited me into their home for the holidays and then fed me while I hunched over my laptop and frantically tried to wrap up the first draft of *Amnesty*, while simultaneously line-editing *Armistice*.

And most of all, my love and thanks to Eliot, who had to live with me while I finished this book. You're a hero, and you kept me sane.

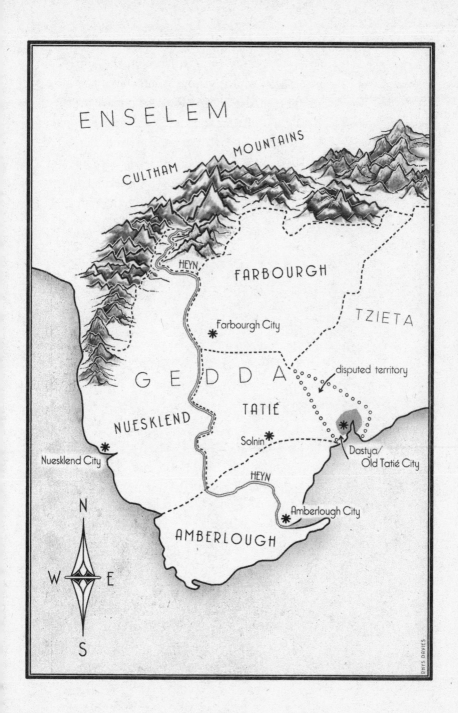

We act it to one another, all this hardness; but we aren't like that really, I mean . . . one can't be out in the cold all the time; one has to come in from the cold.

—John le Carré,
The Spy Who Came in from the Cold

I never knew a man who had better motives for all the trouble he caused.

—Graham Greene, *The Quiet American*

PART

1

CHAPTER

ONE

Aristide didn't hear the bell of his telephone over the racket of radio and ticker tape and typewriter keys. Even if he had, he wouldn't have answered. That was what secretaries were for. Because he hadn't had the benefit of a warning ring, Daoud caught him unawares, head sunk low to a ledger, spectacles sliding down his nose.

"Ari," said Daoud, and when Aristide finally heard his name it had the air of a third or fourth repetition.

"Sorry," he said, blinking as his vision adjusted for the top half of his bifocals. "What is it?"

"Telephone."

Aristide took off the new spectacles and pressed the heels of his hands into the aching muscles around his eyes. Damned new prescription. Damned old body. "Tell them to ring again tomorrow. I'm ready for a drink."

Daoud's lips crimped to one side, tugging the line of his beard askew. "It is His Highness. Prince Asiyah."

Attention pulled him taut as a piano wire. He set his pen aside with unwarranted care. "All right. Send it back."

There was every chance this was the warning Aristide had been ready for since last autumn, when he and Merrilee Cross sent their first cargo of tar to the newly pacified port of Amberlough. Asiyah wasn't vice or port authority by any stretch, nor was he precisely a confederate of Cross-Costa Imports or any of its multiple subsidiaries. Still, he had in the past let hints fall for an old friend. Perhaps out of pity or guilt, since the information Aristide originally cajoled from him led to neither profit nor satisfaction. Cyril DePaul had not appeared from the jungles of Liso.

Or perhaps this wasn't about the tar, but an order to cease skimming Porachin aid shipments. Aristide had done his best to keep *that* from royal or intelligence attention.

It had started small. Defeated at his original purpose and pushed south by fighting once war began in earnest, Aristide brought Daoud south and settled in Rarom, near the airfield. There was a seedy little bar where the pilots liked to drink and soon Aristide had a good rapport with Wedi, who kicked a carton or two his way when she thought they might not be missed.

Merrilee came down from Ul-Mejj when he started to cut in on her market. By then her city was on the front line anyway, so they set up their company in *his* backyard. Fewer unexploded shells.

They did well for themselves, redistributing rice and tobacco amongst the highest bidders. Police and royal agents largely looked the other way if their palms stayed greasy. But a prince would be another matter, especially now that the war was over and the royal family had face to save and laws to impose in the land they had reclaimed from republican control, where Porachin aid was sorely needed.

Aristide was prepared for a friendly tip. He was prepared for a royal summons. He was not prepared for what followed Asiyah's pleasantries.

"I have some news about a mutual friend," he said.

Their shared acquaintances fluttered through Aristide's mind like a handful of shuffled business cards. Pulan? Lillian? He kept in contact, if irregularly, with both of them by post, and sometimes by radio call if a special occasion warranted, though those were expensive and a pain in the rear to organize. Usually it was letters, and occasionally a telegram. In fact, Lillian had cabled him last week, with an invitation to an event he had flatly refused. He wouldn't cut the ribbon on a memorial so she could curry favor with Gedda's ministerial candidates. Not *that* memorial, anyway.

"Sorry," he said, realizing that Asiyah's silence had dragged into expectancy. "Who is it?"

"I cannot say on this line."

Which meant clandestine work. Conspiracy. Espionage. Aristide had less to do with foxes than with thugs these days. Pulan, Asiyah could have mentioned on the telephone. If not her, then . . .

As if the final tumbler of a stubborn lock had given way, the realization snapped into place with metallic clarity. It had been five years, but perhaps the jungle had given up its prize after all.

"Where?" His fingers tightened on the receiver; resin creaked at the seams.

"There is a flight to Dadang tonight," said Asiyah, and Aristide realized he had answered for a different, more pedestrian value of the word.

"No," he said. "Where did you find . . . ?" It wasn't that he remembered *not* to say the name. Only that he *couldn't*.

"Pack a bag," said Asiyah, "and be at the airfield by nine o'clock."

Aristide was not afraid of many things. He'd been in fights and ended them. He'd walked cliffs slippery with rain and sleet in darkness uncut by electric lights. He'd fended off wolves and foxes and folk bent on doing violence to his person. He'd gone hungry, slept in the street, sunk a knife into another man's belly, and put a bullet through somebody's skull.

He still hated flying.

By the time the Mgenu-330 picked itself up from the tarmac—three hours late, thanks to the weather—he had gotten therapeutically drunk. This had the effect of muting his terror when the little aircraft hit turbulence just after takeoff, but also increased his nausea when they banked to turn and the earth sank below the windowpane.

The flight was longer than he would have liked it to be. He should have stayed sober enough to get some work done—there were letters to write, both business and personal. Daoud had gawped at him when he said he'd be back in a few days, and come up with a raft of protests that mostly boiled down to reluctance over dealing with a testy Cross on his own.

But Aristide wasn't sober by any stretch, and terror combined with monotony put him into a numb contemplative state.

Five years he'd been in Liso. When he arrived in Oyoti, drenched by the first monsoon of the rainy season, he'd been so sure of success. Foolish. He could acknowledge that now. If he hadn't let himself get soft, he would have known it then, too. And it wasn't just lush living in Porachis that had dulled his edge; considered retrospectively, his wits hadn't seen a whetstone since he signed the deed for Baldwin Street.

He had achieved all the things he hoped to. Wasn't it what he had always told himself? *When I'm rich I won't have to worry about that.* He'd whispered it to himself until it was true, and then— stupidest of all—bought into the myth. Aristide Makricosta, king of the black market, monarch of the demimonde. Untouchable, untamable. Even the FOCIS's Master of the Hounds couldn't run him down, when it came to it, and instead turned belly-up beneath his teeth.

He hoped he'd learned his lesson. He would have liked to believe he was past arrogance now, only the thought itself smacked of the same.

Two years steaming in the equatorial rain forest, chasing phantoms through a war-torn jungle, had taught him to be leery of even the smallest trace of confidence. Anything that looked promising was likely to lead to disappointment. Anything that billed itself as a sure wager would inevitably end in embarrassment. Aristide had relearned caution in his later years, and greatly resented the lesson.

Yet here he was plastered into a seat ten thousand feet above the ground—oh, perdition take that particular line of thinking—on the strength of a single phone call.

He clutched the armrest as the plane banged through another patch of rough air, and reassured himself: This was not some cutthroat warlord baring rotten teeth, parting with dubious information at an inflated price. This was Prince Asiyah Sekibou, intelligence baron, just this side of an old friend. The last person Aristide knew who had seen Cyril DePaul alive, the last to speak to him, to hear his radio transmissions, and he was asking for nothing at all.

That roused Aristide's suspicions. Asiyah wanted something from him. But as many stones as he turned searching for some reason the prince might be lying—a trap, a ploy, a plot—he found he could not convince himself it was anything less than the truth. That certainty took the bottom out of his belly more surely than the airplane's sudden change in altitude as the pilot brought them down toward Souvay-Dadang International.

Asiyah was waiting on the tarmac in the back of a black auto that would have been discreet at the curb, but was less so parked in the midst of a dozen airplanes.

Dawn had just begun to breathe into the east, paling the cobalt sky where it was not already bleached by the lights of Dadang. A bald woman in aviator sunglasses she did not need held the rear passenger door for Aristide, then got into the driver's seat and put the car in gear.

"It's good to see you," said Asiyah. He did not look as if he had been to bed; stubble textured the skin of his jaw, and there was a small stain on the front of his wrinkled red tunic, as though he had spilled—

"Coffee?" He offered Aristide a green metal thermos.

Aristide took the flask and cranked the lid open. A blast of bitter, fragrant steam cleared his altitude-stuffed sinuses and blunted the edge of his headache. It caught in the back of his throat and made him start to cough: a phlegmy hack that had latched onto his lungs about a year ago, which no mentholated cigarette or mustard compress would dislodge. He should see a doctor, but after his last appointment he was honestly afraid to. Like the plane, it put ice in his belly that even the barrel of a gun would not.

He poured coffee carefully into the lid of the thermos, which doubled as a cup. "Did you expect I might be drunk?" he asked, in between cautious sips.

Asiyah shrugged. "I only thought you might need something."

Aristide poured a second cup and swallowed too quickly, to keep from saying something tart, which his disheveled state would instantly belie. When he had finished, he screwed the lid back into place and, addressing the thermos rather than Asiyah, asked, "Well. Where is he?"

"Safe."

It alarmed Aristide more than it should have, to know there had been other possibilities. "And I can see him? Speak with him?"

"I would not tell you to fly to Dadang, if you could not. But better to wait—it is only half past five now. Most people are not awake. Take a short sleep. Eat breakfast."

"Is there a good hotel near . . . wherever it is?"

"Mm-hm." Asiyah slid the divider between the backseat and the driver and said something in Shedengue that Aristide only minimally understood—an order by the sound of it, but a polite one. She answered, one word, and he slid the panel back into place.

Aristide swallowed hard, tasting coffee already gone sour behind his teeth. "Thank you," he said. "For all of this." That kind of thing only came out of his mouth with ease onstage, and he hadn't faced an audience in a long time. The more he meant the sentiments, the more they stuck in his craw. This time they left his throat aching.

Asiyah made a wordless sound: an acknowledgment of the gratitude that didn't accept it.

Well, he'd suspected as much, but it was still a relief to find this wasn't charity. "What is it?"

"I do not do this for you," said Asiyah. "Do you understand? I can only bring you in because he has already been debriefed. Even now, it is not something I should do. But."

"You want something from me." Slipping into the negotiation was the most comfortable he'd felt since Daoud knocked on his door to tell him who was on the line. "Go on. What is it?"

Asiyah had the grace to look into his lap, aiming an abashed smile at the gilded hem of his tunic where it stretched across his knees. "The aid shipments."

It had only been a matter of time, and the war was winding down now anyway. "Ah well," said Aristide. "The revenue from black market beans wouldn't have lasted forever. I'll wrap up the operation when I get back to Rarom." As he said it, it caught him by surprise. As if, after whatever happened today, he would return so easily to daily life. As if, perhaps, this were not real at all, but a strange dream from which he would wake disoriented beneath the mosquito netting of his bedroom, in the airy stucco house on Blatti Azhed. The flight had certainly felt like a nightmare, and the lingering effects of too much gin put every word and action at a slight remove from reality.

Asiyah's smile faltered, then fell. "It is . . . no. It is more complicated. I do not need for you to stop. Only to work with me. To be more . . . strategic?"

This was the problem with food aid sent to violent places—it turned essentials into bargaining chips, so that rice and palm oil meant guns, power, territory. "You want me to cut off the people who are causing you problems."

"That is . . . correct, mostly. Yes."

"Anyone in particular?" In his head, he began to run through a list of their higher-profile customers, but the car pulled to a stop and Asiyah put a hand to his knee.

"Not now, Aristide. We will talk business later. Over dinner, maybe? Perhaps tomorrow. Now, you have time to sleep. To . . . prepare." Asiyah gave him a card. "Ring when you are ready."

Aristide put the card into his jacket pocket without looking at it; afraid if he knew the number, he might dial immediately. Also afraid that if he held it any longer, he would fling it as far from his person as possible, to save himself this reckoning.

CHAPTER

TWO

_____

The house on Coral Street was cold and empty, running on bare-bones staff, most of the rooms shut. Like the street itself, and the city: still recovering from strife and civil war.

"Ma'am." Magnusson the butler swung the front door open to admit her, like a clockwork figurine timed to her arrival. The effect was rather spoiled by the reading glasses on a chain around his neck. A well-thumbed copy of _Rita Ryder and the Red Midnight_ peeped out from one of the cubbies beneath the bench in the vestibule.

Lillian hadn't wanted to keep two houses at once, on an interim government salary that wouldn't last past the upcoming election. Nor could she truly afford folk to run them. But while Damesfort was less badly damaged, and a necessary retreat at the weekends, she still needed a place in the city to sleep. Heating a bedroom in the house was cheaper than long-term residence at a hotel, even if the place depressed her. And with her schedule, and Jinadh's, staff was a necessity.

Both the town and country houses had been given to mid-level Ospie ministers of some stripe or another. They'd redecorated, re-arranged, sold off priceless antiques. The bottom floor of the house on Coral Street had been ransacked during riots, but the upper floors were still livable, barely. They'd had enough money to clean out the ground-floor library and put a desk in it, though the room was still empty of books.

The Ospies had scratched up every aspect of her life. But now at least she was in residence, and when she was settled and could af-ford it, she would put things right.

"How was your appointment with Ms. Higata?" asked Magnus-son, taking her coat and briefcase.

Rinko Higata had been captain of the Sackett debate team when Lillian matriculated: a woman of unbending will channeled through poise as even as a perfectly weighted blade. She'd gone on to study law, and made quite a name for herself, but left Amberlough for Inorugara when the Ospies made Gedda . . . inhospitable. She was back now, and taking on charity cases.

"None, I'm afraid. I didn't think she'd be able to help much, but at least she would have been free."

All of Lillian's assets had mysteriously evaporated after she fled Porachis. There were no records to prove it had all gone into Ospie pockets, but that was where she'd hoped to bring in legal aid. Rinko specialized in white-collar criminal defense and was a sorceress with financial paper trails, but where all evidence had been destroyed, she could not fit a wedge in.

"And the committee meeting?" Magnusson, a consummate pro-fessional even under budgetary constraints, produced a silver tray— slightly dented—and a glass of whiskey, neat. Filling the library might be an extravagance, but the bar was a medicinal necessity.

"A dogfight, as you might expect. Bihaz isn't sure it's a good idea to invite Makricosta to the dedication—thinks it draws too much attention back to . . . awkward rumors. Distracts from the solemn purpose of the event. And Miles is still arguing against the whole enterprise, though it's a bit late now."

"And Ms. Simons?"

"Honora?" Another school friend, who'd ridden out the Ospies playing nice and smiling at parties, giving what money she could spare to innocuous charities who funneled half of it to the Catwalk. "She apologized for Miles's behavior very nicely once he'd left the room." Lillian put away half her whiskey and sighed. "Bags packed?"

"And everyone else on their way for the weekend."

"Shouldn't you have gone and left Bern?"

"Ma'am," said Magnusson. "I apologize if I overstepped, but Mr. Addas is likely to benefit from a footman's services more than mine, with Ms. Wilce there to see to the house."

"You wanted time to read," she said, and was rewarded with a faint blush high on his gaunt cheeks. It was perhaps a trifle familiar, but adversity seemed to spawn that kind of thing.

Magnusson was a Geddan expatriate who'd married an Asunan woman early in his life and been widowed early, too. He spoke the language fluently and had been a boon to them; worth every cent they couldn't afford when they arrived in Sunho. By the time they left they had been doing well enough: Lillian as the director of public relations for the Sunho offices of Camden Standard Trade, and Jinadh as the assistant culture editor at the Asunan branch of Siebenthal's. Working themselves nearly to death, yes, but they could pay Magnusson to keep their house.

When the Ospies finally crumbled, he wanted to come back: he hadn't seen Gedda in fifteen years. Lillian sympathized. And when Honora reached out to her about a position in the interim government's press and public relations wing, she offered him the chance to come along. Siebenthal's conjured up a post for Jinadh at the *Observer*, a paper they'd recently purchased in Amberlough City. He'd taken a pay cut but so far loved the work.

"The last train to Damesfort leaves in an hour," said Magnusson, "though there's one in half that time you might still catch."

"If it's running," she said. The country's railways were a mess, half of them bombed into uselessness. The Catwalk's strategy of starve, divide, and conquer had been successful in the end, but left chaos in its wake. A fact that both leading ministerial candidates were dealing with in their campaigns. Frye as a piece of her platform, and Saeger as a perpetrator of the bombings.

Despite the upcoming dedication ceremony, the Catwalk weren't heroes to everyone.

"Ma'am," said Magnusson. "Before you go, there was a telegram while you were out." He inclined his head toward the mail tray on the hall card table.

Makricosta.

They kept in spotty touch, but enough that she'd felt comfortable reaching out to him about the ceremony. The whole thing was more Honora's line; Lillian coordinated press briefings, put together public statements for the interim ministers and governing council. Honora threw the kinds of parties that made the provisional government look like it knew what it was doing: luncheons, galas, charity breakfasts. Pomp could put a spark of confidence into anyone's breast.

When the idea for the monument first came up for discussion, it was Honora who had cornered Lillian and asked, almost breathless, "Is there any chance of bringing Makricosta here? It would be like living history."

And though she'd strenuously objected, on any number of grounds, Honora wore her down. Lillian owed her for the job, and hated to owe anyone.

Aristide flatly refused the first time—the telegram had simply read *No*—but the second time he'd nearly set the onionskin alight with ire, which she thought was progress. There hadn't been a reply to her third telegram . . . yet.

The committee was breathing down her neck, asking when they could finalize the list of speakers and start to publicize the ceremony. She couldn't put them off much longer.

Trepidatiously, she set aside her whiskey and slit the seal.

```
CYRIL IN DADANG STOP ARI GONE TO SEE STOP
DIRECT CORRESPONDENCE GRAND LDOTHO HOTEL
STOP D QASSAN END
```

The delicate paper crackled in the rush of her indrawn breath.

"Ma'am?" Magnusson's shoes creaked as he shifted his weight, ready for orders.

Lillian had none. The balance of sounds around her shifted, so the hiss of a car through the rainy street roared in her ears, while Magnusson's voice sounded leagues away. Her pulse slammed behind her eyes, hard enough to ache.

"Ma'am. Ms. DePaul." Magnusson cupped her elbow, pressed a hand between her shoulder blades. "Are you all right?"

Unmindful of propriety or class divide, she clutched at his forearm. "A chair," she said, and he led her to the telephone bench beneath the stairs.

"Bad news?" he asked.

"No," she said. "I don't know."

"A glass of water?"

"Where's my whiskey?" she said, clutching the worn green velvet of the armrest. Her sweat stained the soft nap of the cloth. She lowered her palm and wiped it on her mackintosh, which she had not yet removed.

Magnusson retrieved her glass from the card table. Letting out a stale breath, Lillian forced herself to look again at the telegram. Cyril's name in all capital letters, slightly smudged at the bottom of the *y*. Cyril was in Dadang. Cyril had been found.

She had given him up for dead years ago. There had been a brief flare of hope in Porachis, but then a long stretch of no news during which her own life had become too complicated to admit of a brother who was anything but dead. In the chaos of adjusting to Sunho, securing a marriage license and work permits, scouting for employment, and finding tutors and a school for Stephen, she had not had time nor energy for anything but her old pedestrian grief. Now, guilt seized her, counting the years she could have been looking for her brother, years she should at least have *hoped*.

"Your whiskey, ma'am."

She nearly jumped, but habit stayed her. "Thank you, Magnusson."

"I don't mean to pry," he said, and let it hang.

What was she supposed to rotten tell him? The telegram gave her nothing. So Cyril was alive. Was he coming home? Was he sane? Healthy? In one piece?

"It seems," she began, then shook her head. "I've had some news. I . . ."

Mother and sons, she was supposed to be on the train to Carmody in twenty minutes. What if Daoud sent her another message here?

"Can you stay here tonight?" she asked Magnusson. "Take the train up in the morning?"

"Of course," he said, and though he ought to have been glad of the time to read, he looked more concerned than anything.

"Thank you. I need to send a telegram. Right now. I'm sorry, I know this is leagues below your purview. If Bern were here . . ."

"It's quite all right," said Magnusson, picking up the pen from the telephone bench and tearing a piece of stationery from the pad. "Go ahead."

"It's going to Cross-Costa Imports, Blatti Iynodib, Rarom third zone, Ibdassi. That's Liso. Yes, you know. Attention Mr. Daoud Qassan. All further correspondence Damesfort, Carmody, Dameskill County, et cetera. Stop. Please be in touch with all new developments. Stop. Arrange radio call if necessary. Stop. My name. End. And if anything comes overnight—"

"I'll forward it to Damesfort before I close the house. Or, if it comes late, I'll bring it up."

"Thank you." She finally finished the whiskey, and it struck the bottom of her stomach like a depth charge.

The last train into Carmody got her to the station very late indeed. Martí met her at the bottom of the steps, looking about as beleaguered as Lillian felt.

"I'm sorry to drag you out at this time of night," she said, surrendering her suitcase.

Martí bowed her head, less out of deference than to hide a yawn.

Like many other things, Lillian couldn't afford a driver. But it was that or miss meetings depending on the whims of the railroad and the trolleys, both of which were still recovering from the Catwalk's onslaught late in the Ospies' tenure. Lillian had only taken the train tonight because Jinadh preferred to avoid it; Geddans still felt the sting of the Spice War, and some folk were sour over Gedda's most recent entanglement with Jinadh's natal country.

They needed the car at Damesfort anyhow: Martí was meant to fetch Stephen from school tomorrow. Lillian didn't trust him on the train alone, after the letters they'd been getting from the head.

There'd been one on the mail tray nearly every week this term, ending with the blow that Cantrell would prefer if Stephen took some time away from school. More specifically, all of Leighberth term. Depending on his attitude, and his academic performance gauged by written and oral exams, he might return on sufferance after Equinox to finish out the year. If he failed the exam or—more likely—did not improve his manners, he was out of Cantrell with a black mark by his name, and lost his chance at many of the better secondary schools.

Run down from chasing worry's tail, Lillian had fallen asleep by the time Martí brought them level with the front steps of Damesfort. She woke to the sound of the slamming driver's side door and the pain of a kink in her neck. Warm light grew wider in her peripheral vision and she had to blink when she turned toward it. A familiar silhouette came into focus, already jogging down the steps.

«You're here,» said Jinadh. He sounded relieved. Her schedule lately had required more last-minute changes of plan than she knew he preferred. And he was still adjusting to life in Amberlough; she sometimes caught resentment in his words, like the faintest trace of smoke on the wind. At least in Asu they had both been unmoored from familiar society. In Gedda she was on reasonably comfortable ground; he had no frame of reference, and it made him apt to snarl.

She climbed out of the car and stretched before dipping to kiss his cheek. "Have there been any calls? Cables?"

«It's three in the morning.»

"I know." She took a steadying breath of clean country air, and when she exhaled, it turned to steam. They had left the rain behind, and the skies over the estate were patchy with silver clouds. Bands of stars crossed the pristine sky.

"There has not been anything," said Jinadh, as if saying it in Geddan would convince her more thoroughly. «Come inside. Come to bed. It's freezing.» It was colder here than in the city, where the closely packed buildings sheltered most streets from the wind. Jinadh, born in the tropics, wore a flannel-lined dressing gown over a cabled sweater, and still shivered.

"You go," she said. "I just want to pop into the library for a minute."

He scoffed. «Don't be ridiculous.»

"I'm *not*."

Martí jumped at the hard turn Lillian's voice took. Jinadh stepped back. «One night without this would have been nice.»

"I'm sorry." She put her palm to her forehead, as if she could smooth her thoughts into order. Her marriage had not borne up well beneath the strain of yet another immigration and a badly mannered teenage son. This latest development would likely do no wonders for it, either. "I just don't think I'll be *able* to sleep. I had some news. Just before I left the city."

"Work can wait a few hours, surely," said Jinadh. "Please don't ring them until morning."

"It wasn't—" She stopped herself, conscious of Martí moving bags, of Bern the footman hovering at the open door. "Later."

That softened the irritation in his face to curiosity, which was worse because it was unfamiliar. «If you're going to the library,» he said, and she resigned herself to company.

"Just leave the bags in the hall, Martí," she said. "Get yourself to bed."

"Yes, ma'am. Thank you." Martí tipped her cap and dragged back out to take the car to the garage.

"You, too, Bern." Lillian waved the footman off when he tried to take her suitcase. "I'll deal with it."

"Ma'am," he said, and stifled a yawn.

«What's going on?» asked Jinadh, close enough their shoulders brushed. Proximity encouraged her exhaustion and she sagged against him, nose in his hair. Hostility melted out of her as she breathed his scent. Her eyes prickled and she bit the inside of her cheek.

"They . . ." She had to take another breath. Caution sent her into Porashtu. «Jinadh, they found him.»

There was a beat, a moment where he didn't know who she meant.

"Cyril," she said, so softly only he would hear.

He stopped in the center of the hall and caught her elbow, turned her to face him. Their eyes met briefly and she faltered, so that by the time he had his arms around her she was choking on a sob she should have let out hours ago.

"Not here," she said, cheek wet against his ear.

His hand tightened on her elbow and guided her deeper into her own family's home, as if she had forgotten the way. She almost felt she had. Jinadh flicked the light switch just before they reached the library and plunged the front hall into darkness. The remnants of a fire burned in the library hearth, and the tufted leather sofa was warm. A crocheted blanket hung over one arm, mussed from recent occupancy.

"You were waiting up for me," she said.

He shrugged. Then, sitting by her, «Tell me.»

«I don't know.» She twisted the blanket in her hands, stretching the stitches. «I had a telegram, but it didn't *say* anything. Only that he turned up, and Makricosta went to see him. It was *three lines,* Jinadh. That's all. And my *brother*—» She put her hand over her mouth to stop the flow of words, because there didn't seem to be another way. Jinadh closed his own over it gently, prising her chilled fingers from her cheeks.

«If you need to go to him, you must. We can probably afford to send you. And I know I was very insistent, but Stephen and I can take care of ourselves during the holiday.»

"Oh, temple *bells*," she said, squeezing her eyes shut so tightly she saw stars. "I can't *leave*. The dedication ceremony, Jinadh. And the last months of campaigning. If I want to . . . I can't be in *Liso* for that."

She didn't dare open her eyes after she realized what she had said; she could feel Jinadh pulling away from her.

Part of the tension that had simmered between them since their arrival was Lillian's determination to install herself in whatever administration took the Cliff House. Her position with the provisional government, by its nature, would not last. She was well qualified to shill for the state, and it might help put a shine on the family name, which had grown a bit tarnished in recent years.

Former Catwalk strategist Opal Saeger, erstwhile right hand of Cordelia Lehane, had led the Amberlinian chapter of the Geddan Alliance of Theatrical Technicians for two terms before the rise of the Ospies, representing the sizable local union at national meetings. Political experience, to be sure, but in Lillian's opinion not nearly enough to run a country on.

Saeger was young—younger than Lillian—and her rhetoric naive, which won her a strong following in the university crowd. Her political party, Forward Gedda, centered largely on social programs, leaving large swathes of domestic and foreign policy either unaddressed or thrown together in a confused jumble.

Industrial doyenne Emmeline Frye, former Nuesklend City alderman, already had Lillian's vote. But Saeger didn't need to know that. Lillian would take a press position under either candidate. Jinadh, who had been born into court politics and been greatly relieved to escape it, was not eager for Lillian to reenter the fray.

Even *she* was appalled at her reluctance to go to Liso. But it simply couldn't be done if she wanted to stay on the radar as a potential appointee.

"I had Magnusson send a cable to Daoud, to say any news should come here. And anything that comes tonight or tomorrow he's said he'll bring along."

"Fine," said Jinadh, and she saw him fighting to swallow her practicality. "So they will cable you here. What then? Will he come to Gedda?"

That brought her up like a hunter balking at a fence. "I'm . . . I don't know. I suppose we could have him? Would you mind?"

"Would it be safe?"

The Ospie press had not been kind to the DePauls, following Lillian's flight from Porachis. Her liaison with Jinadh had been blown out of proportion to the tune of espionage, eventually linked—not so erroneously—to Porachin money and Lisoan arms funneled to the Catwalk. She had been able to spin that story in her favor, after Acherby was deposed. What they had printed about Cyril . . . There was less room to maneuver, there.

A multiple murderer and turncoat to all sides. No loyalty paid to the OSP, nor to the FOCIS, which at least would have made him an honorable opponent. The only angle a sympathetic reader could latch onto was his affair with Aristide Makricosta, which had been trotted out briefly as a small detail in a sorry, sordid string of them. Someone in Acherby's administration had clearly realized there was a hook there, and bent it down as flat as it would go.

Lillian rubbed at the stiff spot in her neck. "As safe as it is for anyone, these days. There's been more than enough news in the last five years to bury anything we'd rather stay out of the sun."

«If this scheme of yours plays out,» said Jinadh. «If you end up press secretary—»

«Then I will be perfectly placed to deal with that kind of problem.»

«What about Stephen?»

«What about him?»

«You don't think your brother might be a . . . that he might not be the best role model?»

Lillian rolled her eyes. "They'll probably get along like dogs." Then, seeing Jinadh's confusion at the idiom, she added, «Um, friendly as a wick and a match?»

«Lillian, I'm serious,» said Jinadh. Firelight reflected from deep within his eyes—as deeply as he hid his anger.

«I know.» She put her hands over his. «I'm sorry.»

He shook his head. «No. No, I should be. This is your weight. I'm supposed to help you carry, and I'm scolding.»

"We'll just have to wait and see," she said. "I can't tell you what I plan to do right now."

He nodded, somber, turning his hands palm up to take hers where they lay together on his lap. With an air of resolve, he said, «It will be good, if he comes. I always . . . it hurt, that you had no family for me to meet, and you could not meet mine.»

«I don't think it will be like that. Not . . . not like a happy re-union. I don't know what it will be like. I don't know what *he* will be like.»

«He'll be your brother,» said Jinadh. «No matter what he's like, I'll be glad to have met him. Especially at Solstice.»

CHAPTER

THREE

"I will warn you," said Asiyah. "He is not . . . he is not looking so good, maybe, as you remember him."

They stood in the courtyard of a family compound in the outskirts of Dadang. A fat bottle palm squatted by a well, casting crosshatched shade. Colorful tunics and shawls hung to dry on lines strung between semiseparate houses. Aristide wondered who they belonged to. Surely no one *lived* here. Still, the illusion was admirable. And focusing on the tradecraft kept him from thinking about what he was about to do.

"He spent a long time in enemy territory," Asiyah continued. "He . . . bah." Dropping into Porashtu, which Aristide understood poorly but far better than Shedengue, Asiyah said, «Lived by his wits?»

Aristide nodded, wondering where Cyril had learned to do that.

Thinking of all the questions he never asked: about that livid scar that crossed his middle, the odd habits of watchfulness that haunted his steps as he moved through the world. Where had a desk-bound son of privilege learned such things? What other ways had life marked him now?

"Are you ready?" asked Asiyah.

Aristide hated that he was so transparent in this. He glowered at Asiyah. His anger hid nothing, but it made him feel a little better.

"Come," said the prince, and swung open the door.

The widening arc of sunlight illuminated a comfortable sitting room, pegs scattered around a board where someone had abandoned a game of solitaire. The hush that hung over the house reminded Aristide of an empty film set, or backstage early in the afternoon. A place prepared for drama.

Asiyah stopped at the end of a long corridor, with a door at the other end. Aristide felt laughter threaten, faintly hysterical. If this had been one of his films, he wouldn't have shot it any differently. Maybe a little dolly zoom to heighten the tension. He certainly felt dizzy staring down the hall.

"I will wait here," said Asiyah, and retreated to the sofa and the peg solitaire.

"He knows," said Aristide. "Right? That I'm coming?"

Asiyah nodded once, then pinched a yellow peg from the table and placed it pointedly in a hole.

Aristide hesitated for a moment longer then stepped into the corridor, which stretched before him like taffy until he was, quite suddenly, at the door.

Should he knock? It seemed absurd. But it was a courtesy he expected Cyril had not been granted in some time. And it put off the inevitable that much longer.

When his knuckles struck the wood he checked the blow, then worried it had landed too softly. He was about to knock again, when something rustled behind the door.

Every scrap of air left his lungs.

"Come in."

Disappointment hollowed him out. The voice wasn't right. He could hear it in his memory: its warm timbre and smooth tones as rich and lived-in as a cotton velvet smoking jacket, or the curves of heirloom furniture. This voice was hoarse and curt with ragged edges.

The silence stretched, aching, until it was broken by another rustle. This sound Aristide could pinpoint with ease: a newspaper page, insolently turned.

The crackle of paper, timed perfectly, struck a chord: Cyril at the breakfast table, avoiding an awkward question by the turn of another page—the licked thumb, the moment's pause before the sheet of newsprint swept in front of his face and settled against its fellows. The flash of his eyes in the flicker of paper, like a zoetrope. Sometimes Aristide caught him watching in that slight gap. After, they pretended that their eyes had never met.

When he opened the door, he couldn't help but stare.

It was certainly Cyril. It had to be. Behind the bulwark of the paper, his eyes were sharp and blue as Aristide remembered them: the center of a candle flame. But now they were rimmed in red and sunk deep in shadow, the thin skin around them stained purple with exhaustion.

Cyril's hair, which shone in Aristide's memory as yellow gold, slick with oil and sticky with wax, had been rudely clipped close to his skull, showing dirty scalp beneath the stubble. His face had settled into pouches and pulled into lines. He was nearly ten years younger than Aristide, but looked a decade older.

Muscle had melted from his bones. Aristide would have put him at a little less than ten stone, except for the weight that heavy drinking had hung around his waist. The same had burst capillaries across his cheeks and nose—once straight and sharp as a knife blade, now buckled at the center and healed badly.

Aristide had once marveled that whatever violence had beaten Cyril body and mind, it had spared his delicate nose. Left it for him to stare down in moments of inbred, monied arrogance. Now even that had been taken from him.

He looked terrible.

If Cyril was as—what? Devastated? Astonished? What was this echoing emptiness of an emotion? If he was feeling as strange as Aristide, he hardly showed it. Instead, he folded the newspaper and set it aside, then picked up a cigarette smoldering in the ashtray. He held it cupped beneath his palm, cagey and cramped, as though he expected the wind or rain to put it out. A shame: He had been such an elegant smoker.

Aristide shut the door, too hard. Cyril jumped, then settled back into his chair as if he hadn't noticed his own tic.

They were in what would have been a bedroom, if this had really been a home. It was clear of furniture except for two caned chairs and a plank table. Aristide took the seat opposite Cyril.

"Hello," he said, and immediately felt like a fool.

"Stones," said Cyril. He took a drag on the straight and let it out slowly. "You got old."

It wasn't true. Well. Halfway. When Cyril looked at Aristide he could see everything the other man had been. The years hadn't diminished him: only made him slightly more delicate. He'd always been evasive about his age, and good at avoiding it as a topic of conversation. But in the intervening years it seemed to have caught up with him. There was something brittle in his movements and his manner. Or perhaps that was only the situation in which they found themselves.

And anyway, he couldn't be *that* old, silver hair notwithstanding. It looked good on him: the roots gleamed, and faded into dusty streaks of brown and black at the bottom of his shingle, set in waves.

Still, cruelty comforted Cyril. It was be cruel or come apart, and he knew which option would hurt less.

"You don't exactly look—" said Aristide, then stopped when his voice edged toward breaking.

"Say it," said Cyril, who wouldn't be able to bear it if Ari went maudlin on him. "I look awful."

"Like somebody peeled you off their shoe."

The cadence of his speech, the slang, scooped a chunk from Cyril's heart he hadn't realized he had left to lose. He took another drag on his cigarette to fill the hole. He'd killed his sense of taste, smoking too much, drinking too much, taking tar when other vices wouldn't cut the tension or dull the pain. The cigarette tasted like nothing now; it only burned.

"Asiyah told me you were behind enemy lines," said Aristide. "I knew you had been working for the LSI, but last I heard . . ."

"I was dead." He'd thought he had been, too. And there had been times he wished it were true. A part of him, maybe, still did. "I came close."

"So were you abducted?" asked Aristide. "Or did you run?"

"I haven't had a talent for that, historically." He let the words fall between them caustic as lye, because it was easier to be angry at Aristide than at himself.

And Ari did pull back as if it stung. Cyril could spot all the ways in which he reassembled himself, and wondered if he had honed his observational skills so much more sharply in the time since they had last seen one another, or if Ari was getting sloppy. Or if this was just long-dormant familiarity with the other man's affectations, rising to the surface.

Of the three options he preferred the first. The other two he didn't consider too closely, for different reasons. Now that he had the luxury to think beyond survival and subterfuge, he found his mind was a field of unexploded ordinance.

"So," said Aristide. "It really was republican militants?"

Cyril nodded, slipped back into debriefing mode. "They came in the middle of the night, said they knew what I was doing for the south. Beat me and hauled me back to camp." Here, he glossed over the gruesome pieces, which he had reported in full detail for Asiyah's people. Given a choice—he would always make sure he had a choice, in the future—he would never repeat any of it to another living soul. "They kept me for a week. I didn't tell them anything." Tits, he'd need to work on that defensive tone; it gave away too much. "They would've killed me, but they were close to the border and a raiding party found them. Destroyed the place. Saved my life."

"Why didn't you go back across the border?"

"Did I say they rescued me?" He'd fallen out of debriefing clarity, he realized, into the safety of vagueness. "I woke up in a pile of ashes. They'd burned the place around me. Maybe they thought I was dead, or didn't realize I was there. Maybe they didn't give two dried shits. I don't know."

He pulled another cigarette from the lidded basket on the table and lit it from the end of his expiring straight, which he snuck into the pocket of his waistcoat with the four others he'd already smoked this morning. They'd dug up a gnarled old three-piece linen affair for him, somewhere. Just for this meeting, he suspected. To make him feel more comfortable? Rotten parody. It fit badly. He'd have been more at ease in a tunic and drawstring trousers. Though anything was better than the rags they'd stripped him out of on arrival.

Aristide reached for the cigarette basket.

"They didn't leave me any matches," said Cyril. "No knives, either. Nothing interesting."

"Why?" asked Ari. "Would you have . . . gotten up to mischief?" He stumbled on the playfulness. Cyril analyzed the possible tracks his sentence might have taken: *Set the house on fire? Done yourself harm?*

He analyzed his own answers, and decided not to provide any of them. Only a smile screwed ratchet-tight.

Aristide took a lighter from his jacket pocket and tapped it on the table with a painful, pointed flourish. It was a beautiful object: purple enamel with gold braiding at the cap. Something Cyril would have teased him for, an age ago. Now he had an absurd urge to snatch it, weigh it in his hand, put his tongue to its vivid smoothness. Instead he watched, dry-mouthed, as Aristide lit his straight with hands that trembled, almost imperceptibly.

Ari with unsteady hands. What kind of world had he come back to?

"What happened then?" Smoke barely softened the edges of Ari's words, which were surprisingly curt. Well, Cyril could play that game; had been, since the door opened. Get the barricades up and dig your heels into the mud.

"I've already been debriefed, Aristide." He crossed his arms. "Why are you here?"

"Someone needed to come, and I was closest. I had my secretary send a cable to your sister. Lucky thing we've kept in touch."

Sacred arches. "You've met *Lillian*?" It was too much to ask: return to a world where social interactions weren't predicated on strength, arms, information. Readjust. Meet your old lover; the one you'd almost . . . well. And then find out that, while you'd been embedded in purgatory, he'd been jawing with your sister? "I'll wager *that* went well."

"Better than it might have," said Aristide. There was a world of subtext in the angle of his wrist, the way he stared at the ash on his straight. Silence built like a fogbank, precariously caught on craggy hills. Just before it culminated in something smothering, Aristide blew it away with a change of topic, a change of tone. "I looked for you, you know."

Cyril tipped his head to the side, inviting the rest without evincing any particular interest.

"Not right away. When you didn't . . . when I didn't hear anything. But while I was in Porachis, when I met Lillian, some information came to light. I heard you had been seen in Liso. Asiyah was very accommodating, though he didn't believe you were still alive. It's why I came. This would have been what, five years ago? Anyway, he said you'd been trying to get me out, with your ill-fated machinations. It seems we were working at cross-purposes. I felt . . . compelled to search for you."

It was like walking through a swamp, unsure of the ground in front of him. This was not some heartfelt confession. If Ari was telling him this story, there was a sinkhole somewhere in it. One wrong step would drown him in mud and crush his lungs.

"You didn't find me," Cyril said, because sometimes one could count on facts.

"Well," said Aristide. "I stopped looking, didn't I?"

Cyril didn't want it to hurt. It *shouldn't* have. But it was delivered with theatrical perfection, calculated to pass between his ribs and kill. "Why?"

"Sorry?" Aristide cocked his head, one ear closer to Cyril. "Didn't catch that."

He was being needlessly cruel now. Cyril gritted his teeth and forced the words between them. "Why did you stop?"

"Well, darling." Now he had cut himself with his own vicious edge, and a thread of pain slid through his words like blood. "How long were you out there? Eight years? I wasn't exactly keeping the lowest of profiles, and there are newspapers, even in the jungle. It just finally hit, like a sandbag to my head: Even if you were alive, you never came looking for me."

And Cyril, who had nearly drowned before—who knew the sensation and still lived in fear of it—felt the waters of guilt close over his head. "I suppose you want an apology."

Aristide, apparently feeling better for having got that pettiness out of the way, put the ember of his straight into the ashtray and said, almost cheerful: "I'd settle for lunch."

And because Cyril owed and owed and owed—Aristide, Amberlough, everyone—he went along.

Cyril's intelligence and experience had been gold to cells of royalists in northern territory, but it wasn't worth much to the LSI with the war as good as ended. They'd wrung him like a dishrag over the course of a week holed up in that family compound. They wouldn't have brought Ari to the house if they weren't done with all that it required.

He was free to go.

Liso owed him a pension. It felt very academic. A set of requirements to fulfill so he'd have somewhere to set his carcass down until it died.

In the meantime, he let himself be bundled into a car and driven through the city, and sat on his stool when he was pointed toward it.

Under the low ceiling of a dark taverna, empty at midday, the silence between them seemed compressed, pressurized. Ari ordered a cocktail in rough Porashtu, which the bartender half-spoke—a double martini, very dry, with a twist. Cyril lit another cigarette. The constant availability of something he'd had to scrounge for made it hard to stop. Nicotine hummed beneath his skin. He took a handful of matchbooks when the bartender's back was turned, and put them in his jacket pocket. Perhaps the suit hadn't been such a bad idea. A tunic and trousers wouldn't have afforded him so many spots to stash his spoils.

"You know," said Aristide, after his first martini arrived. "I'm not particularly hungry."

Cyril snorted. "Looking after your figure?"

"And you *do* feel like eating?"

Stones, the arch of his eyebrow put a cramp in Cyril's gut that had nothing to do with hunger. He took a rueful drag on his straight and then rolled it between his fingers, letting smoke flow through his field of vision like fog rolling in. It helped when he spoke; made the world feel far away. "Why lunch, then?"

"Because Asiyah's safe house didn't have a bar." Aristide put the rest of his drink down his gullet and gestured for another one. "Rye and soda, still? I think I see a bottle of Carter Bowles back there."

Cyril shrugged. He hadn't had rye since . . . well, he'd stopped counting. He was unused to preference and frankly, at this juncture, it seemed pointless. "I'll take what I can get."

They sat, unspeaking, as the bartender mixed and poured. It wasn't until Cyril put the first warm swallow of whiskey into his belly that he finally said, "What are you doing in Liso, anyway? Acherby's gone." Dissolved his government and stepped down under pressure, assassinated three days later stepping out of a car. That news had made it even into the jungle. "I'd have thought you'd be back in Amberlough as soon as the Ospie flag went off the pole."

Aristide tugged fussily at the wet napkin underneath his glass. "You'd have thought wrong."

Cyril leaned on the fault before he considered the consequences. "Can't go back, or won't?"

"Haven't," said Aristide, the lines around his mouth hardening.

"Why?" Cyril could feel the sharp edges of the question as he asked it, knew he looked a little rabid. "Scared of what you'll find?"

"I've been very busy." He said it too crisply.

"Getting to know my family?" Despite himself, Cyril was curious about that.

"It was quite a while ago. We were both in Porachis at the same time. The Ospies had her on a bit of a short jess; I helped to get her out of it."

As if the memory were rising through muddy water, Konrad Van der Joost's flabby face coalesced in his mind's eye: threatening Cyril's sister, if he misbehaved.

"I'm not awfully thrilled about the reward for services rendered," Aristide went on. "She wants me to . . . She's got some appointment in the provisional government, and wants me to make an appearance at this ceremony. Shake some hands, make her look capable, and well-connected."

"Sounds like she hasn't changed much." It didn't get the smile that it should have: that cruel curve of thin lips that said they were the only two in on a caustic joke.

"Yes, well. I told her no, but . . ."

And it hung there. No follow-up. Ari had caught him slipping in his bad behavior, the habits more appropriate for interrogation than for small talk, and was going to make him own up to it. He'd have to keep playing the game.

Power struggles. His breath caught. Once, it would have been lust. Now it was a mix of anger and fear, left over from conversations like this one in tone, though weightier in content. Conversations in which the person who came out on top was the one who ended up alive.

"But what?" Cyril asked, the pressure of his fingers putting dimples in the paper of his straight.

Ari stared into the remains of his drink. He'd put two double martinis away faster than Cyril would have credited, if he hadn't seen people do worse, faster. Maybe these eight years hadn't worn on Aristide as gently as it seemed.

Cyril's straight had burnt down to his fingers. He put it out and slipped the butt into his pocket. Saw Ari follow the motion, and caught the flicker of a shadow that passed over his face, the deepening of the wrinkles at the corners of his eyes.

"The ceremony," he said. "Cyril, it's a dedication. For a memorial on Temple Street. Right where the Bee was. For the Catwalk. But mostly, for Cordelia."

So Cordelia Lehane was dead.

Cyril wondered how this should make him feel. Surprised? He wasn't. He'd been half sure he was going to get her killed during the course of their association. Distraught? He was leagues beyond that. Guilty? This was just another bucket into the bay. There were ripples from the impact, certainly—he imagined her face would be swapped in for any number of other faces when he staggered into nightmares tonight—but good luck picking out this particular sin from the general cold depths of his self-loathing.

Cordelia Lehane was dead because of him. So were a lot of people. Nothing he'd done in the jungle had changed that.

He'd helped the Kingdom of Liso keep tabs on militias making incursions over the border. And he'd been tortured for it. He'd escaped that, and helped royalist cells build their networks in the north, undermining the authority of Gedda's puppet government from within. He'd helped the rebels capture Ospie-backed troops and contractors who'd gone on to summary executions on their knees in the mud.

He'd lost sight, after a while, of whether that was a step toward redemption or one more thing he should hate about himself.

Cordelia Lehane was dead, but unlike so many other people dead at his hand, on his watch, with his blessing, at least the people who loved her would have a chance to bow their heads and say goodbye.

"You should go," said Cyril.

"Apologizing to a plaque won't do her any good." Aristide nibbled moodily at a piece of flatbread.

Their meal had finally arrived: brisket, spicy lentils, collards cooked with nigella and fenugreek. Cyril wasn't hungry, but began to eat anyway, out of habit. The part of him that was still hunkered down in Mayaoba—or slinking along the rain-slick game trail between Niallo Benggi and Niallo Kreb—that part told him to eat and keep eating until he filled his belly, because there wouldn't be more coming at regular intervals.

"She's *dead*, Cyril. I could dig her up and piss in her eye and get nothing but mud for my troubles."

"Still." He swallowed too much brisket, nearly choked. "You were her friend."

Ari looked about to protest, but changed tack at the last moment and said, "So were you."

"She wouldn't want me there." He thought of the look on her face when she'd come to his miserable bolt-hole after someone she loved had died—no one he knew, or had ever met, but someone he had helped to kill regardless. He'd tried to mend the bridge between them by saying they both did what was necessary to survive.

You're nothing like me, she'd told him. *Least I been honest about my ugliness.*

"She would. If only just . . . oh, what did she say? So she could slap your teeth out."

"I'd take it, and thank her." Uncharacteristically, Aristide missed the innuendo. Granted, Cyril only caught the joke after he'd made it, and found it in poor taste.

Plucking the twist of lemon from his martini, Aristide began to fiddle with it, worrying the oily rind until it tore in two. He stared at the pieces for the span of a breath. When he let it out, he said, "You're right. I'm a coward. I ought to go."

Cyril shrugged, turned his whiskey on its napkin.

After an interminable silence, Ari began, "The last thing she said—"

"People say all kinds of swineshit when their guts are on the ground." He'd heard most of it firsthand. "I don't think I want to know."

"The last thing she said to *me*," Aristide went on. It was as if Cyril hadn't spoken, except for the graphite streak of stubbornness that colored Ari's tone. "It was several years before she died, but . . . well, you of all people must understand how hard it is to get a letter out when you're on the run." On that, the graphite turned to steel. Cyril let it cut him, silently.

"She said she didn't want to be forgotten. So much of what she did, she did in secret, and she told me she missed the applause." Aristide tossed the remains of his lemon peel onto his plate and struggled for a moment with where to put his hands, finally folding them in his lap. "It won't be what she wanted. People in suits making speeches about patriotism and bravery. Probably there won't even be a band."

"That's why you should go."

"I've let my trombone practice fall rather by the wayside, I'm afraid."

"No, really." Something sharp and unfamiliar stuck in his gut like he'd been impaled. It took a beat too long to realize he was jealous. Of Aristide, yes, for the opportunity to honor a friend who deserved it and more. But jealous of Cordelia, too. How must it have felt, to *want* folk to find out what you'd done? To take pride in your work?

How had it felt to be a hero?

"I honestly hadn't planned on it." Aristide swept his fingertips through condensation on the bar, leaving trails with beaded edges. "Would you come with me, if I did?"

It caught Cyril by surprise. He no longer understood the rhythm of Aristide's caprice, if that was what this was.

Back to Gedda? Where neither of them had been in almost a decade? Back to whatever was left of everything they had destroyed?

The idea made Cyril itch all over, like a million mites were crawling on his skin. Blood pounded in the tips of his fingers and burned at the delicate arches of his ears. Every physical response he had learned to trust in years of gauging danger told him *no,* not this one. Do not go.

"All right," he said. "Take me along."

CHAPTER

FOUR

Martí left for Cantrell before dawn, estimating that she would return with Stephen in time for a late lunch. Bradley, the cook, had planned a menu of all his favorite foods, or near as he could come under the double strictures of the household budget and informal rationing imposed by the aftermath of conflict: price gouging, hoarding, ruined infrastructure.

Lillian was supposed to be working. She had a folder full of mimeos spread across her desk: briefs from her team, and a half-written strategy plan for the provisional government's approach to the election. But despite her intentions she spent the morning looking between the clock and the window, and occasionally calling Magnusson from his own work to ask if the mail had come, or a telegram, or any news at all. Nervous energy simmered through her limbs, combining with the imminence of Stephen's arrival to destroy any hope of productivity.

Still, somehow, she missed the car as it came around the bend. The clock hands read ten past one when she heard the engine and the spatter of small stones against the fenders.

Excitement zipped out from her chest to her hands, chased by apprehension. Stephen's presence tended to highlight—and exacerbate—her differences with Jinadh. When he was younger, it had been less of a problem, as he had less of an opinion and less of a voice to lift in protest.

She hated that he'd been raised by parents first separated by circumstance—and by her own stubbornness—and then united against adversity. The latter had on occasion brought them closer together, but had far more often driven them to outbursts, tears, and accusations.

She had hoped that settling in Gedda, where they all spoke the language, where she and Stephen at least understood the social norms and etiquette, would smooth some of those rough patches. But Stephen, who had been at an international day school in Sunho, was having trouble readjusting to boarding, and to the discipline and academics of the Geddan system. His letters had come infrequently this term, all of them surly. The headmaster's came far more often, but were not much cheerier in tone.

When Lillian couldn't sleep, which was often, the consequences of her decisions dogged her.

The engine cut out in front of the house. She swept her papers into a pile and left her study for the landing. By the time she made the bottom of the staircase, Magnusson had the doors pulled open on a brilliant, bitter afternoon. Martí and Bern struggled up the steps with a steamer trunk, and Stephen stood on the running board with a satchel slung over one shoulder. His pants were too short, revealing several inches of cabled sock over bony ankles. Same with his cuffs, which showed the delicate knobs of his wrists. His growth spurt had melted the last of his baby fat away, turning everything about him angular. The sun made his buttons and boots gleam, but if his scowl had been a heavenly body it would have eclipsed the brightness handily.

Jinadh beat her to the drive and opened his arms. Stephen grudgingly allowed himself to be embraced.

«Do you plan on setting off any bombs now that you're home?» asked Jinadh, when they had pulled apart.

It took Stephen a moment to parse the Porashtu, but when he'd got it he rolled his eyes. "*Dad.*"

"Hello, Steenie," Lillian said.

Stephen's slouch straightened, and his attitude lost its insouciance if not its hostility. He took the steps with gravity exaggerated to the point of satire, and came nose to nose with her, or nearly. When had he gotten so tall?

"Mother," he said, suddenly ten years older. How did he *do* that, the swift shift from little boy to man, and back again? He sat on such a thin edge between the two, and it always cut her when she came too close. She could never tell, either, which side he was likely to come down on.

Jinadh glanced between them, frowning, then made a foray into the stiff silence, pushing Stephen gently over the threshold and into the hall. «Lunch is nearly ready. Go wash up and change. Bern laid out some dhoti; they'll cover your ankles at least. Do they put you on the rack at that school when you misbehave?» He thwacked Stephen's rear with his newspaper.

«*Dad!*» Stephen aimed an affronted glare over his shoulder and muttered a foul curse under his breath.

"What was that?" Lillian asked. Echoing back sharply from the marble floor of the hall, her own voice sounded eerily like her mother's. A wave of emotional vertigo hit her—that she should stand here admonishing her own child, as her mother had admonished . . .

Cyril. She clenched her teeth against panic.

Stephen didn't notice. "Nothing," he said, shoving the word out between his teeth. "Queen's sake."

«*Lunch,*» said Jinadh, propelling Stephen farther into the front hall. Then, more quietly, for her: «Lillian, *don't.* He's just gotten home.»

A reflexive retort coiled in her chest to strike: Did he want his child to speak that way? She swallowed it in the interest of maintaining a détente. Before she could summon something less acidic, the telephone bell shrilled.

"Ma'am," said Magnusson, appearing from the vestibule, "It's for you."

"It's a radio call, ma'am." Magnusson held the telephone in front of him as though it were a precious artifact. "From Aristide Makricosta. It took him quite a while to get through. Should I accept?"

"Yes, thank you," she said, hearing the words from a long way away. "I'll . . . I'll take it in my office."

"Shall I fetch Bern for you, or would you like me to take notes?" Magnusson had done double duty as her secretary in Asu, some days: a duty which now occasionally fell to Bern. Someday she'd have the money to hire a real right hand. She hoped.

"No," she said, "that's all right."

Magnusson nodded and spoke quietly to the operator; his voice faded as Lillian went up the stairs, feeling each variation in the grain of the bannister in exquisite detail while her mind avoided more important things.

Her office door confronted her before she was ready. The black resin of the telephone was cool, and her breath caught in a brief patch of condensation on the mouthpiece.

"Hello," she said. "This is Lillian."

"Lillian." Aristide's voice, though it came through a haze of crackling interference after a long lag, sounded more immediate than Magnusson's, more immediate even than her own. "How are you?"

"Fine, thank you." The small talk came out automatically. At the price per minute of a transoceanic radio call, they didn't have time for it. "And . . . and my brother? How is he?"

"He'd like to come to Amberlough for the dedication. I can arrange his travel."

Words stalled. She wasted precious airtime with her lips parted and her lungs empty. "You could fly into Dameskill county," she said, finally, airless. "The regional airstrip is a short drive from Damesfort. If the weather's good, it should get you here a few days sooner than sailing." Then, "You're coming, too?"

Fraught, crackling silence on the line. Then, "Yes, of course."

"Oh," she said. "Oh, you don't like to fly, of—"

"No," he said. "It's simply—"

The line got garbled, his protest lagging behind and tangling with her apology, until they both went silent waiting for the other to talk. Finally, Lillian said, "I'm sorry. Go on."

"I have some business in Rarom that needs to be wrapped up before I leave. I thought you might like him home before that. So you can . . . catch up, I suppose."

"You'd send him ahead?" Unspoken, the question: Was he whole and competent to see himself across international borders?

"Just by a few days," said Aristide. "If that's all right."

Her little brother. Coming back from the dead. In a state of disgrace and dishevelment at the most inconvenient time, but if that wasn't Cyril all over, what was?

Last she'd seen him he had been in the hospital, just back from some mysterious errand in Tatié: wan with exhaustion so his tan looked dusty. Anger had seemed to be the only thing keeping him awake.

Who was her brother now?

"Of course," she said. "Cable with the details? We've jawed long enough to empty out the treasury, I'm sure."

"Lillian." She heard a loud rasping noise—shuffling papers, maybe, or shifting in his chair. Or a stray storm scrambling the call. "He's . . . I don't know what you might expect, but I think he ought to be treated with some delicacy."

Lifting her hand to brush at a tickle on her cheek, she found she was crying and wondered when that had begun. Wiping the tears away with the heel of her free hand, she said, "Send him ahead, Aristide. We'll take care of him in Carmody."

How was she supposed to face lunch after that? But she had to. It would be the best time to break the news to Jinadh, in front of Stephen. She could frame it as a family affair, a chance for Stephen to meet his uncle. She was bringing Cyril home for Solstice, not to hide him in obscurity until after the memorial dedication. After that, she could . . .

What, send him away again? Or perhaps he could stay at Damesfort. Riskier than, say, the chalet in Ibet, but less callous. And anyway, the chalet had been sold years ago, after the Ospies confiscated everything the DePauls had ever owned.

She could hardly think of the situation except in strategic terms. Anything at a smaller distance plunged her into formless terror and nameless hope. Lunch would keep her on an even keel, businesslike, presenting her plan.

As she came down the hall, she heard Stephen expounding about school in the dining room. He still sounded shrill—his voice hadn't broken yet, though she thought it might in the next year. Queen keep her then. He was already a terror; staggering over the cusp of manhood would only make him worse.

"All the children at school are so *boring*," he said, and she paused in the corridor to listen. "Everyone's always after me to be their friend—I could have lots of friends if I wanted, because I'm so exotic—but everybody's about as interesting as boiled peas."

He called himself exotic without irony, but inwardly Lillian cringed. Yes, he was the son of a disgraced courtier and a defrocked diplomat whose family history was checkered with divisive politics and shadowy deals. But the international day school in Sunho had been full of students from around the world. Missionaries' daughters, correspondents' sons. The children of investors, contractors, expatriates, and academics. Classes had been taught in Asunese but the chatter in the classroom was as varied as the hair, the clothes, the colors of skin.

She imagined Cantrell was a bit hard to stomach, after that. Especially coming in for his final year, when all the other students had knit together closely and there was little room left for a new friend. The best he could hope for, she supposed, was to play the aloof but interesting foreign boy, the prize for everyone to chase to prove that they were cosmopolitan.

How dismally lonesome he must be.

"And Master Wythe—she teaches history—she hates me because of Mum and her brother and the Ospies and Grandmama and all, I guess, but she won't say any of it right out. She just canes me for stupid stuff."

"I'm sure that isn't true," said Jinadh. Lillian, who had been at Cantrell, was quite certain that it was.

Perhaps five years wasn't quite enough time to bury bad news. At least for some people. And it seemed the DePauls couldn't please anyone, on any side of the argument. Just something Stephen would have to learn to live with. *If* he got back into school at all.

"There's *one* boy who speaks Asunese," Stephen went on, "but he's horrid and nobody likes him and anyway he isn't as good as me. I'm going to forget it all if I can't practice."

«We've engaged an Asunese tutor for you,» said Jinadh. Lillian cringed, remembering how much the woman charged.

«I don't *need* a tutor.» The cringe melted in a swell of pride. How easily her son slipped from Geddan to Porashtu to complain about Asunese. «I already know how to speak it.»

Even from her hideout just beyond the door, Lillian could hear Jinadh sigh. «No, partridge, she's a regular tutor. Only she'll teach you in Asunese.»

Before Stephen could whine about the endearment, or launch into some fresh tale of woe from school, Lillian made her entrance. "So sorry," she said, settling into the empty chair at the head of the table and spreading pickle thinly on a slice of bread. "Radio call, from Liso. Expensive, so we kept it short."

«And the outcome?» Over his coffee, Jinadh's gaze hung heavy with meaning. He'd caught on, but wasn't sure she wanted to bring this all up in front of Stephen.

Setting aside her bread unbitten, she decided to end his suspense. Lunch was served cold on the sideboard, so none of the staff were present. That would be another conversation entirely. "Steenie, dear."

His eyes rolled over to her, dragging as if the weight of his suffering held them down. Had she ever managed to look so put-upon, at his age? She had certainly seen the same expression on her brother's face. Would she have matched that memory to this moment, if things didn't stand as they were? "Do you remember Uncle Cyril?"

"The secret agent?" he said. "The one who died?"

"We don't *know* that's what he was. I said he did lots of work he couldn't talk about."

"Duquesne at school said he was a spy," said Stephen. "And a traitor."

"It's complicated."

"'Complicated' just means you don't want to admit it."

"Stephen," said Jinadh, setting his cup into its saucer. The porcelain snapped with an anger that had been absent from his voice.

"Complicated means complicated," she said. "Maybe it will be better for your uncle to explain it himself."

Given Jinadh's expression, she was glad he'd set down his cup before she spoke.

"What?" Stephen's raised brows and open mouth turned him into a poor copy of Jinadh. "How? He's dead."

Mother and sons, she'd meant to handle this more neatly. But she tried to treat Stephen like her child, rather than a press conference, and as a result found him more intimidating than a pack of rabid pen-fencers.

"Well. We had some good news. He was only . . . missing for a while. And now—" she glanced at Jinadh. "He's coming to visit."

Stephen dropped his fork with a clatter. "Here?"

"Yes," said Lillian. "For Solstice."

"No fooling?"

"No fooling," she said, and to her horror felt her throat closing. Stephen didn't notice, but she saw Jinadh catch the change in her timbre.

«Partridge,» he said, «I think this calls for a celebration. Get Magnusson to take you down to the cellar and pick out something sparkly.»

«Can I *have* some of it?»

«Today, yes.» Stephen was nearly out of the room by the time Jinadh called out, «Ask Magnusson for the good crystal, too.»

The dining room door slammed on the end of his sentence. «So,» he said, when they were alone. «You waited, and you saw. What happened?»

«Apparently he told Makricosta he wants to attend the dedication. They're *both* going to come.»

«Have you told Honora?»

"Oh, stones." Lillian pushed back from the table, chair legs screeching on the scuffed parquet.

Jinadh put a hand out, patting the air. «It can wait for a glass of champagne, surely.»

"It really can't. I should ring her. I'll be back down in a moment. She has a score of people waiting on the list of speakers—the printers and radio folk and half a dozen papers."

She saw Jinadh crumple slightly at the shift in her priorities, but she couldn't help it: The tide of work had caught her. Kissing the top of his head, she told him, "Duty calls," and left him alone at the table.

CHAPTER

FIVE

"Well," said Aristide, shutting the door behind him, "That's set. She wants you to—"

He stopped short, the rest of his sentence dying in his throat. Cyril was sprawled on his back on the sofa of Aristide's hotel suite, one hand dragging the carpet. His mouth hung open, jaw loose. On the low table in front of him: an empty crystal tumbler and Aristide's bottle of sleeping pills.

A beam of evening sunshine crossed his supine form, turned his lashes gold where they lay across his cheek. He was utterly unmoving. He wasn't even—

Aristide got across the room before he realized he had moved, and found his hands tight around Cyril's upper arms. He gave the other man a hard shake, and heard his own voice saying Cyril's name.

And then the light moved on Cyril's lashes and his eyes were open, the striations in their shades of blue picked out in exquisite detail, whites crazed with broken veins.

Ice leached from Aristide's limbs, leaving him sore and creaking, weak with relief. He sank down onto the floor between the sofa and the coffee table.

"Stones," said Cyril, slurring slightly. "What's on fire?"

Aristide snatched the pill bottle from the table. It was nearly as full as he'd left it last night. "Everything's fine. I'm sorry to wake you." With shaking hands, he capped it and put it into his pocket.

"That's some strong magic." Cyril hooked his fingers in the same pocket that now held the bottle. The motion made the pills rattle, and pulled the lapels of Aristide's jacket out of line. "Feels like I got sludge poured in my ear."

"You aren't supposed to mix them with liquor," said Aristide, defensive and therefore prim.

High as he was, Cyril still managed a derisive snort and eye roll. "Tell me *you* don't. Your hands shake, Ari. And they're swollen."

Aristide curled the offending extremities into fists and felt the edema in his joints protest.

Cyril's fingers slipped from Aristide's jacket pocket, back to the carpet. "I don't rotten care. We do what we need to."

"Like taking pills that don't belong to us?"

Cyril's eyes fell shut. The lids were purple-red and shiny with exhaustion. "I couldn't sleep."

"It's early yet. Just past dinner."

"I haven't slept for two days. I was so tired, but I couldn't . . ."

As Aristide watched, horrified, tears leaked from the corners of Cyril's eyes and dampened his crow's-feet.

"I'm sorry," he said. Not words he was used to saying, but they fell out of him as though they had been teetering on his tongue, shoved to the brink by everything behind them.

Levering himself up, Aristide settled onto the coffee table but went no further than that. "I spoke with your sister. I'm sending you ahead. I need to go back to Rarom before I leave, for business."

Cyril didn't answer, or move, or even sigh. His stillness was the same stillness that had sunk an ice pick of terror into Aristide's heart not five minutes before. Now he only wondered if the pills had done their work.

From the tension in Cyril's jaw, he suspected it was an act. Or a defense.

"You'll take a plane from Souvay-Dadang, refuel in Hyrosia, and then land at some regional airstrip."

"I already regret this." Cyril reached out with a limp hand until his knuckles knocked the tumbler.

"It's empty," said Aristide.

"Well then fill it."

The worst thing was, if Aristide had been alone, faced with an empty glass, he would have. Shame at his own hypocrisy sent him running for shelter in comfortable habits: criticism, performance, frivolity.

"Tomorrow we'll get you clothes," he said. "I know a good tailor in Dadang, and I'm not sending you anywhere in that scrap of lettuce leaf."

"Just wrap me in a rug."

"Lillian would skin me."

"Lillian's seen me in a rougher state." He rolled and put his face into the sofa cushions. "Let me sleep."

"You don't want to get undressed? Sleep in the bed?"

Blearily, Cyril glared out from under his own arm. "You're not seriously—"

Aristide realized a moment too late how his meaning had been misconstrued, and stood unsteadily from the coffee table, desperate to put distance between them. "Queen's sake, of course not. I just—I can take the sofa, if you like."

"I've slept on worse." Cyril squirmed deeper into the cushions and spoke more softly, so that Aristide almost didn't hear him add, "And anyway. You've got a bad back."

A visceral memory struck him then: Cyril's thumbs pressed into the knot that still lurked at the base of his spine, ready to spring into a full spasm if he stood too long, or sat, or turned too fast in the wrong direction. The way the snarled muscles held their tension under pressure until suddenly, blissfully, they didn't. Cyril's warm hands spreading, palms down, over the tender place left behind in the wake of pain.

Cyril remembered, too, or he wouldn't have said. And that made the memory hurt worse than his bad back ever had.

"Oh," managed Aristide. "Thank you." He took Cyril's empty tumbler for himself, and filled it at the bar before he closed the bedroom door.

It was strangely like being saddled with a child or a pet. Cyril was petulant and cranky, apt to snatch up things that didn't belong to him. At the tailor, when he removed his sweat-stained jacket, three monogrammed pens and a small wooden spoon fell from the pockets, along with several books of matches. The monograms were all different. The spoon, Aristide found upon closer examination, had been sharpened at the handle end.

Cyril shattered the impression of vexing but innocent once he was down to his shirt and trousers.

"You can go," he said, not looking at Aristide. But he clearly didn't mean the tailor, who was holding a book of fabric samples open for him.

"Oh, please. It's nothing I haven't seen before." As soon as it was out of his mouth, Aristide knew it was wrong. First, instead of a saucy note, he'd struck a little to the left of nagging. Second, he remembered Cyril's horror at his perceived flirtation the previous night.

He got no better results this time. Worse, in fact.

"Get out," said Cyril, between clenched teeth.

Aristide retreated to the front of the shop and pushed at the door so that the bell chimed. He stayed inside and waited for it to close, then settled softly onto one of the caned chairs along the wall. Between the slats of the folding screen that sheltered the fitting room from the street-facing windows, he caught glimpses of the process. He lost the conversation after Cyril's first line:

«I do not care a damn what cloth,» he said. Then, one of the only bits of Shedengue Aristide knew, which was *Do you speak,* except instead of saying the Shedengue word for "Geddan," Cyril said the word for Shedengue itself. Whatever information they exchanged after that was beyond Aristide's reach, though from the sound, it wasn't much. In the lengthening silences between the tailor's tentative questions and Cyril's terse replies, the hiss of the tape measure was the only sound in the shop.

Aristide leaned against the wall, changing the angle of his vantage point. A sliver of angled mirror slid into view, and with it, a section of Cyril's reflection.

His undershirt—what Aristide could see of it—was splotchy and snaggled. No wonder he'd worn that horrible suit to sleep, and given Aristide the bottom of his boot just now.

And then he shifted on the riser and put the crook of his elbow into view, the underside of his forearm. Just for a moment but long enough to show livid pink. Track marks? Suicide scars? Did Aristide want to know?

He wished he had gone when he'd pretended to. Now there was no way out—if he truly left he'd ring the bell over the door, and Cyril would believe he'd come back, then figure out his ruse. In lieu of an exit, he averted his eyes from the crack between the hinges.

And something—some shift in the angle of his ribs, the tentative breath he let out as he moved—tickled his chest and woke the cough that had begun to plague him. He felt phlegm catch as he tried to inhale—

"Damnation, Aristide!"

Cyril, sock footed, in shorts and his holey undershirt, slammed back the screen. One wobbly decorative newel met its end and clattered to the floor.

And *that* was what he had been trying to hide. Scars, yes, but not the kind that Aristide had feared. Not the straight lines of a razor, but the ragged, puckered swathes of burns.

"Mother and sons," said Aristide. He had his handkerchief to his mouth, from coughing, and his voice came out rough. He could have been a mourning widow in a scene from a melodrama. A mother whose son had come back from a war. He cleared his throat and put away the hankie.

"I told you they burned the camp," said Cyril. "With me still tied to a post inside. I'm lucky: The roof fell on my legs, not my head."

Attention drawn down, Aristide saw there were scars across his shins as well. These were worse than the incidental marks on his forearms: raised, twisted lesions that still looked painful, even healed.

"It rained," said Cyril. "Or I'd be dead. Only time I was ever glad it did, in that jungle."

Aristide made himself look up, meet Cyril's eyes with indifference.

He wouldn't let himself show pity. He couldn't even *feel* it, really: just the cold, dull ache of horror.

"He said he can rush it for an extra ten thousand mitu." Cyril turned and started back into the fitting room. "Be done in a couple of days. You're paying, right?"

It was like watching him drop sandbags between them, or lay bricks. Aristide got out his billfold, and went to settle up while Cyril slid into his clothes.

Daoud rang the hotel that afternoon. The concierge put the call through to the room while Cyril was sleeping, which he had been since they got back from the tailor. Badly. When he was still, Aristide suspected he wasn't resting but awake and alert and actively avoiding interaction. When he truly slept, it was obvious, because he had dreams. They did not sound pleasant.

So when the phone rang, and the concierge told him who it was, Aristide shut the door to the bedroom and sat on the freshly turned-down sheets. Mosquito netting drifted in the breeze from the open window. The coastal weather was temperate; pleasant even in the early summer. It tempted one to think of home, but if one was careful, one never did. Memories of Loendler Park at lilac time were inevitably shattered by the errant palm frond or shrieking monkey, and the realization that in Gedda, the seasons ran opposite. Frost would have killed the lilac leaves long ago.

In Rarom, at a higher altitude, nights could get positively chilly even when the rest of the country was sweating through the dry season. Daoud still had the down comforter on his bed. Aristide was not proud that he knew that.

"Good afternoon," he said, toeing off his loafers. "How's business in the sunny south?"

"Cross wants to know when you are coming back." Daoud's tone was tart, just this side of needling. "We have some lucrative offers on the table and she needs your signature to go ahead."

"Can you suspend operations for a few days? Let me wrap things up in Dadang and I'll explain it all when I get back."

"Cross will not like that."

"Well, we're equal partners. That just means I need a tiebreaker. And I can count on you, can't I?" A cheap maneuver—a cut to the hamstring, a blow to the groin. But Aristide had always fought dirty.

He had *meant* to end things with Daoud. He *had,* for a while. But after two years of failure in the war-torn border jungles, hope fading and everything familiar left far behind, what was he supposed to do? He sought comfort where it came most easily.

And perhaps he'd kept seeking it, even after he established himself. After he had a home and a company and reconnected with an old business partner. Because it was easy. Because it was reassuring to return to something one understood, even if it didn't exactly satisfy.

"How long," said Daoud, "must I keep Cross's patience?" He sounded on the verge of snapping, though he never did. At least not where Aristide could hear him. Did he have friends to whom he could complain? He worked all the rotten time. Maybe that was why he put up—and kept it up—with Aristide. No chance to cultivate other options.

"Well." Aristide put his hand over his eyes, behind which a headache had begun to build. It was past two o'clock, and therefore long past time for a drink, but he'd been busy. Sweat was starting under his arms and on his palms. A drink, then lunch. Then another drink. That would put his shakes away, and the pain in his temples, too. "I need you to look into flights for me."

"From Dadang to Rarom?"

"Yes, but also." Lady's name, he was going to get into it now, wasn't he? "Is there anything from Dadang to . . . to the Dameskill regional airstrip?"

"Where?"

"It's in Amberlough," said Aristide. "Near . . . near Lillian's estate."

There was a long pause, unbroken by crackle of paper or clatter of pen. "So you are sending him home."

"I'm sending him *ahead*," said Aristide. "I'll sail later from Ul-Weiya."

"You told her yes?" Daoud had been privy to Aristide's rant upon receipt of Lillian's first invitation. He sounded as incredulous as he had a right to.

"I did." He didn't owe Daoud an explanation, and wouldn't give one.

"Good," said Daoud.

"You thought I should go? Why didn't you say anything?"

"How would you have taken it? You said it 'smacked of political striving,' and was 'unseemly, cheap, and disrespectful.' I did not know her as you did, so my opinion did not enter the discussion."

He did not ask the question Aristide had never let himself answer: How else would Cordelia *want* to be remembered? Carmine lips, crass language, hair so bright it could have been mistaken for candy floss.

Daoud hadn't known her then, and he hadn't known her long. But even he had *known* her; one couldn't help but get a faceful when she walked into a room.

If anything happens to me, she'd said, *I just want folk to know what I did. I miss the applause.*

If he admitted it to himself, with the Ospies gone, she wouldn't care who used her name. Not as long as there were posters up on Temple Street, and unlicensed prostitutes in Eel Town could bribe the hounds to stroll the other way. She had got what she wanted.

He had promised to tell people what she had done, and he had failed.

It was a failure he'd been happy to bury. Just one of several. Many. It was easier to tell himself that he was doing the right thing, when really he was just keeping his heart wrapped in cotton, packed in straw.

When he was young, he had never understood how people could feel disgusted with themselves. Even the foulest crimes had failed to stir his conscience, because they were in service to a worthy end: his own security and comfort. Age had given him clarity, on that subject at least.

"When will you return?" Daoud asked, and Aristide wondered how long silence had taken up the line between them.

"I'm not sure. Book me outbound and we'll arrange the rest later."

There was a pause, in which implications settled like stones.

"I will ring the airfield," said Daoud, at last. "For . . . for . . ."

"Mr. Ambrose van Weill," said Aristide. An Enselmese entrepreneur. That was the name Cyril had written on his new passport, supplied by Asiyah in order to avoid any awkward questions that might arise. When Lillian turned tail on the Ospies they dragged her whole family through the midden, and some people had long memories. Acherby was gone now, but the stories had been printed. And no matter where one's sympathies lay, Cyril DePaul lay opposite.

"For Mr. van Weill," said Daoud. "I'm not sure there will be anything tomorrow. But perhaps the day after? Two days at the most, if the weather is fine."

"Two days," said Aristide. As the words traveled through the line he felt a swell of dread. *Two days*, with a man who couldn't speak to him without sneering. Two more days of listening to those nightmares. Of staring at a wall that had once been a door, ajar.

It was much better for him to fly ahead. Sharing a ship voyage would have been too much.

"And you?" asked Daoud, reminding him of the telephone in his hand, hard against his cheek. "Will you be flying to Rarom the same day?"

"Yes," said Aristide, "I suppose I'd better. Cross will tear me up and down, when she hears what I've agreed to."

"She might not be the only one," said Daoud, and rang off before Aristide could retort.

CHAPTER

SIX

Aristide ran errands. Cyril assumed they had to do with him. They certainly resulted in a new suitcase, clean shorts and undershirts, pyjamas, toiletries. He refused to go for a shave, because he didn't like the idea of a razor wielded by a stranger's hand so near his neck. Even less, the idea that he couldn't trust himself to hold still.

On the evening before Cyril's departure, Aristide returned to the hotel with another stack of paper-wrapped packages and said, "I won't send you to your sister like this. If you won't go to a barber, I'll shave you myself."

"Your hands shake," said Cyril from the sofa, where he had remained for too many hours, dug in like a soldier in a trench.

Aristide held one of the offending extremities in front of him and said, too keenly for humor, "Steady now. I've been to the bar."

That shouldn't have been reassuring. "I can do it myself."

"You haven't yet." Aristide set the packages on the sideboard and plucked delicately at the strings that held one of them shut. The brown wrapping fell away to reveal a gold stamp on white cardboard. Aristide's fingers were indeed steady as he unfolded the lid to reveal a badger brush, a silver-banded cake of soap, and a gleaming safety razor packed in pristine white tissue.

"It isn't even a cutthroat," Ari said, lifting the razor with a particular grace that pulled Cyril back through time, to a past that had seemed impossibly distant until this moment. When Aristide raised his eyes he left his chin tucked, so his gaze came filtered through his lashes. "Tell me you aren't *afraid*."

Cyril's throat was dry, when he tried to swallow whatever threatened to rise from his chest. "Not of the razor, anyway. Pour me a drink first?"

What Ari brought him from the cocktail cart was more tranquilizer than aperitif. As he put it away, steadily, he watched Aristide unwrap another package. The slow reveal had an air of burlesque to it. One sheet of newsprint pulled away showed translucent tissue paper and the shadow of a chalk-striped cashmere Cyril didn't remember choosing for himself. Then there was the neatly folded shirt, the sound of Aristide's palms spread across the twill, the teasing slide of one finger beneath the band, and ultimately the snap of paper as it tore.

Cyril drank his whiskey and tried not to be intrigued. He didn't have the energy for it.

By the time Aristide hung his suit and shirt to air and straighten, and laid out a pair of simple cap-toe derbies, Cyril was anesthetized with whiskey.

"I threw your boots in a wastebasket," said Aristide. "There's a few pairs of socks as well—I put them in your bag."

"Thank you, Nanny." Cyril scrubbed at his face; his cheeks felt numb. It was beginning to dawn on him that he had not eaten yet today, though he could have called for room service anytime. It hadn't seemed important.

"Come to the washroom," said Aristide. He had gotten there without Cyril noticing, and turned the water on.

Cyril dropped his glass carelessly onto the table and heaved himself to his feet. He had grown unused to receiving instruction in the jungle and far more used to giving it, which had been exhausting. Debriefing had been all question and answer. It was a relief to simply follow orders from someone who didn't present a threat.

Aristide put the toilet seat down and laid a folded towel over the porcelain. Cyril sat and, without waiting for another towel, or instruction, stripped off his undershirt.

Ari didn't hiss, or flinch, but Cyril still caught the moment of silence, the sudden stillness in the gathering swirls of steam.

He tried to remember what there was to see. The burn scars, which were spattered across his shoulders, too. Various remnants of fights, flights, and accidents. And of course, he was too thin.

Maybe it wasn't anything in particular—only the difference between what Aristide remembered and what confronted him now. Cyril knew he didn't stand up to his memory.

But Aristide said nothing; only handed him a hot towel. Cyril closed his eyes. A dark, pungent scent rose from the shaving soap as Ari swirled the brush through the lather. Musk and vanilla, amber and white flowers.

The sheen of drying perfume on each pulse point; Aristide, naked, in front of an open window.

Damn that scent memory, bobbing up like a dumped corpse rotted free from its weights. Aristide's Padgett and Sons cologne. The soap had the same profile, and once it was on Cyril's skin he would carry it with him until he washed again.

"The towel?" asked Aristide, and Cyril peeled it from his face. Taking an unsteady breath, he held himself taut in anticipation of the brush and was surprised when it didn't come.

"May I?" asked Aristide, and the gravity of his tone was only slightly more surprising than the fact that he had asked at all.

Cyril took another moment to center himself, then dipped his chin in assent. A moment later, he felt Aristide's fingertips just beneath it, pushing his jaw higher, and then the kiss of soap-slick badger hair against his throat. His larynx moved beneath the bristles as he swallowed.

Aristide worked slowly, and Cyril tried to remember if he'd kept a shaving set in the washroom at Baldwin Street, or only ever gone to the barber. It was like trying to remember the props onstage in a play he had watched once, long ago.

Horn rattled against porcelain, followed by the faint chime of steel. Before his brain caught up with his body he went tense. Aristide waited, not touching him; in the swirl of steam against his skin, Cyril imagined he could feel the currents of Ari's breath.

"Now?" he asked, and Cyril realized how closely Aristide must be watching him, to have noticed the minuscule slackening of his muscles.

"Go ahead," he said, curling his fingers beneath the toilet seat. But as soon as the steel edge touched his throat he was standing, one hand over the thin, shallow cut beneath his jaw.

Aristide's expression gave him nothing, so he gave nothing back. For a moment they stood opposite one another. A drop of blood fell from Cyril's chin and sprayed across the floor, turning black against the lapis tile.

Then Aristide wiped off the razor, leaving a pink streak on white terry cloth, and set it on the sink with painful precision. "Perhaps you ought to do it yourself after all."

Left alone with the sound of running water, Cyril felt his failure on so many levels he lost count.

The last airplane they'd put him in had been a military affair: stripped down and freezing cold, dun and green and dirty. The one he boarded as Ambrose van Weill had plush seats and offered cocktails before takeoff.

That didn't make the flight any warmer, or more pleasant. Neither did his hangover.

The suit fit well enough, for something thrown together in less than three days, no second fitting or fiddly bits. Amazing he could remember what it *ought* to feel like, enough to notice the difference in the pitch of the sleeves, the gap at the back of the collar.

Aristide had looked at the ensemble and given a small *tch* of disapproval, but there wasn't much he could do in an hour. Their farewell on the runway had been awkward, stilted. They had not touched one another. They had not touched one another at *all*, save the shaving incident.

Cyril found the first knuckle of his forefinger at his chin, where Aristide had tilted his jaw half an inch higher for a better angle with the badger brush. He cleared his throat, and put his hand into his lap.

His neighbor was a white-haired Lisoan woman in half-moon spectacles. She slept through the first half of the first leg, waking when they hit rough weather over the Egyrian Sea.

She took off her spectacles and rubbed her eyes, then growled, ≈Demon's jism.≈

The emphatic profanity startled a snort out of Cyril, which caught his neighbor's attention. ≈You speak Shedengue?≈

That would teach him to laugh at old women. He'd been hoping to avoid conversation until Carmody, and even then keep it to a minimum. ≈Yes,≈ he admitted. ≈But not well.≈ Five years of immersion hadn't made him eloquent, just competent, with a vocabulary oddly weighted in favor of tactics and violence.

≈You don't look like you can speak it at all.≈ She cased him with sharp eyes. ≈Where are you from?≈

≈Enselem,≈ he said, recalling his papers. ≈But I make business in Liso.≈

≈War business,≈ she said. Not a question.

He had no prescribed story to explain himself, so instead found himself extemporizing. ≈The kind that is better in a war.≈

≈What kind is that?≈ she asked, and he could feel her marshaling her forces for an attack. If he chose whatever she was preparing to be angry about, he might drive her off and have the rest of the flight to himself. But that meant hours spent at hostility's elbow, and perhaps an ugly scene.

So instead: ≈I work with a Porachin shipping company, in Liso for many years. Now, I help move aid into the north.≈ He'd known an Ibetian woman who did the same thing; she passed messages for his people sometimes. It would hold wine better than a sieve, at any rate.

The pinched expression on his neighbor's face softened into satisfaction. She put her hand to her heart, bowed, and flicked her fingers up to her brow and then toward him: a greeting, and expression of gratitude. He'd learned to use it on village leaders, reluctant officials, and long-suffering matriarchs who agreed to take him into their crowded compounds when the weather turned wet.

≈Achela Aowamma,≈ she said.

He made the reverse gesture: fingers to her, to his forehead, to his heart. ≈Ambrose van Weill.≈

≈I'm sorry if I was sharp with you,≈ she said. ≈Many people have been taking advantage of our country's disarray.≈

≈War makes profit,≈ he said. ≈Especially for the . . . hm. Not honest?≈

≈Unscrupulous,≈ she supplied.

≈Yes,≈ he said, thinking of Aristide and wondering what underhanded economics had paid for his expedited cashmere suit.

≈Ah,≈ said Aowamma, as the flight attendant stopped with his cart. ≈I will have arrack and water. And you? Ambrose? Will you have anything?≈

He would, but . . . what was van Weill's drink? Not rye. Not gin. Certainly not a cocktail. Something strong and dark, probably expensive. He felt himself fall further into the character, felt the persona wrap around him like a warm, muffling duvet in the chill darkness of the cabin.

"Peated whiskey," he said, defeated by Shedengue. At least his Enselmese accent was credible. ≈Uh, Calishaughn, if it is there? Or Tolishnaughcaul?≈

When the flight attendant handed over their glasses, Aowamma raised hers and toasted him. ≈If only all neighbors could get along so well.≈

They carried on quite a pleasant conversation for the rest of the flight. And by "they" Cyril meant Aowamma and van Weill. He sat back in his seat and watched it happen from very far away.

"Mack," said Cross, their brand-new blacklist spread in front of her. "These are our best customers."

Facing Merrilee Cross and her dangling cigarillo in the smoke-filled offices of Cross-Costa Imports, the prospect of explaining this change of plans was even less appealing than it had been in Dadang. But worth it. Aristide kept repeating that, hoping he would feel the truth of it sometime soon. Especially now that Cyril was well away, and less like a man than a strange, unsettling dream.

"Nevertheless," he said. "They've got to go. I've cut a deal with someone I'd rather not disappoint."

"I don't want to disappoint *them*." Merrilee jabbed the list with a stiff finger. "Holy stones. We tell Oreeta Ngdoze we won't sell to her anymore, I don't give us good odds on making it through to the rains."

"I think you're handicapping us a little harshly." He'd been running the same calculations since his dinner with Asiyah. Dealing with Cyril had taken most of his time, so that he only found himself free to meet about business after the plane to Hyrosia taxied down the runway.

They had dined in Asiyah's suite at the Waolla-hai. Over pilau and fish curry, Asiyah had given him a list of names that included five of their best customers, and three of their most dangerous.

"I cannot offer you protection," Asiyah told him, when he pointed out the risks. "And I do not think you need it as badly as you say."

Cross-Costa had arrangements with private security, it was true, but, "A couple of hired truncheons aren't going to keep me in one piece if Ngdoze decides she wants me in several."

That got him a shrug. "That is your affair. Now that DePaul is safely on his way to Gedda, I will appreciate a swift show of your gratitude before you, also, leave the country."

He should have been more careful with his telephone calls. Cross would quarter him if she ever learned how widely open he'd left that flank. In fairness—he hated when that phrase was applicable to his own actions, because it always accompanied some idiocy that could have been avoided—*in fairness*, he had been somewhat distracted.

Still was. There had been packing to do, arrangements to be made. And that was just the logistics. The rest of it—the hiss of soap against stubble, sunlight slanting through eyelashes lowered in sleep—he couldn't possibly approach head-on. And certainly not until everything else had been dispatched.

"If it was *us* I was writing up in the racing form," said Cross, "I'd give better numbers. But you're gonna dump my rear and go sailing off to Amberlough for what, the season?"

"I'm not sure," said Aristide, light and brittle as spun sugar. "I haven't planned so far ahead."

"I wish I'd ever gotten knocked so hard my brains fell out the back," said Cross. "I guess DePaul's still got the tackle for deep-sea fishing after all this time."

The secret had yet to be whispered that could be kept from Merrilee Cross. Aristide let the uncouth comment slide, though it scraped off a layer of skin. Daoud, however, did not.

"Ms. Cross," he said, crisply as creased waxed paper, "perhaps we should focus on the positive parts of this situation. For instance, I believe our business interests in Amberlough are due for an expansion?"

"Indeed," said Aristide. "Since we're losing Ngdoze, Otiuno, and the rest, it seems an excellent time to focus on our Geddan offices and ventures. Jamila is too clever to languish doing busywork."

"Well, I won't miss Otiuno, that's for sure." Cross ground out her cigarillo in the overflowing ashtray at the center of the table. "He never did pay on time. And Jamila's last cable said she's got a good lead on a company that can move our goods inland. If you're gonna leave me here to get hacked up, might as well make some money over there for my heirs and assigns." Cross sucked her teeth. "It ain't a bad idea."

"Contrary to your belief, my brain still resides safely in my skull."

He tapped the arm of his spectacles with one finger, then straightened them on his nose.

"The idea," said Daoud, "was mine."

The scolding caught Aristide off guard, and the apologetic grin he aimed at Daoud felt more like a wince on his face.

Cross raised an eyebrow, but only asked "When do you leave?"

"Two days," said Daoud, sliding into the opening she had left for Aristide. "It is a fast ship, and the canal has been reopened. You should dock in Amberlough City early next week. I have cabled Ms. DePaul; she will meet you in the city for the ceremony."

"And what about *Mister* DePaul?" asked Cross, picking an errant piece of tobacco from her tongue. "I don't trust you past your jess if that tow-headed turncoat has a hand free to haul down his zipper. Stones, I wouldn't trust you even if he was in shackles. Maybe less."

Aristide was still composing a response behind his shaved-thin smile when Daoud asked, "And if I went with him?"

"What?" Instantly, Aristide had reason to wish he'd hidden his outrage better. It wasn't that the younger man looked hurt; rather that he looked a tad too smug for Aristide's liking.

"If you are doing business in Amberlough," said Daoud, "it seems you might benefit from the services of your secretary. And it may set Cross's mind at ease."

"Queen's sake," said Cross. "Take a camera and film it. I want to see how this plays out."

Aristide plucked a cigarette from his case to stifle a sharp remark. Once he'd lit it and taken a steadying drag he said, "You aren't worried about being short another hand, in the face of Ngdoze's rage?"

"What's *he* gonna do against her muscle?" asked Cross, jutting her chin at Daoud. "Strong gust'd blow him over."

Daoud did his best to look innocent, but Aristide had taught him to shoot a pistol and seen him put the lessons into practice. He might be a bantam, but he could fight outside his weight class.

"Surely there's not room left on the ship." He was making poor excuses, now.

"You have a very large cabin," said Daoud. "I am certain it will fit a cot."

"I'm a grown man. I don't need a chaperone."

"I'm your business partner," said Cross. "And I think you do."

"*Equal* partners, Merrilee. You're neither my nanny nor my boss."

"It sounds like you need somebody to break the tie," said Daoud, and Aristide saw the irony ten miles out.

CHAPTER

SEVEN

Takeoff from Kenaipha was delayed due to weather, which meant Cyril spent a disagreeable several hours in the ramshackle airfield bar, eating handfuls of pastel, candy-coated almonds. There was no proper food.

Aowamma's final destination was on the island, and she left him to his drinking with a warm farewell he only managed to return in character. When she left the airfield, van Weill went with her.

Hyrosia in the winter was a bleak place: mostly rain, some sleet, incessant wind. Awful weather for flying. Finally, near dawn, they had a brief respite.

Few people were traveling to Dameskill Regional from Kenaipha; more than the meager five who boarded would have surprised Cyril. The pilot, who greeted the passengers as they climbed the stairs, made tasteless jokes about the likelihood of a crash. Several people turned green. Cyril settled into his seat without complaint and promptly fell asleep, thanks to the auspices of several stolen pills. Given the pharmacopeia in Aristide's washroom, he wouldn't miss them.

Cyril only woke as they thudded to the ground at Dameskill Regional. Outside the window, the downs rolled away into gentle hills. The grass was brown, the trees bare. In his memory, Dameskill county was green, and smelled of hay and strawberries in the sunshine. This felt like touching down in yet another foreign country.

But it felt right, too. Freshly mown fields beneath scudding clouds and a blue sky? That was the domain of a different man. A boy, even. How often had he come back to Carmody since school? And it had never been an idyll, then; it had been an imposition. Fraught holidays with aging parents. Then one funeral, and another. A miserable week lying low after the election in Nuesklend.

That was his last memory of the place: dogged by his failure and treachery, wandering empty rooms, sniffling and sneezing amidst the dust sheets as a late spring cold snap froze buds from the fruit trees. No family, no staff. Even the groundskeeper was away—with the remaining DePauls scattered, she only came up from the village one week out of three. Cyril hardly remembered the house lived-in.

A small cluster of cars had gathered in the field that passed for a runway. Unlike the other four passengers, Cyril didn't put his forehead to the window; didn't peer into the gray evening, growing grayer, to look for friends or family or a chauffeur. It would all be on him soon enough.

Likewise, he let the other four shuffle out ahead of him, wrapping their mufflers more tightly as the bitter wind made its way into the airplane cabin. As if it hadn't been freezing already.

He didn't have an overcoat, or hat or gloves. His joints had gone stiff in the chill high altitude, his fingers and toes numb. As a consequence, the cold bothered him very little now. And without a coat he cut, he realized too late, a somewhat more striking figure at the head of the stairs than he would have preferred.

Lillian, standing at the front fender of a shining black car, put her hand to the hood and took a step back when she saw him. She didn't cover her mouth, or gasp that he heard. She might merely have been shifting her weight. But even a decade out, he knew his sister. This, in her, was a dead faint in a lesser being.

She wore a tightly belted camel coat, the collar turned up against the wind. In the last photograph he had seen—she had been holding Stephen on one knee, both of them in summer clothes—her hair had been cut in a chin-length bob. Longer now, it was swept into a twist at the back of her head, drawing her features up so she seemed to stare haughtily down her nose.

All she needed was black robes and a pair of spectacles, and it would be his mother standing there, ready to pass judgment.

She met him at the bottom of the stairs and first took his face between her palms. This close he could see that her hair, like his, had begun to show threads of platinum white. Her red-rimmed eyes were framed by fine lines. Powder covered her dark circles poorly.

Someone else might have said she looked tired. But Cyril had seen tired. He had *been* tired. Still was. Lillian needed a week of good sleep, and food put in front of her. Cyril needed to lay down and die.

"Lady's name," she said. Her hands fell from his face to his shoulders, and then her arms were around him.

He fought his initial impulse—block a knife to the belly, bend to throw her over his shoulder—and simply let her hold him, though he could not make himself relax. The crook of her neck smelled of geranium perfume; the fabric of her collar like cedar and, faintly, mothballs.

"You're so thin," she said, fingers closing on his arms. "And holy stones, you must be *freezing*. Is that all you have? No overcoat?"

"I have a bag with socks," he said. "A few shirts. No other clothes. It was warm in Dadang."

She smoothed the wrinkles her grip had put into his sleeves, then held him and looked at him again. Fading daylight caught in a tear gathering at the corner of her eye. Before it fell, she squeezed him once and turned briskly to her driver.

"Martí," she said. "Is there a blanket under the seat? Will you get it out and air it, please? Yes, just give it a shake." Then, not quite looking at Cyril, "There's poached chicken for dinner. But if you want anything else . . . that is, if Bradley can get it. Given a little notice, of course, anything's possible, but the market these days . . . you understand."

Rationing. Ruined infrastructure. Mistrust. Hoarding. He understood.

"Poached chicken is fine," he said.

That was when she started crying.

It was dark by the time they passed through the gates. Cyril's memory supplied the curve of the lane, and the headlights proved him right. He had not forgotten how suddenly the house appeared from behind the hill.

He *had* forgotten how, at night, the lights of the windows reflected in the rippling water of the Dameskill where it ran along the lane. He had, in honesty, forgotten the Dameskill, and the sound of it rushing over stones where they broke the shallow surface. When the car stopped and Martí came to open his door, he mistook it at first for radio static.

The driver eyed him with the reserved curiosity of domestic staff, and he knew he would be a topic of much discussion downstairs. Maybe he already was. Though, Lillian would have been discreet;

Martí might not even know who he was. If any of the old guard were still in the butler's paybook, she'd find out quick enough, but that seemed unlikely bordering on absurd.

He wondered how many people Lillian could afford to keep on, if it was poached chicken for dinner and that a luxury. And if she could afford it, how many was it seemly to employ, if she didn't want her neighbors to talk? Or did they talk already?

What was life like, for Lillian in Gedda? Did the DePaul name carry authority anymore, or had his bad behavior stripped it of that? From what little he'd bothered to ask Aristide, and the equally scant information Ari volunteered, it was public knowledge that he'd thrown in with the Ospies, and also public knowledge he had thrown them over in turn. Public knowledge, but also old news, eclipsed by bombings, strife, and civil war.

"I told Stephen he could wait up to meet you." Lillian flexed a nervous hand inside her glove, pressing the opposite thumb into her palm so the leather creaked around it. "I hope that's all right."

"How old is he now?"

"Thirteen. And a nightmare. He . . ." Her gaze cut to him, sideways. Since that moment at the bottom of the airplane stairs, she hadn't been able to face him eye-to-eye. "He's in some trouble at school. It . . . well, it was familiar ground. Sometimes he reminds me of . . . you know."

She'd better hope he didn't turn out anything like Cyril, unless she looked forward to losing him one way or another.

The front doors swung open. A silhouette on the doorstep half-bowed. Cyril stared beyond the butler—too young to be someone he remembered, or who remembered him—into the front hall.

The tile was the same: white and cobalt, with small gold accents. But it was chipped in places now, and not kept as clean as he remembered. There had been potted palms when he was young: one beneath each archway. Without them the marble looked austere.

Each pillar bore a lily-shaped sconce, though some were broken. The chandelier, unchanged, glimmered at the end of its chain. At the far end of the hall, made giant by perspective, a Y-shaped staircase curled up to the second-floor gallery.

Golden light spilled down the broad front steps to touch his shoes. They didn't quite fit. Blisters, at least, felt familiar.

"Cyril," said Lillian, his name catching behind her teeth as though she had forgotten how to say it. She had reached the top of the steps, and paused in the unwinding of her scarf when she saw he had not followed. "Come inside. Your teeth are chattering."

He hadn't realized how the chill had gotten into him. In the sweltering north of Liso he'd forgotten what it was, to feel the cold. In the shelter of the house, bare degrees warmer than the night, tension wanted to leak from him. He wouldn't let it. Without that ache of fear in his muscles, they might not hold him up.

She led him—*Where? What was around this corner?*—to the library, yes, and paused at the door to knock. In her own home? Well, he supposed she wanted to warn whoever was in there she had come with him in tow.

Who *was* in there? Just Stephen? But why would he wait alone in the library, which they had as children always been forbidden?

He heard her murmur a sentence in Porashtu, and then an answering low voice, muffled by the door. Not a child; a grown man. Nerves crept up the nape of his neck. He didn't like going blind into a room. He didn't like the empty hallway at his back.

"Here he is," said Lillian, swinging wide the door. Cyril didn't know if she meant the announcement for him, or for his opposite number in the library.

The man on the sofa wore a quilted smoking jacket over a green flannel suit, and red velvet slippers over thick socks. His long, black hair was gathered into a messy knot at the back of his head, from which several tendrils of loose curls had escaped. A thick beard, closely cut, traced the line of his jaw and bracketed finely curved lips haunted by the echo of a habitual frown. The same frown had put deep furrows in his brow.

Firelight warmed his face on one side, bringing out rich clay red in the dark brown of his skin. Where the sharp angles of his cheek and nose cast shadows, only the gleam of his eye showed.

"Jinadh," said Lillian, "this is my brother. Cyril, this is Jinadh. Stephen's father. My husband."

Jinadh unfolded from the sofa and came to Lillian's side. He put out a hand to shake. Cyril missed the moment he put his own hand into Jinadh's proffered one. The man's palm was dry and warm, his grip firm. It was a good handshake, and it was the only thing that anchored Cyril to the moment.

Lillian was *married*. There was someone living at Damesfort who was not him, nor her, nor their parents. Someone who did not fit into his memories of the house or his own family. Cyril was *related* to this man, and the only thing that connected them was this handshake.

As though anything else felt closer than that; as though the rest of the world weren't at an arm's length, and him clinging to it by strength of habit and his fingertips.

"Where's Stephen?" said Lillian.

Jinadh's mouth fell into the frown Cyril had seen lurking. "I sent him to his room. He was being . . . difficult." The lilting cadence of Porashtu colored his Geddan, putting even more emphasis on the euphemism.

"We agreed—" Lillian bit off whatever she had been going to say, and began again, more placating. "Perhaps tonight we can be lenient?" Cyril felt the change in her focus, her weight shifting slightly in his direction.

Jinadh's frown deepened, and he made no secret of looking at Cyril. Still, he said, "Well enough," and untied the cord of his smoking jacket. "I will go tell him."

After he left, Lillian scrubbed her palms down the front of her skirt. "So. That's Jinadh."

"He's handsome," said Cyril, for want of anything more diplomatic. He suspected, from that exchange, that they often fought. But maybe it was only nerves.

Lillian blinked as though he'd spoken in a foreign language. Then said, "You needn't worry about dressing for dinner. We're certainly not going to."

"I wasn't," he said. "Remember? I don't have any clothes."

From the head of the table, Lillian stared across a surreal landscape. Everything was as it should have been for a guest—what was left of the good china, the freshly polished silver that almost matched— and the dining room was as it always had been. Even the occasional brush of Jinadh's elbow, as he dined left-handed to her right, was familiar.

But Stephen had gone from her left hand to the foot of the table, and her brother sat in his place.

Her brother, who she had kicked under this very table when he talked back, or tried to make her laugh in front of company. Who tonight, when Bern bent over to offer a dish of stewed greens, started so violently he nearly upset his glass. Her brother, who had been dead until this week, or as good as.

"Well," she said, cringing internally at the too-bright note her voice struck. "It's wonderful to have a full table, anyway."

Jinadh's smile wavered in the candlelight; he knew her well enough to parse the tone. Stephen made a small noise of disdain. Cyril put a piece of chicken in his mouth.

She picked up her fork. Put it down. "Cyril, there were some of Daddy's things left in the attic—a miracle, really, with everything else we lost. It was very hodgepodge, what the . . . previous tenants took. Anyway, I had Magnusson bring the lot down and air them for you. He was about your size, I think. Daddy, I mean."

He kept chewing, giving her a bare nod.

She had known it would be hard. She had known he wouldn't be who she remembered, and even the brother she remembered had driven the rest of the family to tail-chasing at times. That didn't make this easier. "And I made up the daisy room for you. You remember the daisy room? It's that big one, just off the—"

"I know," he said, and drank some wine.

Silence crept across the table.

"May I be excused?" said Stephen, in a sudden clatter of silverware.

"Not yet," said Lillian, more sharply than she'd meant to. This was not proceeding as she had envisioned.

Stephen sighed and scraped the tines of his fork across his plate. "Let him go."

Both Jinadh and Stephen looked as startled as Lillian felt. Stephen recovered from Cyril's interjection first, and started to get up.

"Stephen DePaul," said Lillian, "sit down this instant." Surprise made her strident.

"But he said—"

"Your *mother*," said Jinadh, "told you to *sit*."

"Thank you," said Lillian, glad for unexpected aid from that quarter. Too often, Jinadh made her the disciplinarian. "Steenie, I thought you were excited for this dinner."

Stephen's glare intensified, and she realized she had revealed a secret he had been hoping would go unacknowledged. Cyril was not supposed to know his visit had been looked forward to.

"*I* thought," said Cyril, "you were going to be lenient tonight."

"What?" said Stephen. "What's that supposed to mean? Can I go?"

Something in Cyril's face had changed. Earlier, he had seemed . . . not quite vacant, or empty, but like a wine bottle in which all the sediment had settled to the bottom and would not be stirred. The substance of his personality had remained compact and hidden. Now he was, if not exactly smiling, at least looking upon his nephew with *expression* in his eyes. The candle flames made it wavering and uncertain, but there was something there. What that expression *meant*, she couldn't say.

Hadn't she said Stephen reminded her of Cyril, at that age? Maybe he saw something there to drag him back from whatever fort he'd barricaded his heart within. She had told Jinadh they would get along like a match and a wick, and at least this fitful smolder-ing was better than what had come before.

"All right," she said. "But mind you clean your teeth well. And do the reading you've been set."

He was out the dining room door before she finished her sen-tence, so that she brought her volume up at the end to chase him.

There was a small noise from Cyril—an exhalation, brief and amused—so that below her annoyance, she felt warmth rise in her chest.

"You see what I mean," she said, to Cyril. "About how he can be?"

Cyril shrugged. "He's young."

"I wonder." Forced banality strung Jinadh's words taut: drawing room charm, sorely taxed.

"What, dear?" asked Lillian, sensing a pitfall.

"Only if Mr. DePaul, in all his many endeavors, has any experi-ence in the rearing of children?"

The small living thing that had been stirring behind Cyril's eyes withdrew so swiftly she might have imagined it was ever there. "I haven't had that pleasure."

Jinadh pressed his lips into a smiling imitation of indulgence. "Well then, perhaps you should leave it to us. Or at least ask for some advice, before presuming."

Cyril aimed the same expression back at him, honed to an even sharper point. He offered no rejoinder; instead, without looking at Lillian, he dropped into deep sarcasm and said, "May I be excused?"

"I thought you *wanted* him here." Lillian yanked her hairbrush through a tangle with unnecessary vehemence. "What was that about?"

Jinadh sat on the edge of their bed and dug for his lighter in the nightstand. Though her parents had kept separate bedrooms, and there was space at Damesfort for them to do the same, Jinadh had leaned heavily in favor of one suite. She now suspected it had less to do with intimate reasons, and more with diplomatic; it forced them to resolve conflicts or go without sleep. Anyway, it was one less room to heat.

"I . . ." he picked at the duvet.

"*You* told me to bring him. You said you'd be happy to meet him. He's my *brother*." She bit down hard on another escalation, and forced herself to swallow it. It burned going down, like raw liquor, and stung her eyes the same. Whatever had torn out Cyril's center and left that husk at the dining table, it wasn't Jinadh's fault.

"I know!" Jinadh stood again, leaving wrinkles in the bedclothes. He lit the straight crammed into the corner of his mouth and took a hasty, irritated drag. "But Lillian, he . . . there is something *wrong*. He needs . . . I do not know what he needs, but I do not think that we can help him. And I am not certain that I want him around Stephen."

"I hardly think he's dangerous," she said, a seedling of doubt unfurling even as she spoke the words.

«How well do you know him?» asked Jinadh, shifting to Porashtu. He often did, when he had something hard to say. She was guilty of the same, in the opposite direction, and she'd been speaking less Porashtu in general since they came to Amberlough. «He's been gone nearly a decade.»

Guilty, she met him on the playing field of his mother tongue. «He's my brother,» she said again, less vehement this time. The doubt was creeping up her walls like ivy. If she didn't strip it away, the mortar of her convictions would crumble. And if she couldn't believe what she told herself, she wouldn't know where to place her trust. Gathering her confidence, she went on more firmly: «He only needs time. Think how hard it was for us. And he has passed through so much more.»

Jinadh stopped in the center of the room, then sighed and came to sit beside her, settling amidst the ephemera of her vanity. She put her brush down and held a hand out for his cigarette.

"I apologize," he told her. "I know. It is only that . . ." He picked up a pot of cold cream and turned it in his hands. "It feels as though since we came to Gedda you have been elsewhere, either in mind or body. Because of your work, and the campaign. And Stephen has been at school, not writing much. I thought we would have time during Solstice. To come together again."

"We will," said Lillian, stubbing out the butt of his straight.

"Even with your brother here?"

"You don't think he can . . . come together with us?"

Jinadh paused in his fiddling with the cold cream to give her a worried look. «From what I know of him, he's better at tearing things apart.»

It hurt all the more for being true. Rarely had the DePaul family gotten through a holiday, a trip, or even a quiet dinner at home without a tussle, Cyril inevitably at the center of the conflict. Gedda was just a bigger, nastier example of his mode of operation.

"I think he's probably learned his lesson," said Lillian, rising from her stool. "Unzip me?"

Jinadh's fingers closed on the clasp at the nape of her neck, then moved down her back with the zipper. «I *am* sorry, moon-eyes,» he said, and kissed her neck.

She put a hand to his head and pressed her cheek to his hair: loosely braided for sleep, soft with scented oil. «Me, too. Bed?»

It wasn't until she slipped beneath the covers that she realized how chill and bone-tired she was. The mattress pressed up to meet her, and Jinadh hissed when she tucked her feet behind his knees.

"Did Magnusson get that stain out of your dinner jacket?" she asked, unable even half asleep to let loose ends lie.

"He did."

"You're sure you won't wear a kurta for the reception?" she said.

He lifted his eyelids a bare several centimeters. «Don't try it on me, too.»

"Try what?"

«You've got Makricosta to dress your set,» he said. «And I've heard you talking with Honora over the phone; the guest list reads like Ospie Gedda turned inside-out. Immigrants and agitators, to an invitation. I'll wear my dinner jacket.»

"Stones." She put her forehead to his shoulder. "I'm sorry. I never should have asked.»

«No,» he agreed. «You shouldn't have.»

"I just need a nod from Honora at the end of this. A letter, a word in the right ear. I can do a lot of the work myself, but it never hurts to have a phalanx at your back. And she's good for ten soldiers at least."

"You will find something," he said. "Even if it isn't the Cliff House. And we will not starve."

"In this economy?" she asked. "Don't be so sure. We'd have to sell off land, at any rate. And with my family history . . ."

«You said it's safe for Cyril to be here. Isn't it safe for us?»

«Safe is not happy,» she said. «Safe is not comfortable.»

«Safe isn't powerful, either,» he countered, with a trace of bitterness.

«Jinadh . . . » She closed her eyes, face crumpling in frustration. «It's not about that.»

«If you could tell me what it *is* about, I might believe you.»

"I just want to get our name up out of the dust. I know it sounds hackneyed, but the DePauls had *honor* once—"

"Honor." He said it not with anger but exhaustion. «What kept us apart in Porachis, Lillian? What made me miserable for years? I'd rather be a father than found a dynasty. I'd rather be happy than honorable.»

"It's just a few more months," she said. "We go to the polls just after Equinox. If nothing comes of it after that . . ." She managed a small shrug, rustling the bedclothes, but couldn't look at him.

He sighed deeply. «I will be *very* glad when this election is over.»

She hoped she would share the sentiment.

CHAPTER

EIGHT

Aristide recognized the harbor in his soul, and at the same time hardly knew it.

The water stank like it always had: oil and sewage and shriveled seaweed. The shape of the Spits stood out sharp against a steely sky, and he remembered a thousand sunsets sinking behind them, seen from the fashionable side of the bay. The dome of the capitol, which had once been visible over the masts and hulls and chimneys in the harbor, was now obscured by scaffolding.

"Still cleaning up?" Daoud stood beside him at the railing, wrapped to the nose in a muffler. "It has been a year of peacetime."

"A year under an interim government," said Aristide. "With many other nasty dishes on its plate."

"Talking of nasty dishes," said Daoud. "When would you like to meet with Jamila?"

"Now, now." Aristide slotted his fingers together, pushing his gloves more tightly onto his hands. "Ms. Osogurundi has done very well by Cross-Costa in the last six months."

«I appreciate that,» said Daoud. «Almost as much as I appreciate the fact she's been doing it here instead of in Rarom.»

"The only reason you don't like her is you're fussy, and she's not afraid to put her arms in the midden to the elbows. Which is what makes her perfect for the job."

"Then it is good she does it, and not me." Daoud shivered. "*Mihaaz*. How do people live in this climate?"

"Speaking for myself," said Aristide, "mulled wine, silk underwear, and an eiderdown duvet. It isn't the worst of the seasons, if you're well prepared."

It made him think of the duvet on Daoud's sturdy double bed, back in Rarom. And that, in turn, made him think of his cabin, which had never seen a cot through the crossing. It made him think of any number of things that could keep one warm in the winter, besides the ones he'd listed.

Shifting his weight, he put another several inches between the two of them.

Daoud retreated farther into his muffler. "And if you are not?"

"Sorry?" His discomfort had distracted him from the thread of conversation.

"If you are not prepared."

Oh. He meant the weather, still. "Rotten miserable."

The ship shuddered as it came to a full halt, leaving them stationary several stories above the docks. Aristide looked down on the milling hats and luggage carts, the clouded breath of hundreds rising with the steam from food carts and exhaust pipes. Abruptly, through the haze of stagnant water and diesel fumes, he caught the scent of fry oil and the salty tang of eel.

His stomach growled, and he thought about brown paper packets of barley fritters. About crispy cardamom rice balls, and hot chestnuts roasted over a coffee can grill fueled with shredded news-papers.

"I hope the hotel has a good kitchen," he said. "And they can get something worthwhile to cook in it."

"Do not raise your hopes too high. It has been bad weather for the farmers. A dry summer. And despite the efforts of West Cultham Rail Company, among others, the railroads are not as good as they were. Too many tracks blown, thanks to the Catwalk."

"Ah well," said Aristide. "I've eaten beans before." Then, "West Cultham. Isn't that—?"

"Jamila can tell you more," said Daoud, suddenly brisk. "*Chii bhale*, or they will give our bags to someone else."

Despite his worries, their bags were waiting on a cart with a por-ter in earmuffs standing attentively by. She helped them find a taxi, and Aristide tipped extravagantly. The tourist trade had likely flagged along with the rest of the economy.

"Hello there," said Aristide, bundling himself and his mink into the backseat of the cab.

"Where are you headed?" asked the driver. Tatien, by his accent. A loyalist, probably, and a refugee now that his state had achieved an ill-fated independence from Gedda.

"Oh, what's the name of the hotel?" Aristide asked, though he had it by memory. He didn't like to sound too eager.

"Sykes House," said Daoud. "At . . ." he consulted his datebook. "Coral and Whitney."

The cabbie whistled low. "Nice piece of town. Even now." As he pulled away from the bustling dockside curb, he said, "This is your first time in Amberlough?"

"Mine," said Daoud. "Yes."

"And you?" Aristide caught the flick of the cabbie's eyes in the rearview mirror.

"In a while," he said. "I haven't been back for some years."

"The war?" asked the cabbie.

"Its . . . antecedents. And you sound like you come from the east."

He made a noise with his teeth: something sucked back he might otherwise have spat. "Foolishness, to leave the federation. And look what it's gotten Memmediv and his folk, ah? If Tatié lasts 'til spring, it's only by the blessing of the Queen."

"Are we still calling it that?" asked Aristide. "Gedda, I mean. 'The federation.'"

"If you listen to the provisional folk, yes. After the election, who knows? Frye thinks we should keep the interstate borders open, tariffs down. She's got interests in the railroads and she'll serve herself first, but it doesn't mean she won't lay a good table. Saeger . . . People like her for herself, you know? Me, I want to hear her talk real policy. Not just bedtime stories. So she wants us all to be siblings in the struggle to end hunger and poverty. Fine. What about the treasury? And our borders? And our infrastructure? Where will all this money come from? It's a choice between a dreamer and an oligarch."

"You haven't always driven a cab," asked Aristide, "have you?"

The driver snorted. "And a cabbie can't talk politics?"

Aristide opened his mouth to pull out his foot, but was given a pardon before he could manage.

"I was a professor at Haverin East," said the driver. "And ran for city council once or twice. Not much city left now, I hear."

He stopped at a signal. Aristide glanced at their surroundings and realized with a start that they had reached the intersection of Temple Street and Seagate Road.

"This is rather out of the way, isn't it?" he asked. "We ought to have turned onto Station a while back."

"It's a mess," said the driver. "Construction at the trolley transfer. Faster to take Seagate to Staunton and then go north. A good memory, if you've been gone so long."

Aristide hesitated a moment, eyeing the red light, daring it to change before he asked what was about to slip from his tongue. But it didn't, and he said, "I know it's out of the way, but would you mind just taking us a few blocks north on Temple?"

The driver shrugged and flipped down the stalk by his wheel to indicate.

It wasn't far off Seagate—a block and a half, if he remembered right. And as the driver had said, his memory for these things was good. He had a map of the city—*his* city—at the ready behind his eyes.

Many of the marquees were dark; more than a few had been converted to picture palaces. Others had been knocked down and replaced with offices or apartments. But others still stood tall and proud. Some had scorched façades, which made Aristide wonder about the extent of rioting and revolution. He'd been given to understand armed conflict was limited, and that "civil war" meant less trenches and gunfire than mob violence and political pressure. Still, Temple Street bore scars. The ugliest of which they were approaching now.

"Stop," said Aristide, abruptly, and they did. "Will you just idle here for a bit? Thank you."

"Aristide," said Daoud, brows furrowed.

"I won't be a moment." When he opened the door, a blast of cold, wet air met his face. Snow oncoming, he should think. Or maybe sleet. His instinctual prediction startled him; the weather had never got into his bones abroad like it had here, and it had been some time since he recognized a shift in the wind and knew what it would bring.

The Bee had stood between a wine bar and a casino, last time he saw it. Now, the empty place where its marquee had been was bracketed by a bad restaurant and a second-rate hotel. The small square left vacant between them was newly paved and populated with wrought-iron benches and holly trees hastily popped into decorative planters. Those wouldn't make it through the winter, not potted this late. He imagined they weren't meant to—their corpses would be replaced with tulips in the spring.

At the center of the square stood a monument shrouded in canvas and rope. He was sorely tempted to cross the street and peek beneath the edge of the covering, but stayed where he was in order not to draw attention, or the ire, of his taxi driver. Besides, two hounds were posted to either side of the park entrance, huddled miserably in their macks. Aristide squinted through the top of his bifocals, fairly certain he could see the shadow of shoulder holsters behind their lapels. ACPD hounds hadn't gone armed with more than a truncheon the last time he walked these streets. He wondered if it was a new standard, or an exception granted for these particular guards.

About Cordelia's end he knew only as much as the next person—whatever he'd heard on the wireless, or read about in the paper. She had been killed in a tactical strike turned sour. Someone had tipped police to a major Catwalk cell receiving a visit from the Spotlight herself, and set the hounds on Cordelia's scent. But what was supposed to be a swift assassination turned into a neighborhood skirmish in the capital city of Nuesklend, just a few miles from the embattled Cliff House. The Catwalk had built a strong base by that point, and instead of a single shot to the head and a body swiftly removed, uncooperative citizenry turned the thing into forced entries, raids without warrants, door-to-door fighting, and finally gunfire in the streets. The result was significant collateral damage, most of it thanks to the Ospies. It looked bad. It made Cordelia into a martyr, and put wind in the sails of a revolution that eventually pushed Acherby from power: first, after he stepped down, and second, after a surviving member of the Catwalk shot him on the curb, on his way out of the country.

In his imagination, Aristide saw Cordelia backed against a wall, behind a crumbling barricade of bullet-riddled furniture. She wore an almost cosmetic streak of blood on one round cheek, and she met the Ospies' guns with a haughty smile and a few shots of her own. When she collapsed, she fell forward as if she were taking a bow. Red had always looked good on her.

He wondered if the memorial captured anything like that.

One of the cab doors opened then shut, and Daoud was at his elbow, closer than he had yet dared to come on land.

"So that is it," he said, soft voice almost lost in wool and the howl of the wind.

"It was," said Aristide, and climbed back into the car.

After a brief stop to collect mail and drop off baggage, Aristide and Daoud hailed another cab and navigated the potholes and saw-horses of the city streets to reach the Amberlinian offices of Cross-Costa Imports.

Even in his heyday, he hadn't kept a proper brick-and-mortar spot to do his business. Why, when he had friends and colleagues in all parts of the city, and could catch a cab or a streetcar to call on them? When there were restaurants, teahouses, opium dens, and absinthe bars that could as easily play host to a rendezvous?

But when one was working across continents, he certainly saw the utility in it. A central hub for the telegraph and ticker tape, a place to take radio calls and direct all the company's correspondence. It was less glamorous than the lamp-lit Crabtree House or the glass-and-silver fountains of Amanti's, but it also drew less attention. Appear to operate above the table, and folk rarely looked beneath.

Aristide had been confident in his own ability to flash his colors and still slip the snares, operating on his own recognizance in a city he knew like the reach of his arms, the shape of his teeth against his tongue. As a part of a consortium, in terrain made foreign by years and conflict, he would rather don the disguise of banality.

Occupying the top floor of a neat brick low rise near the old customs house, the Cross-Costa offices could not have been more boring. The neighborhood smelled like low tide and diesel fumes, and the narrow stairwell reeked of cigars. Climbing up the threadbare runner, Aristide found the source of the latter stench just inside the office door, its brass nameplate in need of a polish.

Jamila Osogurundi, Amberlinian daughter of Lisoan immigrants lately returned home after riding out the Ospies in Rarom, rolled a smoldering cheroot between her fingers as she spoke into the telephone. At volume. Two clerks cringed in opposite corners, heads down at their ledgers as if the conversation were an oppressive cloud akin to the cigar smoke. Jamila held forth in a rolling patois of Shedengue and Geddan, embellished with indecipherable slang: from what Aristide could gather, she was jovially cursing somebody's mother.

The hallway was too narrow for Daoud and Aristide to stand side by side, but he imagined that the younger man was grimacing.

Jamila looked up from her cigar and saw them standing in the doorway. "Ah, bless me," she said, "the holy one has come at last." And then, "No, *pati*, not you. *Juma de sibe la.* Yeah, yeah, you wish. All right, I'll see you. And tell our friend we appreciate his efforts. *Ahundibi.* Yeah. Bye now. Yes, bye." The bell jangled as she dropped the receiver back into the cradle.

"Aristide Makricosta!" she said. "I'm sober as a penitent, so your bones must really be here." She was a young woman, but she talked like a crooked bookmaker and rose from her seat like the has-been wrestler in a fixed fight: palms on the blotter, pressing her weight through her arms. There was a sizable amount to press. Jamila wasn't tall, but she was built like a drum of kerosene.

"Ms. Osogurundi," he said. Her handshake resonated all the way into his shoulder.

"Call me Jamila or I'll quit. Looks like you brought the welter-weight along as well!"

Daoud's smile would have been at home against a leather strop.

"Cross tells me you've been making useful friends." Aristide took his cigarette case from his pocket and offered one to Daoud before he availed himself. A poor apology, and Daoud refused it. "Something about the West Cultham Rail Company?"

"No foreplay with you," she said. "I forgot. At least let a girl get a little wet."

Daoud slapped a leather folio down onto Jamila's desk. "A prospectus for Geddan expansion, based on the assumption of a deal with West Cultham. Will it be possible?"

Jamila stared at him blankly for a moment, until a smile began to build on her face. It was very wide by the time she finished. She slapped Daoud on the back—he made a sound like *oof*—and picked the folio up but did not open it.

"That depends on *you,* my friends. I buttered this roll; you've got to put it on the grill to fry. Hah. Fry, Frye. That's a good one. Though you're going to be dealing with a peach named Frances Custler, not the lady herself. West Cultham is held in trust until the election. And if Frye wins, Custler's the head of WCRC throughout her term."

"Nominally," said Daoud, tone sour.

Jamila jabbed a finger at him. "Hit it in one."

"How short *is* that jess?" asked Aristide.

"That's the question, ain't it? She's been cagey with me. 'Course she wants the world to think Frye's washed her hands of the operation. Saeger's already all over her for mixing profit and politics."

"And you think she'll tell me?"

"Not a chance," said Jamila. "But maybe you can suss her better than me. Anyway, she said she'd bend her knees with you. And that's a start."

They joined Frances Custler at her home for dinner that evening—she was free, and the rest of Aristide's week was promised to the provisional government and Lillian DePaul.

Custler kept a bachelor apartment on Ionidous Avenue. The place looked only half lived-in, and was quite a comedown from Aristide and Daoud's rooms at Sykes House. She could probably afford better. Aristide wondered why she kept the place, and where she spent the rest of her time when she wasn't laying her head down here.

Custler herself was a broad-shouldered woman of perhaps forty-five, short hair styled slick with pomade. Though her rooms were chill, she wore shirtsleeves and those rolled up to show freckled, densely muscled forearms. She had the air of a factory foreman, though her waistcoat and wristwatch read *money* if one could parse the language. Aristide, as it happened, was fluent.

They could have, he supposed, gone to some public establishment, but electoral tensions were high; many eyes were straining to catch a fault. And Custler's landlord kept a serviceable kitchen. He brought them gratin and a roast: simple fare, but good quality cooked well. Where he'd got ahold of it was anyone's guess; the meat at Sykes House had been thin and tough at lunch, a cheap cut dressed up with vinegar and salt. Aristide suspected there were juicier chops available, if one had the cash and the contacts.

Besides, the firelit obscurity of Custler's dining room set a satisfying scene for their conversation. It also meant there was no pretense. No sooner had the wine come uncorked than Custler said, "You're lowballing us on your offer."

"In response to an initial quote that was, quite frankly, ludicrous." Aristide sliced into his beef. It was very pink in the middle, and the juice ran in rivulets across his plate.

Custler smiled into her glass. "I like you already."

"Better than Jamila?"

Swallowing hurriedly, Custler flapped a hand. "No, no. Oso's fine. But if I can deal with the boss, I'd rather. And you just happened to be in town. Lucky me. Written your speech yet?"

The meat in his mouth suddenly lost its savor. He choked it down, and instead of answering he asked her, "Will you be at the dedication?"

Custler snorted, and put her elbows on the table to roll a cigarette. "That's Emmeline's crowd, not mine."

The way she said the name put Aristide in mind of the way Cross sometimes referred to her husband, or the cargo pilot they kept it up with on and off, when he flew shipments to Rarom. An affectionate kind of derision that conveyed unintended volumes about the speaker's intimacy with the subject.

He filed this useful piece of information away, right beside his observations of the dusty mantel and the scent of vacancy that hung about Custler's rooms.

"Perhaps we'll cross paths," he said. "Gracious of her to attend, when the Catwalk wreaked such havoc with her livelihood."

"Are you kidding?" Custler sawed at her beef with gusto. "WCRC's picked up some lucrative contracts from the temps—the provisional government. We're not just running trains, you know. We're building rails for pay."

"Which means," said Daoud, "you ought to be amenable to a lower rate when it comes to shipping Cross-Costa's goods." He removed another leather folio from his briefcase and slid it across the table. An adapted version of the prospectus they had brought to Jamila; shorter on detail than the internal version, and the rest of it polished to shine.

"It speaks," said Custler. "I was starting to think you just kept him to fetch and carry. And maybe to improve the scenery."

Like Frye does you? Aristide thought but did not say.

Custler set her twist in the ashtray beside her plate and took up the folder. There was a protracted silence, broken only by the ticking of the clock. Daoud caught Aristide's eye, then let it fall. Inconveniently, Aristide felt his cheeks warm with shame. He hoped his complexion would conspire with the unsteady light to hide it.

After an interminable overview of the figures provided, Custler set them down, retrieved her twist, and took a long drag. "I don't know," she said. "This is a lot to move, and a ticklish time to be moving it."

"You mean you will not offer a lower rate," said Daoud. "Very well, there are other rail companies in Gedda."

Aristide wished they were sat close enough for a sharp kick to the shin. He settled for sending a quelling glance over the casserole dish, which Daoud took with a bland smile. Anger seared him through, smoldering into inconvenient lust.

"There are," said Custler, watching Daoud closely, then sliding her eyes to Aristide.

"None so discreet," he said. "Jamila tells me you have some experience with shipments . . . similar to ours."

"Sure, we've moved a little contraband here and there. Who hasn't? But this kind of thing, this scope, you're looking at a lot of trust on both sides. When deals like this go bad, folk end up in prison, if not worse. Emmy's running for prime minister; you can understand she might be nervous."

"Emmeline Frye," said Aristide, "is not acting president of this company."

"But how many people will care, if we get caught moving half a ton of poppy tar deep into Gedda? If somebody was suspicious, they might almost think you were trying to load us up with a plant, so when somebody sings we get caught up to our wrists."

"Far be it for me to downplay your concerns." Aristide held his wine, turned the glass, and inspected its legs. Rather thin, for the cut of meat she'd served. "Suspicion has saved me many heartaches in the past. But I am in no way invested in the outcome of this election."

"You were friends with Lehane," said Custler. "So was Saeger. And you're speaking at this Catwalk dedication. I think that argues at least a *scrap* of partiality."

"I am speaking," he said, "out of a sense of deep personal obligation." Truth came to him with difficulty, and the strain told in his tone. Daoud began to look concerned.

"To who? Lehane? Or the temps, maybe? I got word—from where I don't care to tell—it was Lillian DePaul who leaned on you to come."

"She *invited* me, if that's what you mean. Is she mixed up with Saeger, somehow?"

Custler laughed and picked up her long-abandoned twist, drawing on it so the tip burned bright. "She's got her fingers in both pies. A real nice-maker, y'know? I get it. She wants to hammer down a place for herself no matter who ends up on top. That, I understand. I ain't worried about her. I just got questions about you. Why are you here now, offering this deal? Are you Saeger's patsy, or are you just doing a favor for the sister of your old cockmuff?"

Cold steel slid through his middle. It *had* been in the news, some years ago. The Ospies, angry with Lillian, had flung all the DePauls' dirty linens across the lawn. His affair with Cyril was one of the stained sheets.

Then he remembered nobody was after either of them right now; Custler probably didn't even know Cyril was alive, let alone in the country.

A swift sizzle of nerves and elation turned his blood to seltzer: Cyril was in Amberlough, just up the highway in the weald. Cyril was alive and in one piece, and would be arriving in the city soon. He was the reason Aristide had come.

But he would rather swallow tacks than tell Custler that. So what *could* he tell her?

"I was afraid," he said abruptly, the explanation snapping into place with the swiftness and clarity of his most perfect falsehoods.

It surprised her at any rate. "Afraid?"

Gratifying, how that always stunned folk. That Aristide Makricosta might feel the chill of fear like any other earthly creature.

"I'll tell you the truth," he said. "The LSI has clocked a little racket we had going with Porachin aid shipments and told us to cut off their biggest troublemakers in the north. I've pinned some people I don't like to be on the wrong side of. And we're looking for another stream of revenue. Are you satisfied?"

This put a slow smile across Custler's face: a warm and greasy one that spread like melting wax.

"You know," she said, "I heard things about you would raise the hairs on a hanged man. But I'm starting to think you're just a crooked sculler like the rest of us. Damned good one, but a sculler all the same."

CHAPTER

NINE

It snowed lightly the night before they left for the city, so that the drive south took them through an ashy landscape of ice-rimed empty fields, but by the time they arrived at Coral Street the weather had warmed enough to turn the snow to slush. Cyril, in a pair of borrowed gaiters, took the path to the front door slowly. Not because half-melted ice made it treacherous, but because he could hardly be sure it was real. He hadn't been over the threshold of number twenty-four since he was in school.

"It's not . . ." Lillian began, turning back to face him before mounting the steps. "Well. We were gone for a long time. And things didn't go any better here than they did in the rest of Gedda."

The damage wasn't immediately apparent, in the vestibule. Even the front hall only looked a little bare. Pale patches on the wall showed where paintings had hung, but nothing was splintered or broken. The pineapple newel on the bottom of the staircase sent a shock of recognition through him: a sudden vivid memory of the slip of satiny wood beneath his hand, against his short pants; sliding down the bannister, hopping off, catching at the newel to slow himself before he fell.

"I thought we'd put you in the library," said Lillian. "On the sofa. It's just we don't have . . . there are only two bedrooms furnished, at present. They took most of the furniture, or sold it. And there are some broken windows in the back we've just patched up with wood. The library will be warm, at least."

It was that. And also empty of literature. He ran a hand over the tufted leather of the sofa, scarred in places, set on the parquet amidst deep scratch marks.

Too heavy to move, then, and too difficult to get through the door. Unlike books and art, silver and linens.

"They gave it to the Ospies," said Stephen from the doorway. Cyril controlled his flinch, barely; it passed through his body like a sudden chill, leaving him shaky, but it didn't show.

"The house," Stephen went on. "Some Ospie family lived here, and another one at Carmody."

"They stole the books?"

He shrugged. "Dunno. Sold a lot of the furniture I think, or just junked it. Maybe ran with it at the end. And what they didn't grab or get rid of I guess went in the riots." He kicked at the wainscoting, not quite hiding his expression. Cyril was certain that he could have, if he wanted to. But he was leaving an opening, a hint: a light shining under an unlocked door. He was begging to be asked a question.

Some of Cyril's best and bravest informants had been Stephen's age: arrogant boys and girls who were not quite, anymore. Children who stood teetering on the cusp of fully grown. Some of his most dangerous enemies had been the same. He had learned to get the information he needed from them, which required a different set of tactics than he used on people his own age and older.

They craved respect and responsibility. They despised dissembling above all things. Adults preferred comfortable lies and illusions; Cyril had been rudely disabused of this preference some eight years back, and so often found it easier to interact with his younger informants and interrogatees. Being frank with thirteen-year-olds got you the answer you wanted. Try it on their elders and you'd be rebuffed before you could get your breath back. Adults required wooing. People who had not quite become adults? They were desperate to woo.

"Lillian said you were in trouble at school." He ran a hand along the marble mantelpiece. "What for?"

"*Lillian*," said Stephen, with the relish of an angry child using a parent's given name, "has some rotten gall, telling you *that* right out of the gate."

"She's always been like that," said Cyril, settling easily into Stephen's side of things. "A busybody. She knows what's best for everyone."

Stephen's suspicion morphed from purely hostile to partly surprised. "I blew up a pencil sharpener."

Cyril did not laugh, or scold. Just raised an eyebrow and asked "How?"

"Put some potassium in the shavings bin."

"Which you got from . . . ?"

"Chemistry cupboard." Then, more defensively, "Puddle *never* locks it. It isn't even like I broke in."

"Puddle?" asked Cyril.

"Master Tuttle," said Stephen. "Chemistry teacher. Complete fart."

Ah. Pitiable professor. Student eager to impress his peers. Volatile combination. Rather like potassium and pencil shavings. "Did people laugh?"

Stephen scoffed. "Rotten fireworks. Best thing they'd seen since Millicent Rice mooned the headmaster."

"Anyone hurt?"

The scoff faded into sullenness. "No."

"Do you wish they had been?"

Stephen really looked at him, then. Not just a leery sideways glance, but a full-on stare. His nephew's eyes were so dark they swallowed his pupils. Or perhaps his pupils were just that wide. Fear, excitement. Either would do it.

"No," said Stephen, more softly this time, and then looked back at his feet.

For a precarious moment, Cyril thought that might be the end of things. He had just reached for another opener when Stephen looked up again and spoke.

"Mum won't tell me outright, but . . . You were a spy. Weren't you? Even before the Ospies. You did all kinds of dangerous stuff. With guns and all. And coded messages."

"With guns and all," said Cyril, keeping his irony close to his chest.

"What was it like?" asked Stephen. "Did you kill anybody?"

He thought of the ceremony tomorrow. Of Cordelia, and everyone like her who'd suffered for his cowardice. "I did."

"What else?" asked Stephen, no longer sullen or arrogant, but deeply sincere. "Can you do poisons? What about microfilm? Did you ever have to go behind enemy lines?"

"Let's just say that I *could* teach you how to build a better bomb," said Cyril. "But more importantly, I can teach you not to get caught."

A crowd gathered for the ceremony, despite the weather. Gray slush stood an inch deep over the bricks of the small park they'd made where Cyril had once sat with a cocktail and watched the curtain rise.

The space looked smaller than it had when the Bee filled it: grubby walls on three sides, without windows. A patch of low sky dragging its belly, threatening more snow. He lifted his collar, against the wind and any curious gazes that might come his way.

"Neither of us are exactly pariahs," Lillian had told him the night before, when she brought down some blankets for him to use. "They ran a couple of exposés when I first came back from Asu—I gave one or two interviews. Everyone wanted something juicy, a big tell-all, but I tried to keep it bland. Mostly about family and patriotism. People don't care about you if you're boring."

"And me? I imagine my story's a little harder to downplay."

Her smile looked more like a wince. "Well, it's been quite a while since your photo ran, and you . . . don't quite match it anymore. Still, I'd keep a low profile."

"You aren't," he said, trying to decide if he recognized the pattern of the quilt she spread across the sofa. Family heirloom? Or newer acquisition?

"My situation's a *little* more sympathetic than yours, I think." She smoothed wrinkles from the quilt. "I didn't hand the police over to the Ospies like a rotten key to the city."

"Is that what the article said?" he asked.

"No," she said. "It's what I read in your file when they told me you were dead and I'd end up the same if I didn't play along." She smacked his pillow, fluffing it. "The papers made it sound a little more tabletop."

"Like?"

"'Though he showed early promise brokering an understanding between Acherby's government and the ACPD, DePaul nevertheless proved to be dangerously unreliable, owing his loyalty not to his country but to his own deviance.' That kind of thing."

When he asked what the Ospies had printed about her, she asked if she could turn the light off. He said yes, though he hadn't undressed or even gotten under the covers.

They hadn't spoken much at breakfast, or in the car on the way to Temple Street. When Lillian hit the slushy ground she was already on some other level, assembled to wage a charming war. Cyril became an afterthought, and he was grateful for that. Standing at the edge of the crowd, he looked up and down Temple Street. It had always seemed a little seedy in the daytime, then, or at least out of its element. Now it just looked sad. That could have been the weight of winter dragging on the city, but he didn't think so.

The speeches started—he heard applause, the squeal of a microphone—and he turned half-reluctantly from the damp, cold set piece of the street. No one he recognized. Nobody he could imagine Cordelia having known. Not even—Who was it? He'd been poking at the newspapers by the hearth last night, in the small hours when he couldn't sleep. Saeger. Opal Saeger. Cordelia's right hand, apparently. Old Catwalk folk, probably still smelled like cordite. The logical choice to speak at this half wake, half aggrandizement. Except she was running for prime minister, and the provisional government couldn't appear to favor one candidate over the other.

She'd be here, though. Lillian had said as much at breakfast while she tiptoed around speaking directly to Cyril. Jinadh made a sarcastic remark in Porashtu, and Lillian sighed and said, in a long-suffering tone, "I believe it translates as 'brown-nosing,'" which was how Cyril learned his sister was after some attention from Saeger.

"This isn't the kind of thing that would appeal to Frye's base," said Lillian. "But she needs to branch out if she wants to win. I told her as much when we spoke at the Parks Foundation fundraiser."

That was Lillian: hands in every pie to the wrists.

Now Honora Simons took to the podium for her turn to speak: grief and hope, duty to the memories of the deceased. Cyril vaguely remembered Lillian mentioning her in letters from school. Had she visited Damesfort one summer? Her pat phrases were followed by applause, which faded into an expectant hush when she failed to leave the stage.

"So far," she said, "our speakers have been officials, politicians, and policy makers. People who are helping to rebuild our nation, in what we hope was the image carried in the hearts of those we honor here today."

He wondered if Lillian had written this speech. She would deploy cloying sentiment if she thought it would stick. Honora's syrupy delivery wasn't doing it any favors.

"Now," she went on, "I have the solemn privilege of introducing a man who was there at the inception of the Catwalk—"

Cyril realized who was about to speak, and wondered if what she had said was true.

"—Who knew Cordelia Lehane as an everyday acquaintance before we knew her as a leader." Honora was positively gleeful, and hiding it poorly. "A man who shared a stage with her, and can speak about her not as a figurehead but as a friend. Distinguished guests, I give you: Aristide Makricosta."

As the crowd had stood longer and longer in the cold, their feet in icy puddles, audience response to the speakers had flagged. It picked up now, noticeably, though the clapping had a heavy, flat tone: Everyone was wearing gloves. Honora returned to her seat, ceding the microphone to Aristide.

He looked, somehow, warmer and more comfortable than the rest of them, as though he had been carried in a litter over the slush and wore long underwear of a better quality. A life onstage, Cyril supposed, had prepared him for this moment. And probably a significant amount of brandy.

He did not seem to have trained in the same school as the other speakers. There was no hesitancy as he approached the lectern, nor any reverence. "I wouldn't have called her an *everyday* acquaintance," he said, taking a satin rope from a silent stagehand. The rope he would pull to reveal the memorial. "More late nights and weekends."

Startled laughter.

"Nor, I think, would I have called her a friend. Not at first. She could chafe; she didn't have an easy personality. I think sometimes more curse words passed between us than pleasantries."

Some of the laughter had become uneasy. But Aristide, like a sailor testing the wind and moving to suit, shifted his weight and changed his tack.

"But," he said, growing serious, "when called upon to perform a difficult task—last-minute choreography, or taking on the danger-ous burdens of a friend—that difficulty revealed itself as stubborn strength of character."

Cyril thought of her again, weeping with rage as she refused what he'd offered her—a spot working for the Ospies, which he'd thought would keep her safe. Strength of character, of course. And convic-tion. And in the end, she'd even been right.

"It is not easy," Aristide went on, "to destroy your life. To coat the things you love in kerosene and light a match. To wire the halls of your heart with dynamite and flip the switch. The pain does not pale, even when viewed in the light of a greater purpose."

Gulls cried in the quiet; Aristide had made the crowd forget their restlessness, so they stood silent beneath the cloud of their own breath. An image, in the shiny black and white of rotogravure, hung in Cyril's mind: flames curling through the wrought-iron balconies of Aristide's Baldwin Street apartment building.

"Cordelia's aims were great," said Aristide, into the quiet. "And she believed that they were worth every sacrifice she made. That does not mean they did not hurt."

Expectation hung in the air like the exhalations of the audience, everyone waiting for Aristide to say something more. Only Cyril was unsurprised when he gave an odd little shrug, and pulled the rope.

CHAPTER

TEN

The speech was hideously genuine, but Aristide felt he owed Cordelia that much. He'd shown himself just across the aisle from sober to get through the thing. If . . . what was the woman's name? Honora. Yes. If Honora or any of the other grandees had taken exception to his consumption of three martinis and a sizable digestif over the course of their painful luncheon, nobody had mentioned it.

The monument wasn't quite as awful as his speech had been, but he didn't think Cordelia would have liked it. The stone obelisk and copper plaque were too tasteful and staid. She'd have wanted gold plate twenty feet tall, tits out and flag flying.

He hadn't let himself look at the crowd closely while speaking; instead he'd used the old trick of staring just beyond the last row. It made everyone feel as though you were looking straight at them, albeit from a noble distance with your chin cocked high.

Embarrassment would have made him fumble, if he'd seen any familiar faces.

Lillian had rung the hotel the night before to say she'd see him at the reception after, but wouldn't have much time to chat. He made sympathetic noises and accepted her apology, trying to decide if he felt grateful to be spared her small talk.

"Frye was at the speeches," said Daoud, as they drew up to the curb outside the Matrons' Benevolent Society. "I saw her arrive, while you were waiting to go on. I believe she will be here as well."

"A bold move," said Aristide, who had spent the last few days catching up on current events.

Daoud shrugged. "Beside the point. You should speak with her."

"Test the jess she has on Custler, you mean. I don't think I'll exactly be cutting a deal in the MBS ballroom, not when her company's held in trust."

"Just talk to her," said Daoud, sounding tired.

Aristide made a theatrical moue. "Of course I'll *talk* to her. It's a *party*. But I do worry if I buttonhole her for a little jaw, we might get a few sideways glances."

Daoud cased Aristide with a crook to his lips. "You? Everyone will think you are only socializing."

"You have a poor understanding of my position in Gedda."

"I have a very good understanding of your position *tonight*," said Daoud, and for half a moment Aristide thought it was an innuendo. But Daoud continued, unaware of Aristide's discomfort and—hang it—faint arousal.

"These people," said Daoud, "are thinking of you as a symbol. To them, who you were is dead. Now you are . . . a memory. A moving picture."

"Apropos," said Aristide. "I suppose they must have lost track of me after I stopped making films with Pulan. If any of this crowd ever watched them to begin with." He rubbed a hand down the back of his neck, which failed to soothe the tension gathered there.

"Time to go in," said Daoud. "And do not start drinking before you have found some food."

His brief spike of lust had been fading, but Daoud's flippancy blew sudden air into the heart of the embers. "Don't presume," said Aristide, voice low and devoid of mirth. Alarm passed through Daoud's black eyes, like the orange glow of heat moving through a bed of coals. Aristide was going to do something shameful later this evening. But for now, he had business to attend to.

The Matrons' Benevolent Society was a relic of old Amberlough the Ospies hadn't quashed—or at any rate, they'd left the gilding on the walls and no one had put plain plaster over the moulding. How the benevolent matrons had fared, Aristide wasn't so sure.

He parted with his mink at the coat check, loading it into the arms of a girl who didn't look large enough to bear its weight, and ascended the curve of a recently scrubbed marble staircase. The whole place had the air of being hastily cleaned—under the wax and lemon oil, he could still smell dust and damp, a little mildew.

The sound of chatter tumbled down the bannister toward him and he rose to meet it, emerging on a landing outside two double doors thrown open onto the reception.

The room was littered with those impractically small tables caterers always set up at things like this; the tall ones at a good height for nobody, that filled with clutter every fifteen minutes and had to be cleared. If you put your drink down on one of those, it would disappear as soon as you turned your back. He planned to keep firm hold of his, and drain each glass before it left his fingers.

Very few people were in white tie, and Aristide's tuxedo felt less daring than he had hoped. Ten years ago it would have been all tails and winged collars. Some guests wore international dress—tunics and dhoti, sashes and fustanellas. There were women in jackets and trousers, too, some with other women on their arms. More than one man wore lipstick and rouge. The razors and blushboys were making their presence felt: loud laughter, languid hands.

Aristide wondered how many of the more . . . *colorful* guests had been invited specifically to put on this show. He couldn't have been the only adornment to these proceedings. Why did the provisional government feel a need to hammer the point home? Or perhaps Honora had only wanted a theme for her party: *The Ospies are most certainly gone.*

He wasn't sure how many people were convinced. Colors were thin on the floor, and where they appeared they were muted with gray or brown: earth tones, sepia, subdued shades. Few jewels, and nothing ostentatious. Nobody here wanted to disrespect the memory of the dead they'd gathered to honor, but it seemed to go deeper than that; people still carried the weight of fear.

Before he could begin to feel morose, Aristide turned to Daoud and said, "Find Frye for me, will you? While I find the bar." As he turned toward his mission, Daoud caught his elbow.

"There," he said, and gestured. It was not the sort of party where one pointed fingers.

She stood at a distance of about twenty yards, caught in what looked like three separate conversations. A woman of medium height made imposing by tall pumps, she was older than Aristide by perhaps ten years. Silver hair was piled on her head, held with simple pins. Sun had turned her skin to supple leather, warm with a tan even in the winter, tightly creased at the corners of her eyes. She wore a mauve dress that showed a softly wrinkled décolletage, spotted with freckles, framing a single sapphire ringed in seed-sized diamonds. An antique, by the setting, but a fine one. Purchased at auction, perhaps. Camouflage for new money.

And, at Frye's elbow: Lillian DePaul.

Aristide had not seen her since setting foot on Geddan soil. In fact, he had not seen her in five years, not since the lobby of the Grand Ldotho, her face buried in the filthy hair of her son. Stephen, that was his name. Snatched out from under the Ospies' noses by the oddest pair of rescuers ever yoked together.

Aristide briefly felt the chill of the steppe wind, felt the curve of Cordelia's small shoulders underneath his hands.

Horribly, his eyes began to burn. He blinked to clear them and looked at Lillian again. Though she was unquestionably alive, and apparently unscathed, the past clung to her like cobwebs.

She would always be burnt into his memory in the bias-cut gown she had worn at their first meeting. It had suited her: traced her tall, svelte figure in a sweep of storm-gray satin. But fashion had moved on, even in cash-strapped Gedda. The piece she wore this evening was cut militarily straight across the shoulders. Padded slightly, unless he missed his guess. The sleeves fell loose to her elbows, then narrowed at her forearms, tightly ruched. The plunging neckline was the only feature of the gown that revealed skin. Not to say that it was modest—aside from the shoulders, the cut was snug. The skirt twined around the curves of her legs in a tight twist of black silk crepe, gathered at one hip with a diamond buckle. The hem hugged her ankles, showing a pair of simple velvet pumps. She looked gorgeous, frightening, and austere.

And she was deep in conversation with Emmeline Frye, smiling faintly, nodding along, looking very much as if things were going right for her.

Cyril was nowhere to be seen.

"Excuse me." Aristide put an apologetic hand to Daoud's elbow. "Find us some nibbles?"

"If you'll eat them," he said sourly. But by then Aristide was already sinking into the elegant press of people that churned between him and Lillian.

She didn't see Aristide coming. Unpardonable. But he approached from behind and she was putting all her energy into appearing attentive without also appearing in print.

Cyril was off her elbow, at least, so they'd be deprived of that story. He'd showed no inclination to attend the gala, and she hadn't tried to change his mind. He'd stayed behind at Coral Street with Stephen.

The flashbulb throng got most of what they wanted at the ceremony, or on the curb outside the MBS, but there were still a few pen-fencers, and a couple of photographers on Honora's payroll Lillian didn't hold above shilling for the glossies on the side.

Frye had thrown them a cursory smile and a couple of lines—too formal, blatantly rehearsed—and begun to circulate in groups where she clearly had friends. Lillian stalked like a big cat after faltering game and caught her in the back corner of the room, sheltered from the press. They were just circling around a concrete time and date for lunch when a large hand closed on Lillian's shoulder. She jumped and had to play it for laughs.

"Mr. Makricosta," she said, when she turned and saw who it was. "You nearly made me spill my drink!"

"An egregious offense," he said, sliding effortlessly into the act. "Though I would've gotten you a new one." Then, as though he had just noticed Frye—she was certain this was not the case—he said, "My goodness, is this who I think it is? Ms. DePaul, do you mind making introductions?"

"Of course not," she said, quashing her irritation. "Ms. Frye, this is Aristide Makricosta: imports and exports, and an old friend." She bent the meaning of her words like tent staves, so they would support her manners. "Mr. Makricosta, Emmeline Frye, Neo-Federalist ministerial candidate."

Frye had a smile like salt flats: dull, arid, alkaline. Even her eyes seemed sun-bleached: faded hazel, like the brush that grew in the Porachin desert. She couldn't stand up to Saeger's youthful flash, her passion; the trick would be to play on that spareness, build it into a platform of appealing pragmatism.

"I'm not sure we ought to be talking," said Aristide. "I've got a sizable quote from WCRC sitting on my desk right now."

Of course he had an agenda. He was not being charming for nothing. Anger froze her into paralysis. Grudgingly, she admired him.

"I've pulled all my fingers out of that and wiped them clean." Frye flicked the relevant digits like they were wet and she had no towel to dry them. "And anyway, if you want to move something through Gedda, you haven't got many other choices, at the moment."

"Something your infrastructure plans would fix, I'm sure." Aristide examined his nails, campy and casual. "Doing your competitors a good turn. Very altruistic. Of course West Cultham would benefit from an improved and expanded railway system as well. And you'll be well ahead of the pack coming around the bend."

Frye shrugged. "Throw corn for the flock, each goose gets a crumb."

That farmland, black earth, flat-vowel relatability—*that* was what would get her votes. Though where it came from, Lillian wasn't sure. Frye was a suburban Nuesklender born to well-off middle-class types. Nothing close to a farmer. She'd been at university in the state capital and built a small fortune dealing in commodities— enough to throw in with a couple of partners, build a successful railway company, and buy them out just in time for the Ospies' rise to power.

WCRC had been nationalized by the Ospies, then brutalized by the Catwalk. Frye had gone to ground—Lillian didn't think she'd been out of the country, but she certainly hadn't lifted her head. When the dust settled, she showed up to take the reins of her company again. While the rest of the rail companies floundered in a mess of missing money and twisted steel, Frye sank staggering borrowed and personal funds into rebuilding—and privatizing—key lines across the country. She made the balance back within months.

Opponents called her a gouger if they were feeling polite. Lillian had also heard her called a cold-hearted, calculating, dry-bite bobtail. But she looked and sounded folksy, if she leaned into it. People liked that kind of thing. They bought it, brought it home, and ate it up for dinner.

Except for Aristide, who had a sly look on his face that said he wasn't falling for the affectation. Of course not: He was constructed of the stuff. Frye couldn't hope to fool him with his own tricks.

"I was just on my way to the bar," said Aristide, watching Frye through narrow eyes. "Is there anything I can fetch for either of you?"

Damnation. Lillian could *feel* the thing that passed between them: a frisson that held some hidden invitation, and its acceptance.

"I'll come along," said Frye. "I don't trust you to order for me. You seem like the kind of man who likes a girl better when she's drunk."

"I'm the kind of man who likes everyone better drunk. Especially myself." He offered his arm, and Frye took it.

Lillian killed the impulse to stamp her foot. But then Frye tilted her head over her shoulder as she departed and said, "DePaul, my house. Not tomorrow, but . . . the next day? Half past noon."

She smiled and said, "I'll put it in my diary."

———

Saeger was harder than Frye had been.

For one, she was the center of attention. Though she hadn't spoken at the ceremony, everyone knew she had been close to Lehane. The brains behind the Catwalk's strategy. A little older, a little better-organized, with experience wrangling disparate folk to a singular cause. Cordelia had been the Spotlight, but Opal—Gaffer, clandestine code name now worn like a badge of honor—had shone it on her. And now it was Saeger's turn onstage.

It was Jinadh who gave Lillian an avenue of approach. With the flypaper memory and smooth manners of a courtier and gossip columnist, he glad-handed with professional skill. Nobody would guess how deeply he despised the entire enterprise—provisional government, dedication, gala, upcoming election—for its hold on Lillian. Tonight, at least, he had drunk enough to put him in a jovial mood. His white teeth gleamed in the frame of his newly trimmed beard, a beacon Lillian could easily keep in sight.

He was chatting with Daoud near the stage—there had been even more speeches, but at least everyone had dry feet during these—when Lillian saw a shift in the flow of the crowd around them: a mass movement of bodies like an incoming tide that bore on its foam the statuesque figure of Opal Saeger.

Tall, raw-boned, with a jaw angled to cut granite, she wore a structural gown in matte white silk. She did not look like she knew how to move in it, and Lillian scented bad advice. On someone a little less blunt, it would have been a statement. On Saeger it looked like cardboard. They should have put her in a suit, or at least something a little simpler.

She drew up to the third point in what was now a triangle, offering her hand first to Daoud, and then Jinadh. Lillian plucked two coupes from a passing tray and slipped sideways through the crowd, careful not to spill.

"Spice cake," she said, deliberately watching her hands as she approached. "I got you a—oh."

"Ah," said Jinadh. Lillian could hear the disappointment in his voice, but only by virtue of marriage. No one else would pick it up. "Ms. Saeger, this is my wife. Lillian DePaul."

At least he took one of the coupes from her, so she could shake. "A pleasure to meet you, after hearing so much. How is the campaign trail treating you?"

"Better than the Ospies did," said Saeger, and Lillian would have rolled her eyes if she weren't on her best behavior. This woman could be the next prime minister. This woman could give her a job.

Torture-surviving resistance hero was a large part of Saeger's appeal. It played well with angry folk who'd lost something to the Ospies. It got her positive coverage in the *Clarion, Morning Bulletin,* and on a few of the newer call signs cropping up on the airwaves. It didn't sing so sweet with the people burned by the Catwalk's bombing campaigns. Even if the selfsame organization had transitioned in popular assessment from terrorists to liberators, once they started distributing aid along the only rail lines they'd left operational. Aid that went largely to sympathetic towns and cities, or those that could be swayed by a soft hand. Anywhere perceived to have an Ospie majority starved.

The *Telegraph* reliably took a piece out of Saeger, branding her a disorganized upstart. Lillian was surprised to find herself agreeing with their op-eds for the first time in her life.

But politics wasn't about agreeing with people; it was about mutual benefits and compromise. So Lillian smiled through Saeger's grim rejoinder and replied with, "That's not saying much."

"No," said Saeger. "It certainly isn't. Load of good it did them, in the end. Thanks to Pulan Satri. And the rest of Porachis, eventually."

The royal treasury had got behind the Catwalk's bid when things looked likely to swing their way. And it explained Saeger approaching Daoud. Lillian wondered if they'd ever met in person, or if she only knew him by name and reputation.

A camera flashed nearby, capturing their conversation. Lillian fought a wince and won, but barely. "I'd make a comparison to moths and flame," she said. "But they're the ones who are lighting up. Can't seem to shake them, can you?"

"I wouldn't want to," said Saeger. "I'm after good press as much as the next sculler on a ticket."

"Well you won't get it from him. That was Emil van Nuys. He's freelance—Honora hired him—but he sells a lot of his photographs to Chester Chandler." It got her a blank look, badly disguised. Saeger had charisma, but no skills of deception. "The weekend editor. At the *Telegraph*. It's just . . . I've noticed they don't tend to do you favors."

One of Saeger's eyebrows went up. They were dark, under short-cropped honey-blond hair. Much like Lillian's own coloring, though paired with dark brown eyes. She was a first-generation Geddan; Suldatian parents. Both dead before the Ospies, but Saeger often talked about what *might* have happened to them, if they had survived. What had happened to all the other foreign parents of Geddan children.

Good stuff. If she was canny, she'd use it to segue into talk about immigration policy. So far, nothing.

"You're with the provisional government right now," said Saeger. "Aren't you?"

"Press and public relations, yes."

Saeger dipped her chin in a scrutinizing gesture that was almost a nod. "I'll bet you're very good at your job."

"I like to think so," said Lillian, because *I am* was the truth, and selling that was not her business.

Saeger gave another tip of the chin, this one more affirmative. Then she turned to Daoud and said, "Mr. Qassan, it was very good to meet you. Please tell Ms. Satri how grateful I am, next time you speak with her. How grateful *we* were. She made a lot of things possible for us."

Stones, the mash-up of formality and half-shed city drone . . . it made Lillian itch to ring up a dialect coach. A better one than Saeger already had.

"I will," said Daoud, and Lillian wondered how often they spoke. She hardly kept in contact with the filmmaker these days. "And, if you'll excuse me, Mr. Addas . . ." Half his mouth twisted into a smile. «I think I should find my companion before trouble does.»

Once Daoud had gone, Saeger shook Lillian's hand again, and Jinadh's, and then swept off into the thinning crowd. Lillian didn't see her after that. Things were beginning to wind down.

Jinadh, apparently realizing the same thing, let a little of his glitter fade. "Please do not thank me. I hate myself for letting you near her."

"I don't know if it did any good. But I do have lunch with Frye this week."

He closed his eyes, as if against sun glare, and sighed. "Good luck. Will you at least keep the week of Solstice clear?"

"Of course. Well, as clear as I can. Duty may call, with Honora and the rest."

"As long as you are at the table," said Jinadh, casting his eyes afar in a manner she recognized as avoidance. "I do not want to host alone."

"Host?"

"Yes," he said. His fingertips pressing on the rim of his coupe were another small tell. «I've invited my respected brother Daoud Qassan. And also, Aristide.»

———

Since Lillian and Jinadh were out for the evening, Cyril braved the dinner table. Without his sister wrangling the social interactions, the whole thing felt less like an ordeal and more like an opportunity to shovel in some food.

The dining room echoed like the rest of the house, bare of ornaments. The table was not the great sweep of golden oak Cyril remembered, resting on elaborately curled legs. It had been replaced by something square and utilitarian, largely hidden by a plain white cloth.

Stephen showed up a few minutes after Cyril did, flinging himself into his chair with an aggrieved sigh. Cyril waited for the complaint that seemed imminent, but then Stephen's eyes rose from his plate, snagged briefly on Cyril's, and fell again. Silence reigned.

Bern, the footman, leaned past Cyril to put a few slices of stuffed cabbage on his plate. He forgot that he was supposed to say stop, and ended up with too many. Years ago, his parents had banished Lillian's spaniel from the dining room after they realized he was feeding it his scraps. He'd hated the rotten thing, except for its utility under the table. Could have used it now.

Stephen picked at his cabbage. Cyril watched the angle of his head fall, his bony shoulders tucked around his ears.

"What did you think of all that?" asked Cyril, against his better judgment.

"The speeches?" asked Stephen. "The Catwalk?"

"Any of it."

Stephen shrugged. "Big fuss about something done." Then a pause, the tines of his fork creaking pensively against the porcelain. "D'you think that's why they made such a racket about the pencil sharpener? 'Cause it was a bomb, and folk are all het about the Catwalk still? Most I should've had was a switching, or even if they'd kept me out of classes. But instead it's . . . well they aren't acting normal about it."

"How so?" asked Cyril, sipping his water. Magnusson hadn't brought any wine to the table, and there were no glasses for it. Cyril wondered if that was penury or overprotectiveness.

"Mum and Dad have got these letters home from Porks," said Stephen. "The headmaster. I'm out for all of Leighberth, supposed to do a pile of reading and *maybe* get back in, and then keep my marks up and no more demerits or else, and it doesn't seem like it's about the pencil sharpener at all."

"What else did you do? Besides the pencil sharpener."

"How do you know I did anything?"

Cyril stared at him, blinking slowly once. Bern, in the corner, shifted on a patch of creaky floor. Tension rose.

Stephen didn't break fast—a good sign—but he did break eventually. "All right, I've been suspended twice this term for sneaking out after curfew, and I put Duquesne in the infirmary. He didn't tell anybody it was me, but they knew."

"You hit him?"

"With a bowling pin, in the shed after practice."

"Why?"

"He said my family was dirty traitors. The shit Gedda should've wiped off its . . ." It wasn't modesty that kept him from saying it, but rage. "'Cause of Mum working for the embassy, I guess. Before the Ospies went. And . . . because of you, probably. And Dad. He got a couple of digs in there about Porachis. I think I broke his nose."

"And he didn't name names?"

"He's bigger than I am. He didn't want to be embarrassed. And he knew I'd get him back if he told. Plus, even the teachers don't like a tattler."

It sounded as though school hadn't changed much in thirty years.

Cyril gave him a choice. "Do you want to know what they would say if you asked? Or do you want to know why they're really so upset?"

"Both," said Stephen.

"Smart." Cyril turned his water glass pensively in his hands. "If you asked, they'd tell you people could have gotten hurt. And that's part of it; a bomb is different than a bowling pin to one boy's nose."

"It was funny," said Stephen, voice breaking awkwardly on the last word.

"Not to them; like you said, Gedda's had more than enough to do with bombs the last few years." He remembered Lillian saying how Stephen reminded her of him, at that age: sent home at the holidays with reprimands heaped on his head. Scandals and switchings and long hours spent locked away without dinner.

If Cyril was any indication, the boy was on a road to nowhere good; the same road that had gotten Cyril beaten to death's left hand, lying on the docks with a pistol to his head. "But they're really worried because they don't know what to do with you. Nobody wants the responsibility. Nobody wants it to be their fault you exploded a pencil sharpener, or can't pass your exams. It makes them uncomfortable that you can't be fixed, so they'll keep trying to pass you off to somebody who can. Your parents to the school, the school to your parents."

Stephen's fork hung suspended over his cabbage, food forgotten. "What happens if nobody can fix me?"

There hadn't been anyone around when Cyril was that age, to tell him what would happen. To teach him what survival took, in the world that already had its hooks in him. Just his spotless sister and his distant parents, disgusted with their second child's slow slide into failure. His father had pushed him off the cliff into tradecraft, just to be rid of him and his ragged reputation.

Cyril wondered if Lillian could see as far into Stephen's future as he could, and whether she was preparing him accordingly.

"You don't need to be fixed," said Cyril. "You just have to be ready for the moment they stop trying."

Aristide woke in his accustomed state of parched misery, head pounding, and rolled over to find he was alone in bed. If fate was kind, they could pretend—as they often did—this had not happened.

Then he heard the washroom tap and his hopes were dashed.

"You look as though you need some breakfast," said Daoud, emerging with a toothbrush tucked into his cheek. "Or a coffee, at the very least." He was wrapped in a white cotton dressing gown embroidered with the hotel's monogram. Water still shone on his hair, neatly striped by the teeth of a comb.

"You're still here," said Aristide, redundantly. Speaking dislodged a wet chunk in his chest and the words gave way to his habitual morning coughing fit, familiar as his hangover.

«To turn you like kebab and make sure you didn't die in your sleep.» At least, that was what Aristide thought he had said; his words came out indistinct around the toothbrush, and Aristide's Porashtu had gotten rusty at Cross-Costa, where most of his end of the business was conducted in Geddan.

"Also," said Daoud, from the washroom this time, where he had gone to spit. "To talk about Frye." The tap ran again, briefly, and he emerged with a glass of water. "Here, drink that."

Aristide reached blindly for the tin of Aceto powder on the bed-side table. It would be easier to have this conversation if his headache banged a little less forcefully against the inside of his skull.

"What did she say?" asked Daoud.

"Nothing of consequence. You could hardly expect that." Aristide swirled Aceto into the glass of water. "Still, even though she walked on cat paws all the way around it, I think we're liable to hear from Custler soon, and positively."

"So you think they are still in contact?"

Aristide smiled—almost leering—into his cloudy gray analgesic. "I have suspicions."

Daoud cleared his throat and looked expectant. Aristide sighed, and made a vulgar gesture with his fingers.

"Ah," said Daoud. "That is good. I am happy to have it done."

"Not done yet," said Aristide. He drank the noxious dose of Aceto in one long swallow, bringing on another coughing fit. "But nearly."

"Nearly," Daoud repeated. And though they had reached the end of the conversation, he did not leave to dress and begin his day.

Aristide set aside his empty glass. "Was there something else?"

Daoud sat gingerly on the foot of the bed. The pause before his next sentence put Aristide's fine hairs on end. "Jinadh Addas invited us to their country home for Solstice."

If he had been drinking the Aceto now, he would have choked. "I beg your pardon."

"For the holiday." Daoud waved vaguely. "It is only a few days. We don't have plans. I told him yes."

"You told him—on whose say-so?"

"My *own*." Daoud scowled. "You do not need to come." A piece of his hair fell forward across his forehead and he flicked it away with an impatient jerk of his chin. The gesture gave Aristide a pain in his chest before he realized why.

Surely Daoud had done exactly that before. But with Cyril's ghost so freshly risen and veiled in flesh, Aristide made an association he had never made before. The gesture was not so much a practicality as a finely honed nostalgic knife.

There was a part of him that was . . . curious? To see Carmody, where he had never before had occasion to go. To spend a long holiday in the country, with a *family*, as though he *had* one.

Every moment would cut like shattered ceramic, of course.

Would make him sick and sorry for himself and angry. It would be like a flaying. And yet he could not refuse.

He thought of every time he'd left a welt on Cyril's skin. The tears and cries and pleas for more, harder, *Yes, yes, I'm so sorry, yes*, and suddenly, he understood the urge.

"I will," he said. At which Daoud looked, incredibly, more miserable than he had before. "I don't have to, though, if—"

"No." Daoud shook his head, put a patronizing hand on Aristide's knee. "Of course. It will be wonderful, I'm sure."

CHAPTER

ELEVEN

Lillian hadn't given Saeger a card. They'd talked for perhaps two minutes. And yet, when she struggled from bed the next morning, hoarse and mildly hungover, she found a telegram waiting by her breakfast plate.

Pointedly, with great discipline, she poured her coffee and took a sip before she set aside her cup in favor of the onionskin.

MEET HALF TWO AT LYLES STOP OS END

Which was how she found herself at the top of a set of treacherous stairs on a side street off Temple, beneath a buzzing neon sign that read LYLE'S TAPROOM.

Not her usual sort of haunt. Thanks be Martí had known the place and been able to take her there. Just another odd stop in the long line of them her work over the years had called for. At least at Lyle's she would not be attempting seduction, or sedition.

The stairs were an adventure to navigate in pumps, but she made it down and let herself in. A bell over the door thwacked dully, short a hammer. A team of metro workers sat at the bar, still in coveralls, hard hats upturned on the floor beside their stools. The trolley lines had been under nearly constant construction since Lillian returned to the city, and the dusty teams were a ubiquitous sight.

A young man with a notepad and half a pint at his elbow scratched aimlessly at a table with the nib of his pen. Two middle-aged razors occupied the corner by the jukebox, veiled in a cloud of smoke.

Out of her eye-catching gala finery, Saeger looked more comfortable, and more compelling. Lillian had never been particularly susceptible to the sway of charisma, but Saeger certainly had . . . something. An intensity that made her difficult to ignore.

A useful tool, already winning her support among the more impressionable of the voting populace. Lillian could help her temper it with strategy, wield it to best effect. Hopefully that was why she had been invited here: to offer her opinions and advice.

A couple of hangers-on about Saeger's age occupied the table with her: two men, likely brothers, and a broad-shouldered woman in a sheepskin jacket.

"Lillian," said Saeger, and the informality struck Lillian as awkward but understandable. The surname might catch somebody's attention.

"Opal," she said, because a ministerial candidate was even more likely to be recognized than a minor scandal.

"Anything to drink?" Saeger tipped her pint glass. She didn't introduce the hangers-on, and they didn't move to do it themselves. Were they protection? Campaign team? Friends?

Lillian smiled and shook her head. "No, thank you. Or perhaps just a shrub?"

Saeger snorted. "I don't think they do those."

In denim and canvas and a collarless work shirt, instead of stiff raw silk, she also spoke more easily: the barest hint of a nasal city drone, and soft, almost nonexistent consonants that let her words run together. Her mouth had a crooked cant, so her sentences came out of one side. Lillian wagered it was the same side smoke came out of, when she had a straight lit up.

"Why Lyle's, may I ask?"

"Old haunt," said Saeger. "And we're not likely to run into—what was his name? The snapper?"

"Van Nuys?"

"Or anybody else like him. Not that I'm ashamed to be seen with you. It's just—"

"*I* can't be seen with *you*. Conflict of interest. The same reason we couldn't put you onstage yesterday."

Saeger nodded, sipped her beer. She looked so at home here, and so in her own skin: much more than she had at the gala. "*That* was a hard time, listening to it all and keeping my teeth shut. Delia would've been firing smart remarks like a chain gun, with all those swells telling made-up stories about her."

"You don't think she'd be pleased to be remembered?"

"Pleased? Absolutely. Polite? Not a chance. She wasn't exactly tactful. Or tactical. Me, you didn't hear a peep, and I smiled through it. I know about grand gestures. Spent enough years lighting 'em. Back when this place was Curtains."

"Stagefolk bar?"

"Only the name's changed really. Though there's fewer strippers and all that now." Setting her glass between them, she put her palms on the table and leaned in. "But I didn't want to talk to you about old times. The party's called Forward Gedda, after all."

Lillian tipped her head: a nod, barely.

"You've noticed the press doesn't treat me kindly. How do I change that?"

"I'm afraid as far as the *Telegraph* goes, you're scratched. But you might get a better class of censure if you actually matched Frye policy for policy. If she talks about her tax plan in a debate, you'd better have a rejoinder." The first one, a month ago, had been a joke. "Rallies are one thing, but when they put you opposite Frye you need to be able to counter her points."

"My policy is to help Gedda," said Saeger. "Delia used to say she just wanted to get the Ospies out, get things back to normal. But I'd always tell her if the house fell down the first time, why build it back the same?"

"And what did she say to that?"

"She said that's why I was the brains of the operation. She told me when we scratched Acherby, I ought to be in charge. She meant it for a joke, I think, but after she . . . I just kept hearing her say it. The way she used to tell me to round up our folk, there was a train tonight that wouldn't make the station."

"A mission," said Lillian, despairing.

"Maybe. But it ain't just for her. I don't want my country run on bribery and favors, welfare gutted to line somebody's pockets. I want a better, cleaner Gedda, but I don't want to sound like Acherby when I say it. I just want something that works for us all."

Idealism. Lillian held down a shudder until it died. "That's all very fine, but Frye has clearly outlined foreign policy plans. She has a stance on international trade. She has donors, too. With deep pockets."

"I've got the labor unions," said Saeger.

"Which are still in tatters. You'd be well advised to seek out some softhearted philanthropists who want a sop for their guilt."

Saeger's frown had been deepening as Lillian spoke. "I asked you here to help me. And this is what I get?"

Lillian had slipped, but she couldn't quite bring herself to walk it back. "I am helping. You need to hear it from someone."

"All right," said Saeger, squaring her shoulders. "In my place, what would you do?"

If Lillian had brought a folder, this is when she would have opened it and spread the papers. "The wealthy despise you, and so do Tatien loyalists. Older folk are divided—some of them are nostalgic, some of them are suspicious. You're playing on your youth; your Catwalk credentials; your ties to the unions, the workers, the poor."

"And the Chuli," Saeger said. "We blew those guard towers. The camps came down because of us, and we put guns in their hands."

"The Chuli," said Lillian, "can't vote."

"They'll be able to once I'm in office; that's a promise."

Lillian held back a sigh of frustration. "I wouldn't bring it up until after the inauguration."

"That's cheap," said Saeger. "I've got integrity."

"Yes, but that doesn't win you an election. The *appearance* of integrity will do you wonders, but you'd better stay slippery until the polls close. Your numbers might be better than Frye right now, but she's still got a solid base. Stealing some of them from beneath her will serve you well, but they won't be swayed by voting rights for stateless nomads."

"I don't want to win on lies," said Saeger. "I want to win on my convictions."

"It would be wonderful if that was how this went," said Lillian. "But those odds don't invite a wager."

Saeger shrugged, and Lillian saw a wall go up between them. "It worked for Delia, didn't it?"

———

Lunch with Frye was a more dignified affair, and one she hoped would get her into less trouble. After all, it was her only option now.

Lillian presented herself at the agreed-upon time, clicking up the concrete steps of a town house on Fountain boulevard. A maid in a spotless apron led her to the parlor and brought coffee. Frye appeared shortly after the tray. Unlike Saeger, who had been ill at ease in formalwear and more comfortable in work clothes, Frye seemed equally at home in a tweed suit as she had a ball-gown. The open lapels of her jacket showed a conservative collar of pearls.

Lillian stood and offered her hand. Frye shook it, smiling, and sat down at a right angle to Lillian, so that they were both leaning on the arms of their chairs to speak. It felt conspiratorial, and this gave Lillian hope. If she had a choice, she'd rather join the Frye administration, since she seemed to know what she was doing better than Saeger did.

"I hope you were able to get a little rest yesterday," said Frye. "I know how hard you've been working."

This meant Frye had been keeping an eye on her. That was good. "I had a slower day than usual. Which isn't saying much."

"I wish half my team had half your work ethic," said Frye. "We'd be polling three times as high."

Lillian sipped her coffee and shrugged. "It's not that I don't appreciate the praise . . ."

"But?"

"I'm not sure you have what Saeger does. Even if you put in more hours and more money, you're missing something vital."

Frye cocked her head, touching her pearls with one contemplative finger. "She does have a . . . an aura. A pull. I'm not sure what I'd call it. It's not enough to run a country."

"No, but it might be enough to win her an election."

Sighing, Frye dropped her hand back to her lap. "Sometimes I hate how sentimental folk can be."

"You may hate it," said Lillian, "but you'd better learn to use it or you'll end up giving a concession speech."

"And you have an idea."

"Several."

That got her the small nasal huff of Frye's laughter. "Start with one."

"Nostalgia is a strong emotional hook," said Lillian. "And Saeger doesn't even have to work for hers: She stands for the lights on Temple Street. For the cherry trees on Talbert Row. She ousted the Ospies from power, and not metaphorically. To at least a third of the country, she's a folk hero."

"And the other two-thirds?"

"Half of that's your base," said Lillian. "People angry at the collateral damage caused by the Catwalk. People suffering from the destroyed infrastructure. People who don't like the idea of their taxes funding welfare. Maybe a few people with some lingering Ospie sentiments."

Frye made a despairing noise at odds with her conservative pearls and the refined appointments of her parlor. "Those stone-sucking sow-shits just won't lie down and die. One fart out of them and a whole room's foul." She sighed, heavily. "I apologize for my language. They just gnaw at me. As I'm sure they do you."

"In different ways, I think. If you want to keep their votes, you have to make them feel sure of you without pandering, because pandering will lose you the rest of Gedda. You have to balance on the edge."

"And you?"

"I'm not running for prime minister," said Lillian, looking into the rippling black mirror of her coffee cup. "My best option is to keep my past quiet and do my best in the here and now. My parents did it—not with the Ospies, but they made their way after Grandmama and the Spice War. It's a matter of compartmentalization. And humility. You take what you can get, do it well, and strive for better, all the while making people like you now instead of hating who you used to be."

Frye made a *tch* noise, tongue behind her teeth. "That must chafe."

"It comes more naturally to me. My brother has always had a much harder time." As the words left her, she felt the same horrified inevitability of watching a glass fall from a table, a child run in front of a car. Time slowed. She had made a grievous error.

"Forgive me," said Frye, disconcertingly casual. "I did know you had a brother, only . . . I was under the impression he had died? I remember reading something, several years ago . . ."

Lillian's lungs felt atrophied, unable to pull in air. Her hands on the saucer and coffee cup went numb. "Yes," she said. "I did. I mean, I do." *Breathe.* In Porachis she had learned how to escape a pit of quicksand—a problem sometimes in the upper waters of the Shadha. Once it had you, struggling would only pull you further in. Calm was the key to escape.

"When I . . . exited the foreign service," she said, weighing each clause carefully, "the Ospies made a lot of my family's missteps. My brother had been pressed into collusion. Blackmailed, really. Threatened. We were all under the impression they had executed him, in the end, but happily—" an inadequate adjective, which failed to convey any of the myriad complications Cyril's reappearance had occasioned, including this one "—those rumors have proved false."

"That must have been a surprise," said Frye. "He just . . . showed up?"

"He did," said Lillian. "And in the middle of the worst possible time. But that's how he's been since he was born. Mother went into labor when she was in the middle of a closing argument."

This got Lillian another small laugh. A modicum of tension went out of her shoulders, and she could feel the warmth of porcelain through her fingertips again.

"Born a nuisance?" ventured Frye. She was smiling. Lillian began to breathe normally.

"That's Cyril. But like I said, I'm not running for prime minister. I can afford nuisances. You can't. Or, if you've got them, you have to make people look the other way."

"And what do you suggest?"

Stones, it felt good to be on solid ground again. She set Cyril aside, along with her cup and saucer. "You have more experience, a better campaign, better people behind you—you ought to win this election. But if you're going to win against Saeger, you've got to get people angry about something. You need to make them cry. Get at their hearts and you can have them."

The mantel clock ticked loudly in the silence after Lillian wrapped up this little speech. Caught in consideration of the idea, Frye sat still as if she had been carved from wood. Only the glittering of half-closed eyes gave her away. Under that hooded gaze, Lillian felt doubt creep in at the edges of her confidence. Had she miscalculated? Did Frye dislike the approach she had outlined? Or had she made some other misstep and lost this opportunity?

Then, softly, the candidate began to clap her hands. "Worthy of the stage," she said.

Lillian let out her breath and allowed herself a modest smile. "I've stood behind my fair share of podiums."

A soft knock on the parlor door heralded the maid, who bobbed a curtsy and said, "Lunch is served."

"Just in time," said Frye. "Ambition makes me hungry."

PART

2

CHAPTER

TWELVE

Cyril watched his sister dart in and out like a stitching needle for the next few days. She spent hardly an hour in the house over the course of the week. And Jinadh worked late at . . . whatever it was he did. Some kind of newspaper job?

At the end of the week, he made it home in time for an aperitif. Lillian was still out, making gears turn, but Stephen and Cyril were both in, and practicing a particular aspect of tradecraft: reassuring the target and soothing their suspicions.

Stephen laid flat on the rug in the library, nose stuck in one of his assigned texts. Cyril was close at hand on the sofa, cigarette smoldering in the ashtray, the *Clarion* propped on his knee. He'd even shaved, and put on a clean undershirt and a cardigan Magnusson had unearthed for him. From the look on Jinadh's face, the cardigan was his.

"Don't you two look cozy," said Jinadh, when he had recovered his equilibrium after noticing the sweater. He poured himself a stingy drink and collapsed into an armchair, setting his feet on Stephen's rear as though the boy were an ottoman.

"Hey!" said Stephen, and wiggled out from beneath him.

Jinadh asked something in Porashtu, to which Stephen responded, "A *book*, obviously."

Leaning forward, Jinadh tipped the cover to read it. "Kandeep," he said, impressed.

"It's on my list," said Stephen. "I thought it'd be boring but Uncle Cyril said he remembered it from school and it was the only thing he liked."

Over the rim of his glass, Jinadh cased Cyril with bloodshot eyes. "Really?"

He shrugged. "It's good." This was true. Mazul Kandeep's history of warfare and alliance between the southern continents had been the only book that kept Cyril halfway engaged in class discussion at Cantrell. It had given his teacher several weeks of false hope before the class moved on to less brutal and less interesting historical periods.

"Hmm." Jinadh put back a bit of his drink and sank farther into the upholstery. "I'm certainly pleased to see the house still standing, anyway."

Stephen's expression, at an angle visible to Cyril but hidden from Jinadh, was thunderous verging on tears. Cyril put this down to embarrassment. It was one thing to blow up a pencil sharpener for the entertainment of your classmates. It was another for your parents to make jokes about it while you were in exile pending possible expulsion.

"Please," said Cyril, stretching his legs out and sighing. "I'd never let him blow up his *own* house."

He had guessed on this one—that if he turned Jinadh's joke

around, made it about himself and not Stephen, he'd win some gratitude. And it worked; Stephen's mouth twitched and he turned his face down toward his book.

By contrast Jinadh looked off-balance, as if he hadn't considered that Cyril might take responsibility for Stephen, or let him blow up *other* people's houses.

Smiling thinly, Cyril snapped the creases of his newspaper and pretended to resume reading he had never been doing in the first place.

But Jinadh had gotten himself back in the saddle, and said, "If either of you are going to be arrested, at least wait for the arson until after Solstice? I do not want to make things awkward for our guests."

"Who's coming?" Stephen put his book aside, curiosity overwhelming his pique. "Mummy's work people?"

"No," said Jinadh, sounding slightly too pleased with himself and pointedly ignoring Cyril, who probably wasn't going to like the answer. "Old friends."

"Yours?" asked Cyril.

"Actually, yours."

The newspaper was loud in the silence, when he folded it and set it down. "Lillian agreed to this?"

"Of course." There was too much cheer in it, which meant there had been some argument. He wondered if her initial reluctance had been on his account or her own.

But she had acquiesced in the end. And despite what he'd said to Stephen, about being ready for the moment the adults around him decided he couldn't be fixed and had to be gotten rid of, he now found it was much worse to be dragged out of obscurity, roughly polished on somebody's sleeve, and newly assessed as fixable after all.

———

It began to snow about halfway between Amberlough and Carmody. When the train pulled into the village station, Daoud and Aristide stepped onto a platform festooned with mistletoe and holly garlands, a wreath over the ticket counter and tinsel hanging from the clocks. It was still several days to Solstice, but the village was prepared well in advance. The smells of pine and coal smoke threaded through the air. Aristide breathed in, and felt the chill catch in his lungs.

"Ah," he said, when he had come out the other side of a wet and painful coughing fit. "The country. How invigorating."

Daoud checked his watch. "We are a little late. Lillian was going to send a car, correct? It should be here now."

A porter brought their bags, and they found a black auto waiting out front. A woman in a smartly pressed gray jacket leaned on the hood with a cigarette between gloved fingers.

"You're from Damesfort?" Aristide asked.

Startled, she flicked her cigarette away. "Mr. Makricosta? Mr. Qassan? Sorry. Lost track of time. Help you with your bags?"

"And your name?" asked Aristide, letting her take his larger case and heave it into the trunk.

"You can call me Martí."

"Your surname?"

"Yes, sir." She opened the rear door for him, and held it for Daoud to climb in after.

"That's Tatien, right?"

"It's as Geddan as I am," she said, and put the car into gear. Her tone meant she was finished with the subject. Aristide pressed on.

"Naturally. You were on this side of the border before the split? Or did you choose to emigrate after?"

Her eyes nailed him from the rearview mirror. "Does it matter, if I can drive this car?"

"Aristide," said Daoud.

"I'm only curious," he said, to both of them. "I meant no offense."

"Of course not," said Martí, and they drove on in silence.

Only rarely, in the past, had his business taken him outside of Amberlough. He had certainly never driven in broad daylight through the rolling downs of Dameskill county. This late in the year everything was brown or gray, though the snow had started to stick in shady places, and to stone. Dry stack walls along the roads all bore a dusting. Ravens gleaned the fields. The last of the wild geese crossed the low gray sky, heading south for somewhere warmer.

Turning off the main road, the driver took them over a small stone bridge across a deep ditch, onto a gravel lane. A pair of gates stood open at the bridge's far end, admitting the car to the DePaul estate.

The lane was a long, winding affair of white gravel, and the house appeared from behind a hill like a bank of fog. The sun found its way through the clouds for a moment and struck the gray-white granite at a sharp angle, limning the eaves and edges in silver. It was a very grand piece of architecture.

Aristide hated to be nervous. It made him feel weak and foolish.

«It's not quite Hadhariti, is it?» asked Daoud, and his mischief had an air of consolation to it, as if he knew Aristide's heart. That only made Aristide feel worse.

«You be polite,» he said. «Please.»

«If you'll do the same.» Daoud crossed his arms.

Martí parked the car and opened the door. Her bow was stiff, and she made no small talk. That was fine. Aristide didn't feel quite capable of reciprocating, at the moment.

The two big doors at the top of the steps swung open, showing Lillian at their center in gray flannel trousers and a cabled sweater of heather tweed. It was early in the afternoon, but she already had a cocktail in her hand. Aristide wondered if it was festive or medicinal.

"There you are," she said, coming down to greet them. She had on sheepskin slippers, he realized, and was stepping carefully in order not to slide on the stone. When she reached the gravel she stopped and held out her free hand in a hybrid gesture that seemed to invite both kisses and a bag to carry. Aristide settled for the former, as Martí seemed to have the latter under control. Lillian's wry smile was too like her brother's. In the past it would have cut him cleanly, a sorrow he understood. Now it left a ragged wound, and he had to hold back a grimace.

"The boys are in the back," she said. "Jinadh is testing his throwing arm."

"Hm?" Daoud cocked his head. "His—"

Before he could finish, a gun discharged very nearby. Lillian didn't flinch; Aristide did, and saw Daoud do the same. Both of them regained their composure before Aristide's next heartbeat. Exposure didn't inure one to the initial shock of unexpected gunfire, but it did teach quick recovery time.

"Trap," said Lillian. "The coveys are barren, I'm afraid—the, um . . . the interim occupants didn't keep the grounds up. But Cyril found a pile of clay pigeons in the garden shed and Stephen had never—"

Another shot rang through the still, cold air. Sparrows took off from a leafless tree by the stream.

"Anyway. Come in and get warm. There's punch. Mother and Daddy used to keep a big bowl on for weeks at the holidays. It's a bit extravagant, I suppose, but I thought we'd ask Bradley to revive the tradition." That dull knife of a smile again. She knew they'd need the social lubricant.

Aristide took his punch from a tray proffered by the—butler? Footman? How did one tell them apart? He'd only learned by exposure at Hadhariti—and followed Lillian into the house.

The hall was not much warmer than the outside, despite a large fire in a massive hearth at the other end. Even here, shots from outside were audible.

"It's warmer in the drawing room," she said, and led them through a set of heavy doors. Aristide noted that the gilding on the panel edges was peeling. And there was a moth hole in Lillian's sweater, showing pale skin between the frayed ends of the yarn.

Old money shabbiness. Maybe. Not very many people in Gedda were doing well, these days. And what had she meant about interim occupants?

The punch, at least, was strong and sweet.

It *was* warmer in the drawing room, though barely. Daoud went to the fireplace to chafe his hands. Lillian hovered, not quite visibly nervous. Aristide set his punch on the sideboard. A good two hundred years old, probably, and with those lines it looked like a Marquette. In his limited experience dealing antiques—some fraudulent, some genuine—it should have been part of a set, but none of the other pieces were present. In fact, the furniture was a hodgepodge, some of it better suited to a boudoir or a billiards room.

The house was big enough that he imagined it had both. But he also imagined they stood empty now, pillaged of their furnishings. He had begun to get a sense of just how things hung at Damesfort.

The DePauls' country home was situated at the inner curve of a valley, hidden from the road by a hillside but set far enough above the lowland for a view, which the drawing room windows showed to great advantage. A winter-brown lawn swept down from the house to the stream he'd seen earlier, which wound its way through copses of bare trees. Thin smudges of smoke rose from the village, hidden by a small wood on the other side of the snow-dusted fields at the valley floor.

Much closer at hand, perhaps ten yards from the house, stood a small group: Jinadh by a stack of pigeons, Stephen bowed awkwardly around the stock of a shotgun, and Cyril smoking beside him. They all wore brown-and-gray country clothes. Cyril had gone so far as to snag a flat cap crookedly on his skull. Aristide wondered where he'd gotten the clothes, which almost fit him.

Jinadh wound up and flung a target high over the fields. Stephen followed with the heavy gun, too slow. He missed. Jinadh said something inaudible through the distance and the glass, but his expression was readable: encouragement, perhaps a little desperation. His breath clouded as he spoke. He looked cold. Stephen, on the other hand, looked stubborn. Until Cyril tapped his shoulder and held a hand out for the gun.

After watching Stephen struggle with its weight, Aristide found the grace with which Cyril handled the weapon almost uncanny. He took it one-handed from his nephew and broke it without hesitation. Stephen handed him two shells from the pocket of his own jacket.

Cyril tucked his cigarette grimly into one corner of his mouth, loaded the gun, and snapped the barrel back together.

Jinadh watched all this without expression, without breaking focus to stamp his feet or breathe into cupped palms. If he moved at all, it was only to grow stiff and start to frown. Now Cyril turned to him and cocked his head, indicating he should throw a pigeon.

His expression closed as swiftly and as surely as the shotgun's barrel, but not fast enough to hide the irritation that flashed across his face. He tried to smile. Cyril tried it back at him. Neither quite managed, though Cyril's attempt at least had the benefit of irony.

With time-consuming care, Jinadh selected two targets from the pile. Unperturbed, Cyril held the gun against the leather patch on his shoulder, motionless and patient. If he found the weight cumbersome, it didn't show. His eyes were locked on the middle distance. The only thing that moved, finally, was his mouth, to speak one short word.

This time, when Jinadh threw the pigeon, he put his back into it. Cyril tracked the target and pulled the trigger. The pigeon disappeared, snuffed from the sky, leaving only a trailing cloud of smoke.

The second target followed so closely that Jinadh must have thrown it before Cyril shot the first. But slick as greasepaint in summer, Cyril traced its path over the trees and blasted it from the sky.

He handed the gun back to Stephen, who staggered under its weight, then took his burnt-down cigarette from the corner of his mouth. Licking his thumb, he pinched the ember out and put the butt into his pocket.

Dusk came quickly, silencing the gunshots. Lillian's pulse jumped in the quiet; there was an awkward situation in the offing, and she would have to manage it. From what she'd seen of the afternoon's sport, her brother had not endeared himself to her husband.

Stephen was another story, though. Since the dedication ceremony, and their subsequent days together mewed up in Coral Street, Stephen and Cyril had developed exactly the sort of bond Lillian had thought—and hoped—they might. And that would endear Cyril to Jinadh even less than his own surliness.

Typical Cyril. A charmer when he needed it, he could switch the power on like a man with a generator. But it must burn up fuel he didn't have right now; the light behind his eyes was fitful at best.

A door slammed on the other side of the house, and what trivial conversation they had managed—"Is that sideboard a Marquette?" "Why yes. A wedding gift to Grandmama, I think. Pity to have lost the rest."—died at the sound. The void was filled with the clatter of footsteps and voices, indistinct but growing louder. Mostly Stephen's. Jinadh now and then.

"We're in the drawing room," she called, though the door was shut against the draft. Magnusson would tell them, if they couldn't hear her.

Sure enough, moments later the door opened to admit the sportsmen, still in their damp tweeds. The snow had begun to fall in earnest toward the end of the day and soaked them through. It was falling still; light from inside caught the flakes that came closest to the windowpanes.

When Jinadh saw their guests his features fell out of their pinched, enduring expression into something much more like pleasure. He went to Daoud first, saying, «Bléssed Solstice, respected brother.»

«The same to you,» said Daoud, and looked truly happy for the first time since Lillian had greeted him in the drive. Funny what exile could do: bring a Belqati man and a member of the royal family together at the holidays.

"And Aristide," Jinadh went on, "I am glad you could come as well." He offered his hand to shake and Aristide, staring over his shoulder, missed the cue. Daoud cleared his throat, and Aristide jumped to.

"Queen's sake," he said, taking Jinadh's hands. "They're like ice! Careful you don't break one off." A little stiff, a little too affected.

Stephen lingered at Cyril's side until Jinadh called him over to meet their guests. He came, with a quick glance behind at his uncle. Cyril did not return it, or perhaps even notice. Lurking at the threshold, he held one hand over his pocket as though checking for a watch or cigarette lighter, but did not then withdraw anything.

How had Lillian never noticed it before? Patting a jacket pocket looked just like pressing your palm to a gut wound. The look on her brother's face certainly fit the image.

"Cyril," she said, to cut the tension. "Punch?"

He jumped at this name then slowly turned to face her. "No, thank you."

"I will take some." Jinadh flopped into the armchair Lillian had left warm when she stood to welcome them in. "Tossing those awful things has given me a pain. I used to throw discus, in school, but that was many years ago and I am out of practice."

Magnusson, who had entered as though rolled in on silent casters, circulated with the punch tray.

Cyril refused in favor of neat rye, poured from the bar. Magnusson eyed him with censure. Aristide pretended not to watch. Daoud stared at Aristide with the same harsh judgment as the butler aimed at Cyril. Mapping the glares drew a cobweb of malignancy across the room. You could strangle in a snare like that.

In the center stood her son, dripping on the rug.

She knew what was coming. He always begged a cocktail of his own before dinner, and usually ended up with half of one, or a sip of someone else's, generally only after badgering and begging or sometimes subterfuge.

With the clairvoyance of a medium, or at least a married man and father, Jinadh said, "Stephen, what do you say to a glass of punch?"

When Lillian made a surprised sound, Jinadh shrugged and said, "It's the holidays."

But Stephen, too, was watching Cyril swirl the glass of rye. Finally, he tore his eyes from his uncle and stood up straight. "Actually," he said, "I think I'd like some whiskey."

Dinner was more of an ordeal than some beatings Cyril had endured. At least when someone was hitting you, you knew exactly where you stood.

But thinking that, and then seeing Aristide a few seats down, fork flirting with his dinner . . . well. Those memories belied the comparison. The exception, then, that proved the rule.

The food itself strengthened some of his suspicions. Meatloaf made of mostly breadcrumbs, served with garden greens. No proper beef, no fish. Not even poached chicken.

That would in part be due to scarcity. Magnusson kept a store of old newspapers downstairs for window cleaning, shoe polishing, and other tasks. Cyril had raided this to do some catch-up reading and found the past several seasons had been hard on farmers. Imports were expensive; key trading partners alienated by the Ospies were still reluctant to engage with an unstable Gedda. Shipping by sea was possible in coastal regions, but the railroads and highways were still recovering from Catwalk depredations. It was simply hard to find food and to move it. The DePaul fortune should have made this a negligible concern, but Cyril was starting to wonder if there might not be such a thing anymore.

Finally, mercifully, the meal ended. Stephen was sent to bed and the liqueurs came out. Cyril refused and made himself scarce.

He found Stephen at the top of the stairs, leaning back on his elbows. The indistinct sounds of conversation rose from the dining room, flowing more freely now that Cyril had gone.

"Bad acoustics," he said.

"There isn't a better spot." Stephen sat up and put his elbows on his knees. Over the sharp bones, his skin was pebbled by the pressure of the carpet. "I tried to find one at the summer holidays, but this is it. Sometimes if they get loud you can make out the words."

It was true; Cyril remembered from childhood. There were places in Damesfort that made eavesdropping simple. The dining room was not one of them. "What rooms did Lillian put the guests in?"

This occasioned some pursing of the lips and a little bit of thoughtful tooth-grinding. It was a show; Cyril had seen this boy at the dinner table more than once, and knew how well he hid what went on in his head. He wanted Cyril to be impressed. "Best ones in the north wing," he said at last.

Which weren't nearly as nice as the worst in the south. They were dark, and caught a draft. There were empty bedrooms in better parts of the house. He smelled spite. She was displeased at Jinadh's invitation.

"Are they close together?" Because the way that bearded twig of a boy had been watching Aristide all night, the careful placement of his hand on Ari's elbow as he made a point . . . those meant something more than "secretary."

"I think across the hall. She gave Mr. Qassan the hill room, and Mr. Makricosta has the, um . . . the . . ."

"The El," said Cyril, who had lived in this house longer than his nephew, though many years ago.

The El was a two-room suite: a study attached to a bedroom, which was technically not in the north wing at all, but the central part of the house. The office door would be across from Qassan's bedroom, which gave them a shred of deniability. It also meant that, from the right room in the north wing, the bedroom window would be visible.

"Come on," said Cyril.

Stephen didn't question him: just got up and followed.

The room he was aiming for had been . . . . Oh, Great-Grandfather's reading room? He couldn't recall. It was unused now, thick with dust, and freezing cold. Sheets shrouded what furniture remained—Lillian had pinched some for the rooms she kept open, apparently having lost a great deal to the Ospies. Obviously no one had used the room since the family took up residence. Too expensive to heat the whole house, probably, and not enough staff to keep it clean.

Their feet would leave prints in the dust. Unavoidable. With luck, no one would check on this room after they left it. At least not for a long while.

"Window seat," said Cyril, and pointed. Stephen sat, and sneezed. Cyril leaned over him, checking the view from the window. Exactly as he remembered.

It took half an hour of waiting before Ari's bedroom light flicked on. By then Cyril's toes had gone numb and Stephen had begun to fidget. But that died away with the lamp's flare, and the sudden appearance of a figure in the window perpendicular to theirs.

"It's him," said Stephen, whispering. His breath clouded the glass before his face.

Cyril made a noncommittal noise as they watched Aristide prepare for bed. Alone. He'd been half expecting Daoud to act as a valet, too, but Aristide removed his cuff links on his own, and unwound the bow tie from beneath his collar. Because they *had* dressed for dinner this evening, with company, except for Cyril. His father had not lived to see the advent of black tie, and left behind only tails. Given the choice between stiff formality and ill-fitting chalk-stripe, he chose the latter, though to put it on was to remember Aristide had ordered it for him. That he wore Ari's money and Ari's taste against his skin.

Across the corner of the courtyard, Aristide hung his jacket on the valet stand and unbuckled his cummerbund. His rings were next, and then the pearl drops from his ears. He looked around the room, made a pursed face, and turned back to his jacket. From one pocket, he withdrew a small, round flask and emptied it down his throat. He had just begun to pull the studs free from his shirt when he paused, turned his head, and said something.

From this angle, Cyril couldn't see the newcomer entering from the office. But he could imagine. Reality matched up shortly.

Daoud was already in pyjamas, a quilted dressing gown belted at his waist. Aristide looked . . . not exactly pleased to see him, but didn't throw him out. They had a short, terse conversation. At the end of it, Aristide shrugged and dropped his hands from his shirt-front so that Daoud could take over. Stud by stud, Aristide came unwrapped. Daoud had to stand on tiptoe to kiss him, and when he pulled away he made a face.

The flask. Daoud, who had glared at the butler for refilling Ari's glass again and again, would taste it on him.

Aristide, looking angry now, was the one who did the kissing next.

In their frigid blind, Cyril felt a strange frisson through the air. Stephen's interest in the scene across the courtyard had shifted to something less than analytical, but from his posture, he had half his attention on Cyril now: wariness, tension, embarrassment.

Of course. At that age, how would he have felt to be observed and aroused? To watch what was happening through that window with a parent or his sister at his back, watching it happen, too?

He hardly wanted to watch it now, but couldn't make himself look away.

"You should leave," he said to Stephen. Why had he even taken them on this little mission, when he knew how it would end?

"What? Why?" A note of relief belied Stephen's protest.

There were several answers to this question, all condescending or disingenuous. *Because I said so. Because we ought to give them privacy.* The kind of answers either of his parents might give. But Cyril said, "You're not stupid or ignorant. You've seen enough to know what happens next."

Stephen slipped off the window seat. His knees were covered in dust. He brushed at them ineffectually before looking up at Cyril. "You're not leaving, though."

He didn't have a good response to that, and so said nothing. Stephen, from the shrewd look in his damson eyes, read more in that than Cyril would have liked.

He did not enjoy what he saw. It wasn't voyeurism; it was only more information. It didn't seem, from his vantage point, that the two of them enjoyed it much, either. And that was information, also.

CHAPTER

THIRTEEN

The days before Solstice dragged for everyone else in the house. Or at least, Lillian got that impression when she could haul herself out of her office and away from the telephone. The work of the government—even a temporary one—did not stop for a little thing like the rebirth of the sun.

Anyway, holing up with work gave her an excuse to avoid the various interpersonal tensions ratcheting tighter and tighter in the halls of Damesfort.

On the day preceding the longest night, however, she could no longer use work as an avoidance tactic: everyone else had gone home, rung off, closed up. If tasks were unfinished, they would have to wait until the new year began tomorrow.

When she emerged, the house echoed as if empty. A change that would have been pleasant if she didn't find it so unnerving. She wandered the halls trying to find any of her family or guests, but only encountered Bern bringing in an armload of pine boughs, his shoulders and bundle dusted with snow.

"No idea where anyone's gone, ma'am," he told her. "I've been out running errands."

Finally, she turned up Aristide in the drawing room, a book on his knee and music on the wireless, wrapped in a cigarette haze.

"Welcome back to the present time and place," he said, knocking the ash from his straight into a full tray. "Provisional government still performing as we'd like?"

"It's still performing," said Lillian, aiming for the bar. "'Like' depends on who you ask."

Aristide made a noise into his book and flipped a page she felt fairly certain he hadn't read.

"Where is everyone?" she asked, plucking the stopper from the whiskey decanter.

"Jinadh offered to take Daoud into the village," said Aristide. "I believe their ultimate destination was the pub."

"Jinadh hates the pub."

"Nevertheless," said Aristide, discarding the butt of his straight.

"They ought to be back soon; everything will close down early." Whiskey poured, Lillian tucked herself into the curved arm of the divan. "And my next of kin?" Levity distracted from the faint unease that clung to any thought or mention of her brother, her fear of saying his name in Aristide's presence and seeing what it did to him. Humor helped her pretend the situation was normal.

Still, he shifted in his seat. Closing the book and setting it aside he asked, "Is there any gin over there?"

"And vermouth," she said. "No olives, I'm afraid. Nor lemons. Mr. Qassan said you preferred a twist, but . . ." Lemons were rather dear.

His smile was pinched, and he didn't answer her question until he had his back to her, face hidden. "Out," he said. "They went for a walk in the woods."

"At least they'll work up an appetite." Lillian was glad Cyril was getting exercise and some fresh air. "Speaking of, I'm ravenous."

"I wouldn't dare," said Aristide. "I asked for a plate of something a while back and I think I've earned the cook's undying hatred. Things seem a little frantic downstairs."

"Thank you for the tip. I'll leave them be."

"Your driver," he said. "Martí. She's Tatien, isn't she?" The bar spoon chimed against the beaker as he stirred.

"Yes, of course. Why?"

"Was she at all mixed up with Memmediv's messy little venture?"

"You mean independence? I think not. Magnusson tells me she's quite a patriot. Apparently she was out of service for some time, volunteering with her hometown militia to fight the separatists. Her most recent reference is some five years old." And she had come cheap, because of that. "Still, good at her job."

Aristide returned to his chair, setting his feet up on the ottoman and letting his cocktail rest on his midriff. "I think I might have pinned her rather sharply."

"She's sturdy; she'll recover." The whiskey had settled in her empty stomach, making her reckless with her reminiscence. "You never heard from Memmediv, did you? After Hadhariti?"

Before he answered, Aristide tipped the better part of his martini down his throat. Fist to his sternum, he closed his eyes against some sudden pain: an ulcer, a rising belch. What finally came out was a strangled cough, wet and throaty. Even then he made her wait, rising to refill his glass.

Around the curve of his elbow, she watched him pour: mostly gin, a miserly splash of vermouth. More liquor than she thought might fit into his glass. "I last saw him on the border. I think . . . Cordelia would have kept in some kind of contact." He said the name like he worried it would break. "But he certainly didn't have anything to say to me. Likewise, frankly."

"Not even to do business?" she asked.

"My business is based in Liso."

"Imports *and* exports," she said.

"A euphemism." The lid of the ice bucket struck home too hard. Then, a small concession: "I never worked with him. Not once. We aren't in the arms game, anyway."

"I'm glad to hear it," she said, though whatever games Cross-Costa played were still likely to be dangerous and dirty. "Have you told Cyril what you know?"

Until now he had neatly avoided eye contact with movement and a mobile expression. Now he met her gaze, unwavering. "Have you?"

Breath cooled her palate; she realized her mouth was open. As if she might answer his question.

Before she could decide, she heard the door and voices raised in song. A familiar foreign mode, the tune wavering like water or flame between each note. The singers were loud, their Porashtu slurred and indistinct.

"It sounds as though the pub has closed," she said, "and the party has come here."

Jinadh was much drunker than Daoud, and Daoud was certainly not sober. But neither was morose, thanks be. By and large Jinadh got laughing drunk, but if he started out on the wrong foot he could stumble into a foul pit of moodiness. She'd worried, hearing he'd turned to the village pub, but drinking with a countryman apparently made the place more tolerable.

Magnusson brought coffee for the two revelers to settle them before dinner, which was imminent. Just in time for the dressing gong, Stephen and Cyril straggled in with soaked feet and filthy clothes. No sharp glances passed between her husband and her brother: the former too merry and distracted, the latter . . . well, unchanged. Aristide did not bolt from the room, nor sharpen his tongue on anyone present. His tipsy secretary did not turn possessive. Hot punch was poured down everyone's throats before they were sent to change.

Lillian began to have the wonderful, familiar feeling of gliding on clockwork: the feeling she got when things came together well and everything went the way it was supposed to. This rare, sweet sensation was usually limited to her professional sphere, and it was both pleasant and strange to feel it in the confines of her childhood home. Especially given the circumstances.

At exactly the stroke of eight, they all sat down to tall white candles nestled amidst pine boughs and holly berries. Waxy garlands of mistletoe wound between the place settings.

A roast goose, basted golden, sat queenly over casseroles and roasted vegetables. Most of it came from the estate, she knew; the turnips and potatoes were from the kitchen garden. Until yesterday, the goose had probably been living a quiet life on the local pond. The most expensive things to get had probably been the cooking oil and the sugar for the glaze. But unless you knew all that, it looked like a sumptuous spread.

She'd have to ask Jinadh if the household budget could afford a bit extra for the staff's Solstice fête. Or perhaps it would be better just to slip them all a little envelope of thanks.

Silence settled over the diners, but it was not the awkward pall it might have been; people were simply eating and drinking.

"This is superb," said Aristide, tipping his glass close to a candle flame. "Cestinian? An ontichialo?"

A mercy: The cellars had lain largely undisturbed since Daddy's funeral. The wine was the one true luxury on the table. The interim tenants' depredations had been patchy; someone without taste or knowledge, probably, who had left them a fair selection of good vintages. Small blessings. And another mercy: Each bottle drew out the effects of whatever Solstice magic had descended on her house.

Porashtu mixed with Geddan—nearly everyone at the table understood both. Jokes switched languages halfway through.

«You know Belqati Solstice custom, right?» A lock of Daoud's hair had fallen from his wax, and he'd lost the stiffness that usually held him at right angles. «For married couples?»

"Oh no," said Lillian, laughing.

«The longest night of the year,» Daoud went on. «You have to spend it like you want to spend the rest of them.»

"Holy stones," said Stephen, putting his face into his hands. Lillian's attention had wandered, and it seemed Magnusson had been . . . *festive* in pouring for her son. Oh well, it was only once a year.

«Just married couples?» asked Jinadh, leaning in on one elbow. «Heaven and earth, the things the court got up to on Solstice night would sizzle your small hairs.»

"I think it was similar for some families in the village," said Lillian. "Of course, not *our* parents." Cyril didn't return her smile; she hadn't been expecting it, really. "But I know some women thought it was a good night to conceive."

"Stopped premature births," said Aristide. "Kept the baby longer in the womb. That's what the older women always said, anyway."

Something about the rhythm of his speech shifted slightly when he said it, in a way that Lillian could almost place. "And when were *you* conceived?" she asked, wine-daring.

He gave a little shrug. "The only people who could answer that question are long dead."

Damnation. She'd put her foot through the fragile glass of flirtation and merriment. Striving to regain sparkling ground, she said, "Well, what did you do for Solstice when you were young? Before they went?"

"Mother died when I was born." He delivered it like any other small talk, with a wry twist to his mouth. He knew it wasn't what she'd hoped for. Perhaps this was revenge for her probing questions this afternoon. "My father would go down the mountain to the pub and drink 'til he was sick. Sometimes I went along, when I got older. Not to drink so much as to get him home safely. And the tips were always better that time of year."

"Tips?" asked Jinadh, looking trepidatious.

"The first boards I ever tread," said Aristide. "Solstice was the only time my father saw me sing. And the only time he didn't beat me for it. He didn't like me to go down to the pub. Embarrassed, I think."

Like everyone else at the table. Pudding course finished, brandy poured, there was nothing in the offing to end the eggshell silence that had crept between the plates.

Until Cyril, who had been silent through the meal, said, "Why don't you sing something now?"

He didn't say it kindly, nor as though he expected Aristide to take the suggestion. He tossed the words into the center of the table like a lit firecracker, or a live grenade.

Despite all that, she thought for a moment Aristide might do it.

Then the hour struck and the sound of the clock made him start. He closed his mouth so sharply she could hear his teeth.

"Time for coffee and liqueurs, I think," she said too loudly, and the moment was lost in the scraping of chairs.

Cyril wasn't trying to conceive a child or ensure good fortune for the rest of the year, or even make sure the sun rose the morning after the longest night. He simply couldn't sleep.

He kept hearing the faint shift of Ari's vowels, moving to the front of his mouth. Wondering why he'd parted with so many hoarded gems of information so swiftly, just because Lillian pressed him. Kept seeing the soft opening of his lips as if he really meant to sing.

It had been cruel; he'd known even as he said it that it would destroy the fragile idyll his sister had managed to tweeze from this thorny imitation of festivities. But he'd watched Aristide lay down facts about his childhood deliberately as coins on a counter, at Lillian's slightest suggestion, and something about it slid under his skin like splinters.

Back then, all he'd ever gotten for his troubles with Aristide was a smile. But how much trouble had he really taken? They had kept any confessions they might have made hidden behind their respective roles.

None of it really excused ruining dinner. But dinner didn't mean much to him besides another chance to eat he might not have again. His stomach ached, though he could hardly remember the taste of anything he'd put into his mouth. How long would it take to stop thinking of food this way?

To occupy the time until dawn, he made himself a mission: to open every door in the house, and assess how much of it was being used. Excluding the master bedroom, in which he could hear the sounds of Solstice being celebrated. He found Stephen's room by accident; the boy was soundly asleep, sloppily spread across his pillows. He'd have his first hangover tomorrow. After that it was empty room after empty room, all dusty as the one that looked into Aristide's windows. Which were lit, barely. No movement. And no sound, when Cyril crept down the hall and around the corner to put his ear against the door.

This was the one he'd meant to open all along. The knob turned, when he tried it.

Wrapped in a rug and a dressing gown Aristide reclined in an armchair, head raised from the book in his hands to watch the door open. The room was lit only by the lamp beside him and the glow of embers. His spectacles caught the light and shone it into Cyril's face, obscuring his eyes.

"You might have knocked," he said.

Cyril shut the door behind him but kept his back against it.

"Have a seat?" Aristide opened his palm, indicating the dormer window adjacent to his chair.

Cyril didn't accept the offer. "Why did you come here, Aristide?"

He made a show of checking his page number before he set the book aside. "I was invited."

Cyril shook his head. "No. Why did you really come?"

Aristide looked at him, too intently. "Why did *you*?"

A question he had been trying not to ask himself. He could say Cordelia, but putting her name between them now felt cruel, to Aristide and himself and the memory of her chemically red hair, her laughter and her freckles. Her face when he'd pulled a gun in her dressing room. Her anger when he offered her an out.

And anyway, he knew she was only a part of it. Had he only come because Aristide asked him? Because he wanted to come home, and believed this might be it?

Had he come because some deeply buried part of his mind—a prideless, animal shard—knew that solitude in Liso would be a good excuse for slow suicide? Or perhaps not so slow. He no longer had a pistol; that had been taken during debrief. But he had the skills to find another, or some other method. Dying wasn't hard.

That idiot shard that clung to life didn't understand what he owed. But it was stuck deep, and it throbbed with longing.

His laugh, when it came, felt like being sick. "Are you in earnest? I wouldn't have missed that dinner for all the world. Your cockmuff flirting with my brother-in-law, and all your quaint little childhood stories."

Aristide blinked twice, surprised, and then said, "Quaint? Is that what you heard?"

"I never knew you were a country boy." The snide sound of his own voice was familiar: the kind of disdain he dropped during an interrogation, when shame seemed the likeliest iron with which to break his subject. The only difference was that this time, he hadn't used it on purpose. It had used *him*. "You shook that mud off your shoes and shined them."

"Yes," said Aristide. "Your point?"

"Why tell her? All of them? Why now, tonight, and never—?" He stopped himself, just, with the quick application of fingernails to palm. He was losing his footing, yanked along by hurt like a rider dragged behind a frightened horse. He should not have opened this door.

"So that's what this is about." Aristide fussily rearranged his blanket. "Do you want to know what I *didn't* tell them? Would it make you feel better to know just a little more about me than your sister does?"

"Never mind," said Cyril, reaching for the doorknob. "I don't—"

"I didn't just earn onstage," said Aristide. "My father said he beat me for singing, but we both knew what the blows were really for. What I got up to out the back door, against the wall." His accent was slipping, pressing up against his teeth, and Cyril had *heard* this before: Ari's hands tangled in his hair, spitting curses when he came. When he was startled. When he was afraid.

How had he never guessed that Aristide came from the north,

from the mountains? Chuli, by his looks, or part—that piece fit neatly now. Wise of him to hide it: before, during, and after the Ospies. From what little Cyril had gleaned from old papers and overheard conversations, aid had been slow in coming to the shattered tribes up north. Acherby had fallen, but old prejudice died harder than dictatorship.

Still, why had Cyril never seen past the elaborate stage name, the carefully constructed persona?

Because he hadn't wanted to know. He'd preferred some secrets then. Now he wanted light to shine in every darkened corner, so nothing lurking there could hide.

"Tips *were* better at Solstice," Aristide went on. "For walking the boards. But I made less at the holidays, for all that. Folk aren't after paid teeth on their tackle so much, that time of year. Made 'em feel ashamed, maybe. As if they oughtn't to the rest of the time, knowing how my pa came after me about it."

"*Ari.*"

The nickname stopped him cold, halfway through inhaling to continue his tirade.

"There." Powder and silk returned to his pronunciation as it sank back toward his soft palate. "Now you've heard it. Did you find it quaint? Filled with rustic charm? I'd have thought you already had your fill of *that*, with your tweeds and your guns and your country house."

Cyril realized he had pressed himself against the door so hard the panels were putting divots in his back. "Do you think you have some sort of monopoly on childhood horror?"

"I never said it was horror. It simply made me what I am."

"As if this didn't?"

"This?" Aristide sat forward in his chair and swept a hand through the air in front of him, as if encompassing the whole of Damesfort. The weight of the house, the family, tradition: It felt as though that hand had hauled them from the dust and laid them across Cyril's shoulders. "It turned you into *something*, I'm sure."

Cyril took a deep breath and bore up under the weight, then let it fall to force his next words out. "You have *no idea*."

"Why don't you tell me, then?" He flung it across the space between them as though it meant nothing, but Cyril heard the faintest nasal resonance beneath the rough edges of his anger: sadness, held hard in check. An aching, upturned end to the question.

Afraid that he might answer, Cyril opened the door behind him. "Goodnight," he said, and left Aristide to wonder.

CHAPTER

FOURTEEN

Aristide and Daoud left early, and if Lillian thought any of her relief had shown she would have been mortified. But she had been trained almost her entire life to hide emotions like that, and so instead of embarrassment, she only felt privately ashamed.

The rest of her brief break from work passed in a well-fed blur, and suddenly it was time to return to the city. The family's last night in Damesfort found them in the drawing room: Lillian with her stocking feet on Jinadh's lap and the evening edition of the *Clarion* across her own. She had given the ciphers to Jinadh, who was frowning over the crossword with his pen against his lip. Ink had left a spot there, like a freckle. Stephen—miraculously—was buried in a book with a pad of paper next to him, studiously copying down chemistry notes. The wireless played low, music and advertisements mingling with the soft sounds of the fire.

Cyril had disappeared after dinner. He'd stayed cagey and quiet in the days after Solstice, keeping mostly to himself.

She didn't know what to do for him. And she didn't know what to do *with* him. It might be possible to quietly keep him at Damesfort through the election; it didn't seem likely he would go into the village. The only tricky matter was the staff. She trusted Magnusson, and he would have impressed upon the rest of them a strong need for discretion. But would they abide by his authority? And how loyal would they be to an employer they had only known six months, whose budget they understood to be somewhat strained? An employer who might let them go at the end of the season to cut costs?

It would be better to get Cyril out of her house; out of the country. Some peaceful, quiet place where he could calm down. Possibly a retreat, or sanatorium. Somewhere they could help him with whatever made him jump at loud sounds and slip food into his pockets. She'd seen him doing that at meals, when he thought no one was watching, and later noticed grease spots on his jacket.

There were some places in Ibet that might do, or Suldatia. Mountains and fresh air and no-nonsense nurses. She was leery of alienists as a general rule, but perhaps in Cyril's case psychological intervention might be helpful.

When she would have time to take care of it all, and how she would pay for it once she had . . . She sighed into her paper and turned the page.

"'Coming home sans quarry,'" said Jinadh. "Eight letters. Starts with *O*, sixth letter *X*."

"Oh, you know I'm rubbish at these things." But she reached for it anyway, to look.

"Better than me," he said, "at least when they are in Geddan." Which was true. She wouldn't have dreamed of attempting any word game in Porashtu. She could speak and write it with fluency, but the kind of linguistic and cultural nuance a crossword puzzle required? Beyond her reach.

His, too, from the scribbled-out letters in each box. How he could keep his answers straight from his mistakes, she didn't know. "This one, here?" she asked, pointing. He nodded.

On the wireless, a mournful little foxtrot number wound down and was replaced by the chimes that heralded an hourly news broadcast. Lillian looked up from the paper toward the radio, as though watching its dial would clarify the signal.

"Good evening to the folks at home," said the anchor. "This is *Hour by Hour*, and I'm Marlowe Flanders with your late-breaking nightly news."

Flanders had a smarmy Amberlinian drone that put Lillian's teeth on edge, though it probably played well with city-born listeners.

"Do we have to—?" said Jinadh, but Lillian shushed him.

"Now normally," Flanders continued, "I'd lead up to the big story with a lot of little tidbits from today. But today the tidbits have been blasted out of the water by a story I only got a whiff of this afternoon."

That was a bit . . . *sensational*, for the hourly bulletin. Lillian sat up straighter, crossword puzzle forgotten.

"Hunting down Ospies hasn't been a priority of the provisional government," said Flanders. "If anything, they've decided to let bygones be bygones. In fact, as some of you may know, former Ospie foreign service member Lillian DePaul is a part of the provisional government's press office."

Lillian's hand, holding Jinadh's pen, fell to the paper in her lap.

"If you were keeping up with the news under Acherby, you saw her fall from favor. But you also know she didn't drop the Ospies for the greater good. DePaul collaborated with the Ospies in Porachis for three years before eloping to Asu with a Porachin noble.

For three years, she did due diligence keeping up Acherby's image in the world at large. Coerced, she says: forced to do their dirty work to save her son."

Stephen shifted, staring intently at a spot on the carpet.

"And that was good enough for some of you," said Flanders. "I won't judge. We all had a hard time of it under Acherby. But the story I've got for you now makes that a much harder sell."

Ink flowed from the pen's nib into the fibers of the paper, soaking them black in a spreading circle. She stared at the empty boxes Jinadh had asked her to help fill, and knew what was coming next.

"Ms. DePaul may have her excuses," he went on, "but there's none can be made or honored for her brother. Another story news-noses might remember from the same dustup that dirtied Ms. DePaul. A helping hand in the Ospies' coup, Cyril DePaul forked the ACPD over to Acherby, ensuring the swift destruction of the regionalists. He should be brought up on charges. Instead, a reliable source relayed to me he's sitting snug and safe within the borders of the country we had to claw back from his old friends."

Outfoxed. The word was *outfoxed.*

"Hear the full story tomorrow morning," said Flanders, "from my colleagues on the *A.M. Bulletin.* For now, this is Marlowe Flanders, leaving you in the capable hands of Cary Reiser and his Swingin' Six."

The three tones chimed again, in descending order this time. A smooth-voiced advertisement for Scandal cigarettes played over the opening strains of Cary Reiser's band.

Lillian lifted the pen from the paper and set the cap over the nib with a crisp click.

"Stephen," she said, hearing her own words from a long way off. "Go and get your uncle, please."

———

Though Cyril would not see reason, she would have gone on argu-ing. For every one of his refusals, she would have thrown herself harder against his stubbornness. After all: This was her fault. Her slip of the tongue with Frye had led to this, and now she would be the reason her brother hanged. Or whatever they did to traitors these days.

Eventually Magnusson opened the drawing room door and stood silently on the threshold until the shouting died away.

"I apologize," he said. "I didn't want to intrude. Ma'am, Ms. Simons is on the phone. I tried to put her off, but—"

"No," said Lillian. She had heard the word so many times in the last hour that it sounded like meaningless gibberish. "Of course. I—"

Cyril walked out then, slipping the yoke of further conversation. His shoulder checked Magnusson as he pushed past, throwing the butler slightly off-balance. Magnusson recovered quickly and did not acknowledge the incident. "You'll take the call?"

"Please," she said, dreading it.

Honora sounded calm, collected, sympathetic. Everything Lillian did not feel.

"Lillian," she said. "I'm so sorry."

"Thank you, Honora." Her professional persona settled in her veins like ice, slowing the frantic beat of her heart and cooling panic from her cheeks. "I . . . I should have told you he was . . . it hap-pened suddenly. And I was trying to keep it quiet. It wasn't my idea."

Immediately, she wished she had not tacked the last bit on. It sounded both petulant and pathetic.

"I'm sure you'll handle this with grace," she said. "Just like you do everything."

Lillian bit back sardonic laughter. "With things as they stand, I don't know if I'm the best person to run your press conference this week."

"About that . . ."

Of course. They would never keep her on after this.

"We had a cable just now from the sitting minister," said Honora, "and . . . well, I'm afraid we have to let you go."

"Don't worry," she said, as if reading from a script. "I understand."

"Thank you." The relief Honora breathed into her end of the line turned the words ragged, and Lillian pulled her cheek away from the receiver. "I truly am so, so sorry. If it was up to me . . ."

Lillian would still be sacked, but someone else would have made the call. "Goodnight," she said, and rang off.

In the silence that followed, she heard a faint tap at the window. Then a second, building to a glassine susurrus that shifted with the wind. It had begun to sleet. Ice struck the windows like small ordinance. The smell of Solstice evergreen still lingered in the air as she sat facing another catastrophe from which she would have to rebuild her life. At least she had plenty of practice.

If someone had asked Cyril, an hour ago, if he planned to stay in Gedda, he'd have shrugged. He might even have said no, though he wouldn't have been able to say where else he might go.

Now, he felt as if he had grown roots.

There was every possibility that he would die if he stayed. Lillian had made that very clear.

"Your—our—only hope of thriving, even surviving in Gedda was predicated on keeping things quiet," she told him. "If one of the candidates decides to run with this banner behind them—and at *least* one of them will, believe me—it will probably turn into a tent show. You could end up on the scaffold. In front of the squad. And if somebody takes matters into their own hands before that, do you think I'd have any chance of justice?"

He hadn't said it to her, then, but he had thought it: What about everyone else's chance at justice? What about the people who had fled or fallen or died because of him? What about Cordelia?

For the first time in a long time, purpose filled him. A heavy one, and not the one he might have chosen for himself, but a purpose nonetheless. And it was such a relief to look up and see a satisfying end to this whole parade of horrors.

Who would be hurt by that? He had only ever inconvenienced his sister when they came close enough to interact. She probably hadn't wanted him here for Solstice in the first place. And now look how his presence had embarrassed her.

He didn't think she was completely heartless—it would hurt to lose her brother. But might it not also be a relief? Like the death of an aging parent or an expensive invalid.

And Aristide? Would survive. Had *been* surviving. Had decided Cyril was dead years ago. Even if he had come looking, he had also—wisely—given up.

The fact that he had looked at all . . . that fed some part of Cyril he would rather starve. The stubborn part. The animal bit of him that had dragged him back to Gedda, to his family, with Aristide. The part of him that didn't want to die.

In his drafty room, he emptied out his pockets. Crusts of bread, Jinadh's lighter, a melted piece of hard candy gone sticky in its wrapper. A penknife. A pocketknife. A knife from the table, still marked with a sheen of grease.

He wasn't that man anymore: the one who slunk through the jungle and put scraps in his pockets. He didn't need to carry knives. It made him feel naked to do it, but there was something luxurious in the feeling, too. A kind of horrible freedom.

Last of all he dug out a handful of cigarette butts. Shreds of charred tobacco stuck in the creases of his palm, clung to the lining of the pocket. With a turn of his wrist, he cast them into the grate to burn.

Aristide had been expecting the call, half dreading it, since he woke up to the story on the wireless. When it finally came it was a relief.

"He won't go." Her voice was matter-of-fact. "He won't leave. He said he's staying."

Aristide looked down at the papers on his hotel desk, though he didn't register anything that was written on them. Just a mess of black hatch marks, numbers and letters jumbled, the rustle of his elbows in their midst. "What?"

"I told him it would be easiest to get out of the country the sooner he went and he just stared at me. I said I'd pay for him to go, find someplace for him to stay."

"To be clear." Aristide put the pads of his fingers against the blotter and pressed as if he could push the situation into order. "Did he say nothing, or did he say the word 'no'?"

"Nothing at first. But . . . well, I may have . . . once things deteriorated from polite conversation, he did actually refuse. Vehemently."

"What did he say, exactly?"

"He just kept saying no, and finally when I couldn't stand it anymore and started shouting he . . . Mother and sons, he got this *look* in his eyes and asked where else he deserved to be."

Aristide breathed deep to quell a surge of anger. Anger at Cyril: undeniably a traitor, an Ospie collaborator. Also, an idiot. Anger that he refused to flee. Anger that he had to.

When that subsided, he asked, "How did it get out?"

Breath turned the line to static: a fast exhalation, either laughter or a choked-off sob. Knowing Lillian, the latter shoved into the former's clothes. "Stones, I'm an idiot."

"Lillian," he said, chest so tight he wondered if he oughtn't to have accepted the amyl nitrate his last doctor had suggested. "What have you done?"

"It was Frye," she said, too quickly. Then, "No, I mean . . . we were talking and I . . . it just came out."

He realized he had stopped breathing, and sucked in air through a dry mouth, triggering a coughing fit.

"You," he gasped, in between hacking. "You told Emmeline Frye . . . that Cyril—"

"It's so much worse than that," she said, and now she really was laughing. "You haven't the smallest conception. Aristide, I told her she needed a *hook,* something to appeal to people's emotions. In the very same conversation. And she took *my* rotten advice, *and* my brother. I didn't even *sell* him, Aristide. I gave him away for *free.*"

Inured as he was to using people as leverage and currency, this should not have struck Aristide so deeply, in such a vulnerable place. Yet he found himself standing, shouting into the telephone, "He isn't a commodity, Lillian. He's worth more than whatever you were hoping you would get!"

And she was talking over him, too strident to be shrill, "You can't have it both ways! You have no idea what I'm going through right now, and if you did you'd—"

The door opened, revealing Daoud draped in a thick muffler and chesterfield, briefcase in one gloved hand and snow melting on his beard. He cocked his head, silently inquiring.

Aristide caught the rest of his rage behind clenched teeth and said, "What exactly did you ring me up for? Just to tear me tips to tail?"

He heard Lillian gather herself similarly, heard the restraint in her voice when she said, "A favor."

"Oh? What kind?"

"Talk to him."

Aristide's bark of laughter made Daoud start, mussing the careful pile of folders he had taken from his briefcase and set at Aristide's elbow. He raised his eyebrows, but Aristide shook his head. "What would I say?"

"Tell him he'll be hanged," she said. "What he did was wrong, but to die for it? He was cornered and coerced. He can't shoulder the blame for everything that happened after. And what good will it do to let himself be executed? It isn't as if his death will bring back the old federation."

It had the rhythm of a litany. "You've told him this already. It won't do any good for him to hear it from me."

"Then tell him whatever you like. Whatever you think he'll hear. He might listen to you."

"I think," said Aristide, forceful and precise as a nail driven home, "you have greatly misconstrued my relationship with your brother. Good day."

When he rang off, the force of the receiver into the cradle made the ringer jangle.

"Lillian?" said Daoud.

In answer, Aristide closed his eyes and ground his teeth.

"How is she?"

"As you might expect." He fell back in his chair, sighing heavily as if he could purge the conversation, and nodded at the folders. "What are those?"

"Customs forms," he said. "Cargo manifests. All things associated with bringing a vessel into this harbor and unloading our wares. I had thought we might review them, but if you need . . ." He trailed off, as if unsure *what* Aristide might need in this situation.

In fact, even Aristide wasn't sure. To go forward with the deal would put money in the pocket of a woman who had as good as tied a noose around Cyril's neck. But to falter now would break Cross-Costa to little purpose. Aristide did not like grand gestures if they were also useless. A boycott that accomplished nothing wasn't a statement; it was pathetic. To that end, "No. I'm quite ready to look at them."

Daoud sat down gingerly across from him and lifted the cover of the first document. He paused halfway, clearly struggling with words that wouldn't come. "Aristide. I apologize, but . . . I overheard the last part of your conversation and . . . what *is* your relationship to Mr. DePaul at this time?"

That wasn't even a conversation he was ready to have with himself, let alone with his . . . secretary. Or whatever Daoud was to him. So. "Certainly nothing to do with imports and exports. Shall we begin?"

Frye's numbers in the polls began to rise. She had followed Lillian's advice to the letter—or her campaign manager had—and entered onto the scene well-armed with a point-by-point implementation plan for a series of tribunals: retroactive justice for all the folk who had been wronged by the Ospies. And the whole state of Amberlough, the whole rotten country, had been grievously wronged by Cyril.

Saeger played a poor game of catch-up after Frye's strong start out of the gate. This was where her Catwalk connections ought to have served her best, but Frye had been given lead time, leaving Saeger floundering in the dust. There was no way she could approach the issue without agreeing with the opposition. Her efforts made her sound conciliatory and slightly pitiful, which—like white silk— looked ill on her.

«You'll make yourself crazy,» said Jinadh, when Magnusson brought Lillian's habitual stack of papers to the breakfast table.

"I'm not already?" she asked, trying for levity and missing by a hair. Jinadh made a face she might have taken exception to, if the news had not been more important.

The *Telegraph*, the *Clarion, Federal Call, Farbourgh Times* . . . she'd revised her subscriptions in the wake of the disaster after Solstice. International affairs had fallen rather by the wayside, in her order of priorities.

She traced a headline with one finger. «Frye is proposing judges already, and she isn't even in the Cliff House. If she's elected, she's really going to do this.»

«Starting with your brother, I assume.»

«That's the implication.» She had kept many of their conversations in Porashtu over the last week, half out of caution and half out of embarrassment. None of the staff could speak it, so it gave her some scant privacy in dealing with Cyril's disgrace, and her own.

Jinadh watched her over his coffee, brows drawn together. «How flexible do you think her definition of 'collaboration' will be?»

«Do you mean, will it include me?» She put a little milk in her porridge. «There is no way to know without more . . . hmm.» A switch, to find the word. "Context."

«Ah, so it's wait and see. Your favorite thing, I know.» His smile coaxed an answering one from her, though it wavered badly.

«I think I will be safe,» she said. «I think most people will be. This is a stunt. She will follow through to make good on the campaign promise, but after—» She couldn't make herself say after *what*, «—After, she may not push very much.»

«She might lose control of it, if people latch onto the idea. Have you read the opinion pieces yet? Or any letters to the editor?»

She raised an eyebrow over the top of her paper. «How did you get to them before me?»

«Only the ones in the *Observer*,» he said; the paper where he edited arts and culture. It currently sat somewhere in the middle of Lillian's stack. «I snuck a proof copy. And speaking of . . . » A glance at the clock, and he dropped his napkin onto his plate. «I'll see you this evening, moon-eyes.»

He kissed the top of her head on his way out of the dining room, to polish the pages Lillian usually set aside. It was tempting to turn to them now, to read about marriages and parties and theatre and art, but that would be avoidance, which would not serve her in the end.

An essay in the *Clarion* proposed several people who, in the author's opinion, deserved the judgment of a tribunal as much as Cyril did, if not more. There was something perversely comforting in that. He wasn't as hated as Karol Kramer, for instance, warden of the largest Cultham internment camp, or Acherby's erstwhile adviser Victor Hale.

Kramer's name came up again in an interview with Saeger, who wanted to know what had inspired Frye's sudden pivot into compassion for victims of the Ospies, when she had let that aspect of recent history lie largely silent in her campaign.

Kramer killed good friends of mine, said Saeger. *Or at least stood by and watched them die of dysentery and exposure. More Chuli died on his watch than their people could really afford. There's hardly a whole family left in the Culthams now. If we're going to start stringing up Ospies, he would be my first choice over DePaul any day.*

Unfortunately, neither Kramer nor any of his contemporaries seemed to be in the country right now. Or, if they were, they had gone very close to the ground, leaving Cyril standing solitary in the field and ready to be struck by a mortar or bullets or a bolt of lightning.

Whatever was coming, it would hit him first and hardest, and he would not be prepared. Because he refused to be.

His guilt she could understand. But this misplaced sense of duty . . . it was going to get him killed, and the blood would splatter her and her family. If he wouldn't protect himself, she would have to do it for him.

Lillian had left strict instructions that Cyril and Stephen were not to leave the grounds of the estate.

Jinadh went with her to the city—work wouldn't wait for a family crisis, especially if Lillian had been sacked. Which she had been. Overhearing that conversation from the hall, Cyril gleaned Honora's half of it from Lillian's responses. Given his inferences about the family's financial situation, Cyril could understand why Jinadh left Cyril alone with his son. But he could also tell the man didn't like it one bit.

"Be good," he said to Stephen on the steps of the house. "Like your mother says." Then he cast a narrow-eyed glance at Cyril. His mouth moved as though he might speak, but in the end he only gave a tense nod and joined Lillian in the back of the auto.

The car pulled away, leaving Cyril and Stephen standing at the top of the wide front steps.

"Go for a walk?" asked Cyril. "I'll pack a picnic."

Stephen shrugged.

Magnusson cleared his throat.

"Don't worry," said Cyril. "We'll stay on the grounds. And we won't get into any trouble."

Which was how they ended up in Cyril's childhood haunt: a clearing at the center of the far windbreak. When the overbearing expectations of Damesfort and the DePaul family had grown too strangling, he had run out here to play soldier, hero, hunter, spy. It was the greatest distance you could put between yourself and the village, yourself and Damesfort. The nearest ears belonged to sheep, and even those were at the far end of the field for the moment.

"What are we doing out here?" asked Stephen. He reached into the pocket of his knickerbockers and pulled out a toffee. When he dropped the wrapper, Cyril snatched it from the ground and tucked it roughly back into the pocket from whence it had come.

"Bad as a cigarette butt," he said, patting his newly empty pocket out of habit. "Folk come by and see a stack of toffee wrappers, they know they didn't just fall from the sky."

He saw a teenage retort build, stall, and crumble before Stephen gave a nod very like his father's and kept his own counsel.

"Give me one?" Cyril asked. "A toffee, I mean."

Stephen handed one over. Cyril examined it, almost put it in his pocket, and then remembered he wouldn't need to save it for later. There wouldn't be much of a later, for him. He unwrapped the candy and put it in his mouth. It was slightly stale, and hard, so it went into his cheek to soften while he unloaded the mouse-eaten game bag he'd brought along.

"What'd you bring *those* for?" Stephen asked, as he removed a short length of copper pipe and a sack of furniture tacks liberated from the pantry, a hand drill likewise swiped from the garage, cigarette papers, and a box of the old shotgun shells he had discovered in the shed.

"These," said Cyril, shaking the tacks, "are shrapnel. This—" the pipe, "—a housing. We'll use the papers to make a fuse. And these?" He picked up a shell and pulled the brass cap from the tube. Gunpowder escaped in a fine spray across his fingers. "Explosives." Then, a loaf of bread, some cheese, and two leathery keeper apples came out of the bag. "This is just lunch."

"Temple *bells*," said Stephen, eyes huge in his skinny face.

Cyril shrugged, and sat down on the frozen ground to get to work. "I told you I would teach you how to build a better bomb. No time like the present."

"Why don't you want to go?" asked Stephen, when they'd finished emptying the shells—very carefully—into a piece of parchment paper.

"Hold this steady," Cyril said, handing him the pipe. "And I mean *steady*."

Stephen gave him a very teenaged look. When Cyril didn't yield, the look shifted briefly to concern and then to concentration. Cyril picked up the parchment paper at either edge and placed the narrowest point of its curve on the lip of the pipe. One end was sealed already with a cap. The other cap sat by in a nest of copper shavings they had made drilling a hole for the fuse.

Both of them held their breath as the gunpowder hissed against the metal, the steady stream of it building slowly to a solid layer of black.

"Stop," said Cyril, when they'd filled half the pipe. "Tacks."

Eyebrows relaxing beneath the brim of his cap, Stephen said, "Really, why don't you want to go? *I'd* leave."

"You're smarter than I am," said Cyril. Cold had seeped through his body, turning him pleasantly leaden and impervious to small pains. He had heard that freezing to death was the easiest way to go—that hypothermia induced euphoria so sweet you met your death with a smile.

But that would be too easy. More than he deserved.

"What did you actually *do*?" asked Stephen, pouring a dozen or so tacks into Cyril's palm. "Nobody's ever said outright. Not to me.

I think I've got about half of it from books and the news and things, but they leave the real bits out. You know. And it's no good trying Mummy."

What did that question mean? And where even to begin?

"Nothing good," he said, and began placing the furniture tacks one by one into the powder.

There was a part of him that *knew* it wasn't true. Three months ago he'd pulled a girl no older than Stephen through a minefield after her leg was blown away below the knee. Before that, run a dangerous comms mission for a man whose wife had just gone into labor. Gotten a family out from under the falling heel of a republican platoon on the march, in the very nick of time.

But that part of him was sealed away under glass, so that its mouth screamed silently. If he didn't look at it, he didn't notice it at all.

"This blast won't be very big," said Cyril. "It's just proof of concept. Normally you'd want phosphorus, or ammonal. Lay out some of those rolling papers. Overlapping."

Stephen did as he was told. Cyril constructed the fuse quickly, wrapping the paper around the contents of a few more shotgun shells. One end, twisted tightly, fit into the hole they had drilled. The top of the pipe he capped delicately, wary of sparks.

He stood from his preparations. Movement made his cold joints ache. "What do you *think* I did?"

Stephen looked down at the bomb: half nervous, half impatient. A clear trail of mucus marked his upper lip, where the hair had just begun to darken and grow thick.

Cyril did not move to light a match.

"I think," Stephen said, "you did some kind of work for the Ospies. And whatever you did, it was *really* bad. So bad nobody wants to know you."

Cyril struck the light. Stephen opened his mouth to say something, but Cyril cut him off. "Get back to where we marked."

Sprinting across the clearing, he stumbled on a root, then hopped over the rotten log that had been decomposing since the Spice War. Cyril bent to the fuse, lit it, and walked at his normal pace. He'd left it long enough for leisure.

Stephen flinched at the blast. Cyril, too, though his was less awe and more ingrained reflex. His hands began to shake, and he stuck them in his pocket. Bad as Aristide, with his DTs.

"That was *it*," said Stephen, scrambling back over the log. "There's tacks *everywhere*. It blew the pipe to bits! Rotten *tops*!"

Cyril half-followed him, settling between two soft stumps where branches had decayed away. He watched the boy—his *nephew*—scrape through the frozen leaf mold for a few minutes before he said, "Except you."

Stephen looked up from a handful of tacks. "What?"

"Nobody wants to know me, except you."

"Obviously you didn't *want* to do whatever it was." His scorn and confidence were the kind people generally lost after the world kicked them in the teeth a time or two.

"How do you know that?"

"There are all kinds of people who did what the Ospies told them and hated it." Shrapnel held carefully in one hand, Stephen climbed up onto the log beside Cyril. "Mummy, for one. When she was in Porachis . . . I was little, but even I knew something wasn't right. She doesn't talk about it much. She and Dad, both: backed into a corner so they'd do what the Ospies wanted. And I know there's kids at school whose parents are the same. Folk try to keep it quiet: Nobody wants to end up like you."

It was not the answer he had been expecting, and it hamstrung him.

"It makes them feel good to see you shamed." Stephen was speaking to the jagged pieces in his palm now, pushing them around with his finger. "Because they can tell themselves they're not that bad after all. Which means you must have done something awful."

Breathing hurt—the icy air scoured his lungs, and his ribs felt as though a vice had closed around them.

"It's going to come out anyway," said Stephen, young and smart and terribly matter-of-fact. "On the wireless and all. Why don't you tell me now? Like you'd want me to hear it."

Playing for time, Cyril held out his hand and made a *give it* gesture. Stephen looked perplexed for a moment, then poured the slurry of copper and tacks and forest floor from his cupped palm into Cyril's.

The threatening edges and keen cold points of metal focused him. No one else was going to teach Stephen about these things. And Cyril knew how hard it was to learn in the field; experience imparted its lessons well, but its methods could be brutal.

"All right," he said, closing a loose fist over the remnants of their blast. "I will."

The cold kept him brief, cutting the story down to its most essential parts. But that, he realized as he told it, was how he would have wanted Stephen to hear it first: facts unvarnished by opinion. He'd already proven he was capable of forming his own.

CHAPTER

SIXTEEN

Rinko Higata had returned to Gedda several months before Lillian. She had been in the Niori peninsula, staying with her father's family for the duration of Ospie rule. Now that she was back in the country, she still hadn't established a private practice. Instead, she had been working off and on as an independent consultant to the provisional government and spending much of her spare time at the Yotoi temple mission on Porter Street, offering pro bono legal assistance to Niori immigrant families.

"Penance," she had called it, looking rueful.

Lillian hadn't spoken to her since their meeting before Solstice, about the prospect of recovering DePaul money from the abyss. She was loath to ask another favor, but at least this one was firmly in Rinko's line.

Devotees in simple clothes welcomed her to the temple with kind smiles and soft words. She wondered if that would change if, for instance, her photo started running in the papers. Or if she ended up in front of a tribunal.

Rinko, the mission director said, was with a client just then, but would be done in half an hour. Would she take some barley tea?

She would, and did, and sat in the pleasant silence of the mission's administrative office, listening to the echoes of chanted litanies from the small adjoining temple. The director left her alone, returning to his typewriter. The half hour she passed there, kneeling in her stockings on a quilted cotton pad, drinking toasty, steaming tea, was the calmest scrap of time she'd had since Jinadh handed her his page of ciphers and asked for help. She was almost disappointed when Rinko appeared, opening the door for a wan-faced woman whose eyes sat deep in dark circles. She sent the woman on her way with a few last words in Niorese—what little of that language Lillian had learned only served to translate *goodbye*—and then turned to face her next task.

"DePaul," she said, hands on hips.

"Higata." Lillian set her teacup aside, hands kept steady by concentration.

"I imagine you aren't here about debate club reunion."

"Astute as always." Lillian rose from her cushion and smoothed her skirt.

"Don't tell me you've fallen on times hard enough you need a free legal consultation."

"I'll pay you," said Lillian. "Though given you've had a look through my finances, you know exactly how much you can bleed from me before I faint."

At that, Rinko laughed. Too loudly, for the mission director's taste: He shot a dirty look in their direction.

"Come into my office," said Rinko, holding out an arm to Lillian. "I can guess what you're here for, and you'll want something stronger than that tea."

"Your brother always was an idiot," said Rinko, after she poured a second whiskey for each of them. Maybe that was why the insult didn't land too heavily. Or maybe it was truth that kept Rinko's assessment from stinging; hadn't Lillian said the same thing about him any number of times?

"Wasn't he sent down from Ellerslee?" Rinko went on, capping the bottle and settling back in her chair. "I remember hearing someone mention it."

"Nearly. He did take his degree, but it was complicated. I know after, Daddy was very keen to get him into a line of work that would . . . shape him up. I always assumed that's how he was funneled into the FOCIS. I never got many details."

"That's good. If it comes to a trial, I can use that. If I get a little more information."

That took Lillian slightly aback. "I was really only here for a consult. Or to see if you knew someone. I . . . you're largely corporate defense, aren't you?"

"There isn't much precedent in this country for the kind of thing Frye is proposing, and therefore very little applicable law. There would be lots of room to maneuver. Lots of room to improvise. Besides, is it such a leap from corporate to war crimes? Taschen, Taschen, and Nooz certainly defended contractors accused of worse than what your brother has done."

"And it would be a good way to get your name into a couple of books, I imagine."

Rinko shrugged, and sipped her whiskey.

"You have an idea already, don't you?"

Her laugh came out a little huffy, like she was insulted Lillian thought it would take her any more time than this to create a defense strategy for a hated Ospie collaborator. "Don't you? I kept an eye on your career when you were in the corps. I wanted to see what you did. And you were *good* at your job, but I taught you most of it."

"People like stories," said Lillian, remembering late-night preparations before debates, Rinko's hair escaping from its pins, papers strewn across the floor of a lecture hall, half the team asleep on the benches. "The law likes facts. But the law is made and held by people. The transitive property applies."

"So, what story would we tell about your brother, if it came to it?"

"He endured horrors," Lillian said tentatively. Then gathering confidence, as though this were an oral exam. "And continues to endure them."

"Start earlier," said Rinko. "It has to feel inevitable, or he's still at fault."

Lillian cast back to childhood. They had been close when they were young, united against loneliness when their parents spent weeks or sometimes months away from home. School had ruined that. Lillian took to Cantrell like a fish slipped into the sea, and couldn't understand why Cyril had such a hard time. At university, Cyril sent her miserable letters that she answered with sympathy but little comprehension. Worse was her gradual transition to her parents' side of the front; she wasn't sure when being the good child became something she aspired to, a set of expectations to meet, rather than simply a tool she could use when she and Cyril got into trouble.

When she graduated from Sackett and started traveling, missing holidays and summer trips to Ibet, leaving Cyril alone . . . that was when things had gone sour. Shame on the household, secrets hastily covered up so that even she had never understood exactly what her brother was guilty of.

"A promising young man," she said. "Neglected by his parents, smarts left to fester. And of course, he got into trouble." By now she was not thinking about Cyril, but her own son.

"And I will guess," Rinko said, "that the FOCIS did not treat him any better. Even if the Ospies gave him a compelling reason to turn, if he was loyal to the service he would have resisted."

"Whatever he was doing for them, he ended up in the hospital." Vivid memories showed her the thin, purple line of his lips, gashed through the green-white mask of his face. The black stripes of stitches marked neatly over a livid red wound. "Again, I don't know the details."

"We can get those later," said Rinko. "So. He turns. But only under duress, I assume?"

"Yes. You know Vasily Memmediv?"

Rinko's eyes widened, showing white all around the near-black iris. "The separatist?"

"Yes. He used to be a part of the FOCIS, and he knew Cyril then. Before the Ospies."

"What's he like, in person?"

"Slippery," said Lillian.

Rinko *hmph*ed. "And now he's slipped one too many times. Fallen out of favor over there. How politics pulls people apart! They say he used to be good friends with Ianiźca before the schism, and now she's calling for his arrest. Do you think he'll flee Tatié?"

Lillian shook her head. "No. He'd bleed out into the earth if he thought it would help his . . . country, now, I suppose."

"Funny," said Rinko, "how far people will go for a lost cause."

"Excuse me?" She knew what Rinko meant; it had simply taken her by surprise. The other woman had seemed so confident as she outlined her ideas.

"If Frye is elected and moves forward with this tribunal, what are you hoping for?" Rinko folded her hands around her glass and leaned in across her desk. Papers slithered underneath her elbows. "Acquittal? Exoneration?"

"I thought—" she started, then began again, astonished. "But what about everything you just said?"

"That wasn't a legal defense," said Rinko. "There is no legal defense for what your brother has done. There are records showing his confessions to treason and murder."

"Ospie records," said Lillian. "Coerced confessions. Probably under torture."

"This country wants to see your brother hang. I might be able to keep him off the scaffold, but do not ask me to set him free. It is beyond my skill, or anyone's. And that is something you need to understand from the outset, or we will be working at cross-purposes."

Speechless, Lillian watched Rinko tip her glass back, gray pearl earrings sweeping the skin of her neck. When she set it down she said, "Now, may I come up to Carmody and speak with Cyril?"

"You're welcome to try," said Lillian, hearing her own words at a distance through the ringing in her ears. "But who knows if he'll talk."

CHAPTER

SEVENTEEN

West Cultham Rail Company had a warehouse near what had once been the bad end of the harbor and didn't appear to have gotten much better. The only thing that had changed was the graffiti. No Ospie quartered circles, or regionalist yellow and blue. Still dirty jokes and scatological sketches, of course, but here and there Aristide saw a motif of parallel lines hatched at regular intervals. Train tracks, with Saeger's name scrawled beneath them in dripping paint. Or, sometimes, Cordelia's.

Swathes of the neighborhood had once been his territory, under a different name than the one he used onstage. A gnarled wen on the city's ass made up of vast hangars and the piss-stinking alleys in between. A place where anything might be bought or sold: flesh, drugs, false documents, and foreign currency. Shipping containers could conceal a multitude of sins. Such as the poppy tar now biding its time in orderly rows, listed in the harbormaster's books as tin, cloth, and exotic woods.

"Humble, ain't it?" Custler asked, leaning heavily on the railing of the screeching metal gallery that ran around the warehouse walls. "We're sitting on a hoard, and yet you'd never think to look. Canny art, that."

"Indeed," said Aristide. "But never one I strove to master."

She cased him from the sides of her eyes. "I don't think it'd look as good on you."

He thought of the patchy beard he'd grown in the Culthams. The uneven tangle his hair had made as it grew out in the bowels of the steamer to Hyrosia. "You'd be quite right."

Side by side for a moment, silence settled between them like a lanky, dour bird with evil eyes. Aristide had just begun to worry when Custler said, "Your, um . . . your pencil pusher. He ain't here?"

"Back at the hotel answering letters, I'm afraid. I'm capable enough without him, when it comes to certain things."

"Sure, sure." Custler put a hand over her mouth, scrubbing at her jaw. "I just . . . ah, swineshit. He's real young, and pretty. And I thought maybe you two were . . . yeah?"

Aristide turned his head a fraction of an inch and nailed her with a chilly glance, eyebrow raised. "Like you and Frye?"

"Tits." She turned white.

"Don't worry," he said. "I'm sure you're not as obvious as we are. Otherwise someone would have clocked you when she turned the company over."

It took her a moment to recover from that, and when she did, she came on more matter-of-fact. "I know it ain't my business. I only ask 'cause of this mess with the DePauls."

Aristide's complexion would hide a blanch better than hers had. That didn't mean his blood didn't drain—he felt it in the coldness of his cheeks.

"Paperfolk said you used to spark a little with the brother. Maybe keep each other up. I only asked about the secretary 'cause I want to know if you're over that."

"It was a *very* long time ago," he said.

"Good. Good." Relief gave him an idea of what she was going to say before she said it. "You might hear some nasty things about Emmy from his sister. You two are friends, I think? I just don't want it to turn *our* dealings sour."

"Of course not," he said. "Business is business. I stand to gain as much from this as you."

Custler let out a long breath. "Mother and sons, I'm glad to hear you say it."

As he was to hear *her* say *that*. He'd had to allay one set of Frye and Custler's suspicions already, when they brought up Saeger and the Catwalk. If they thought he was pinned with them over this late-breaking news—and he was, Queen save him—he'd have a brand new round of ruffles to soothe, at greater personal cost than previously. He had no stake in Saeger, except that she had once known Cordelia and he might have liked to ask her . . . Well. Any number of things. But that wasn't enough to incite him to espionage on Saeger's behalf. Not enough to play at threats and blackmail.

Anyone less professional would have let their jaw drop open, stunned by their own stupidity.

He wanted Cyril out of the country as badly as Lillian did. Eight years ago he had simply done the work as necessary, and would have succeeded if not for Cyril himself scratching the whole enterprise. And whatever work Aristide might do for him this time around, if it was tabletop Cyril would turn his nose up at it.

Perhaps he ought to be trussed like a contrary sheep and taken forcibly from Gedda. But Aristide could guess enough about what Cyril had endured to know that this would be unforgivable. The only other option seemed to be changing Gedda to suit Cyril, and it was a little late in the campaign to put his name on the ticket.

But he didn't need to run for office to effect change. To put a halt to the proposed tribunals, he only needed to scratch the prospects of the person who'd proposed them. Or ensure her success on his own terms.

Custler, bless her, had dropped this neat idea straight into his lap. Now, all he had to do was pick it up and give it a shine.

"Hm," she said, casing him like a breeder eyeing horseflesh. "You're real quiet all of the sudden."

"Headache," he said, and pushed back from the railing. "They come on suddenly sometimes."

"Really? You should see a doctor. My brother-in-law had aches like that and took real sick and died. When they cut his head open he had a tumor like *this*." She made a fist. "Gave him delusions, too. Real bad."

He smiled thinly. "I'll take it under advisement."

Daoud was still elbows-deep in paperwork when Aristide returned to the hotel. A smudge of ink colored his cheekbone, just above the carefully barbered edge of his beard.

"Sell all my shares," said Aristide, flinging his gloves onto the sideboard.

Daoud looked up from his work, eyebrows furrowed. He was going to need spectacles soon, from the pained wrinkles at the corners of his eyes. «Once again?»

"My shares in Cross-Costa. Sell them. Yours, too, if you like."

Shaking his head like he was trying to clear water from his ears, Daoud asked, "I—all of them?"

Reconsidering, Aristide sank onto the sofa and stretched out.

"Oh, all right. Maybe half. Keep our fingers in the pie for verisimilitude."

"Veri—" Daoud paused. "Aristide, what are you planning, that we need to tell a lie?"

"I didn't have to plan a thing," he said. "Custler came up with this one all on her own, and dropped it neatly into my lap."

Without looking, he felt the intensity of Daoud's skepticism on him like a spotlight. "Whatever you are going to do," he said, and Aristide heard the rustle of papers collected into a pile. "Cross is not going to like it, is she?"

"It will destroy our Geddan business, if not Cross-Costa Imports entirely. Bring me a drink while you're up?"

Because he had risen from his chair in alarm. Now, taken aback, he hovered with his hands slightly raised.

"A brandy, please. And don't skimp. I know you're liable to."

Daoud's body moved toward the bar, but he watched Aristide the whole way there. When he had a glass down and the bottle uncorked, he said, "The tar. Something to do with the tar, and the election." Then, midway through pouring, "And DePaul."

Aristide held his hand out over the back of the sofa, open and curved for the crystal. Daoud sat it there, then stood with his hands on his hips while Aristide—pleased with himself and apt to be theatrical—sipped his drink to draw out the moment.

"Hmm," he said, tipping the globe so the brandy caught the light. "Not the best I've had."

"Aristide."

"Yes, of course." He set the glass aside. "Frye never truly ceded control of her corporation—she's knocking Custler, for the Lady's sake. And now West Cultham is moving tar. Would *you* want that all to come if you were running for prime minister?"

Aristide knew that Daoud wore a mask with him: a cool, ceramic-smooth aloofness, occasionally smeared with irritation or indulgence.

It reminded him, almost, of the sweet servility he had affected for Pulan. If not in form, then certainly in function. It was maddening, and Aristide had tried many tactics to break it.

This time he succeeded without trying at all.

"You cannot do this," said Daoud. "This is madness."

"It's perfectly reasonable," said Aristide, setting brandy aside in favor of a straight.

"If you expose her and Saeger wins, will there not still be a tribunal? It seems inevitable, at this point."

"Well then, she has to win, doesn't she? What percentage of her campaign costs do you think the sale of my shares will cover?"

Daoud didn't move, though Aristide had breathed a cloud of smoke in his direction. "You are being hasty. You have not thought this through."

"Of course I have. There are plenty of people and shells between me and that tar. I'll be perfectly insulated if it comes to light. Don't tell me how to do my job."

"It is *not* your job!" He finally broke from his freeze, throwing his arms up and striding back to the desk. "This—" he grabbed a bunch of papers from the top of the stack, clipped together at one corner and marked with a metallic seal. "*This* is your job! Cross-Costa is not your . . . your . . ." He slapped the papers down. «It's not your little empire. You aren't the King of Crime, or whatever stupid nickname they used to call you when you lived here in the golden years. Other people depend on this company for work. For money. For their lives. If you do this, your own employees will be arrested, probably jailed.»

Aristide ashed his cigarette. "You seem to be under the impression that I intend to go straight to the press but, my dear, that defeats the point of blackmail."

"*Bhishna solkatay ahshaleh!* Do not be so . . . *itu* with me right now! So fey! I am serious."

"As am I." He sat up, back a pry bar against the temptation of the tufted upholstery. Drawing long on his straight, he exhaled fully before he continued. "If it comes to exposure, the hounds will round up my employees. Fine. When I was the monarch of the demimonde, I let them take my friends."

Daoud stood for a long moment staring, lips parted: an expression of shock he might have worn after being slapped by someone he trusted, before the flush began to rise.

More fool him. He'd had years to learn where he could place his trust, and should have learned that Aristide struck those closest to him all the harder.

A woman came up to Damesfort at the weekend—or, Cyril thought it was the weekend; he hadn't been paying attention to the days. She appeared in time for lunch, crisply dressed in a green plaid suit. Silver liberally streaked her dark hair, which was drawn into a twist so tight he worried her cheekbones might cut through her skin. The angle of her chin was high and crooked, and her epicanthic eyes narrow with unspoken judgment. Where the black edge of her gaze caught, it cut like volcanic glass.

"Mr. DePaul," she said, nodding a greeting as she sat down. And that was all she said to him until the meal was over. He gathered from the conversation that she was some kind of school friend Lillian knew from Sackett, but the cool-friendly way they spoke made it seem she wasn't here for a social call.

That, and the thick briefcase none of the staff had taken from her.

He was ready for it, then, when they had all made an effort on the cold cuts, cheese, and pickles. Ready for her to set aside her napkin, exchange a glance with his sister, and then say, "Mr. DePaul, I wonder if I might speak with you privately?"

"If I say no, will you go back to Amberlough?" he asked. "Or stay here until I break?"

Her smile had the same edge as her eyes, though her teeth were white as bicarbonate of soda. "Lillian's hospitality is tempting, and we have lots to catch up on, I'm sure."

"You're a lawyer," he said, for her answer had not answered anything, even as it implied intent.

"Yes," she said. "I'm yours."

And so after lunch he found himself sitting on the sofa in the library, staring into the fire rather than look at Rinko Higata as she spoke to him.

"I understand you have undergone something of an ordeal," she said, removing a thick folder from her briefcase. Paper hissed on paper, faintly reminiscent of a knife against a whetstone.

"Only compared to some," he said.

"Noble," she said. "I would not have expected it, knowing what I did about you, through Lillian, before . . . this."

"Told tales on me, did she?" He took a straight from the basket on the end table and a match from the tin beside it.

"You certainly didn't make your family's life very easy. And it seems you continued the trend well into adulthood, affecting rather more people."

He was glad of the straight; midway through lighting it, he could feign intense focus on the flame. If it had already been burning, he might have ripped it from his mouth to tear her up and down. As it was, he only inhaled sharply, making the tip of his cigarette flare.

"If you're here to school me about my flaws," he said, once the ember had caught, "let me assure you: I already have them memorized."

"Good," she said, and shuffled a clipped sheaf of papers to the bottom of her stack. "Less coaching."

"Ms. Higata," he said. "I'm not sure you understand—"

"That you'd rather hang? I think I've caught on by now. Lillian said you refused her offer to send you abroad. You could easily have gone. You could still easily go, though time is running out."

"Frye hasn't even been elected yet."

"And you think Saeger will let this kitty sit on the table? There will be a reckoning no matter who takes the Cliff House. And here you sit on your sad, self-pitying rear, waiting to walk up the gallows stairs."

He said nothing. Just drew on the straight.

"Dying will not fix what you did," she told him.

Guilt crawled through him like black mold. "That isn't the point."

"What is?"

He looked at her, finally: a long, hard stare.

"Would you be satisfied," she asked, "with life in prison?"

"What?"

"I said, would you be—"

"I heard you the first time."

She put the folder on her knee, and placed her hands on it in a deliberate stack. "I told your sister I think I can keep your neck out of the noose."

"You're assuming I won't plead guilty."

"I'm not entirely sure they'll let you. This is going to be a show trial; no plea bargains, no going quietly."

"I wasn't aiming for a plea bargain," said Cyril. "I shot an innocent man in the back of the head."

"And poisoned two others before that, yes. The *Telegraph* has the stories on microfiche. Anyway, those are criminal charges. You'll have to deal with them sometime, but I doubt they'll come up in this particular court. The point is you were hemmed into a corner. The last of many."

"That doesn't make it *right*." Sacred arches, this woman was getting under his skin like splinters.

"I agree," she said, giving him another case of whiplash. "Everything you did, you did under threat. Fine. You still did it. We've all seen what it meant for Gedda."

"And you're supposed to be my lawyer?" he asked. "Tits, why not take me out in the yard and hang me now? There's a nice tree in the orchard. Branch the right height. Not that I've been looking."

Higata's expression remained placid as he ranted, faintly aloof, shaming him finally into sullen silence. When he had retreated to his cigarette and returned his gaze to the hearth she went on as if he'd never spoken.

"Now you have to tell them what the consequences meant for *you*. Nobody likes it when a traitor gains by their actions. But I have done my research. I have read the file the Ospies kept on you; after the CIS was dissolved they declassified many documents. You gained nothing, and lost much more than most of us. So mortify yourself. Show us how you've been hurt by what you did. You have suffered horrors, as your sister says, and you will continue to suffer every day you breathe. It is not worth their while to kill you; your life is your punishment."

"And that's supposed to convince me?" he said. "To work with you?"

"I didn't say it was true. If we are lucky, this will play well with the judge and you will get a tough sentence, but not death. We can always appeal. What you put yourself through, in your own heart? That is up to you."

Cyril flicked ashes into the tray on the side table. "So you want me to get up there and read a litany of every torture I've endured since the Ospies caught me running?"

"Oh, no," she said. "You are thinking far too small. I want you to take the stand and recount how life has utterly crushed you at every turning."

"No deal," he said, and ground out the butt of his straight.

Of course, Stephen eavesdropped on the whole thing. Cyril had shown him which upstairs hearths had the best acoustics to overhear conversations carried on below. So after Higata went back to Amberlough—a pressing appointment early the next morning, so sorry she couldn't stay for dinner, no matter what threat she had almost leveled earlier in the day—Stephen found Cyril smoking at the back gate, staring over the barren fields down toward the hidden village. The sun had mostly gone, and every so often the wind parted the trees in perfect alignment so that the winking lights of the shops and houses shone through.

"Is it true?" asked Stephen, folding his arms on the top rail of the fence.

"Which part?"

"Even if Frye doesn't win, you'll go up. And if they charge you, you're looking at the gallows."

He shrugged and lifted his hand to take another drag. Dry skin across his knuckles split, a fine thread of pain so delicate it merely itched. In the silence, a train whistle soared through the purpling sky. Evening robins called from the fencerows and the fields.

"You know I got a black eye over you," said Stephen. "People call you all kinds of names. Mariah Peavey and her gang tried to duck me when we first came over from Asu."

"You didn't let them, did you?"

Stephen sent a piercing sideways glare in his direction. "How do you think I got the black eye?"

"Good. Let them duck you once, you stay wet the rest of your life. Mother's *tits*." Overcome by the truth of it, he pitched the butt of his straight into the field. Sparks danced in its trajectory. "None of it should matter. Not like it does."

"What, ducking and all?"

"Ducking, Cantrell, university, any of it. You're thirteen. A bunch of other kids throwing you in a fountain shouldn't mean more than wet shorts."

"It does, though," Stephen said. His tone had taken a turn from teenage pique to disturbing gravity.

Cyril sighed. "And don't I know." He could feel his nephew staring, wanting to ask but hardly daring.

His secrets weren't for the judge or the jury. They weren't for his lawyer or his sister or the press. He'd had enough hauled out of him in his life to know the value of keeping what he could close to. But he'd decided to teach his nephew how to better live through what had nearly killed him. Perhaps Stephen deserved those pieces, even if it cost Cyril his pride, and dredged up old injuries.

"University," said Cyril. "I made it that far, anyway. I was a miserable student at Cantrell, and all the teachers hated me, but I got along all right with my class and I was never ducked. I only slipped in the midden once I got to Ellerslee."

"What happened?"

"I had a good professor. The only one I *ever* had. Most classes I couldn't keep my head in the lecture; none of it seemed *important*. But he . . . well. It happened slowly. A few of us found ourselves in a study group. We met at his house in the evenings. It wasn't really studying, though. Just talk. But when you got in the room with him it was like someone had flipped the switch on a current and even the *air* was humming. He had that much presence. Which was why, I'll wager, the Tatien government had him recruiting fresh-faced troublemakers. He had a knack for finding the students who chafed in school—the ones too clever for their own good, all ready to chuck what they'd been told they should want and take up something new.

"My last year, he led a research trip to Tatié, to the border. Had some work he had to do there. He needed cover, and he needed help.

He didn't *call* it espionage. I don't know if he asked any of the others, but . . . when he asked me, I said yes.

"I was caught, of course, but too late. I got done what he asked me to. If I hadn't managed it, if I'd crumpled a little more quickly when they asked what I was about, maybe everything would have turned out different. I wasn't good enough to go all the way, then, but I was three-quarters there and I suppose someone figured they could drag me the last hundred yards."

"But did you get in trouble?"

"Of course I got in trouble," he said. "I'm still in it. One giant slog of trouble from then 'til now." He could feel it all stuck to his boots with every step. "It had to be kept quiet. Especially since my father was in the corps. Interstate espionage was a serious crime—still is, I suppose. My father practically tied me in a bow when the FOCIS came calling; he made a deal and I had to take it to avoid prosecution."

"That's when they stopped trying," Stephen said. "The moment they stopped trying to fix you. You think it's going to happen to me."

He shrugged. "Anything *can* happen. I don't try to predict it anymore; I just try to be ready when the dice come down where they do."

Stephen considered this, digging at the base of the fence post with his toe. The snow had all melted a few days ago, followed by a hard freeze, and he made no visible progress except to scuff his shoe leather. "What about the teacher? Did you pitch him?"

"Give him up? Of course. Everybody does, in the end. He was packed off back where he came from." He'd been from some western suburb of Dastya, where rioting and revenge killings were commonplace. "By then he had a reputation, and it was hostile territory. I never heard from him again."

CHAPTER

EIGHTEEN

It was harder than Aristide would have liked, approaching Frye. It seemed she wasn't taking telephone calls from just anyone who rang, and lurking outside of her home was liable to get him shot or at least arrested; a rotation of ACPD hounds had set up on the street. He wondered if Saeger had such a thing, wherever she holed up at night. Maybe the labor unions ran her security detail.

He couldn't ask Custler to put them in touch, either; she would want to know why, and this was a lever better applied without warning, to the top of the chain of command.

In the end he turned to Jamila, explaining the situation in sufficiently veiled terms. Because she was clever and keen, she read the white between the words and clocked he was up to something not quite tabletop.

"You want to catch her a little loose, hang around the Corderey. I've got a pair of eyes on the waitstaff says she spends a few evenings and most late nights holed up in a private room. And she actually works. No whoring or booze like most of the big fish with their names in the book."

"Thank you," said Aristide. Then, belatedly, "Do I need *my* name in the book?"

The telephone line made Jamila's laughter into white noise. "I'll make the call. It'll be written down by the time you get there."

And it was. He felt a twinge of guilt, remembering everything Daoud had said about others suffering for his schemes and knowing that Jamila would undoubtedly be one of them.

The Corderey had bay windows overlooking the south end of Talbert, near Staunton Street. Neither the club nor the neighborhood had received much of Aristide's attention in his day—he had more to do with the docks, the theatres, and folk with money who skirted the crumbling edge of respectability. Members of the Corderey had never so much as glanced over that cliff; they were too far inland to know that it existed. Likewise most of them had never been backstage; they sat in the balconies and watched through opera glasses.

Still, from Aristide's limited exposure—an afternoon stroll along Talbert beneath the skeptical gazes of old money at lunch—the block and the bay windows hadn't changed much. The Corderey had probably skated along through the Ospies much as it had under dozens of regionalist administrations. The places and mechanisms of power rarely changed; only the folk who wielded it. And those rarely.

He presented himself at the door in a sober suit of tobacco brown, swaddled in a cream-colored scarf and vicuña coat. The mink had been left at home in deference to the atmosphere of the club. His fedora—rabbit felt with an unfinished brim—still got him a raised eyebrow at the cloakroom.

Settling into an armchair in one of the bay windows, Aristide ordered a brandy from a passing waiter. Shortly thereafter, a different waiter arrived with his drink on a tray.

"Compliments of Ms. Osogurundi," he said. "If you'll come with me?"

Dispatching half of his brandy before he rose, Aristide fell in line behind the neatly pressed young man and followed him through the narrow halls of the Corderey.

His escort stopped at a door deep down a third-floor passage and knocked softly before opening it.

"I didn't order anything." Frye sounded irritated. "Didn't even pull the rope."

"I'm sorry, ma'am. But you have a visitor." The waiter ceded the doorway to Aristide, who passed him a roll of bills for risking his job. Frye would likely complain to management when he was through with her. Maybe Jamila could find the man something with Cross-Costa if he was sacked here. Though if Frye didn't take this threat seriously, he'd likely be out on his rear again soon after.

Setting all of that aside, Aristide draped himself against the doorway. "Emmeline."

Frye's hand came around the back of her chair like a grappling hook, digging into the upholstery and dragging the rest of her around.

"Makricosta." Her eyes were narrow as chips of granite.

He smiled. "It's so good to see you again. I trust you had a happy Solstice?"

"Leave us alone," said Frye to the waiter. "And unless I pull that rope, don't you dare barge in here again."

There was a second armchair in Frye's private room, at an angle to hers, both of them facing the fireplace. She had a pot of coffee on the table in between them, and a half-eaten apple gone brown. Aristide settled into the empty chair and set his brandy on her tray.

"Have a seat," she said, alum-dry.

He wriggled a little in the soft belly of the chair, getting comfortable and playing it up. She cased him long and hard, but *he* certainly wasn't going to make the first move, if that was what she was after. Instead he sipped his drink and watched the flames eat away at an all-night log: the kind as big around as a man's waist, heavy and solid through. This fire would go until morning. He could sit here to match it.

At last Frye exhaled, exasperated. "I assume whatever it is, Frances couldn't handle it?"

"I didn't even ask," said Aristide. "I don't think it's exactly in her line."

She sipped the remnants of coffee in her cup and made a face. Cold, he imagined. But she didn't ring for a new pot. "You know how many people want things from me now? And let me tell you: They aren't liable to get them."

"I think you'll find it in your heart to make an exception for me," he said. "Knowing as I do several of your dirty secrets."

"Mm." She placed the cold coffee cup back in its saucer, deliberate, pressing the pads of her fingers into its rim briefly before lifting her hand away. "I thought you might be pinned about the DePaul gambit. Custler told me you swore you'd keep it businesslike. I almost thought you might. I'm a little surprised. And disappointed."

"You know," he said, and paused to sip his brandy. "I don't mind disappointing people. Perhaps that's a flaw in my character, but I think it has rather more to do with other people's failure to manage their own expectations. And everyone seems to have such varied expectations of me; how could I hope to fulfill them all?"

"I'll remind you I put the company in trust at the beginning of my campaign," she said. "Ms. Custler will bear the brunt of this."

"Cold," he said. "Do you think she'll still tickle your pear once she's been dragged through the midden, and your affair made front page news? It hardly savors of plausible deniability."

That knocked Frye off-balance for a moment. Then she steadied. "I'd like to know what proof you have of that."

"I'm sure you would," he said, and because bluffing had been his business since he was in short pants, it came out smooth as butter.

"Queen and cairn," she said. "I knew this was a bad idea. I knew *you* were a bad idea. But Frances would push and push for it."

"And you knew you could make me pay, I suppose. Campaign debts. I hear they can be positively crippling."

She put bony knuckles to one temple, pressing so the fragile skin around her eye stretched. "Let me make a guess: You want me to walk back my position on these tribunals."

This time it was his turn not to answer. In the hearth the big log shifted, showering sparks through the grate.

"I can't do it," she said.

He smiled, unkindly. "I'm sure you can."

But she was already shaking her head. "I can't give you any guarantee; I haven't been elected yet. I might not be. Do you have any daggers that would fit Saeger's back?"

Aristide removed his checkbook from the inner pocket of his jacket and laid it on the table between them. "I can decrease the odds of needing one. But first I'd like a promise."

A loud pop in the fireplace, as a pocket of sap boiled away. Aristide realized there was no clock in the room to disturb the quiet with its ticking.

"I can't renege on the tribunals," said Frye, smoothing her skirt across her lap. Aristide bit back another insistence just in time, seeing it was not an ultimatum, but an entrée. "Those are a foregone conclusion, no matter who ends up in the Cliff House. The danger of catching the public's imagination."

"You are not convincing me," he said.

"If you'll sit on your mitts through all of that," she said, an edge of caution or anxiety coming into her voice, "let the tar move along as planned, and come through with your cash, I can promise you a pardon if I end up inaugurated. Will that satisfy you?"

"I exist in a state of perpetual dissatisfaction," he said, considering his brandy. "But it will certainly stay my hand."

Aristide didn't know his way around Amberlough's press corps anymore. He couldn't pick his quarry based on past work or favors owed, or on the understanding that the owner of their enterprise would like them to do one small thing for a gentleman who would call tomorrow.

He asked Jamila, but that got him a shrug—apparently her influence in the city extended largely underground. Well, she'd only been here six months or so—give her a little while and she'd have them all on strings, and the strings tied to her belt.

Unfortunately, he didn't have a little while. Briefly stumped, he finally remembered Lillian's husband was some stripe of paperfolk. He'd left things badly with her, but Daoud had spent Solstice drinking and jawing with Jinadh, and hadn't lately gotten into a shouting match with the lady of the house. Still, he wasn't keen on Aristide's plot, so best to approach it from an angle.

"Didi," he said, over steak and eggs in the Sykes House breakfast room. "What paper does Mr. Addas write for, again?"

"The *Observer*," said Daoud. "Owned by Siebenthal's. And he's an editor, not a columnist. Why?"

"I was hoping he could put me in touch with a few of his colleagues. I find myself in need of a pen-fencer."

That got him a raised eyebrow. "What for?"

"Insurance," said Aristide, which brought the eyebrow back down to meet its fellow in a worried frown. "You might inquire for me. You seemed to be quite friendly by the end of our Solstice stay."

"And Lillian will not speak to you," finished Daoud. "Or anyway, you have not tried."

"I'm not in the mood for a lecture this morning." Aristide sliced into his steak, or tried to. Sykes House may have had a very good kitchen, but the cook's morals apparently prevented them from buying on the black market, where they might have found meat that would yield beneath his silverware. "Ask Jinadh if he knows anyone who might be starving for a big break. Someone hungry. The political pages, or perhaps crime?"

"If you tell me what you want this for, maybe I will do it."

Aristide paused in sawing. "I'm sorry, darling. Please remind me who signs your checks?"

"Cross-Costa," said Daoud. "I act in the company's best interest. And lately I fear that you do not."

A bite of steak finally gave way. "Ask him today," said Aristide, and put it in his mouth to forestall further conversation.

CHAPTER

NINETEEN

Jinadh left on the same train as Rinko, to be back in the city for work. Lillian remained behind, unenthusiastic at the prospect of the city: election rallies, Catwalk graffiti, more threatening letters like the one that had been pushed through the slot last time she was at Coral Street. The *Telegraph* had run a front-page story after it came out that she'd been sacked, printing a photo of her from the gala at the MBS opposite a much older photo of Cyril, in which he was still handsome and slyly smiling. Nobody had managed to get a more recent one. She might have been grateful for that, as it meant he would be harder to spot on the street. Except the spread made them both look haughty and cruel: people who ought to be punished. After it went to print, she felt eyes on her wherever she stepped outside.

So she holed up in the library at Damesfort to quiz Stephen about his reading, when he wasn't running around in the woods with

Cyril, tearing holes in his clothes and tangling his hair. He was not an eager pupil, and on this particular afternoon they were very near doing one another physical harm.

Magnusson saved her with news that she had a telephone call. When he told her who it was, she set aside the book she had been holding, though she knew Stephen would take any out he could find. "Mr. Qassan? Did he say what was the matter?"

"No, ma'am. Will you take it?"

"Yes, of course. Stephen—" He was already on his feet when she held out the book to him. "—Finish your reading for the week."

He slumped, and snatched it out of her hand with a sigh.

"I'll take it in my office," she said. "Thank you."

It was colder upstairs, but more private than the hall. The receiver felt clammy on her face.

"Mr. Qassan?" she asked, and heard Magnusson hang up. «This pleasure is unexpected.» Perhaps irrationally, given their slim association, she liked the young man: He was competent and quiet and kept himself to himself. And he had made Jinadh smile, during the course of their Solstice celebrations.

«I had hoped to reach Mr. Addas,» he said, «but your majordomo tells me he's in the city.»

«Yes. Did you ring the house on Coral Street?»

«I tried here first.»

«Do you have the exchange?» She gave it to him.

«Thank you,» he said, but did not excuse himself or hang up.

«Was there something else?» she asked, tucking her free hand between her thighs to warm it. Up here, her breath made mist.

«I'm worried,» he said.

That made two of them. «About?»

«Aristide. He's . . . he's up to something, I think.»

The cold that crept through her veins had little to do with winter. «I do not doubt he is.»

«It hurts to say, but he's not thinking clearly. He has not been well balanced, since we had the news about your brother in Liso. So, I worry. He's a very smart man, but he doesn't have enough distance, in this case. And he's worse for drinking.»

«Does he often drink as much as he did at Solstice?"

«More. He was on his best behavior, then.» A heavy sigh, on the other end of the line. «I think before Cyril came back, he had finally become resigned. I've never known him as a happy man, but now I'm afraid of what he will do, trying to . . . to . . . »

She twisted the telephone cord in her fist. «What do you think he is going to do?»

«I *know* he's going to blackmail Emmeline Frye.»

"What?" she asked, aghast enough to fall back into Geddan.

«I'm more afraid of what he'll do if she doesn't step like he tells her to.»

«Blackmail her for . . . for what?» Even as she said it, she knew. «*How?*»

«She's moving some contraband for Cross-Costa. Or, her company is.»

«And he's found a way to tie her to it?»

«He has. Frye and her deputy . . . anyway. That's why he asked me to talk with Mr. Addas. He needs a journalist. Insurance, he said. If she doesn't do what he asks, he'll break the story.»

«He'll . . . he'll . . . » Metaphor failed her in Porashtu. "He'll tear the country up." Then, «If this comes out . . . Saeger doesn't know how to lead a country.»

«I don't think he cares,» said Daoud.

«Of course,» said Lillian, crumpling the crease of her trouser leg in one angry fist. «The Amberlough he knew is gone. Why should he mind what happens to this one?»

"Laurie Kostos," Daoud told him. "That is who you want."

Aristide tipped vermouth into the cocktail shaker and began to stir. "At the *Observer*?"

"Lately, yes. But no longer. There was, it seems, some acrimony in the parting. Now he is the anchor for a new nightly program on FWAC."

Aristide tapped the spoon to dislodge a drip. "I said hungry. He doesn't sound it."

"The program is only in its first few months, and likely to be taken off the air if he does not make it sell cigarettes, or what you like."

"Better," said Aristide, savoring the word before chasing it with gin. "Where can I find him?"

"He broadcasts from the Icepick every night at eight o'clock."

Aristide glanced at the clock, downed his martini, and called a cab.

The Icepick had been the Keller Tower, not so long ago. Built by an Ospie industrialist eager to bring wireless technology to Gedda. For a long time the only radio listeners had been hobbyists—many of them Ospies—setting up hack networks here and there across the country. Leading up to Acherby's coup, if you'd had an antenna to catch the signal, the air would have been buzzing with party music and opinions. Of course, Aristide hadn't. He'd been of the mind that wireless was gauche and lacked artistic merit.

More fool him, for not keeping up with the times.

He was frankly amazed the Icepick had made it through the fall of the regime. Its façade was smeared with graffiti—Catwalk train tracks, filthy slogans, *Spotlight Lives*—but it still stood, all forty floors of it, complete with gargoyles, scalloped arches, and the eponymous blinking transmitter tower. Keller's name had been chipped from the arch above the entrance; he had fled the country, and nobody wanted to remember him.

The lobby had not fared as well as the exterior—it smelled of stone dust, fresh paint, and plaster, but showed none of the benefit. Plywood blocked off most of the space, covering whatever ornamentation might have made the entryway more welcoming. A few mismatched folding chairs were strewn unevenly across the marble floor, which was badly pocked and, in one place, shattered.

"Can I help you?" The young man behind the desk was round-faced and plump, much tidier than the rest of the lobby. His dark skin didn't show a cold-flush, but from his fingerless gloves and the hunch of his shoulders, the initial shock of warmth Aristide had felt upon entering the lobby was only relative compared to the outdoors.

"I'm here to see Laurie Kostos," he said.

"He's still broadcasting. But you can go up and wait. Oh, sign the book?"

Aristide did, with a flourish, and headed toward the single lift that stood free of plywood or scaffolding.

The studio was small, which surprised him, but it was also very high in the Icepick, where floor space was at a premium. According to the directory by the lift, the station offices occupied several floors below. The single receptionist looked up when he came in and almost moved to shush him, but just then the red recording light flashed to green. Moments later Kostos came out yawning. The receptionist jumped up and took his hat and coat from a rack in the corner, giving Aristide a curious look as she did.

"Thanks, Marlene," said Kostos. "Who's this?"

She opened her mouth to answer, but Aristide cut her off. "My name is Aristide Makri—"

"Oh, Makricosta, yeah. I clock you now. You were at that memorial ceremony a couple of weeks back. I broadcasted live from there, listened to your speech." He shouldered into his coat. "Pretty good stuff. Who wrote it for you?"

Aristide let that strike him and pass through, ignoring the ache it left behind. "I had hoped you might have a minute to chat."

"About?" Kostos looped his scarf around his neck. "'Night, Marlene."

She bobbed a nod, alarmed and sparrowlike, and let them leave without a word.

Before Aristide could answer Kostos's question, the elevator operator, still parked on their floor, levered the grate open. Kostos stepped on. Aristide did likewise.

As the doors closed them in together, Kostos said, "Does this have to do with DePaul?"

The elevator operator stiffened, fist tightening on the lever.

"No," said Aristide. Although it was a lie, and the question wasn't what he had been expecting, he did not hesitate in answering. If it came out a little snappish, could he be blamed?

Kostos put his hands up in surrender, hat facing out like a shield. "Tits, just asking. I did a little digging, when the family started cropping up in the news again. Only reason I could think you'd be here."

Straightening the bar of one cuff link and sinking into the velvet-upholstered depths of a Central City drawl, Aristide said, "Then your imagination must be *sadly* lacking."

They bumped to a stop back in the lobby. The young woman at the lever cranked the grate open. Aristide handed her a tip and waited until she met his eyes, then gave her his best flirtatious smile. Her hostile frown broke into confusion.

Rubbing the brim of his hat thoughtfully with his thumbs, Kostos stayed for a moment in the lift. He already had a canny face—a skeptical squint ironed in by years on whatever beat he'd covered to end up here—but a shadow of suspicion threw its planes and wrinkles into sharp relief. "What's your angle?"

"I want to talk," said Aristide. "And I want you to listen."

"Usually I get to ask a couple of questions somewhere in there."

"We may get to that," said Aristide. "Let's see how the evening treats us."

Kostos took him to an all-night automat down the block, dead besides a group of drunken students, two prostitutes in laddered stockings passing a bottle in a paper bag, and a rag man smoking a scanty twist. A matted dog slept underneath his table.

Aristide had seen the seedy side of Amberlough, in his day. But this was something else; no energy crackled underneath the surface of this scene. The ponies kept quiet over their cheap liquor; even their makeup looked dull. Something had gone out in the city's soul.

The students didn't laugh, except once, cruelly and too loud. He noticed a few of them wore armbands, or cloths tied around their foreheads: ragged edges and different colors, but all painted or embroidered with the Catwalk's train tracks. Saeger's sigil. Had there been a rally in the city this evening? The sound of it hadn't carried to his hotel.

"I told you it was my treat," said Aristide as they settled at a table. Kostos had a cup of coffee and a slice of plum cake with an unpleasant sticky sheen on its surface. "And this is what you picked?"

Kostos held out his hand. "I'll take whatever change you've got in your pocket, if you like."

"It wasn't meant to be a bribe," said Aristide. "That comes later, if you're interested."

Kostos fished a crumpled pack of brown cigarillos from the pocket of his overcoat, which he had not removed. Under the harsh lights of the automat, he looked gray and old and Aristide almost pitied him before remembering he needed this man's help. Then, he felt ashamed, and suddenly conscious of his own age and appearance. He forgot, often, that he was no longer in his prime.

"So what do you got for me?" asked Kostos, lighting up. "'Cause if it ain't your half of the DePaul scoop, it better be rotten good."

Aristide took his own case from his pocket and picked a straight from beneath the band. "Oh, it's good. And lucky you; I hear you have to get your numbers up or it's curtain call."

Kostos poked a bent fork into his food. "Should have stuck to print. I ain't got a radio voice. Or at least that's what they're telling me. But if Marlowe Flanders can reel folk in with that Eel Town drone of his, why can't the city settle in with a little first-precinct sass?"

Something shifted behind Aristide's ribs like broken glass, and it took him a moment to place the pain. It had been some time since he thought of Cordelia as a guttersnipe out of the bad end of the first precinct; that version of her had been eclipsed by the maimed and furious fighter, making arms deals with people she hated, far away from home. Still, her pragmatism had pulled through. And those flat vowels, the tongue held close to the roof of the mouth. The way Kostos spoke, he could have grown up down the street from her.

"How would you like to tear up Emmeline Frye?" asked Aristide.

Kostos put his fork down, still heavy with uneaten cake.

"Not that I presume to understand your personal politics," Aristide went on, pressing his memories down beneath banter. "But I used to tread the boards. I know a thing or two about drawing a crowd. However you plan to vote, you know this will have folk tuning in."

Either pushing through his shock or shaking it off, Kostos finally bit into the plum cake. His next words came around a mouthful. "You got something that'll scratch her?"

"Perhaps."

He swallowed, wiped his mouth on a cheap paper napkin. "All right. Let's hear it."

"It's come to my attention," said Aristide, "that Frye's company is moving a large quantity of illegal narcotics, currently stored in one of their warehouses in Amberlough."

Kostos took a long drag on his cigarillo and then set it on his saucer. Addressing the ash sprayed finely across the cheap ceramic, he said, "That'll get her tied up in some nasty inquiries. I don't see it taking her down. That company's not under her name anymore."

"No. But the woman whose name it *is* under is . . . under Frye, if you take my meaning."

Kostos raised an eyebrow, then made a lewd gesture with his hand.

"Exactly," said Aristide.

"You got proof?"

"I can tell you where the drugs are. I'm afraid the incriminating photographs will be up to you."

Kostos exhaled smoke and licked his teeth, then picked a stray piece of tobacco from his tongue. It sat between his fingers, wet and black, the object of some scrutiny while he considered what Aristide had said. "What do you want for this? 'Cause it seems too easy."

"I want you to sit on it," said Aristide. "And not to breathe a word."

Kostos made an abortive gesture, as though he would speak, before putting a knuckle to his teeth. It was another moment before he said, "You do know that I'm on the wireless, right? That I report the news? That's why you came to me."

"Of course," said Aristide. "But I'm trying to blackmail someone. You're my insurance policy, and you're not worth anything if you pay out too soon."

"How long do I gotta wait?"

"That depends. But I'll make waiting worth your while. And when you do get to break the story—" because once Cyril was pardoned and they were out of the country, he was more than happy to detonate everything behind them—"I'm sure it will turn out you've got a voice for radio after all."

CHAPTER

TWENTY

The marshal came to the front door of Damesfort in a fast black car, surprising Cyril. He'd thought they had at least until the election; the provisional government seemed happy to let the new crop of scullers crash through this particular bramble.

Maybe this was one of the candidates, afraid he'd scurry far and fast, making her move a little early to keep him where he sat. No good to make a fuss about hanging a villain if the villain vanished before you had a knot tied in the rope.

They needn't have bothered. Still, it was almost reassuring to know things in Amberlough still worked like he remembered them: there was the letter of the law and there was the truth, which stood a little to the left of it. Someone was worried he might run while he was still a free agent, so they'd pulled some strings to tie him up ahead of his time. Leverage didn't stand on ceremony.

Two Carmody police officers had come along for the show. Staring at them Cyril felt as though thirty years of his life had suddenly turned transparent, and through them he could see the officers who'd come up to the house when he and a couple of the village kids set a bucket of paint over the schoolmaster's door, which not only stained his clothes but got him six stitches.

This encounter would lead to something more serious than scrubbing a doorstep and fetching and carrying for a concussed teacher.

"Those are Jem and Paley," said Stephen, chin resting on his hands. They were up on the roof, where Cyril had spent several days teaching Stephen surveillance techniques.

"The hounds?" asked Cyril.

"Mm-hm."

"How do you know them?"

"Slingshotting over the neighbor's wall. Broke her window. They marched me back home like I was for the—" he stopped, sending a sidelong glance at Cyril. "They're full of themselves, is all."

"Small-town terriers," said Cyril. They were probably hard as kitchen pokers right now, standing at attention to either side of the dour woman below. Proximity to power they had never dreamt of.

He couldn't see her well from this angle, but she was older, with brown skin and her skull shaved bald so he couldn't tell if her hair was silver or dark. If it hadn't been for the pumps and stockings, he'd have sworn Ada Culpepper had come back for him, to see her own justice done.

"They're here for you," said Stephen. Cyril ignored the slight wobble on the last word—it might have been a question, to which the answer should have been obvious. If it wasn't a question, it was something like fear or sorrow, and Cyril did not have the strength for that.

"I suppose I'd better go down then." Cyril sat straight and brushed snow from his jacket.

Stephen sat as well, and regarded Cyril solemnly, working up to something. Cyril lit a cigarette while he waited, in no hurry to go to his fate.

"It's stupid," he said, finally, and in those two words was a world of grief, confusion, anger.

Cyril laughed. "Most things are."

Stephen stayed on the roof, when he went down.

In the drawing room, the marshal sat in the wingback chair he had once thought of as his mother's. She couldn't have known how fitting her choice was. Cyril had received punishments from that chair too many times in his youth. The indiscretions had been somewhat smaller, then.

Her escorts, Jem and Paley, stood to each side of the fireplace. They turned at the sound of the opening door, and snapped to sloppy attention.

Jinadh sat forward on the sofa, back straight, at an angle to the woman who had come to take Cyril away. There was a silver pot between them, on a tray.

"Hello," said the marshal, setting aside a steaming cup.

Of course Lillian had served her coffee.

His sister made an entrance then, trailing cold air on her open coat. "*There* you are," she said. And then, to the marshal: "I'm sorry to keep you waiting."

"Oh, for Queen's sake," said Cyril. "Let's not do polite conversation."

The marshal's ironic smile made him almost like her. "Cyril DePaul," she said, rising from the chair. His mother never had— all her edicts were issued from behind a paper, book, or brief. "I'm Marshal Sadie Yamitad, with the Interim Federal Commission for Justice, and I'm arresting you for willful misrepresentation."

"What?" It came out before he could stop it. Then he caught up with himself. It was a stand-in charge, of course. They needed to nab him for something if they wanted him locked up tight until these proposed tribunals actually came together, under whoever's government the people chose.

"Fraud, Mr. DePaul. You entered this country under a false name, with false documentation. That's a crime, and I'm arresting you."

"But," said Lillian, hovering awkwardly between the threshold and the center of the room. "But I thought . . . ?" She had not caught on yet to the utility of this accusation.

Jinadh stood and went to her, a sudden movement in the middle of a still tableau. It seemed to startle her back into herself, or the suit of armor she wore.

"Will handcuffs be necessary, Mr. DePaul?" asked Yamitad. "Or can I trust you to walk quietly to the car?"

He shook his head. "No cuffs."

"I'll telephone Rinko," said Lillian. "And if there's bail to pay, we'll—"

"Lil," he said, and shook his head again.

Her jaw turned stiff and her eyes hardened. "We'll do what we can." He could hear the unspoken end of the sentence, haunting the air between them: *Even if you don't want it.*

"Come on," said Yamitad, angling her head in the direction of the hall. "It's a long drive and I don't want to make it in the dark."

He went where she had indicated, and felt everyone else group behind him for the long trek through the front hall.

That was when they heard the bomb.

Cyril didn't remember flinging himself to the ground. He remembered stepping into the hall, and then his cheek pressed against the cold marble floor.

He was the first one up, because when his brain started working again it told him that the bomb had not been large—the sound at least said that much. He could still hear. The front of the house had not been damaged, not that he could tell from inside.

Back on his feet, he ran to the front doors and hauled them open, the marshal shouting after him. Jem and Paley were slow to give chase, no doubt still shaking in their boots.

The car was in one piece, though barely. Its windows and windshield were gone and noxious smoke poured through the openings. The interior had been destroyed. From the state of the front steps, there had not been much shrapnel beyond the broken windows—the stone remained intact, not even pockmarked. It was not a bomb intended to kill or maim. It was a distraction; a point made.

Stephen was very wisely nowhere to be seen.

"Damnation, DePaul," said Yamitad, coming up behind him. "I thought we said you wouldn't need hand—mother's tits."

A change in the breeze blew cordite smoke in their direction.

"You're lucky the tank didn't blow," he said.

"Officers," barked Yamitad.

Jem and Paley, so stuffed up at the beginning of this affair, were white-faced and wide-eyed now, scurrying sheepishly up to flank the marshal. When they saw the car, one swore and one just let his jaw drop. Cyril wondered which was Paley and which was Jem.

Lillian and Jinadh, who had not so far as Cyril knew ever been in law enforcement or enemy territory, recovered more slowly, and crept up to the door with more caution.

Lillian blanched when she saw the damage. "Temple bells," she said. "Marshal, I—" Then, hand flying to her mouth, "Mother and sons, where's Stephen?"

"I'll find him," said Jinadh, putting his hand briefly on Lillian's arm before he hurried back into the house.

It was not suspicion, on her part, but fear. His sister had not automatically picked out her son as the bomber, as Cyril had. She was only worried that he had been hurt.

Yamitad was less sentimental, and had her hands firmly on the reins once more. "Who's responsible for this?"

"Me," said Cyril. Some grit on the floor had cut his cheek when he dropped. Not deeply, but enough that the scrape had begun to burn.

"You couldn't possibly—" Lillian began but he turned a look on her that had its roots in their childhood together. The one that said *Shut up or they'll find us out.* It had evolved somewhat, given his circumstances in later life. But she recognized it and shut her teeth.

"Took me a minute to come when you called, right?" In truth, he hadn't heard her calling at all. Just lingered awhile on the roof after he saw the marshal arrive. And left Stephen alone, once he descended. There had been enough time—just—for a quick-footed boy who had done all his preparation beforehand. Cyril wondered where he had built the bomb. The shed, probably, where they had found the clay pigeons and the old boxes of shells that, miraculously, still fired.

Cyril had, indeed, taught him to build a better bomb. But he'd also tried to teach him not to get caught. While he was nowhere in evidence now, there weren't many other people to paint the blame on. Stephen was conspicuous by his very absence. And so, Cyril claimed it.

"It won't do you any good," said Yamitad. "We'll call the station in the village for another car. Or requisition hers." Here she jerked her head in Lillian's direction. From her face, this would be an unwelcome turn of events. He wondered how much more she resented him now than she had five minutes ago.

Jinadh's footsteps echoed as he came jogging across the hall. "He's fine. In his bedroom. I asked him to stay there, for now."

"In that case," said Lillian, as if she had not just set aside maternal terror, "I can drive you to the village."

First coffee, now a lift? "What a gracious host," said Cyril.

Earlier, he had plucked an eloquent look from their childhood lexicon, and now it was her turn. This one said, *One more word and you are dead.*

And even though he was, already—whatever Rinko said—he shut his teeth and let them put him in the car.

"Stop *shouting*, Aristide!" Lillian put her hand over the earpiece of the telephone, aware she was doing exactly what she'd ordered him not to. "Fraud, I said. They've arrested him for fraud. Yes, exactly like they said on the wireless."

She could feel the house around her, echoing with the events of the afternoon. Her brother's absence was like an amputated limb: a sudden queasy lightness, the expectation of movement where there wouldn't be again.

She had expected to lose him; she had been preparing for it. She had not expected it to happen quite like this.

Aristide rang her up at the top of the news cycle, when Flanders chimed his hourly update and the whole country—or the folk who had radios, at least—heard the news that notorious Ospie collaborator Cyril DePaul had been charged with fraud and taken into custody.

"It's got to be Frye," he said.

"Why?" asked Lillian. "She hasn't got that kind of power. She can't just *order* someone arrested because she wants them in jail."

"The charges are tabletop," said Aristide. "That passport's LSI work; I got it from Asiyah. But that's not what I mean. She did some digging—or Custler did—and dropped a word in someone's ear. She wanted him locked up tight because she's worried."

"About what?"

"Saeger, for one. If Cyril had run, or shot himself, or robbed Frye of her little campaign promise, she'd have been out a chunk of popular appeal."

All right, he had her there. But Daoud's worries had settled in her chest and now they rattled, waking. "And two?"

A long pause.

"Aristide," she said. "If you've done anything, said anything to Frye . . . You're going to cause more trouble than—"

"Don't say than he's worth."

"You didn't let me finish. He's my *brother*, Aristide, and whatever he *was* to you, he's still that to me."

Someone knocked on her office door. Magnusson, and he looked worried. She held up a finger, begging for a moment.

"What possessed you?" she asked. "What did you possibly think you could accomplish?"

"Possessed me to do what, exactly?" his voice was poisonous over the phone, the sibilance turning into static, the hard consonants to cracks. "Please. Elaborate."

"You know *very well*," she said. "And Mr. Qassan knows, too. You told *him* instead of me, when you chose to meddle in the affairs of *my* family—"

"Daoud is my secretary. There's no point in keeping secrets from him."

"What a miserable excuse. I had a right to know!"

"No," he said, "I don't believe you did."

She took a shaky breath to stop herself from outright screaming. "If you insist on carrying on by yourself, in this slapdash secret manner, it's only going to make things worse. You always have. Before Acherby, even. Before the coup. Your schemes make middens out of people's lives."

"*Those* schemes," said Aristide, "would have gone off without a snag if your mud-fisted brother hadn't cast his own line and tangled it with mine."

"Or if you had told him you had one in the first place!"

"Lillian."

Jinadh's voice recalled her from the depths of her rage and she surfaced as if from icy water: clenched all over, desperate for air. Aristide was still yelling into the telephone, but as she lowered it from her cheek the noise became tinny and indistinct.

Magnusson had gone, replaced by her husband, but the worried look on his face was the same. "You should come downstairs," he said. "There is a special bulletin on the wireless."

"About Cyril?" she asked. The receiver slipped into her lap and she realized her hand ached from gripping it.

He shook his head and she almost relaxed, but something in his expression held her in a state of unease.

"What is it?" she asked.

"An explosion," he said. "In Amberlough."

CHAPTER

TWENTY-ONE

Aristide had grown accustomed to success, as he had to luxury.

There had been a time when he could hardly afford to eat, but he had left that far behind in favor of bespoke suits, silk lingerie, and a weekly manicure. All of it was, of course, unnecessary for survival, but on occasions when he had been suddenly deprived of it he felt as if the earth had turned to quicksand underneath his feet.

This swift disillusionment felt discomfitingly similar.

They had heard the blast, faintly, even this far across town: a crack that echoed into juddering ripples. The window of their shared parlor looked south, and so they had a decent view of the smoke rising into the painful brightness of the winter sky. Smoke coming from the docks, near the train yards.

Aristide already knew what had happened, fifteen minutes before the special bulletin interrupted *Margaret Tse's Melody Hour* midway through an advertisement for Snyder's Straights.

"I told you," said Daoud, as they sat listening to another iteration of Aristide's failure on the wireless. "I said it would go badly."

"Please," said Aristide, drunk and irritated. Half a martini sat on the glass-topped table at his elbow; he'd lost count of how many he'd had. "You didn't. You couldn't even have known."

"It was a stupid idea." Daoud stood from the sofa and stalked to the desk, littered with papers. He picked one up by its corner and frowned at it as though it were a slimy thing pulled from a gutter. "You have lost a heap of money and any leverage you might have had." With that, he sunk into the chair behind the desk. It squealed beneath his negligible weight, which meant he must have fallen with some force. He had grown older in the last five years, but not much stouter.

"I followed you into Oyoti," said Daoud, putting a beleaguered hand to his head. "Into Niallo Benggi. I picked chiggers out of your feet. And all I have ever earned is scorn. What is it about this man? Why does he make you act this way?"

Aristide's laughter turned into a wet cough, which made him breathless and dizzier than the alcohol would have done alone. At the end of it, he swallowed phlegm and finished his martini. Fishing inelegantly for the lemon twist at the bottom of his empty glass, he asked, "Jealous, are we?"

"I would be insane." It wasn't cruel or vindictive. If anything, Daoud sounded surprised Aristide would suggest such a thing. "I am only trying to understand. All my life I have worked hard, done well, given others everything they asked from me. And I get nowhere. I get *nothing*. Cyril DePaul has betrayed, failed . . . he has *floundered* through his life. You were famous, and wealthy, and you threw away everything for him."

"Yes," said Aristide, and though he was drunk, anger made his diction sharp as broken glass and dragged the sibilance across it into tatters. "Twice."

"Why, Aristide? You are so canny about everything else. Why does he make you act so mad?"

Aristide swallowed another fit of laughter, wary of aching lungs. "Maybe I just like a challenge. And Didi, you are anything but."

Aristide only caught Kostos by the grace of a loose-lipped receptionist at FWAC. She told him when news was likely to drop after dinner, Kostos drank his at Sarah's on Adler Street, just south of Ionidous Avenue.

The place had been something else before—Aristide tried to remember and it eluded him. Something he hadn't had much interest in. Bad restaurant, perhaps, or a soda fountain. Something inoffensive where he had no important business. Now it had become a smoky bar with a low tin ceiling, kept too warm by ugly radiators. The place teemed with men and women not unlike Kostos: fast talkers and hard drinkers with cynical expressions and wrinkled shirts.

The man himself stood at the bar over a greasy piece of newspaper covered in the remains of something fried. The smell of vinegar was thick as Aristide approached, mingling with sweat and cigarette smoke.

"You stand out a little bit," said Kostos, taking in Aristide's fur collar and the razor crease at the front of his flannel trousers.

Aristide likewise cased Kostos's rumpled jacket and loosened tie. The top button of his shirt was open, revealing stubble and the loose skin of his throat. "I should hope so."

"I can guess what you're here about." He swiped a chip through mayonnaise, leaving streaks across yesterday's news. Aristide saw Saeger's name, read . . . *rallied today, optimistic despite Frye's gains* . . . between oil spots and egg white. There was a picture of a young man lifted on the shoulders of a crowd, holding a ragged flag marked with Catwalk train tracks.

"My editor don't go in for hearsay," Kostos went on. "And that's what I got now. Not a story."

"You've still got the affair."

But Kostos was shaking his head. "Nah. The peach resigned this evening. You ain't heard? Frye works fast. Can't say I don't admire her get-it-doneness."

Aristide's extremities went cold. "Double martini, please," he told the bartender.

"I don't trust the gin at Sarah's," Kostos said. "Stones, nor the whiskey neither. But whatever they cut it with, at least it don't repeat on me."

Indeed, it seared like paint thinner. But it put his problems at a bearable distance and slowed the beating of his heart.

"You look like you're gonna faint," said Kostos. "Take a seat. Supposed to be something coming down from the hounds any minute. I'd've gone to the station, but they're keeping the numbers clamped down for security. There's a peach with the *Evening Expo* who's got an in with the chief—or he's got it in with her—and she said she'd come 'round and tell us after. She'll keep all the crispy bits for herself and her scoop, but maybe you'll hear something good."

Expediency trumping decorum, Aristide downed the rest of his drink in one swallow. "I very much doubt it."

Awareness of a commotion at the entrance spread through the crowd like wind through grass, making voices rise and fall, heads turn. Folk shouted, then hissed at each other for quiet, until finally, Aristide asked, "What's going on?"

But Kostos had hopped down from his seat and nabbed a colleague. They were both craning their necks to look over the sea of oiled hair and pillbox hats. "Is that Oleksa who just came in?" asked Kostos.

"Can't tell," the other man said.

"Hey!" Kostos might not have had a radio voice, but it carried. "Olek*sa*! What'd you hear at the kennel?"

"Laurie," said the bartender, "don't you go shouting like that in my place."

Four people turned around to shush her.

"Polanka says it's Catwalk." The woman Kostos had addressed, who was the cause of the commotion, climbed up on a chair and flipped a notebook open like she was giving her own impromptu press conference. "I already filed it, scullers, or I wouldn't be so free with my spoils. Our pal Chief Polanka says early investigations turned up three crispy bodies and explosives similar to those used by the nice folk who ousted Acherby and tore up half the country in the meantime."

Some shouted protests, swiftly put down by people eager to hear the rest of the story.

"Yup," Oleksa went on. "Emmeline Frye's private interests look to be the target of Catwalk terrorism."

In one fell swoop, Frye had made herself the victim of a grievous wrong, taken a chain gun to Saeger's chances, and ruined Aristide's prospects for blackmail. If he wasn't so utterly furious or empty of hope, he might admire her.

"Say," said Kostos, leaning in. "You knew Lehane. What d'you think she'd make of this?"

"This big swell knew the Spotlight?" asked a woman sitting next to them. "Knock me. Hang on, Laurie is this that sculler . . . Makricosta, right? No swineshittin'?" She pulled out a steno pad and pencil. "Yeah, what would she say? You were friends, right? Good friends. You think she'd have backed Saeger?"

Kostos half-managed to look sheepish.

"Hang on," said the bartender. "You were friends with *the* Spotlight?"

"That dry-bite bobtail killed my cousin," said the barback.

"Shut your teeth." The bartender snapped a towel at him. "*She* didn't do it herself."

"Her folk blew his train. And he weren't an Ospie. He just shoveled coal."

"Three dead today," said the first journalist. "None of them Ospies, either. Come on, Makricosta, what'd she think?"

It spread just like the news of Oleksa's arrival had, only now the heads were turning his way. Eyes found him, and questions clogged the air. He couldn't breathe. The rancid gin was burning back up his throat and he just had to get out, get *out*—

How he made it to the street, he wasn't sure, but awareness found him on all fours under Kostos's shadow, vomiting into the gutter. There was little in his stomach to bring up but acid.

"Told you not to trust the gin," said Kostos, offering him a handkerchief.

Aristide eschewed it in favor of his own, which would be ruined. Small price to pay for spite.

"I'll get you a cab," said Kostos. "Least I can do."

"Thank you," said Aristide, spit sour in his mouth. "But I prefer to walk."

PART

3

CHAPTER

TWENTY-TWO

Despite the bombing, they shuttered Damesfort and came to town. It was too expensive to keep both houses open and travel between them, if they were going to be paying a lawyer as well. Jinadh needed to be in the city for work—keeping his unmarried name had saved his job. Fewer folk clocked him straight off. His sections sold papers, and his writers liked him and turned their stories in on time. He was an acceptable risk to his employers. Lillian was thankful, as his income kept them from drowning too quickly.

They let most of the staff go, and none of the outgoing employees seemed terribly torn up. Magnusson remained, accepting a cut in pay. "I've always been sympathetic to the DePauls," he said, "ever since the Spice War. The women in your family make hard decisions, and they don't make them lightly."

Lillian could have kissed him.

Stephen kept his head bent on the drive into town, reading

books for a spring term he might never see. At least not at Cantrell. Even with Rinko offering an old friend's rates, it was a serious question whether they could afford to send him back, the results of his probation notwithstanding.

They would find a way. If there was not one hidden somewhere in all this mess, she would will one open. There were *some* things, surely, she could still control.

An encampment of journalists had sprung up outside the front door of twenty-four by the time they arrived. Didn't they have anything better to report on, besides her family's comings and goings? Saeger would be eager to talk to any one of them; with a month and a half to go 'til the election, she needed to reach the voters by any means available. She'd wrangled a slot on *Backchat* the day before and issued a scathing rebuttal to the verdict that the Catwalk had bombed Frye's warehouse.

"I think it says more about her than it does about me," Saeger had said. "Is she afraid of me? Worried folk like what Forward Gedda stands for, more than they like what she's proposing? Worried her gambit with these tribunals won't pull her far enough ahead? We didn't bomb that warehouse, but I'd like to know who did. And I'd like to know why the hounds are lying about it."

Lillian could have given her a hint. Or several.

Why didn't they cover the rallies at the university? When she woke the next morning she could hear them from the house. Hordes of students backing Saeger, screaming their lungs out over the accusations.

Of course, as Jinadh would remind her: there were more than ten pen-fencers in the city of Amberlough. The ones clustered outside the door of Coral Street just happened to have drawn her straw in that week's editorial meeting.

The other reason they'd come back to the city—the obvious reason—was that Cyril had been locked away just at the edge of town. Shearan-Sterner Penitentiary, south of the city limits, would have been the more appropriate option, but it had been one of the Catwalk's later targets. They'd steered clear of the cell blocks and mainly taken out the administrative wing. Denied bail but not yet arraigned, Cyril was being kept in the city jail attached to the Department of Corrections, and looked likely to remain there for some time.

So when Lillian awoke in the city to the sound of not-so-distant rhythmic chanting, her first order of business was to ring up Rinko Higata about the possibility of seeing her brother in prison.

In the badly lit visiting room, its walls painted an unattractive shade of green, Cyril looked not just pale but sick. She sat across from him and asked, "Are you all right? Your color isn't good."

He brushed her concern away with a wave of his hand. The knuckles were chapped. It was cold even here; the cells likely weren't much better.

"Do you have any cigarettes?" he asked.

She turned to the guard who lurked in the corner and lifted her shoulders in a beseeching shrug. He rolled his eyes and looked pointedly in the other direction, so she opened the case she didn't often use and picked two straights from inside of it. One of them, she supposed, could have secreted a lock pick, but Cyril leaned in for her to light his rather than stashing it on his person.

As if he could—he had no pockets now to fill with odds and ends. Only a drab green smock and loose trousers. He hadn't shaved since his arrest, and the skin below his eyes hung empty and bruised as if something had drained from beneath it.

"We'll need to clean you up a bit before your arraignment," she said.

That got a laugh out of him, smoky and bitter. "I don't think it'll do much good."

"It will make me feel better," she said. "Will you at least consider that?"

He looked around for somewhere to tap off the spent end of his straight. Lillian, momentarily at a loss, fished a handkerchief from her pocket just in time. A spray of ash fell across the linen, obscuring the monogram and freckling the painted steel tabletop.

"Sorry," he said, touching the rolled hem of the hankie. It put their hands close together. She almost covered his with her own.

"Do you think there's going to *be* an arraignment?" he asked. "Or a trial? Or is this just the prelude to the wall and the squad and a hole through my head?"

She fought the urge to cover her mouth, controlling her nausea by force of will. "You were arrested for fraud, Cyril. That's hardly a cause for summary execution."

"No," he said. "But treason might be. And who knows what other charges they'll heap on when we get to the *real* reason I'm in here. You know the fraud is an excuse, Lil."

"Do they let you read the news?"

"A day or two late," he said. "But I'm keen enough to catch a whiff when something smells off."

She wanted to tell him whose fault it really was: his arrest, the bombing. She wanted him to hate Makricosta as much as she did. But the guard in the corner had two ears and a mouth, and Lillian's profession had taught her to be wary of spreading a story without intense analysis of the consequences. Instinct told her the effect would be destabilizing. She thought of the chanting students, Saeger's forceful voice through the wireless, Frye's newly revealed ruthlessness. Bombs, riots, anarchy.

Enough chasms had opened up beneath her lately; she needed solid earth to stand on or she'd never get anywhere she wanted to be.

"What are we going to do?" she asked. It could have meant any number of things, but Cyril only heard one.

"I think you've done about as much as you can. The smart thing would be to cut me loose like a dragging anchor."

But anchors couldn't drown. People could. "I'm already a traitor in my own right. By some folk's definitions, anyway. Cutting you loose won't change the choices I made."

"You had Stephen," he said. "You couldn't have made a different choice. I could have."

There had come a point in her life—some time during university, or perhaps just after graduation—when Cyril began to try her patience, as he had her parents'. His irrational passions, his self-obsession, his obstinance. Every conversation she had with him inevitably reached a point of exasperation. Neither time nor distance nor death nor resurrection made a difference.

Maybe she didn't understand what he had been through. Maybe she never would. But neither would he understand what she had done or what it had cost her. "Why are the rest of us held to such a lower standard?" she demanded. "Why are you special?"

"What did I have to lose? Who would have suffered if I had said no? You all thought I was dead; I just would have gone sooner, and ruined less."

"You aren't Caleb Acherby," she said, and saw the guard in the corner come to attention: either at the name, or at her tone of voice, which had gone acidic with vexation. "You did something reprehensible, yes, but Cyril . . . who didn't?"

A beat, a heavy pause. Lillian knew what he was going to say half a breath before he said it.

"Cordelia."

"A political martyr?" she asked. "The woman who toppled the Ospies? That's a high bar to set for yourself."

When he looked up from the ash on the tabletop, his eyes were bleak. "Is it? She was a *stripper*, Lillian. I don't know if she ever finished school. As far as I know she didn't own stockings. And she wore this awful rosewater perfume . . ." His voice wobbled, precarious. "But she didn't fall in line, which is more than either of us can say."

"I hardly think you can judge someone's character by their stockings," said Lillian. "Or lack thereof."

"No," said Cyril. "I guess you can't." He took a long drag on his straight, staring at the far wall as he inhaled.

The resultant cloud of smoke he sent over his shoulder, toward the guard, who cleared his throat and gestured at the clock with his truncheon. "Time's nearly gone."

"I'll try to come again this week." Lillian stood from the table.

Cyril gave no indication of having heard her. Smoke curled from his crooked nose. "How did she die?" he asked, still watching the green-painted brick.

"Door-to-door fighting." Lillian looked down at her hands, watched their clasped stillness and imagined making fists. Then she looked up again, so she could deliver it professionally. "They tried to kill her quietly and she turned it into a brawl."

When Cyril smiled, his dry lips split. "Yes. That sounds about right."

Lillian let herself stop at Grafton's before she went home. No one would grudge her a drink, after that. Surely.

The place was a Staunton Street institution. When her father was in the corps, and when he was at home, it was where he did his drinking and a fair amount of his diplomacy. There was no sign on the door—how anyone knew to call it Grafton's was a mystery. Perhaps that wasn't even its name. She didn't know what it had been under the Ospies, but it was hardly worse for the wear. Unlike some things.

She was a little leery, going in, but the clientele was nothing if not discreet. If they wanted to judge her, they would do it silently as long as she was within earshot. And anyway, it would hardly be busy at this time. Grafton's was strictly a lunch and after-hours haunt, and when she arrived the low sky was still the color of white laundry washed accidentally with indigo. The days were growing discernibly longer, just.

Several serious drinkers in suits had their heads together over fans of paper spread where they could catch the last of the winter light through the large front windows. One woman, alone on a leather sofa, read an official-looking folio. Half a soggy sandwich sat forgotten in front of her. The place wasn't well known for its food, but it often did in a pinch for the busiest residents of Embassy Row.

Homesickness gripped Lillian like a seizure. Absurd. She was less than half a mile from the house where she'd spent half her childhood. But suddenly Grafton's seemed like the only thing that hadn't changed beyond recognition. Lillian turned slowly to drink it in, heart wrung tight as a dish towel.

In the quiet, to the rhythm of a waltz on the wireless, the bartender polished glasses with a white cloth. Just past her working elbow, slouched over a martini, was Aristide Makricosta.

Lillian hadn't seen him since he left Damesfort after Solstice, hadn't spoken to him since she let the receiver fall back into its cradle still buzzing with his fury. Had hardly given him a second thought, except to curse his name each night before she went to bed, for bringing her brother back to Gedda wrapped in a nice neat cashmere package for the press and everyone to tear apart.

She paused inside the doorway, the bell still ringing behind her. No one looked up except the bartender, who gestured with the glass in her hand, leaving the empty seats to Lillian's discretion.

She could choose any one of them: the small round table in the front window, with its padded bench seat and two curly stools. The armchair in the back corner, under a commercial calendar turned to a lurid advertisement for shirt collars. The straight-backed chair by the radio would afford her a good chance to listen to any news bulletins, if they came on. Even knowing she would hear nothing good, she still followed along obsessively. The hill up from habits, as Porachins said, was slippery.

There were many seats she could choose that were not next to Makricosta. But like Grafton's, he was a relic. A piece of the world the rest of them had lost or been torn from. And their last conversation had been rudely interrupted by a bombing. So she sat down beside him and ordered an aquavit with vermouth.

"Aristide," she said. "Trying to insinuate yourself into international politics again?"

He jumped when she spoke, but recovered quickly. "Good afternoon, Lillian." The words bled into one another, and she realized he was drunker than he appeared at first glance.

"Really," she said. "What are you doing drinking at Grafton's?"

"It's close to my hotel," he said, and finished what was left in his glass. "I didn't know it was your spot. I didn't even know you were in *town*."

"It isn't," she said. "My spot, I mean. Just near my house." She hadn't realized he was in the neighborhood. But then, had she ever asked where he was staying? She had been juggling so much, perhaps that particular piece of courtesy had fallen by the wayside.

"I'm surprised you're speaking to me." He winced, and pushed his empty glass away.

"If I weren't speaking to you, how would I express my disappointment?" She sipped her cocktail without dropping her gaze. "I've just been to see Cyril."

He closed his eyes, as if in pain. "I deserve your twisting that knife."

"You're lucky I don't stick a real one in you," she said, and heard that she was dangerously close to losing her control. She must be tired, if she hadn't caught herself before speaking. "Cyril's lawyer says I ought to be ready for a warrant. They're looking for that passport. The one you said was—"

"And are they going to find it?"

She arranged her expression into a flawless mask and delivered the scripted line. "I never saw the thing. They're welcome to search the house. Both houses. For all I know, he burned it."

In fact, the pile of charred odds and ends in the hearth of the daisy room had not contained the remains of Cyril's passport. The police and the federal investigators were welcome to sift through it if they liked, along with every other hearth and the spaces under the flagstones and floorboards. Their hopes would go unfulfilled. A family like the DePauls knew how to hide a safe.

Confusion crept into the wrinkle between Aristide's eyebrows, followed by dawning realization. She watched, fascination almost overtaking anger. In their acquaintance, she had come to know him as a man whose internal workings were largely hidden: a meticulously constructed machine beneath a shining enamel cover. She had never had the opportunity to witness his mechanism at work.

How long had he been sitting at this bar?

Her anger wasn't exactly doused by pity, but rather temporarily displaced by it. "You shouldn't drink so much."

"You needn't scold me." He lifted his empty glass, peered into it, and then put it back down on the copper bar with enough inept force she worried the stem might snap. "Daoud's done enough of that."

"How is he?" she asked. "Well, I hope."

Aristide put his face into the tripod of his first two fingertips and thumb. "Queen's cunt. Who knows?" Then, lifting his head and letting it swing toward her, he saw the abandoned aquavit. "Are you going to drink that?"

She swallowed the rest of it in one go and said, "Why don't I walk you home?"

It was getting dark now, and bitterly cold. They headed west on Staunton, past gated chanceries with their colors struck for the evening. Their shoes crunched on ice pockmarked by scattered salt. Lights still burned in the buildings, many of them stately old homes that now housed diplomatic missions. Representatives of many nations were exiting to head for home, all swaddled into uniformity by mufflers, heavy coats, and hats pulled low against the wind. Naked tree branches rattled together over the quiet street. Saeger's mobs of angry supporters had not penetrated this deep into the Central City's heart.

When they had passed through a small gaggle of bundled-up diplomats and had the sidewalk to themselves, Lillian said, "I don't suppose you have any other plans in your pockets?"

Aristide, sobered somewhat by the cold, still had to pick his way carefully between icy patches. Lillian found herself waiting for him to catch up before he answered. "None at present, no. Are you pleased?"

She let it lie, because she wasn't sure of her honest answer, nor of her ability to answer dishonestly.

"I was sure it would work," he said. Then, more quietly, "I wanted it to work."

"And you've always gotten what you set after," she said, shaking her head. "How old are you?"

He lifted his chin with affronted dignity that verged on satire.

"Fifty?" she asked, unaffected. "Fifty-five? It's long past time you learned this lesson. Your hair is gray. Don't act like a child."

He stared at her, cold as the wind slicing through her coat, then pushed past. Surprised, she let him have a yard or two.

"I'm not the one acting like a child." He threw the words over his shoulder, and she hurried over the treacherous pavement.

"*Please* don't shout," she said. "The last thing we need is *this* in the news as well."

"You're the fool," he said, "for imagining anything like acquittal."

"I'm not; Cyril's lawyer was explicitly clear on that point. All I want is to keep him off the scaffold."

Aristide gave a bark of laughter that caught somewhere inside his chest and tore, becoming an ugly cough. When he'd recovered, he said, "And how much is that costing you?"

"I don't see how that matters." She had only meant to see him back to his hotel. How had they fallen to fighting again?

"How much?" he demanded. "You only had three rooms open downstairs at that country house of yours. All the others were done up in dust sheets, except where you'd poached furniture. And a handful of people doing jobs fit for a full set of fingers and toes. Have you sold your land to pay his lawyer? Hired out in Eel Town? Or is that next week, after you indenture your son?"

Sudden fury stuck her to the spot. "How *dare* you."

"You'll be bankrupt before he hangs."

"Enough!" She put her hands to her ears, and realized they had both gone numb: there was more pressure than sensation against her skin. "Why should I hear this from you? What right do you have? You've barely even *spoken* to him since you dumped him in my lap. Just stuck me with him and then got on with your own life. Your own *business*. As if that were more important."

"I put my business in the kitty for him," said Aristide. "And I lost everything I bet! That was *my* tar in Frye's warehouse."

"And now it's all of us in a kettle, ready to start shrieking. You gave Frye a scare and you gave Saeger a grievance. Now one of them's mounted a tight defense and the other's on the march, and neither of them are primed to play kindly with my brother." Pettiness, which had been building at a steady boil, overspilled from her now and scorched in the flame of her anger. Why shouldn't he hear what Cyril had made her listen to? "He doesn't even want to be *saved*, Aristide. He's going to let them put a noose around his neck and happily."

"Don't be dramatic."

"What? You mean you don't know? He didn't say anything to you? Or maybe he hasn't had a chance, since you haven't bothered to speak to him since Solstice."

He stopped walking, but kept his back to her. "Who said anything of the kind?"

The aquavit in her empty stomach made her unpleasantly dizzy, and she put a hand out to the iron fence of the—What? Cestinian embassy?—to keep her feet. "Nobody had to."

She only caught the slight turn of his head because it put his spectacles at an angle to catch the stoplight up ahead. The signal blinked from red to green, eliding whatever expression he wore beneath the reflection. She didn't have time to apologize before he stepped into the street and hailed a cab. But she had never intended to, anyway.

CHAPTER

TWENTY-THREE

Aristide could have humbled himself, to find out from Lillian where they were holding Cyril, and how to go about visiting. But that was asking quite a bit after their last interaction. After their last *series* of interactions.

So he got Daoud to do it for him.

This won him no admiration; in fact it earned him scorn, but that was nothing new. And gin repelled scorn like wax did water.

"The city jail," said Daoud, when he got off the telephone. Aristide had heard Jinadh's voice on the other end, and from what little of the quick and colloquial Porashtu he could catch, the conversation had been at least partly social. "Apparently Cordelia's people caused some trouble at the nearest appropriate prison."

"And who do I have to bribe to get in?"

"You are on the approved list already."

That tripped him up. "Really? Why?"

Daoud shrugged, and it was not exactly all ignorance; at least one quarter had been given over to sarcasm. "Who knows. *I* certainly would not want you visiting *me* in prison."

"That's because you've never been."

"Have you?"

Aristide had nothing to offer against that. He had never been caught. The thought of it curled his toes, and he drew his feet up onto the sofa. Drafts had penetrated even the steam-heated atmosphere of Sykes House, which for all its bad food and harassed service had at least started out pleasantly warm.

"Twist that valve, will you?" he asked Daoud, burrowing more deeply into the white fox collar of his dressing gown. "It's freezing in here."

Daoud glared at him, but knelt on the floor to do as he was asked. His flannel trousers, loose when standing, pulled tight across his rear. While he was facing the radiator, rather than Aristide, he asked, "When do you plan to go?"

"This afternoon, I suppose."

"Will you want me?"

He heard it first as a carnal question, depressingly practical and resigned: a courtesan's question to his keeper. It was only after Daoud stood, brushed his hands together, and repeated his question that Aristide realized he meant at the prison, as a secretary. He could have hit himself.

"No," he said, and it was true on both counts. Shame had killed whatever erotic interest the spectacle of tight trousers had aroused. Lady's name, how had he burrowed so far down into the midden? They had started fresh, at first: arriving in Liso as partners in a venture, nothing more. It was only repeated, demoralizing failure that had pushed Aristide back into something he had always known wasn't good for either of them, and of which he felt faintly ashamed. Now it was less the affair he felt ashamed of than himself.

"Didi," he said.

"Hm?" Having moved on from the radiator to neatening the piles of paper on Aristide's desk, Daoud glanced up from a drift of letters in need of replies. He seemed distracted, beard due for a trim, utterly unaware of Aristide's assumption and subsequent disgust. "You needed something else?"

"No," said Aristide. "No, I only . . . oh, never mind."

Looking skeptical, Daoud turned back to tidying.

"What will you do?" asked Aristide, the question out of him before he had time to consider it. Gin would do *that*, as well.

"Pay bills," Daoud said. "Balance the accounts. Perhaps pick up the dry cleaning, if it does not snow. The walk would be nice."

"No, not . . . not while I'm out. I mean, after . . ." Aristide waved a vague hand and felt his cheeks grow warm with frustration and embarrassment.

Straightening from his busywork, Daoud stared. "After what, Aristide?"

The vague hand fell into his lap, shot down like a game bird.

"No, I am curious. After what? This tribunal Frye has promised? After whatever your next scheme may be? What am I waiting for, Aristide? And will it ever happen?"

Aristide felt cool air on his tongue, and realized that his mouth was open. No words were forthcoming. He wasn't sure Daoud wanted answers, really. His questions had grown introspective at the end.

As if he had realized this, Daoud shook his head. The motion faded into a drop of the chin, a glance at his watch, and a look out the window. "Perhaps I will go to the cleaner's now," he said. "While the weather is still good."

"Gentleman caller for you," said the warden, slouching against the bars of Cyril's cell. "Hope you wore your lacey things today."

"I save those for you, Markert," said Cyril, sitting up. The mattress hadn't gotten any better, but he'd slept on worse. That didn't mean he liked it.

He didn't ask who the gentleman was; there was only one it might have been. Stephen was on the list, but he'd likely only come with his mother, and Markert would hardly call him a gentleman.

Cyril lifted a hand to smooth his hair. The last shear he'd had in the jungle had grown out slowly, but it *had* grown, and without the guiding hand of a barber. Now it had a tendency to flop in his eyes and stick out at strange angles. There was nothing in the cell he could use as a looking glass—the windows were too high, and they certainly hadn't given him a mirror.

As if it mattered. Hand-combing his uneven mop wasn't going to make him look any less a prisoner.

Maybe he *would* ask Rinko about getting cleaned up a little before they hauled him into a courtroom. When she came next—was that tomorrow? Would he have asked her sooner if he expected to get *gentleman callers*?

"Let's *go*," said Markert, banging his truncheon on the bars. So Cyril went.

A fine scrim of smoke already hung in the still air of the visiting room. Its source was a slim turquoise straight, gold-banded, held in Ari's kid-gloved hand. Purple kid, too: the color of heavy red wine. Under the smoke, Cyril smelled a faint trace of white flowers and an animalic base. Had Padgett and Sons made it through and carried on selling perfume? He wondered if any Ospies had been partial to vanilla musk.

Aristide wore a mink coat with the collar turned up, fur thick enough to sink into. A mauve ascot embroidered with metallic thread was tucked not-quite-neatly into his open silk collar, and there might have been a touch of rouge on his cheeks.

Even older, out of makeup and offstage, he carried the sweep of the spotlight with him, the echo of applause.

Without breaking eye contact, he took a long drag on the ridiculous straight and said, "We have *got* to stop meeting like this."

Cyril dropped into the opposite chair and said, "You never gave me a chance to come see you."

"*You* didn't try very hard to catch me, or I might have."

"Careful," said Cyril. "What's the statute of limitations on . . . oh, I don't know, pick something. What didn't you do?"

"Nothing so bad as you."

It punctured the soap bubbles of their banter. Aristide looked away first, though he was the one who had said it. Once he'd recovered, he asked, "Would you like a cigarette?"

"More than anything. Even if they are . . . what, green?"

"There are pink ones, too. Or purple, if you'd rather." Aristide flipped his case open.

"Hey," said Markert.

"Relax," said Aristide. "I've paid your little sop, and I mean to get something out of it. Stand there if you must, but please be silent."

Cyril took a straight, and as Aristide lit it for him he glanced at Markert to see how he'd taken that drubbing. Not well; he'd gone a shade of purple not so different from Aristide's ascot.

"Thanks," said Cyril, knowing it wouldn't go easy with him later. "He never does that for me."

"And it's rubbing off, I see. You're much chattier now than you were at Solstice."

That brought him up short, like looking down midway across a chasm. To be reminded he was . . . making conversation? Flirting? It spiked him where he stood.

"Dear, dear," said Aristide. "Hit a sore spot, have I?"

Cyril inhaled smoke and let it sit too long, so that he was dizzy when he said, "Maybe I've been a little lonely."

"With me to keep you company?" asked Markert. "Sure you have."

Rage looked better on Aristide now than it ever had, and it had always looked good. A length of iron rod rose up his spine, and his chin flicked to a haughty angle that made light flash across his spectacles. One stiff kid-gloved finger pointed at the door. In withering tones he said, "Get out. And send someone who's less inclined to be snotty."

After a piano wire pause, to Cyril's great surprise, Markert did as he was told. There was a brief exchange with someone in the office—with the door open and his eyes still on Aristide and Cyril—and then he traded places with his colleague Dorfner, a taciturn man who appeared perpetually worried.

How much money had Aristide parted with, on his way in? And what did he have to say, that was worth such a sum?

"Why don't you stutter anymore?" asked Cyril, because it was an easier question than any others banging around inside his skull.

Aristide gave him a curious look that said he understood exactly the tactic Cyril had just deployed. "I am well aware that with increasing age comes the potential for absurdity. Therefore, I have . . . *dampened* my affectations, somewhat. I shouldn't like to be taken for a clown." Despite the rouge and pastel cigarettes, he said it without irony. There was none to be had: His presence did not admit of it.

"It never made you sound like that. *You* were never that."

Aristide shrugged: a liquid motion beneath his mink. "It was my character, then."

"I always liked it."

"I know you did. But do you see a stage?"

"You never needed a stage," said Cyril. "Would you do it for me now?"

He raised an eyebrow. "What do you want me to say?"

If it was an opening, it was one he didn't know how to take. "A bit of one of your routines, maybe. From the Bee."

It was the wrong thing. "Cyril, I—"

But suddenly, presented with this glittering apparition from a life he'd left far behind, that was what he desperately wanted. A moment of escape; thirty seconds of the past. "They're going to hang me, Ari. Tell me one of your rotten jokes."

"They aren't going to hang you." He suddenly looked tired. "Fraud isn't a capital offense."

Cyril tapped his straight into the ashtray at the center of the table. Another luxury Aristide's cash had bought. "We both know exactly why I'm here."

It put a peculiar look on Ari's face that piqued Cyril's curiosity. An atrophied muscle, that, and it ached like one. "Ari?"

But he shook the question off, and shed the strange expression that had crept across his face. "I read an interview with your attorney," he said. "In which she wondered why the nation felt the need to punish a man who already suffered agonies of guilt every waking day. Is that true?"

Cyril flicked his burnt-down straight into the ashtray and sat back, arms crossed. "What do you think?"

There was a pause before he said, "I hardly know." And then another. "Lillian says you don't want to be saved."

"If Frye's judges don't put me on the scaffold, it'll be at least twenty-five years. Probably life. Do you think that's what they want from me?" He waved a hand as if to indicate a mob of angry citizens. "They don't want a gavel and a sentence. They want a corpse."

"And you want to give them one."

"They deserve it. And I don't want to spend my life in prison." He said it casually, but perhaps that was the very reason Aristide reacted as he did.

"This is nothing but a lazy suicide," he snarled, grinding his cigarette savagely into the tray. "You'll ruin your sister, and you'll ruin me. Why don't you save us all the trouble and expense and end it now?"

Cyril looked up, shocked at Ari's anger, his suggestion. "Don't think I haven't stood on that ledge a thousand times."

"Then why haven't you *jumped*?" And now Cyril could hear it, underneath the fury: pain, and pleading. "Surely if you haven't killed yourself by now, you have some reason. What's kept you from pulling that trigger?"

Not much. Not nearly enough. And yet, "I don't get that luxury. I owe too much. If they hang me, at least my death's a kind of payment."

"*Swineshit*. Who's better off once you're at the end of that rope? This whole circus isn't selfless; it's selfish. You can't even do the deed yourself."

Something in him, which had been bending beneath a great weight for too long, finally snapped. He stood so suddenly his chair fell backward. "Would you rather I did? Do you want me to?"

Dorfner was shouting, had his hands on Cyril's arms. When had he crossed the room? Cyril let himself be pressed roughly back into his seat.

"Thank you," said Aristide. "That's enough."

Dorfner retreated to his corner.

"Of course not." Ari's fists were tight enough that the leather of his gloves puckered at the joints. He pressed them hard against the ugly yellow tabletop and addressed them solely when he spoke. "But you're making the people who love you *pay* to see you *killed*."

The pieces of Cyril's pride fell to the ground, hardly clattering, and he sagged against the sharp metal frame of his chair.

Aristide rose, gathering his mink about him. "Perhaps I should go."

It took too long for Cyril to work out what he ought to say, and in the end he just pushed out whatever words were on top, to keep Aristide from walking out the door. "I knew you were alive."

He didn't come back to his chair, or turn. Or even speak. But neither did he leave.

"I saw you in a newspaper," said Cyril, and it sounded like begging. "Probably a month after it went to print, but I saw your face. I knew you were alive."

Silence, still.

"You want to know why I never looked for you?" He paused but got no answer, and so blundered ahead. "I was ashamed."

"Ashamed?" Aristide's voice was tight as a trip wire.

"Of course," said Cyril. "You got out, you made your way. In the photo, you looked so . . . How could I come to you, after all I did? After I—stones." He let his head drop, so his fist in his own hair was the only thing that held his face off the table. "I made such a mess of things." The words strangled on unshed tears.

"You should have known better."

It stung enough that Cyril pulled himself together and looked up, grateful for his anger. "Oh? You'd have wanted me? Even then, crawling back and cringing?"

A light kindled in the depths of Aristide's eyes, an ember catching a draft. "Of course," he said, and even his voice had grown warmer. "Haven't I always liked you on your knees?"

Whatever filled Cyril's heart, it hurt like blood rushing past a loosened tourniquet.

Higata had told him that his life was his punishment. That it wasn't worth their time to kill him because he'd suffer a thousand times worse if he lived. But now he saw the truth of it. The instant before death would be worse than another thirty, forty, fifty years of guilt because in that instant an infinity of failures would unfurl before him: all the things he might have done and would now never do. All the opportunities to do better that he would turn away, in paying a symbolic price for past wrongdoing.

If he lived, at least he could limit his errors to the logical progression of his own decisions. And if he was lucky, temper them with a success or two. If he was very, very lucky, he could make amends.

Cordelia was dead, put up on a plaque and made into a symbol. He could die and be the same: her opposite number, like Ari used to be onstage. Pathetic traitor to her keen and clever saint. But if he lived . . .

He could not fix all the wrong that he had done; too many of those doors were shut. But this one—the one that led to Aristide—might at least stand ajar.

A shame that it was far too late to see what lay on the other side.

CHAPTER

TWENTY-FOUR

The bombing of a warehouse full of merchandise was, of course, cause for a company meeting.

Cross being in Liso, she sent a telegram that Aristide and Jamila should handle things and arrange a radio call only if necessary.

So although he had many other things on his mind—Cyril looked sick in prison greens; Cyril had lost weight he could ill afford; as soon as the election was over, Cyril would become a spectacle and then a corpse—Aristide found himself climbing out of a cab with Daoud at the unremarkable offices of Cross-Costa Imports once again.

«You are going to tell her what I did,» said Aristide, shoulders hunched more in misery than against the wind.

«Of course I am.» Daoud went ahead of him, and didn't hold the door.

Jamila welcomed them with open arms, jollier than anyone

Aristide had interacted with in the recent past. She wore a smile and a napkin tucked into her collar. A paper plate of flatbread and curried peanut lamb sat steaming on her desk.

"Boys!" she said, slapping the blotter on either side of her lunch. The two clerks jumped, one of them starting so violently he struck the carriage return. "Have a seat. You two—" this to the clerks, "—stroll off."

They ran like startled hares.

"You are in a very good mood, considering." Daoud sat sulkily across from her.

She laughed. «Respected little brother—» there was an ironic tinge to the diminutive Porashtu honorific "—this may look bad, but the gods saw fit to gift us with a blessing called *insurance*." She scooped up a bite of curry and, still chewing, said, "The payout's the value of the goods we shipped on paper, which I was clever enough to pitch high. Not because I *expected* a disaster, see, but because I always like to be prepared. And!" She finally swallowed, then paused for a belch. "It's risk-free now. No tar sitting around for any hounds to find. No moving it, no distribution. A pain for all the folk who would have made money on it selling, but for us? It doesn't hurt near as bad as it looks."

"Not for the company," said Daoud, still slightly sour. "But I think Mr. Makricosta would tell you a different story."

"Cheer up, Didi," said Aristide. "You were never worried about me anyway. If I recall correctly, all your care was for Cross-Costa."

Jamila's good humor began to drain at this exchange, replaced by suspicion. "What are you two jawing about?"

"That bombing was not Catwalk," said Daoud. "It was a cover-up."

"What for?" She put down the scrap of flatbread still in her hand and leaned in on her elbows.

"Blackmail," said Aristide, at the same time Daoud said, "Stupidity."

Jamila surveyed each of them, ran a thumb beneath her nose, and then sat back. "All right. Sick it up."

"This—" Daoud cast a withering glance in Aristide's direction. His first few obscenities and aspersions were such technical Porashtu Aristide didn't catch them, but he latched onto the sentence when Daoud levered himself back into Geddan with "dizzy, prick-led *moron* threatened Emmeline Frye with exposure. The results being, there is now no more tar to expose."

"Please don't forget she was knocking her second-in-command," said Aristide, too helpful, verging on sarcastic. "I would never have made such a pedestrian attempt as Daoud describes."

"Nor will I forget the cash-out," said Daoud, rising to meet Aristide's faux-pleasantry with a steel-edged smile. "All his shares, Jamila. And the money went to Frye's campaign."

"You wanted a puppet," she said, crossing her arms. "Why?"

Aristide opened his mouth, but Daoud slipped in before he could say anything.

"Cyril DePaul, infamous Ospie collaborator, and brand-new resident of some rat-infested jail in Amberlough. Haven't you heard? Mr. Makricosta does not prefer a safe and comfortable love affair. He prefers to be dragged through shit in the gutters, whipped and spat on all the way."

"As you well know," said Aristide, "I prefer to do the whipping."

Jamila sucked on this for a moment, much as she might have a piece of bone with particularly sticky marrow. Then she said, "That sculler on the radio? The one they arrested a while back?"

Excruciatingly courteous, Aristide opened a hand to Daoud, inviting him to speak first. He was rewarded with festering silence and had to answer for himself. "The very same."

"Men." Jamila shook her head. "Anything to shuck an oyster."

Neither of them deigned, or dared, reply.

Daoud rather conspicuously spent the rest of the day running errands. Aristide spent it with a bottle and a book, one of which got more attention than the other.

He dwelt, drunkenly, on Cyril's choked-off *In the photo, you looked so . . .* What? So happy? He had been numb or miserable for much of his time with Pulan. Forbidding? Surely not.

But however he had looked, it sent Cyril into the depths of the Lisoan jungle, almost losing him forever. Twice would be too many times.

Later that evening, rather deep in his cups, he got a call from the desk. Fumbling the receiver, he finally put it against his cheek and said, "Yes?"

"Sir, there's a woman here to see you. Jamila Osogurundi. Should I send her up or would you prefer to come down?"

Aristide looked around the parlor: a room service tray, listlessly picked through. Dirty glasses. Him in a dressing gown open over rumpled, sweaty clothing.

"I'll come down," he said. "Thank you."

When he picked his way to the bottom of the grand Y-staircase, freshly if somewhat sloppily dressed, Jamila was waiting in the lobby flipping through a magazine he couldn't imagine she was interested in.

"Ms. Osogurundi," he said. "Will you join me in the bar?"

She cased him over the magazine, one eyebrow raised. "You sure you need it?"

He refused to look down at himself, but did wonder if he'd got his buttons off by one, or left his fly open.

"I will order a coffee," he said, enunciating carefully.

Once they were settled in a booth, far at the back, she said, "I had that call with Cross."

Aristide reached for his watch, found he had left it upstairs, and said, "It was late in Rarom when we came to you."

"I woke her up."

Ah. This was not going to go well for him.

"I ain't even gonna roll this in sugar for you," she said. "You're out. With a boot print on your rear. You sold your shares, so Cross has the say-so, and she says *so*. I bet they picked her up on every receiver between here and Rarom. You're lucky our insurance paid out, or she might be on her way across the ocean with a dull knife and some pliers."

Aristide sipped his coffee. Still too hot.

"I don't think she'd mind if you left town." Jamila went on. "Maybe Gedda. Go somewhere slow and sit there quiet for a while, out of mind. She says, it's about time you retired from the life."

"Does she really?"

Jamila had never struck him as a squirmer, but she came close. "Qassan's got an open invitation to stay on," she said. "He's a good worker. But if you want to take him with you . . ."

His cup snapped back into the saucer with too much force. "I think we both know the answer to *that* question."

"Right." Jamila wouldn't meet his eyes.

"If that's all—" he began, rising from his seat.

But she shook her head. "Hang on, hang on. Listen."

"If it's about Daoud, I'd rather put a hatpin through my ear."

He saw her press down annoyance and gather herself overtop of it. "No," she said. "Sit back down."

"Please?"

"Damnation, Makricosta, I'm trying to do you a good one and you're making me regret it."

Slowly, he lowered himself back into the booth. "How so?"

"How are you making me regret it? I don't got enough fingers."

"Jamila."

She sighed heavily, dropping her shoulders and head into a weary slouch as though he'd placed a great burden on her. He thought this a trifle dramatic, as she was the one who had volunteered the favor. But he kept his mouth shut lest the situation escalate further into farce.

"This muff of yours they got in lockup," she said, voice low enough he had to lean in. "I asked around."

"Whom did you ask?" he asked. "And what about?"

"The kind of folk with names you don't just throw like seed," she said. "*My* folk. You ought to know; I hear you used to have the same kind of people yourself, back then. When you caused the right kind of trouble."

Under the table, his swollen hands made aching fists.

"They're taking him to the courthouse in a couple days. Dunno what for; my man ain't a lawyer. Point is, he knows when the transport leaves and he knows what route it takes."

The hairs on the back of Aristide's neck prickled as they rose.

"Now normally," Jamila went on, "you'd be sunk—they'd take Station Way straight through, under the Queen's eyes and everybody else's. But there's a big patch of trolley line still busted up where the Catwalk blew the Capitol transfer—where Armament meets Station. Concrete barriers, blocked-off intersections. They've got to go around."

Of course. He remembered the same situation on Temple Street, his cabbie cursing the drawn-out construction project.

"I ain't advocating anything, understand?" Jamila pulled out her billfold and thumbed thoughtfully through the cash therein. "Just saying, if you're on your way out of Amberlough anyhow . . ." Licking her thumb, she peeled a bill from the clip and set it on the table by her empty beer glass. "That ought to cover yours and mine."

Faintly, he said, "They'll charge it to the room."

Jamila smiled, like she knew what he was thinking. "I didn't want to sack you and then make you pay."

"Please," he said, voice gathering strength. The surface of the money was slick beneath his fingers, and it slid across the table toward her as if greased. "One good turn deserves another."

In better days, he would have fallen straight into the telephone, the details, the favors owed he could now call in. But there was barely time to consider all the details, and nobody in Amberlough owed him favors now.

Besides, he was paralytically drunk.

He put his carcass to bed, but hope and despair conspired to keep him from sleep. Horizontal in the darkness, at least his head didn't spin so badly.

Jamila had helped him, and might continue to do so, if he didn't ask too much. He might get a few spare hands off her, as long as her name didn't enter into things. He set that aside for the morning.

If they came out the other side of the escape unscathed, they wouldn't be able to stay in Gedda. He considered the options. Ports were bottlenecks and boats were traps. A land border would be better.

The idea of Enselem made his chest tighten, an iron band of irrational panic that made him think again of the prescription for amyl nitrate that he'd hastily torn to bits. He didn't like to think of himself as superstitious, but he wouldn't plan on crossing those mountains again.

Besides, he had friends in Tatié. Or, if not friends, the kind of contacts he no longer had in Amberlough. And in a war zone it was very easy to get lost.

Going by car would afford them flexibility, but cars needed fuel, which meant stops along the way: opportunities to be spotted. He also didn't currently *have* one. Nor did he have time to buy one tabletop or ready cash for anything illicit. Unfortunately, trains out of Gedda no longer stopped in Tatié, not unless you had a stack of papers as high as your head and months to wait around for clearance. And he didn't feature flinging himself out of one at speed before they hit the Ibetian border.

He lost track of the time making mental circles. The hour was very late when he heard the parlor door and the sound of boots toed off against the floor.

"Didi?" he called out, gin and loneliness overcoming his better judgment.

A long pause. He imagined Daoud standing, sock footed, considering his options. Maybe sighing. Then, "Aristide? You are still awake?"

Aristide didn't bother to answer. The bedroom door swung open, just wide enough to show a slender silhouette against the parlor lights. "Are you ill?"

"I need you to make a phone call."

"Right now?"

Aristide levered himself up and swallowed against a surge of nausea. "Yes. I know it's late. Early. But . . ."

"What is this?" asked Daoud, pushing the door open wider. Aristide blinked. Blind, he felt Daoud sit on the foot of the bed.

"Call Lillian," he said. Sacred arches, his head hurt.

"Aristide, it's half three."

"We're both awake. Call her right rotten now."

"To ask her *what*, exactly?"

"She knows Saeger. They've talked. Might know where to reach her."

"Absolutely not. What are you—?"

He stopped abruptly, because Aristide had gripped his upper arm. Tightly. As tight as he never had when he really wanted to. Through the layers of Daoud's coat he could feel the give of flesh, the stubbornness of bone.

"Saeger was Catwalk," said Aristide. "The Catwalk threw in with Tatié. I need to cross that border and she can help me."

"Why—? Aristide, please." He tried to pull away. "Pulan could—"

"She can't. *You* can ring some other folk for me to make travel arrangements—from the office; make it sound like a business trip, maybe. I'll write you out some notes for what I need." The cruelty of it caught up with him a little late, and by then he was barreling on. "The Tatien border, though, I have to handle soonest, and I can't be cabling back and forth with Porachis. That's bound to put a hound or two on the scent we don't want sniffing."

"Sniffing what? That *hurts*!"

Aristide let go, hand aching, and the momentum of Daoud's struggle pitched the younger man back.

"I'm getting out of Gedda one more time," he said. "And I won't leave him behind."

Daoud, held up on one elbow and spread across the bed, blinked once before comprehension made him crumple, then stand up.

"I will call," he said. "But only so you get some sleep."

"Lyle's," Daoud told him. "That's what the majordomo said. He wouldn't wake her, but he said there isn't an exchange in her date-book. She has met Saeger once, at a barroom called Lyle's just off Temple Street. That is all I can give you."

With that information in his possession, Aristide did not go back to bed.

He arrived at the place just past closing, scared a few regulars off their barstools, and mustered all of his old self that he could. Not the man Malcolm Sailer had hired to make bawdy jokes. Rather, the man who'd haggled Zelda Peronides to the bone, brought honest hounds around to graft, and scared scullers' guts clean if they even dreamed of cheating him.

He brought it to bear on the bartender, who eventually yielded to the manager, who fell under the onslaught and gave up an address.

By the time his cab pulled up out front of Saeger's building, dawn was seeping into the eastern sky. He tipped lavishly, half wondering if he'd be able to do so in the future. He'd given a lot of money to Frye's campaign for nothing, and didn't look likely to earn much more in the near future. What he was planning now was bound to be expensive, too.

A couple of bruisers, wearing Catwalk armbands and union pins, stood at either side of the stairs to Saeger's second precinct tenement. The building was unremarkable, slotted between two more just like it on a street of dry cleaners, bookmakers, and a green grocer's store. She hadn't let fame go to her head, apparently. Or perhaps it just hadn't reached her wallet.

"Nobody goes in," one of the bruisers said when he approached the steps. "'Cept when they've got a key to the building and we know their face."

"How much will it cost to give you knowledge of mine?"

"Nah," said his fellow. "We ain't like that."

"Does the name Cordelia Lehane mean much to you?"

"Much as it does to anyone. You ain't special for knowing it."

"Oh, but I am. Go on. You can ask Saeger if you like. Tell her Aristide Makricosta wants to see her. I'll wait down here."

And he did, until Saeger appeared on the doorstep in a sweater hastily thrown over pyjamas, rubbing sleep from her eyes and looking not in the least ministerial.

"Makricosta," she said. "I . . . not that it ain't a pleasure to meet you, but . . ."

"The pleasure's all mine," he said. "Or at least, I hope it will be."

"I don't like the sound of that." she said.

"We can get rid of him, if you want," said a bruiser.

Saeger shook her head, then chafed her arms. "Temple bells. It's too cold to stand here jawing."

"Well then, I guess you'd better let me in," said Aristide.

Looking more bemused than aggravated, Saeger stood aside and waved him up the steps.

"The thing that you're asking me to do," said Saeger, a little while later, "it could ruin me."

She was in the kitchen, making coffee. Aristide sat at her dining room table, taking in the spare apartment with its single bed. From the scrubbed table and counters, the bare floors, and recently beaten rug, he guessed at any other time those rumpled sheets would have been folded tight, the quilt tucked in at the edges. But he had hauled her out from under the covers at an inexcusable hour. Of course she hadn't made the bed for him.

"Forgive me for saying so—ah, thank you." The mug—enameled tin—nearly burnt his fingers. "But you're already ruined. Frye as good as nailed a terrorist attack on you."

"That wasn't my folk."

He bit down on *I know*. That wouldn't get him anywhere he wanted to be.

"Stones," said Saeger. "'My folk.' They ain't even that anymore. There ain't a Catwalk. Those hatch marks are just a handy flag to wave."

"No Catwalk?" he said. "Really?"

She shrugged. "Sure there's folk who *were* Catwalk. But Gedda don't need that now. And it ain't like bombing trains gives me any right or sense to lead a country." She blew on her coffee, staring despondently at the wall. "I ain't just a fighter. I wish more people clocked that."

"I'm not asking you to fight," he said.

"No. But you're asking me to take a few steps back toward it. Talk to those people. And a lot's changed in Tatié since we were yoked together. It's even odds or worse I could get ahold of someone who could help."

"But would you try?"

"Why should I? 'Cause I ain't got anything to lose? Stroll off. There's plenty past the Cliff House they can still take away from me. This could see me thrown in prison. It could get spun up as sedition, treason, espionage. The folk you want me to talk to, they're traitors to the nation of Gedda. I could be prosecuted."

"Then you'd better be very careful."

She put her cup down hard, so coffee sloshed across the scrubbed-raw surface of the table. "You got a lotta nerve. I ain't even looked sideways at saying yes."

"Not even for Cordelia's sake?"

"Don't bring her into this."

"She was brought into this eight years ago. She *chose* it. The person I need to get across the border was . . . was her friend. Like we were. And he didn't have a choice."

She shook her head, not looking at him. "People always have a choice. And if you're talking about who I think, he made the wrong one. She didn't."

In the pause that followed, Aristide took a steadying breath. "Ms. Saeger—"

"Queen's sake, just call me Opal."

"Opal. We're both from the same world, or close to. And so I hope you'll know it isn't vanity when I say you must know who I was. Or you must at least have heard of me."

She sipped her coffee, making him wait for her answer. Then, swallowing, she nodded and said, "Yeah. I knew your name. And enough about you to steer well clear."

"Probably wise." He removed his spectacles and pinched the bridge of his nose. "I only bring it up to make a point."

"Which is?"

"I was proud. Still am, with less reason. And I have rarely been a man to beg. But if you ask me to, I will *prostrate myself*. I will lie flat on the floor at your feet, and plead for your help like a Hearther penitent before an icon of my saint."

She considered him across the gray wood of the table, staring over the linen runner and the saltcellar, an ashtray full of butts. "Poetic. But then, you were in front of the curtain, not behind. Or up above. You know how to play to the punters."

"Almost my entire life has been an act of one sort or another," he told her. "But not this."

She leaned back in her chair. Sunrise struggled through the overcast outside, limning the fine hairs that outlined the contours of her face. He waited for her to speak, but she didn't. Only stared as steam rose from her cup.

If he had been on the boards, it would have been easy to slide from his chair. He would have been wearing pads over his knees, and the impact would not have sent a jolt through his bones straight into his teeth. Doctor Footlights would have cured his hangover, the ache in his heart, and the banging in his head.

If he had been under a spotlight, he would have been someone else. Only putting on a show. But he wasn't stagefolk anymore. He meant everything he did this time, and felt it.

"Oh, for . . . Makricosta." Saeger set her mug aside and held out her hands, as though she would grab him and stop him from taking the gesture any further.

"Cordelia died fighting for the things she lost." When was the last time he had wept? Is this what it had felt like? "Lillian put a whole new life together. But I didn't have the courage to die or change, and now he's the only thing that's left for me."

"Get up," said Saeger, voice ragged. "For Queen's sake, get off the floor."

"Please," he said, hanging his head and sinking lower. "I don't know how else to say it. Please."

"All right," she said. "All right," and scooted back in her chair as if afraid he might fall forward into her lap. Instead, he sat on his heels and lifted his face, eyes closing in relief.

"I'll make a call," she told him, standing up. Her palms she wiped on her thighs, as though they were soiled. "But not because it's right, and not because of Delia. I'll only help you two get out because this country ain't got room for cowards anymore."

CHAPTER

TWENTY-FIVE

Magnusson knew his way around a range well enough, but he was no Bradley, to stretch meager supplies into a meal worthy of the linen it was set on. Still, he'd gotten up something edible for dinner.

Lillian had no appetite for it, but Jinadh gave her that grandmother look he did so well, and so she managed a slice of toast and beans.

At her left hand, Stephen chewed in silence. When had he last spoken to either of them? Really spoken, and not some sharp remark in response to a reasonable request. Was this only growing pains, or was something really wrong? How was she to know? And where would she find the skills to fix it, when everything was crumbling around her?

"Have you done your reading this week?" she asked.

Stephen looked up from his plate, food stuffed into one cheek, and didn't answer.

"We had a letter from the school; they'd like to schedule your assessment exams."

"Why bother?" he said, into his beans.

"I'm sorry?"

He swallowed, overdramatic, and jammed his fork into the baked potato on his plate. "You *heard* what I said."

"Stephen." Jinadh laid his silverware down and glared at their son.

"What?" asked Stephen, digging out a lump of potato and mashing it with his beans. "There's no point in it. Everybody'll hate me. I'll never get into secondary, not after all this swineshit."

Jinadh scowled. «You *will* be respectful when you speak to your mother.»

"Don't turn all Porachin *papu* on me," said Stephen. "You hate that. It's why you rotten left."

Jinadh's mouth opened, but no sound came out. Lillian drew a breath, readying a scolding or an edict of banishment or some other castigation she never got to level, because glass shattering in the front hall cut her off.

"What—?" Jinadh began, half rising. But he was interrupted by a loud series of *bang*s, like gunfire but not quite.

Stephen was out of his chair before either of them, with the agility of the young and a mix of enthusiasm and relief that put a hot splash of anger through Lillian's gut. Their house had just been *attacked,* or something of that stripe, and he was glad to get out of a scolding?

And then she remembered he was thirteen, and a handful, and he would take any excuse to avoid a serious conversation.

Jinadh got out after him and Lillian followed, smelling cordite. Magnusson met them still wearing an apron streaked with soapsuds. Cold wind howled into the front hall through the broken front window, tearing smoke from a set of exploded firecrackers. The tile was scorched, and the rug smoldering, but beyond the window nothing was damaged. Thanks be, the house hadn't caught on fire.

Stephen was already poking at the husks of the explosives. "Jumbos," he said, eyes wide. "These are the *big* kind."

Lillian remembered a boy in Carmody who'd once stuffed a firecracker into a toad and hurled it after her as she ran. Nausea threatened, filling her mouth with spit.

"Ma'am," said Magnusson. "I'll fetch a broom. And some cardboard for the window. Would you like me to ring the police?"

"No," she said, imagining the scene, the story in the papers, the satisfaction it might give the bomber. The ideas it might plant in other people's heads. Better to keep this to themselves if they could. "But thank you. Stephen, put that down."

He had picked up a heavy stone from the center of the wreckage—smoking red paper, crumbling fuses, the tatters of a brown paper sack—and was weighing it in one hand. Soot streaked his palms.

"Lillian," said Jinadh, and inclined his chin toward the rock as though it deserved closer attention.

It was jagged at the edges, gray and mostly flat. Limestone, maybe, or a chunk of cement. The detonating firecrackers had marked it in places, but not scorched the surface beyond recognition. *Out of Gedda OSP rat*, it said. Stephen flipped it over with blackened fingers. Parallel lines on the other side, hashed regularly along their length. Train tracks. Crude but recognizable. The Catwalk, or what Saeger's supporters had made of it. That was who had bombed her home.

A memory surfaced: Cordelia Lehane lingering in the gallery of the entrance hall at Hadhariti, her face gone pale with shock as the gruesome puzzle of Cyril's past came together. Then, Lillian had compared her to a ghost, a haunting. She had been a piece of a lost world, and half lost herself: grieving, defeated, confused. For her— for all of them—the boundaries between friend and enemy, right and wrong, had been blurred by necessity.

Alive, would she have thrown a bomb through the front windows of Coral Street? Lillian didn't think so. It was death and narrative that had warped her memory into an avenging revenant. A poltergeist.

Would Saeger herself have thrown this incendiary? Lillian thought back to their few interactions. The candidate stiff and formal in her gala dress, then burning with frustration in a basement pub, afraid that all her hopes for her country might be thwarted if she lost this election. She might not be a canny politician, but she knew firebombing people's houses wouldn't win her votes.

Nobody Lillian knew had thrown this through her window. And no one who knew her. Someone had seen her as a symbol, too. To them this was just like defacing a monument, or tearing down a flag.

In bed, in the small hours, Lillian tucked her cold feet beneath Jinadh's thigh and felt him flinch awake.

"Sorry," she said, and made to pull away.

He laid his hand on her ankle underneath the covers and held her where she was. «They'll warm up.»

She chewed at her lip and felt dry skin split. After too many years in the tropics, she had forgotten how the cold could turn skin into paper, tearing where it creased. «Jinadh.»

He made a sleepy sound.

«Should we stay?»

Silence.

«In Gedda,» she said, in case he hadn't clocked her.

A pause, before he rolled over. In the dark, she could only make out the curve of his cheek against the lighter black, the reflection of faint moonlight in his eyes.

«Do you *want* to leave?» he asked.

She hesitated, though she had asked the question. «It *does* make sense. If Stephen doesn't get back into Cantrell, nothing keeps us here except your job.»

«I can't ask to be transferred again so soon. Especially not right now, with . . . these complications. I can't expect special treatment; the opposite, perhaps.»

«Could you not just speak to them? Explain this is a matter of—» She let it hang, implying rocks through the window, firecrackers smoking on the rug. All the things that might come afterward, much worse.

«I think it will have to be something more extreme than this, for me to make that argument. And I'd prefer not to reach that point.»

«You don't want to leave?» She pushed herself up on one elbow. «But you hate it here.»

«I like my work,» he said. «I like Siebenthal's, and the *Observer*. I don't want to lose this job, and I don't want to start again with nothing. Especially not now, with Stephen . . . » A flash of light as he cast up his eyes, toward the bedroom ceiling or the heavens. «I don't think it is a good time to put him through another transition.»

«And you think he will fare any better here? School will be . . . he will not have an easy time.»

«None of us will have an easy time,» he said. «No matter what we do. And our finances won't support a move.»

«We could sell the house. Or . . . or Damesfort.» She said it swiftly so her aching throat wouldn't close around the words.

He looked at her gravely. «Lillian. The estate?»

"Hang the estate. It's only property." But her voice broke when she said it, cracking against memories of hide-and-seek, fresh strawberries, the last time her family had been under one roof and some semblance of happy.

«*You're* the one who doesn't want to leave,» he said. «We could have stayed in Sunho, but you wanted to come back. You started to talk about it the day Acherby's government fell.»

Heat crept up her cheeks, and she cursed and welcomed it equally. No one but Jinadh could make her blush like this. Rarely did anyone matter enough to her that they could make her feel ashamed. "I'm so sorry." She sagged back into the pillows, hiding her face against the flannel case. «I didn't know how badly it would go. And I dragged you into it.»

«I was not dragged,» he said. «I have learned to dig in my heels, a little bit. I'm here because I love you, and it made you happy to come home. Heaven's eyes see my own home is far from perfect, but if the same thing were somehow possible for me . . . » His voice hitched, there, threatening to come apart as hers had. «I would hope for the same consideration from you.»

It never would be, though: Porachis was lost to him forever. He had wanted so badly to escape, but she knew there were things and people that he missed, that he would likely never see again. Her compassion and loyalty would never be tested as his had. She reached for his hand under the covers, and his grip made her bones ache.

«You will have to work,» he said.

«I know.»

«What will you do?» And then, with a tinge of despair, «Will anyone take you?»

Head heavy on the pillow, she wondered the same thing.

Jinadh fell asleep again easily. Lillian, less so. The sound of breaking glass played in her memory like a skipping record. Every breath convinced her there was still gunpowder in the air.

Maybe if she read a little bit, or just went down to lie on the sofa in the library. Sometimes a change in scenery killed her insomnia. The cushions weren't as soft as the bed, but she didn't need comfort: only distraction.

The draft bit at her elbows, and she dug for the quilted dressing gown she kept folded at the foot of the bed, beneath the covers where it would stay warm. Slippers, too—she anticipated the icy floor with dread. It was warmer here than in Carmody, but barely.

When the library door swung open she met the wary eyes of her son, who had apparently heard her coming in time to scramble up from the sofa, but not in time to do much else. He held the afghan to his chest with two tight fists and stared at her.

"Steenie," she said, one hand over her heart. "Temple *bells,* you scared me."

"Sorry," he said. Slowly he grew less frozen, and she realized she had scared him, too, though he was not going to admit it.

"Can I sit with you?" she asked, a little awkward in asking permission. If he had been younger, sweeter, his growing limbs less sharply lined in firelight, she would have simply sat beside him. "I can't get to sleep."

He nodded, and settled uneasily onto the sofa.

She took the arm opposite, a safe several feet between them. "You couldn't sleep, either?"

He glared at her, and she relapsed into silence. Sitting near him was a privilege. She had not been given leave to speak.

In the quiet that fell between them she heard the radio on low—a late-night drama of hushed voices, faint sound effects. Probably something she wouldn't have let him listen to, if he had asked. Now, she let it go. It seemed less important than it might have, under different circumstances.

She wanted very badly to fill the silence; she had never been good at letting other people speak first. But a growing tension from the other side of the sofa told her Stephen was incubating something important, so she bit the inside of her cheek and stared into the coals.

"They just wanted to scare us," he said, and it sounded like he was trying to convince himself. "They could have made a real bomb. They could have blown up the house."

A gunshot from the radio, and a woman's exaggerated scream. Both of them jumped. Lillian let out a nervous huff of laughter, and suddenly—

"It wasn't Uncle Cyril," he said. "The police car. It was me."

She blessed her exhaustion; it kept everything she might have felt far away, behind a fog. Fear, surprise, outrage. All she could manage was a sigh, and her hand cupped to catch her falling head. "That's a bit bigger than a pencil sharpener."

"I didn't think it would stop them or anything." He didn't look at her as he spoke, and she was glad; his anger would have burnt hotter than the hearth into which it was directed. "I just wanted . . . it wasn't fair. And I knew how to do it, so I did."

"You knew how . . . Cyril, I suppose." He didn't answer that. She didn't need him to. "Someone could have been hurt," she said. "Killed."

This time he did turn toward her, and gave her a look that made her feel she'd missed a lesson and just given an unpardonably stupid answer to an easy question.

"I knew what I was doing," he said. Not arrogantly, but with affronted confidence. "Uncle Cyril taught me. I did it right."

"You blew up a *car*, Steenie." And then, mother love her, she began to laugh.

He regarded her suspiciously until she wiped her eyes, and then asked, "Aren't you angry?"

"I'm *furious*," she said. "I just . . . Oh, holy stones. You didn't think at all." Her head fell back against the upholstery, giving her a good view of the ceiling and the dusty medallion around the lamp. In the quiet, she could hear the squeak of coals shifting in the grate.

Stephen, perhaps knocked off his high ground by her hysterics, pulled himself out of his slouch and drew his knees to his chest. "If I don't go back to school, what will you do with me?"

She paused, considered, and wondered where this was headed. "Well. If you can't finish out the year at Cantrell—which I hope you'll be able to do—there are still any number of secondary schools I'm sure would take you. If not in Gedda, then abroad."

"You're going to send me away?"

"That isn't what I said at all."

He had found a moth hole in the afghan and begun to fret with it, worsening the damage.

"What's this about?" she asked. "Really."

"Uncle Cyril," he began, and of course it was. "He told me when he messed things up, at school, Granddad sort of . . . packed him off. And that's how he ended up how he is. That Granddad made him be a spy and all."

"What did he tell you?" She had been smart enough to guess at half of it—that her father had something to do with Cyril being packed off to train as a kit for the FOCIS. Now it sounded like Stephen knew the whole. She felt cheated, somehow. And exiled from her own family history. She felt less like a DePaul, for only finding this out now. She felt less like Cyril's sister, and it hurt more than she might have thought.

Stephen finally met her eyes. "That Granddad gave up on him after he was nearly tossed from school. Because of that stuff in Tatié— the teacher who spotted him and all. He made a deal to keep him out of jail, so the family wouldn't look bad." After a long pause on Lillian's part, he said, "Didn't you know?"

The simple answer was yes, of course. But she hadn't, really; none of the details. And she hadn't ever asked.

Cyril had been in Tatié, a school trip. She had been home after her first assignment. After three years pushing paper and supporting the beleaguered consul in Gurunda-rai—her father could have seen her placed somewhere more comfortable, but he insisted the experience would build skill and character, and he'd been right— she had only wanted a peaceful summer before her next foray.

She had arrived to strangling tension. No screaming fights—that had made it strange. Only closed doors, low voices, a palpable air of fury and disaster. The abbreviated explanation was that Cyril had well and truly torn it up this time, might be sent down, could even be arrested, and needed something to straighten him out. These were not new sentiments, but this time there was an air of finality to it all; a new determination.

He disappeared a week later, for "a job with the state," and the promise he'd be gone for a good long while.

"I . . ." The radio played footsteps, the creaking of a door. "Stee- nie, I'm not going to . . . I didn't know." She wanted to tell him she wasn't like her father, but that was patently untrue. She had striven every day of her adult life to emulate his skill, his poise, to live up to his name. A name that was now poison, which Stephen would have to bear. "They never did get along," she said, instead.

It was the wrong thing. "Like us."

"I *love* you, Steenie." It got her a sideways glance, which was all she could have hoped for. "All right, you're a tangle in my reins. I won't say you aren't."

His shoulders came up around his ears. "So you don't *like* me."

"Steenie," she said, and wanted to put a hand on his bare foot where it lay, just inches from her hand. He should be wearing socks;

it was too cold for skin. "I . . . I don't think I know you well enough to answer that."

"I'm your *son*," he said, indignant.

"Do *you* like *me*?" she asked.

His mouth did something that reminded her neither of Jinadh, nor of herself, and the truth of what she'd said struck her squarely in the heart—he was becoming his own person. It was terrifying, and incredible; she had made and raised someone who had grown opaque to her. A stranger.

She opened one arm. Stephen peered at her skeptically, so she raised her eyebrows and said, "Don't be a beast, beastie." It was what she'd called him when he was probably too small to remember, when Stephen or even Steenie seemed too big a name for such a tiny thing.

Almost managing to look put-upon, he shifted across the sofa cushions so she could settle her arm around his shoulders.

"What's the jail like on the inside?" he asked. "Are there bars and all?"

He wanted to know about Cyril, and of course he wouldn't ask. He was a DePaul. Why come at anything straight-on?

"Dull," she said, because she couldn't stand to tell him what he wanted to hear. "Cold. The furniture is ugly."

"Can I go sometime?"

"We'll see."

He made a small, assenting sound, and the weight of his head relaxed against her shoulder. The next time she looked down, he had fallen asleep.

She didn't manage the same, and was still awake to say good morning when Magnusson came to stoke the coals.

CHAPTER
TWENTY-SIX

Aristide swept his hands across the recently cleaned desk of his hotel suite. He had forgotten what color the blotter was. Boxes and sealed envelopes were stacked against one wall. Some were bound back to Liso for Cross. Many he would consign to the incinerator. Or rather, consign to Daoud for incineration. Various bribes, rewards, and remunerations—a healthy chunk of his remaining funds—were among the ephemera, ready to be distributed as his needs required. He hoped he wouldn't need most of it, but he did like to be prepared.

Daoud was taking inventory of the boxes in his little blue notebook, checking their labels against some list he had scribbled earlier, presumably while he packed. He kept his nose firmly pressed between the pages, eyes cast down. Tension made the air thick as set aspic.

Reaching the end of the row of boxes, Daoud made a last tick mark and pinched his book closed so fast the paper snapped.

"That is everything," he said. "You are well set to leave Amberlough City."

"Good." Aristide opened his jacket, and took out an envelope. "That's for you."

Daoud watched him from across the room, but made no move to come closer. His eyes grew cold, and a certain haughty lift came into his posture.

"Severance." Aristide dropped it on the blotter—a very nice shade of sage green, really. "More than generous, I think, given the terms of your contract."

"I am remaining with Cross-Costa, Aristide. You are not. I do not think it is your right to sack me."

Familiar pain from a bad tooth plagued Aristide when he clenched his jaw. "Take the rotten money."

"Why? To ease your conscience?" Daoud sneered. "I am not a whore."

"Don't be so dramatic."

"Dramatic? I am not the one who is planning some sort of *jailbreak*—"

"*Didi*," he said, because the pet name came more easily. He hadn't realized, until then, how hard the dental consonants could crack against his teeth in anger.

Apparently, neither had Daoud. He stopped abruptly, and the blood drained from beneath his dark brown skin, leaving his face flat and hollow.

"You aren't going to cry, are you?" Embarrassed, Aristide retreated to the firm ground of cruelty.

The notebook was out of Daoud's hand so fast that at first Aristide didn't understand what had struck the far wall. And then Daoud was in front of him, palms pressed to the desk, eyes decidedly dry and alight with fury. "What is *wrong* with you, Aristide?"

"Not a damned thing," he snapped. "I know it was you who told

Lillian about Frye. I'll thank you not to run out to every society lady you see, begging them to take me on for the sake of charity."

"Then do not act as though you need it! How many times this month do you remember putting yourself to bed? And the mischief you get up to . . . *bhakchala*, Aristide, if nobody looks after you, you will drown in your own sick."

"And you think it should be you? Because you clearly find it so rewarding."

"Nobody is going to do it for you in prison! And I doubt that Cyril DePaul will manage!"

"Lower your voice at once," demanded Aristide, looking over his shoulder as though someone might have overheard.

Daoud snatched up the envelope between them. "I do not follow your orders anymore. Not if you truly wish me to take this."

"You'll take it and turn tail." Aristide didn't know when he had stood from his chair, but he suddenly realized he was towering over Daoud, talking down and at volume to a man who had never grown past his slight adolescence.

It deflated his rage somewhat, and made him, paradoxically, feel small. Sinking back into his chair, he let Daoud's glare push him deep into the upholstery. Eventually, the strength of it even pushed down his eyes. Staring at his fingers, steepled before his lips, he spoke to the garnet on his pinkie.

"I'm sorry," he said. The words dragged through him like barbed wire, but he pulled them out all the same. If this was the last time they ever saw one another . . . life had taught him the utility of closure. "Daoud, you've been very . . . useful to me."

He laughed, one harsh exclamation, and said, «A convenience.»

«No.» Aristide assayed it in Porashtu though he was bound to fail. «A . . . a firm place. A great help. And a friend.»

"I expect an excellent reference," said Daoud, and walked out the door.

"Ma'am," said Magnusson, from the door to the second-story office—she had begun to inhabit it, as though sitting at a desk might translate to work, and pay. How Daddy would have blanched at the thought.

But Daddy hadn't been quite the good example she had made him out to be. Never had been.

"Yes?" She looked up from the household accounts, which she had spread across the badly scuffed blotter. The previous tenants had left the desk, but taken or sold the leather seat and filing cabinets, so she had brought a dining room chair up for the moment.

"That young man is here to see you. Mr. Qassan."

Odd. He hadn't rung, and she hadn't spoken to Aristide in some time. What could he be after? "Bring him up, please."

Daoud's appearance did not inspire confidence: a coat thrown over his suit, but no scarf and no hat on his head. The weather was warming, slightly, but it had not grown so temperate. Bloodshot eyes at the center of a pinched face cemented her suspicion that he had not come bearing good news.

"Mr. Qassan," she said, standing from her chair and realizing too late there was no other to offer him. "Perhaps we could repair to the library? It will be warmer there."

He managed something between a nod and a shrug, then bit down hard on his lower lip and dissolved into tears.

Alarmed, Lillian froze for a brief moment before compassion got her across the room. Daoud was small in her arms, not much bigger than Stephen, and since she was in pumps, his head fit just beneath her chin if she stretched up a little way. Weeping took ten years off his age, and if she guessed right he had not yet reached thirty.

"Queen's sake," she said, rubbing circles on his back. "What's happened?"

He tried to breathe, but lost it to a sob. She felt his fist close on the loose knit of her cardigan.

"Magnusson?" she called, over his head.

The discreet butler reentered her line of sight from his post to the side of the door. "Yes, ma'am?"

"Fetch some whiskey, will you? Mr. Qassan is, er . . . indisposed."

By the time Magnusson returned with the liquor, she had got Daoud settled into the straight-backed dining room chair, and was leaning one hip on the corner of the desk. Magnusson poured two glasses and left the decanter.

"Now," she said, once Daoud had gotten a swallow down his throat. "What's the problem?"

He pulled an envelope from inside his coat and dropped it onto his knees. "Severance pay, of a sort. I . . . I am still employed by Cross-Costa, but Aristide . . ." His face crumpled.

Lillian drank her whiskey to give herself time and then, as tenderly as she could manage: "Threw you over?"

His free hand made a fist, grinding into the top of his thigh. «Nothing so simple as that.»

He was too far away to comfort easily with touch, and anyway, now he looked too proud. Lillian set aside her glass and pressed her fingers to her lips, half in thought and half in sympathy.

«I'm sorry,» she said, joining him in Porashtu.

He shook his head. «No, it was long past time. I needed . . . we needed to end it. Still, I should be furious. I *am* furious. But also, terrified.»

«Of what?»

«Ms. DePaul—»

«Lillian,» she insisted. They had been through enough for that.

«Lillian. He's already done something very foolish for your brother . . . »

«And you think he is going to do something else.»

He closed his eyes, and she saw the lids were shiny with fatigue, stained purple and threaded with broken blood vessels. «I know he is.»

She waited. He was going to tell her, or he wouldn't have come.

«When they take Cyril to the courthouse, Aristide has . . . I was not part of this. I only booked their passages, found room in a hotel. I rang up some of Pulan's people, and put him in touch with—»

«Daoud.»

She saw him right his wobbling voice, steady his panic. «They're going to run.»

"Sorry?" she said. Then, «Wait, no. Please, don't tell me. I can't . . . the fewer people who know, it is better.»

Roughly, he wiped at his cheek with the back of his hand. "I apologize," he said. «But I can't talk to him anymore. And I needed to talk to someone. What do I do? I don't know what to do.»

The edge of the desk pressed into the backs of her thighs as her weight sank into it. Defeated? Relieved? It was hard to tell the difference. «Why do you need to do anything?»

Daoud stared at her, poleaxed. «He's . . . he's going to be arrested.»

Guilt, exhaustion, but yes. Horribly, the feeling was relief. «Whatever he does now, it is not your concern.» Was she talking about herself? Not quite. Cyril had not planned this scheme. More, she was speaking to the sense of grasping, the need to steer the course of events according to her own map. «It will work, or it will not work. You cannot stop him. All you can do is . . . » She tapped one finger on the surface of the blotter, searching for the word. "React. That's what you control. Your own reaction to events. Not him. Not the world. Only yourself." Tears made tiny prickles of pain at the inner corners of her eyes.

"I hate that," he said.

She laughed. "Perhaps we should found an association."

Daoud sipped his whiskey, then spoke to it. «I don't know what I'm going to do.»

«Do you want to go back to Porachis?»

He shuddered like a pony shedding flies. «Heaven's eyes, for what?»

She shrugged. «I just thought to ask. Will you stay with Cross-Costa?»

«For now, though not forever. I don't suppose *you* need a secretary?» He had the decency to put his hope behind a scrap of humor, so it didn't look quite so naked.

«Even if I could afford it, I would not hire you.» He looked stung, and rightly so, but she put up a hand to stop him interjecting. «How old are you?»

«Twenty-seven.»

«And what have you ever done for yourself?»

«I pay my way,» he said. «And send money to my parents.»

She shook her head. «I am not talking about money. When you worked for Satri, I rarely saw her without you at her elbow. I imagine it was the same for Aristide.»

«It was my job.»

«Was it your job to drop down on him?» The Porashtu idiom had always struck her as needlessly vulgar, but she employed it now for effect and it worked. Daoud's anger curdled into grief and shame.

«Did you love him?» she asked.

He drew a breath as if to speak, then shook his head. «It was . . . he seemed like he needed something to hold onto.»

«And you like to be useful, very much.»

«You make me sound pathetic.»

«I didn't mean to.»

But he was shaking his head. «He told me that I wasn't a challenge. And I think he's right.» She saw him shove aside a fresh bout of weeping. «I'll go,» he said, moving to discard his half-drunk whiskey on her desk. «I'm sorry.»

«No.» She put her hand to his glass and stopped him setting it down. «Please.»

«Why?»

She cast around the bare, chilly room for an excuse, but nothing convenient presented itself. That left her with the truth. «I said I did not want you as a secretary. But I would like to keep you as a friend.»

Daoud stayed for dinner, and made no comment on the quality of the food. In fact, by the end of the meal he seemed almost happy— to be speaking his own language again, as an individual at a table of equals, out from under the shadow of his erstwhile employer.

After Stephen went upstairs, ostensibly to study for his imminent reentry exam, they adjourned to the library for drinks and the welcome warmth of the fire. Lillian, who had been looking at the accounts when Daoud dropped in, mourned the last of a decanter of Tolishnaughcaul. That was an extravagance they couldn't sustain.

«Will you go back to Sykes House tonight?» Lillian asked, watching Daoud navigate the complexities of the peated whiskey.

He cleared his throat. «I should. My things are there. And it is too late now to go looking for new accommodations.»

«We would offer you a place here,» said Jinadh, who had been briefly apprised of the situation. «Unfortunately, the spare bedrooms aren't exactly inhabitable right now.» As in, they both lacked beds, and most other necessary accoutrements.

Daoud shook his head. «It's all right. I'm a grown man; I shouldn't mind.»

«If only that were how aging worked.» Jinadh tipped the rest of his whiskey back and then said, «Bad manners, but I'm afraid I need to get to bed. You two stay up as long as you like.»

«No, no.» Daoud stood, too. Lillian noticed he had not finished his drink. She was above pouring it back into the decanter once he'd gone, but certainly not above finishing it for him.

There was an awkward moment in which Jinadh and Daoud didn't quite know how to say goodbye—Daoud put his hand out for a shake and interrupted Jinadh's attempt at a cheek-to-cheek air kiss. If this had been an embassy ball or some other diplomatic occasion, Lillian would have blanched. But instead it gave her a spot of sorely needed mirth.

"Before you go," she said, after Jinadh had left them, "I have a favor to ask."

"Of course."

"In the future," she said, sweeping the library ladder from the corner, "you might ask what you're agreeing to. I've avoided too many scrapes to count, that way."

His laugh was rueful. "I will make a note."

She lined the ladder up beneath the third decorative panel from the wall and climbed past empty shelves. Depressing a latch disguised as an ivy leaf, she released the panel from the wall to reveal a combination safe. "Hold this?" she asked.

Failing to hide his surprise, Daoud took the panel from her.

She spun the dial through its paces and the safe swung silently open to reveal a velvet box containing Grandmama's medals, her mother's diamond collar, and her parents' wedding rings. If the previous occupants had found this safe, she imagined it all would have vanished along with the paintings and the furniture. She might have to sell the jewels herself, if fortune didn't fill the family's sails and soon.

Under the baubles was a small pile of papers. Her wedding contract, Stephen's birth certificate, the deeds to Damesfort and to Coral Street. Beneath it all, in a plain brown envelope: a passport for Ambrose van Weill.

She slipped this free and locked the safe again, then climbed down and gave the little booklet to Daoud. He flipped the passport open to Cyril's photograph: half starved and all wrung out.

"I know you don't want to speak to Aristide again," she said, "but since you said you'll be going back to Sykes House . . . I don't know if it will do him any good, with the fraud charges and all, but I thought it was better he had it. In case it can be of some use."

Daoud put the passport into the pocket of his greatcoat. "I will give it to him."

«Thank you,» she said, and meant it. Then, «You might take a roundabout route, getting back. Just to throw them off the trail.»

«Who's sniffing?» he asked.

«That pack of vultures out front,» she said. «And heaven's eyes see whatever else.»

«I'll swap cabs,» he said. «Maybe stop for a drink somewhere. So hopefully, we won't find out.»

Cyril was resting his eyes, half wishing for a newspaper and knowing he wouldn't be able to concentrate on any printed page, when he heard the clang of a steel door and, beneath its echoes, a tense, whispered conversation in the corridor perpendicular to his cell. Markert, and some other guard. It had the rhythm of street market haggling, by which Cyril surmised it might be a discussion of bribery.

The whole thing ended in under thirty seconds, with Markert's declaration—so loud Cyril heard it clearly—that this had better not happen again. It struck a false note. He must have come out wealthier in the deal.

A freckled, brawny guard—Pryzbieza, fond of Cyril because he could pronounce the surname none of her colleagues could—came to unlock his cell.

"Visitor," she said. "Your sister. Markert didn't want to let her in after hours, but . . ."

"I hope you kept a little for yourself."

"Enough to drink on, after work. Come on, let's go."

He let her handcuff him and went meekly down the corridor, wondering what Lillian wanted.

Her face gave him no clues. When he sat, she produced a single cigarette from her coat pocket, which he took gratefully.

"How's it turning?" he asked, around the straight.

"As it has been." She had a book of matches, too, and struck one for him.

"What brings you to my humble drawing room tonight? And how much did it cost?"

"Rather more than I can afford, these days."

"Is that why you haven't been visiting?"

She didn't blush; instead, shame made her mouth grim.

"Don't feel bad," he said. "I'd rather keep the money out of Markert's pocket."

It didn't cheer her up. He leaned in, setting the straight on the edge of the table with one finger on the end to steady it, keep it from falling. Lillian had not merited an ashtray.

"Lil," he said, "is something wrong?"

"No." She marshaled her expression, and though she favored their mother in the breadth of her face and the shape of her eyes, suddenly he saw Father in her: the puppeteer's control, the careful presentation.

If she had put on her professional mask, something was very wrong indeed.

"You're all right," he said. "Is it Stephen? Aristide?" Then, belatedly, "Jinadh?"

The delay earned him a rueful look, her mouth twisted to the side by a hook of pained amusement. "Everything is fine, Cyril. Can't I come see you without news, or an ulterior motive? You're my brother."

There. Something flickered beneath her practiced polish. Like the flash of a startled fish in dappled water, it was gone again before he knew what he had seen.

But she didn't want to talk about it. Or . . . He cut his eyes toward the wire-crossed observation window, to the bored-looking guards behind it. One woman smoked; another picked at her hangnails. Only Markert, supervising his more junior associates, still watched them closely. And then there was Pryzbieza, leaning on the wall not ten feet away. His conversations with Rinko were ostensibly private, by law. His conversations with Lillian did not have that privilege.

Whatever it was, maybe she *couldn't* talk about it here. And he would have to guess her purpose.

"Your brother," he said. "I am. And a heap of good it's done you."

"I don't know." She managed a smile. The glare of the bad lights over her eyes showed him they were wet, though the tears didn't make it to her voice. "I think you gave me a good example of what *not* to do."

"And somebody convenient to blame all your mischief on."

"Cy," she said, suddenly grave. "I'm so sorry for what Daddy did to you."

Surprise put a rod down his spine. "What do you mean?"

"Stephen told me, about . . . after Tatié. I never knew." She struggled with her words for a moment, then said, "No. That isn't true. I guessed. I just . . . I knew I wouldn't like what you were up to."

"That's why you never asked?" When she'd come to his hospital bed, she'd straightened his blankets and said empty things. Never wondered aloud how he came to be there. Never asked why they'd had to haul his guts out of his belly, or where he'd been, or why he hadn't written. Why he had stopped speaking to his father, except in small sentences, when they were forced together by circumstance.

"If I had," she said, "would you have told me anything?"

He wondered if she had been more afraid he wouldn't tell her, proving some deep connection between them well and truly severed, or more afraid he would, revealing his absolute lack of integrity. Perhaps she feared whatever character defect he had was catching.

"I was walking the edge of that cliff anyway," he said.

"Still." She laced her fingers and he saw the skin where they touched go white with the pressure of her grip. "He shouldn't have pushed you off."

"Why are you apologizing for him?" This was a betrayal of everything Cyril had ever understood about his sister. The diplomat, the perfect daughter. The DePaul worthy of the name that he, Cyril, had summarily destroyed.

"Because someone has to. Somebody has to apologize for our entire rotten family." Anger made a thin line of her lips, pushed her gaze down and to one side. "I just wanted to do it before . . ."

"Before what, Lil?" The arraignment? Whatever came after the election? She had plenty of time for that, surely.

Pryzbieza cleared her throat. "Time's up."

"See you in court, I suppose," he said, trying for a smile.

She failed to return it, and shook her head. "I truly hope you don't."

That threw him. "Lil?"

But she shook her head and buttoned her coat and only said, "I love you, Cyril. Goodbye."

CHAPTER

TWENTY-SEVEN

Aristide woke before dawn, aching and nauseous, heartburn claw-ing up the back of his throat. A lesser—or maybe better—man would have been defeated by the sensation, but Aristide was habitu-ated to hangovers. Struggling from sweaty, tangled sheets he reached for the glass of water at his bedside but found it missing.

He had on last night's clothes. The light was still on. His head spun when he sat up.

He hadn't been able to sleep. Why had he been awake so late? Why had he opened the fresh bottle of gin on the bar cart?

Ah. Because today, today he would meet with two of Jamila's un-official employees, Tabby and Chido, at the corner where they had spent the two days previous mapping escape routes, obstacles, ad-vantages.

Two days had not been enough time. Jamila had come to him late, had given him no time for the kind of planning this venture required. There were bribes he would have liked to pay, if he knew to whom they should go. He had his Erikh Prosser passport—unused since he traveled to Porachis, always kept close in case of need—and a ticket under that name, but no papers or itinerary for Cyril. As it stood, there was half a plan for the extraction, a hotel two countries over, and Saeger's word somebody would help them get there. After that, if they made it so far, things would go more smoothly.

Then again, when he had time and resources, all his plans had gone awry. Maybe this strategy—or lack thereof—would serve him better.

Leaning on the doorframe, Aristide looked out at the gloomy parlor, empty of its boxes now. Daoud's coat was still missing, and now his hat and scarf had gone as well. Silence hung over the room, disturbed only by the occasional chime of a distant trolley bell.

And in the center of his otherwise empty desk, a flimsy booklet. Perhaps three inches by four. Aristide wove across the room and dropped heavily into the chair.

Thick green card stock embossed with the Enselmese national crest, placed on a piece of the hotel stationery. A note, in Daoud's hand: *From a friend*.

Aristide opened it to reveal a haggard photograph of Cyril De-Paul, partially obscured by visa stamps, above the name *Ambrose van Weill*.

Well. That would solve some problems, maybe. Not as it was, of course. This passport was a piece of evidence in Cyril's convenient fraud case. But perhaps, if altered slightly . . .

Mother's tits, it had come to this. Forgery had never been a strong suit, for the monarch of the demimonde. The closest he had ever come to caught was forging cheques, early in his career. Once he could afford it, he hired folk to make his fakes for him. What he wouldn't give for Zelda Peronides now.

Scamming in this city used to come as easily as breathing. But this was the only gasp of air he'd gotten, so he'd better take it.

Cyril had borrowed Aristide's pen to fill out the pages of the passport, so the nib and ink wouldn't be a problem. The penmanship, however . . .

It occurred to him that he couldn't remember what Cyril's handwriting looked like, and whether or not this was it. He had never learned to copy the other man's signature or calligraphy. Why would he have needed to know?

Letting out a ragged breath, he held the passport close to his eyes to study the idiosyncrasies, and then realized the text was blurry because his spectacles were still beside the bed. Once he had retrieved them and held them in his hand, he realized the offending extremity was shaking.

That would never do.

In deference to the hour, he chose a can of tomato juice to mix with his gin instead of vermouth. It went down pasty and tasted mostly of salt. He cleared his throat and poured another shot, unadulterated, which he took back to the desk with him.

On a scrap of hotel stationery, he fiddled with *Ambrose van Weill*, adding letters where they would fit, modifying others. Perdition, why had Cyril chosen such an awkward name? Though Enselmese Ambroses were common as Jacks in Gedda, so really that left the surname, with its bothersome preposition. The *v* could be changed to an A, perhaps, and . . .

Yes. Ambrose Adam Wallis. That was doable. Perhaps one of his parents came from the Hellican Islands.

Aristide put the pen down, breathed deep, checked his hands were steady. Then picked it up again and put it to the paper. The less thought that went into this, the better.

In victory, he reached for his gin. Heart hammering and fingers numb, he fumbled and watched in horror as the glass wobbled and then tipped, spilling across the fresh ink of his forgery.

Terrified and still a bit drunk, Aristide sat behind the wheel of a box van hauling a load of soiled laundry. Ahead of him, Tabby rode shotgun in the cab of a fish truck beside Jules, a driver Aristide had only met this morning. Chido was hidden amongst the mussels and twitching crates of pollock.

Aristide hadn't driven a van in decades. He had never broken someone out of jail. It was much more expedient to buy people's freedom with money and favors, and less likely to see him locked up in turn.

It wasn't jail, he reminded himself, idling behind the fish truck in a narrow alley waiting for their target to come by. It was just a kind of carjacking. He'd done that. Back in the foggy moors of his past, yes, but he'd absolutely stolen a car out from under its driver.

This time, all he had to do was provide cover. Park the box van behind his conspirators to partially block them from sight while they got the job done. He wasn't even carrying a gun. Better not to be found with one, if it came to that. Which it wouldn't.

None of it would be his responsibility. Which meant none of it would be under his control. He didn't know whose dirty laundry he was hauling. Didn't know where Chido and Tabby had found Jules, or where they'd gotten the vans. He felt like he'd pushed a sled down a hill, hopped in, and was now at the mercy of the landscape.

He did not like that this feeling had become familiar.

Ahead of him, the fish truck coughed into motion, turning left out of the alley and into the jerky flow of traffic redirected from

Station Way. Aristide stomped on the accelerator and trundled after them—the steel-toed boots of his disguise made him clumsy.

A cab tried to cut him off but he leaned into the horn and pushed past, keeping close to the fish truck's bumper. Angry drivers beeped and made rude gestures. He gave a few back, and almost rear-ended Tabby and Jules. Stopped for a moment, he imagined Chido hidden behind those canvas flaps, wondered if he was cold. Hoped the crates of seafood would hide Cyril from at least a cursory search.

If they got Cyril into the truck at all.

They were coming up on it, now: the spot they'd earmarked as the best bet for a clean getaway. The intersection of Shaw and Pur-lieu, where DeCarr split off just before the light. If luck favored them—Aristide sent a prayer up to the Queen—Chido and Tabby could do what they needed, and the vans would pull off Purlieu and head south toward Harbor Terrace. Tabby knew a man who ran a scrap depot at the bottom of Ionidous where they could pull in, change plates, and swap sensitive cargo. Then she and Chido and Jules would head back to wherever they needed to be, and Aristide would take the coastal highway northeast and out of town.

Easy. Simple. He felt like he might vomit.

Traffic jerked forward, stopped. Jerked forward. Stopped. The fish truck came level with DeCarr and inched forward. Aristide held off, despite honking behind him. If they needed to reverse to make the turn, he'd give them room.

Any moment the cars would come to a standstill. Surely. Maybe even . . . now.

They sat for half a breath before Chido jumped down through the flaps of canvas, gun already drawn, silencer heavy on the bar-rel. Chido disappeared around the front of the fish truck and Aris-tide realized he was desperate to draw breath: He hadn't in some time.

He couldn't see anything. Couldn't hear anything. All he could do was wait.

Cyril was surprised they let him shave himself. But the razor was a safety blade, and Dorfner stood behind him to keep watch.

"Don't look much better," the guard told him, when he'd rinsed away the soap.

"I do what I can," said Cyril. "And whatever my lawyer asks me to."

"I would, too, let me tell you. She looks like she'd stomp any toe you put out of line."

"Which is why all of mine have stayed where they're supposed to. Shall we?"

They put him in the back of a van with two guards and no windows, so he couldn't see what the streets looked like. Pity. His days in Amberlough were ticking down and he would never get a look at the place. It would just be the jail, the van, the courthouse. Eventually the gallows.

Vaguely, he remembered the rotunda; remembered that the official entrance soared into sunlit marble arches, and that the floor was inlaid with a bronze seal, and probably some sort of platitude about justice.

He preferred the jail, and the bare metal of the transport van. These at least were honest.

For a while, he tried to keep track of the twists and turns, but the reality was he didn't know which side of the building they'd come out of, and could be wildly off-base. Still, he knew in which direction they were headed, and the uninsulated walls of the transport let in sound. It was early, still, and the traffic around them light.

No horns sounded; only the putter and grunt of engines navigating intersections.

Would there be a crowd, at the courthouse? Would they let reporters in? How many photographs of his razor-nicked face, his ill-fitting suit, would show up in the evening editions, or on tomorrow's breakfast tables?

The van rolled to a stop and idled, frame juddering. Cyril looked up from his hands, cased both guards. One stared vacantly at a spot on the ceiling. The other picked her fingernails.

Just for a distraction, he ran his odds. Two against one, and him in handcuffs. Locked doors. And then the driver and likely another guard up front, once he got out. After that, the city on foot, with his hands still bound; yet another problem to solve.

It was a very long shot. He wouldn't have put money on it. And Rinko would have been very disappointed.

They jerked forward. Stopped. Jerked forward. Stopped. Some kind of traffic backup; must be. He let his weight fall back against the side of the van, resting his head.

Then, the van lurched and his skull smacked the metal. And again. He felt it settle strangely, tilted toward the front. Flat tires. Two at once.

A commotion in the cab: shouting, slamming doors. Alert now, Cyril heard—though barely—the insectile *zip* of one silenced shot, and then another.

Both guards jumped to their feet but stumbled when the van shook again. Something squealed at the rear door, then let loose with a ringing crack.

The guards had drawn their guns, and when the door swung open they fired. But whoever had busted the latch had wisely taken shelter. A delivery truck close to the bumper blocked Cyril's view of the street.

He half-rose for a better angle, but the nail-picking guard pushed him back down. Both guards stepped forward to the open door and as he watched the first one jerked and fell forward, hitting the pavement outside. The second had time to lift her gun, but followed her companion before she could shoot.

A mountainous slab of human appeared from below the bumper with a pry bar in one hand and a pistol tucked into his belt. How had he got all those shots off from his position?

Then Cyril noticed the passenger in the delivery truck, unscrewing a silencer from her own sidearm. The driver had both hands on the wheel.

"Come on," said the man with the pry bar. "Out. Or do I gotta drag you?"

Cyril only gaped for a moment. Then he was out the back of the van, trying to avoid the corpses on the asphalt and keep his balance with cuffed hands. His rescuer—probably two hundred pounds, looked Lisoan but spoke like an Eel Town sculler—steadied him and then half-carried him around the back of the delivery van. He cringed, afraid of being spotted by whoever had pulled up behind, but saw yet another box van behind this one. The driver, a middle-aged Chuli man in a flat cap and spectacles, waggled his fingers in greeting.

Cyril stared hard through the windshield, disbelieving. But before he could confirm his suspicions, he was bundled into the midst of cold, wet, and briny stink, and the canvas flap pulled down across the light.

CHAPTER
TWENTY-EIGHT

"I'm glad you could take the time to drive all this way," said the headmaster—Merritt, not Porks, as Lillian had to keep reminding herself. Stephen's irreverent slang was infectious.

She bit down on the darkly humorous response that threatened—What else had she to do, these days?—and also on the very serious complaints. Petrol was expensive, and so was spending the night in a hotel. The school could easily have sent a proctor to the city for Stephen's exams, but she had the sense this was a test: Would she jump through these hoops to see her son reinstated at Cantrell?

Yes. She would. Because if everything else was out of her control, at least this was something she could throw her energy behind.

And anyway, it was an alibi. Cyril was meant to be arraigned today. Meant to be. Jinadh was at the courtroom in her stead, though he had offered to come to Cantrell. She had insisted, pleading her influence as an alumnus. He didn't seem convinced.

"Frankly," she said to Merritt, "I'm surprised you still wanted Stephen to come."

"I won't lie to you." He looked down, frowning, and spoke to his blotter rather than to her. "There was some dissent among the faculty. But ultimately, the majority came down in Stephen's favor. If he places alongside his peers, academically, and rectifies the . . . irregularities in his behavior, he's welcome to return for the spring term. After all, he isn't his uncle, is he?"

"No," said Lillian, "he isn't." *Nor am I my father.* She wondered if Merritt had been one of the dissenters. From his embarrassment, she didn't think so. He was ashamed of his colleagues. If he had been overruled, he would be angry.

"No. Of course. He's just a child. And it's this school's job to see he fulfills his potential."

Lillian did not remind Merritt that her brother had attended Cantrell at Stephen's age, and certainly fulfilled *some kind* of potential.

"When do you think you'll know?" she asked. Stephen was due to finish up with the proctor soon. Lillian would pick him up from the hall after this meeting.

"We should have an answer back to you within a week, I think. Perhaps two. Plenty of time to plan for spring. Whatever the results."

"Thank you," she said, and rose to leave.

Merritt shook her hand, and added, "Ms. DePaul, I do want you to know: I hope to see Stephen on the platform at commencement."

She felt some satisfaction that she had read him correctly; she still had the knack for that, at least. "You're very kind, Headmaster Merritt."

He shook his head. "My elder brother was in Liso. In the Spice War. The way that he was treated, when he came home . . . I think for him it was worse than the fighting. As if spitting on a soldier could right the wrongs of nations."

"I'm so sorry," she said, hovering awkwardly between the coat-rack and her chair, unwilling to rush out on the one person in Gedda who'd shown her some sympathy. Or at least shown Stephen some.

Merritt shrugged. "He does all right these days. But there was a time . . . well. I would like to spare your son some of that, if I can. Not to say he will have an easy time here, or whatever secondary school you choose next year. You know how they are, at that age."

And how they stayed, most of the time.

Glancing at the clock above his office hearth, Merritt said, "You'd better go—he'll be wrapping up any minute. We'll be in touch."

She finally pulled her coat down from the rack and slipped it on. "I look forward to it."

Stephen was waiting on the front steps of the main hall, breath steaming. It was a fine day, for the time of year: searingly blue sky, frost lingering in the shade. The green tongues of daffodils had begun to appear around the fountain in the quad. The cross quarter was behind them, Equinox looming, and the election was not far off.

"I'm *starving*," said Stephen, as soon as she came within hearing distance.

"Sorry," said Lillian. "Merritt kept me back chatting. Late lunch at the Akill Stairs?"

"Kind of expensive," said Stephen, frowning.

Lillian, who had been brought up not to talk about money, kept her flinch on the inside. Of course, you could only raise a child like that if you had enough you never fretted or fought over it. "You let me worry about that."

The Akill Stairs was a local institution—a pub on the north corner of the town square, its front windows facing south across the green. Prices were kept high—the town saw a lot of comings and goings, and most of that went through the Stairs at one point or another. It was a mainstay of families visiting for matriculation, commencement, the beginning and end of term.

As such, it was nearly empty now. Just a few village people, who clearly knew the owners, gathered around a wireless set at one end of the bar. A middle-aged woman in an apron saw them enter and broke off from the crowd.

"Sorry about that," she said. "Shouldn't all be knotted up around the radio, but it's a slow day in here and a fast one on the wireless."

Lillian felt a current up her spine, and it straightened her. "Has there been news?"

"You haven't heard yet? DePaul's done a runner."

"What?"

"He's gone. Left this morning and they're only just telling us. Should have got the word out earlier, so folk would know to look for him."

Queen's sake, if the woman had known what to look for she'd be down Lillian's throat already; hadn't people always said that she and Cyril could pass for twins?

"Mum?"

Lillian put her hand on Stephen's shoulder, pressing slightly too hard for affection. It meant *silence*, and he obliged. She didn't dare look down at his face.

"Pity," she said. "But perhaps they had their reasons." She didn't expect Makricosta had enough sway in that quarter to hold the hounds off for so long. He might have once, but now? Likely they had only been embarrassed.

"Anyway," said the woman, "what can I get for you?"

"Just a quick lunch. We'd like to get back to the city before supper."

"Of course. But it's a week or so until the end of term! What are you doing getting out early? Lucky nubbin, are you?"

"Uh," said Stephen.

Lillian squeezed his shoulder. "A death in the family."

"Oh, poor lambs. I'm so sorry. I'll leave you alone. Two fish pies all right? The trout's from the Akill itself, and smoked by my lady. Mellie, two fish pies. Will you, love?"

A stout woman with graying dun hair looked up from the radio. "Now, Sam?"

"News won't change in the next ten minutes. If it does, I'll give you the form when you come back. Now shake off the dross!" She turned back to Lillian. "Sorry. She can be a sow, but this time at least she's got good reason. Her sister was Catwalk, and died of cholera in the camps. She was truly looking forward to his hanging. Anything to drink?"

"Burdock and seltzer," said Lillian, faintly. "And . . . um, pint of the session?"

"At the table as soon as you are. Have a seat. You look pale all of the sudden."

"I skipped breakfast."

She didn't remember sitting down, but there she was quite suddenly, facing Stephen over a water-ringed table against the back wall. The sound of the wireless reached them there quite easily, so they heard the repetition of the bulletin on the hour, and then the rapid patter of a reporter. For once Lillian took in none of the news; the landlady's words were still running circles in her head.

Her sister was Catwalk . . . died of cholera in the camps . . . looking forward to his hanging. How could things get so twisted around? The founder of the Catwalk had been Cyril's friend. She had hung on his arm and charmed the deputy commissioner: there was a report about that in Cyril's file, written in his own hand. And a recommendation—never sent—that the Ospies approach Lehane and bring her into the fold as a fox.

But that would never come to light in Lillian's lifetime. Not while Gedda wanted a dead hero to worship and a living villain to hang.

Sam brought two glasses and set them down, adding to the collection of circular stains on the wood. "Pies in a moment, nubbins."

When she had gone back to the small crowd at the radio, Lillian leaned forward over the table and their glasses and spoke softly to Stephen. "Eat fast and don't make a fuss. We need to get through this without a scene."

One of those shifts came over him, pulling him back from the cusp of grown. His eyes turned wide and fear made his face slack and soft, unsure about the mouth.

"Buck up, beastie," she told him. "We're undercover."

And even though she'd just told Merritt that her son was nothing like his uncle, even though she hoped he wouldn't meet his uncle's fate or be forced into any of the same corners, she was proud to see how quickly he pulled himself straight and put on a mask.

They made it back to Coral Street just before plates were due on the table. There were cars parked all along the block, and lurking shadows on the stoop of number twenty-four. Luckily, the old carriage house had been converted into a garage. Lillian turned into the narrow, cobbled alley that ran behind the town houses and prayed none of the pen-fencers had set up here. A prayer that went unheard: Her headlights passed over two slouching figures to either side of the carriage house who swiftly unslouched themselves to reveal a man and a woman. Each of these took a window of the car and began to hammer on them.

Lillian leaned into the horn, refusing to meet the eyes of her assailants. Eventually, Magnusson would—

Yes, there were the doors. She struck the accelerator with too much force and bounced into the garage, scattering journalists. Magnusson had a harder time shutting the sliding doors so quickly on his own. Lillian got out of the car and went to help him.

"Ms. DePaul," said the woman, shining a torch in her face. "Were you aware of what your brother was planning?"

She put her body weight against one of the heavy slabs of wood, which squealed on its casters.

"Ms. DePaul," said the man, "did you assist in his escape?"

Magnusson grunted. There was a shriek of rusty metal, and doors struck home. Lillian shot the bolt and let a breath out into the darkness.

"Ah," said Magnusson. "Apologies. I was in a hurry." Somewhere to her left she heard him shuffle, and then the snap of a switch. Light from a dim bulb warmed the garage, showing Stephen half out of the passenger side. One of his hands clutched the door, the other the back of his seat. He had that trembling lip again.

The passage to the house stood open, and Lillian heard footsteps and then saw Jinadh. He nearly fell down the bare plank stairs, and Stephen did not protest when his father gathered him into a tight embrace. Over Stephen's head, Jinadh gave Lillian a look that said she was next.

If he could catch her. She had been thinking, as she drove. And now, she had work to do.

What she had told Cyril was true: Someone needed to apologize for their family. Their ambitious, ruthless, mess-making family. From Grandmama the general all the way down to Stephen's blown-up car. And it wasn't going to be Cyril, clearly.

"Ms. Higata has been ringing," said Magnusson. "And the police have come around. They had a warrant, but found nothing."

Stones. In all the upset, Lillian had forgotten to reach out to Rinko. At least she'd had a good alibi: She had been standing in front of the judge. Though that wouldn't keep her safe from the rest of the investigation. It was *one* place to start apologizing, anyway. But Lillian had some bigger fences to clear first.

"I'll speak with Ms. Higata later." She went around the driver's side, avoiding the comfort she knew Jinadh wanted to bestow—if she had it now, she'd fall apart. "In the meantime, will you bring a pot of coffee up to my office? Thank you."

She couldn't look at Jinadh, but not looking didn't phase him; she felt his hand close on her wrist before she got through the door.

«Moon-eyes,» he said, tugging gently. «At least let me kiss you. I've been worried past endurance.»

Probably furious, too. He wouldn't say in front of Magnusson or Stephen, but she wagered he had clocked her—that she'd been out of the city on purpose for Cyril's disappearance.

But he really did look awful: face slack, bags beneath his eyes. If he was angry, it had long ago yielded to his fear. So she paused on the threshold and let him gather her in his arms, surrounding her with the smells of tobacco and leather and Marygale soap. His kiss was bitter. He'd been smoking, which he didn't, often. Nerves.

«I love you,» he said.

"I've got to make a call." When he frowned, she kissed him again and said, «I'm sorry. You know I love you, too.»

Getting ahold of Opal Saeger at this hour, on this evening, took some ingenuity. Lillian had no card; Saeger had sent her a telegram to arrange their last meeting. And her number wasn't listed in the directory.

She went through Honora, who was flustered to receive the call, but was eventually convinced to give her the home exchange of a campaign liaison. The liaison, in turn, prevaricated nearly past Lillian's endurance. Eventually she said—did *not* snap—"If you're worried, why don't you ring her up and ask if she'd like to speak to me. I'll wait here by the telephone. All night, if necessary."

She hadn't even finished her coffee before the ringer went again.

"Lillian?" It was Saeger, on the line. "What's this about? Rauleigh said you want to meet."

"I do. I . . . do you still need a campaign manager?"

A badly muffled snort. "I know I'm slipping in the polls, but I'm not sure how much you'll help."

She turned her cup in its saucer, watching the surface of the coffee shiver. "I'll admit I don't look good on paper."

"You don't look good *in* the papers, either. I'm already down by a pile of chips in that game, and we've just about reached the last hand. What are you angling for, exactly?"

"I know who blew up that warehouse," she said. "And I know why."

Silence ate the line up for far too long. "And you're only going to tell me if I give you a job."

Lillian wrestled with her ambitions and anxieties and it came to a draw. "I'll tell you," she said. "I'll tell you and you won't owe me anything. But . . . I would appreciate your consideration. Either before the election or after, if the gambit I have in mind succeeds."

"All right," said Saeger. "You've got it. Provided you aren't in prison yourself for aiding in this jailbreak."

"I was out of town all day," said Lillian. A truth, swiftly followed by a lie. "I had nothing to do with it."

"Lucky you." There was irony in that, but Lillian failed to catch its meaning. "Nine tomorrow morning?" Saeger asked, businesslike once more. "Better make it unofficial. Lyle's again?"

"Is it open at nine?"

"It can be."

"Lyle's, then. I'll be bringing someone along, if that's all right."

"As long as they're not packing a snubby."

She couldn't promise—given Daoud's line of work he might well carry a gun. But she was fairly sure he wouldn't aim it at Saeger. "Nobody's going to be shot."

"Good enough for me." And she rang off.

Sykes House was next, but they regretted to inform her Mr. Qassan was no longer in residence. Cursing, she reached for the telephone directory and flipped through it at speed until she turned up Cross-Costa Imports. It was far past business hours, but maybe, if fortune's wind filled her sails . . .

"Cross-Costa Imports, Jamila Osogurundi speaking. Because you've called long past business hours and my clerks are gone. What in damnation do you want?"

"I'm so sorry," said Lillian. "I'm trying to find Daoud Qassan."

"Qassan? Hundred to one. You ever try craps? He's sleeping in the office tonight. Tossed out on his rear. Unlucky in love." Lillian heard the impact of a palm over the mouthpiece, and then a muffled "*Qassan! Telephone!*"

Another series of shufflings, and then: "Hello?"

«Daoud. It's Lillian.»

«Oh.» She heard his steadying breath. «Is . . . is everything all right?»

«As much as I know, yes. I am only calling because I want you to meet someone. Tomorrow, at nine in the morning. Are you free?»

«Meet who?»

«I do not want to say on this line. If the ACPD had any inkling what Cross-Costa got up to, it would be tapped. And they'd find someone who spoke Porashtu. «Only tell me yes or no.»

«What is the favor?»

«Sorry?»

«Someone told me, just the other day, I would be well advised to learn what favor was being asked of me before I granted it.»

She made a fist and tapped it with great restraint against the pages of the directory. He was right, and she owed it to him. But how to say?

«You said you did not think you were . . . » She tapped her fist again, not frustrated this time, but searching for the word. «Challenging. I am offering you an opportunity to be that.»

A hesitation. Then, «I'm interested.»

«Come to my house at half eight, then. Around the back; the front is going to be a pack of vultures. I will explain, and then you can decide.»

CHAPTER

TWENTY-NINE

Between the fish and the dirty laundry, Cyril vastly preferred the latter. It was a little rank, but at least it was warm. In the half hour he'd been crammed amongst the crates of ice, hiding under a string bag filled with clams, every extremity had gone numb. His suit was soaked through, and even his socks were wet. Hauled out to change vehicles at a way station he hardly registered, he stumbled when he hit the ground and had to be lifted bodily into his next conveyance.

The doors on this one were more substantial, too. The canvas had let in a draft, and street noise including police sirens. These grew more frequent, and then less so, the farther they got from the site of the . . . rescue? Kidnapping? Prison break?

All of the above, perhaps.

When he finally dared emerge from his cocoon of dirty linens, he saw the sky outside the van's rear windows had gone dark. They had been driving for hours, and the quality of the road had deteriorated in the last few miles.

The bins of laundry rattled on their wheels, frames creaking, as the tires took on some rough terrain. Then the whole cargo, Cyril included, lurched forward once and settled when the truck came to a halt.

The cab door opened and then shut, shaking the van on its axles. Cyril burrowed back into the sheets, still leery. The rear doors creaked open and a frigid wind blew in.

"Are ye back there, darling?" asked the driver, in a northern burr so thick it almost obscured the words.

Cyril stretched tentatively. A savage cramp dug claws into his shoulders, but in spite of it he raised his head above the linens again and said, "Darling?" He hadn't exactly expected endearments.

In the smothering black of countryside night, he couldn't make out the man's expression. Not even his face. Couldn't be sure it was really Ari.

Not until he said, "Oh, sorry, that en't your name anymore. It's van Weill now. Or, say rather, Wallis."

"What?" he struggled out of the bin, shoes squelching. "Who's Wallis? Ari, is that you?"

"Perdition," said Aristide, before he dropped the act. "And here I thought I could still manage Currin if I put my mind to it. How are you feeling?"

"Like someone peeled me off their shoe."

"You look it, too." He held out a hand, which Cyril took as he stepped down from the bumper. Frost and gravel crunched beneath his shoes.

"Where are we?" A violent shiver chased the words. Once he started shivering and couldn't stop.

"Here," said Aristide, and handed him a cardboard suitcase. Inside were thick tweeds and a scratchy three-color sweater. "Your shoes will do all right, I think. But there are warmer socks in there. And dry."

Sitting on the bumper of the van, Cyril struggled out of his cashmere trousers and into the tweed ones. He couldn't get much colder, even bare-skinned. The double-breasted chalk-stripe he pitched in with the rest of the soiled laundry. His teeth were still chattering. "Where'd it come from?"

"Never you mind." A hint of the burr came back with that, and Ari shook his head as if to clear it.

Cyril pulled the sweater over his head and the jacket over that, but it did no good. "Mother's tits, it's rotten *freezing*."

"I don't recall that you swore this much." Aristide reached into his own jacket and produced a battered steel-and-leather flask. "Brandy?"

Cyril got down half the stuff in one swallow and began to feel better at once.

"You can polish it off if you like," said Aristide. "I have more in my rucksack."

"You're carrying a *rucksack*?" He couldn't picture it.

"Well, I wasn't going to drag all my luggage through the country-side in the back of a laundry van. It's been sent ahead."

"To where?"

"Dastya."

Cyril choked on his second pull of brandy, and had to clear his throat. "Aristide, that's a war zone."

"Nonsense. It's just on the other side of one. Tatié lost it to the Tzietans months ago. East of Kareniv, we'll be fine. There's a Cestinian postal ship due in Dastya three days from now. If we scurry, we'll be just in time to join my steamer trunks and sundries for the next leg of our journey."

"What about the border?" asked Cyril. "Borders. I'll be shocked if we can cross into Tatié at all, let alone from Tatié into Tzieta."

"Luckily, we'll be traveling to Ibet, at least on paper, with only a stop for document checks at the Tatien border."

Cyril swore. "Passports."

"Mine is for Erikh Prosser, my mother's son."

"But I don't even *have* one."

Ari smiled. "Check your pocket."

Cyril put a hand inside the lapel of his jacket and found the inner lining stiff. He withdrew the relevant document, its cardboard covers warped with a dried spill.

"I'm afraid to look," he said, but did so. "Ambrose Adam . . . Wallis, I suppose. What in damnation happened here?"

"You spilled your gin on it."

"Wallis is a gin drinker, is he?" Cyril pulled a face. "Is this how I live out the rest of my days?" The truth of it struck him then, and he began to shake. "I suppose I should be grateful that I get to. But mother and sons, Ari. This'll hold wine about as well as a sieve."

"You aren't *frightened*, are you?" Ari sent a flirtatious glance sideways beneath the brim of his flat cap, and suddenly his disguise had the air of a stage costume. Cyril remembered watching him strip, peeling away the layers of his character in unexpected ways, becoming something different with each item he removed.

He swallowed against a feeling that wasn't quite arousal; there was too much sadness in it, and too much nostalgia. "I suppose it won't be any worse than Liso."

"Fewer botflies, anyway. Hop back in the van."

"It's not a bit conspicuous?"

"We're going to dump it in a couple of miles and walk to Tarbycliff Station."

"The train?" asked Cyril, incredulous.

"Of course," said Aristide. "Who would think to look for a De-Paul in third class?"

The laundry truck lay hidden at the bottom of a deep ditch off a lane, its front bumper sunk in the mud. New growth forest had crept close, and at least in the dark it would be hard to spot the abandoned van from the road. Cyril wondered if anyone lived in the house at the other end of the drive.

The moon was new. That would help them go unnoticed. In the countryside quiet, he could hear the rill of the little stream along the road: some unnamed tributary to the Heyn. He wondered what time it was, and when the first train left.

It all felt horribly familiar. He could almost smell the gunpowder on his hands, the remnants of a hasty assassination. Briefly, he thought of Finn Lourdes dead in his bathtub, of the guards shot to the ground this afternoon. How many more people lay ruined in his wake?

"Let's stroll," said Aristide, and started down the lane. Cyril did not follow him.

His conscience had been left behind in the back of the prison van when the prospect of freedom presented itself so nakedly. Now it had suddenly caught up with him, and hooked the back of his collar so he choked on it.

"Don't you feel guilty?" he asked.

Aristide paused on the footbridge to the road. "What for?"

"Whisking me away like this? What about everything I did? I'm going to disappear and leave that all lying on the ground behind me for other people to pick up."

"Gedda hates you," said Aristide, turning so they faced one another across the plank bridge, water running between them. "Neither prison nor a hanging will change that."

"It isn't about whether they hate me." He could hear the pathetic note in his own voice, the flatness of his platitudes. That kind of thing would never stand up against Ari.

"Isn't it?"

"No, it's—"

"Please." Aristide took a step closer, back toward the road, one sturdy boot on the half-rotten wood. "Don't you dare say justice."

Even Cyril heard the answer in his silence.

"What's that supposed to be, then? It's just some way of salving hurts that we can never truly heal. If a murderer is hanged, what good does it do the victim?" He took another step, coming half across the bridge. "They wouldn't have forgiven you in death. I'd rather you learned to live with your guilt. Perhaps that's selfish, but I seem to have fewer scruples than you do, these days."

"Hard-earned." Cyril had come closer to Aristide, somehow. He didn't remember leaving the safety of the verge.

"I wish you hadn't. Earned them. We'd have been on our way five minutes ago." Aristide came back to the near bank and considered Cyril for a long moment. When he spoke next, his diction lost the crisp edge of argument, and his blasé tone dropped into a different register: softer and more somber. The last of his Central City drawl fell away. Cyril remembered when he used to stutter, and the times the stutter faltered, fled. When he was very serious, or very scared.

"What's keeping you here?" said Ari, and Cyril realized he was standing not two feet away: as close as he had come since Liso, when Cyril startled underneath the razor and drew blood.

"I just want—" But his thoughts fled, shying away, refusing order and exposure. To speak aloud was to commit himself to a course of action, or at least the promise of one. Indecision ached in his gut as badly as a boot.

"Cyril," said Aristide. Horribly, he sounded . . . querulous. Almost afraid. At his sides, his hands curled into fists. "Cyril, don't—"

"I want to do the right thing," he said, all in a rush. "For once. And I thought . . . in prison I thought it was you. I thought you were the only thing that I could fix. Cordelia's dead and the country's in ruins, but you're still here, and so am I."

"Yes." Breathless now, all pride gone.

Cyril couldn't bear to look at him. "Is this the right thing?"

A shaky inhalation. "Is that rhetorical? Or would you really like my answer?"

"Really," said Cyril. "I need someone to tell me."

Moonless shadows shifted at his feet, and he saw the toes of Ari's boots in the mud and melting snow. "*I* think the only justice in this world is what you make yourself. So do better this time. We'll *both* do better."

The words plucked a string in his memory. "Small lies."

Aristide made a soft, pained sound, as though he had been stabbed, and suddenly his arms were around Cyril, who this time didn't tense or shy or try to block a knife. He held Aristide so tightly that his biceps ached, and the muscles in his palms cramped from making fists at Ari's back, the nape of his neck.

"Cyril," he said, too soon. "We don't have the time."

Taking a deep breath, smelling Aristide's throat, the fold of his collar, no perfume or greasepaint to cut the scent of him, Cyril pushed back and nodded once. "All right."

Aristide crossed the bridge in three strides, then turned and held a hand out: to steady Cyril. Or perhaps, to make sure that he followed.

CHAPTER

THIRTY

«You want me to do *what*?» Daoud nearly dropped his coffee cup.

Lillian checked the clock; she had perhaps ten minutes to convince him, and that was if she drove quickly and hit all the signals green. «I want you to help me destroy Emmeline Frye.»

He shook his head. «You want me to destroy Cross-Costa.»

«Cross-Costa smuggles narcotics,» she countered. «They are not saints or heroes.»

«Good people work there. *I* work there. What am I supposed to do once I am . . . » He made a face, pivoted into Geddan, and said "out on my rear?"

"Anything you want. What was the last thing *you* decided to pursue? What was the last turning you took that was all your own choice, and no one else's?"

Daoud sipped his coffee and refused to meet her eyes. "Would this be mine?" he asked, the base of his cup grating softly on the saucer as he set it back down. "If I agree, is it for me, or you?"

"I can't answer that," she said. "I'm just saying, it's a bold move. A challenging one."

«I don't need to impress Aristide Makricosta,» he said. «I don't need his approval. If he's smart, I'll never see him again. And you had *better* hope he's smart, for your brother's sake.»

"Of course," she said. "I didn't mean to imply—"

«Yes you did.»

She bit the inside of her cheek, as was her habit when repressing unwise words. He knew her angle to the half degree.

«Daoud,» she said. «I married a Porachin man. I know it can be hard to see beyond those rules, beyond your duty. The . . . the fences you grew up inside.»

«You married a nobleman. I'm Belqati, and turned. It's different.»

«But none of it matters,» she said. «You are not in Porachis anymore. Not you, and not Jinadh. You do not have to please anyone you do not want to.»

«Moon-eyes!» As though summoned, Jinadh's voice echoed down the hall from the dining room. «I'm leaving.»

"In the library," she called.

Soon after, he appeared in the doorway, hatted and wrapped in a muffler, briefcase banging his knee. «I thought you had an appointment soon. Good morning, Mr. Qassan.»

"I do." Lillian looked at Daoud. "We do. I think."

He didn't answer her unspoken question. He was looking at Jinadh, carefully, as if cataloguing details. Lillian tried to put herself behind his eyes, to see what he might. Purpose? Professionalism? Fatherhood? Marriage? Or maybe just a well-cut coat, ordered under better circumstances.

Jinadh took this scrutiny gracefully, with a hint of amusement, given he was on his way out the door. Finally, Daoud asked, «Are you happy that you left Porachis?»

Jinadh considered his answer for a moment, then said, «No.» Lillian swallowed hurt and waited for him to go on. This was not her conversation.

«Would you go back?» asked Daoud.

Tilting his head, Jinadh sent a sidelong glance at Lillian. She gave him nothing; she didn't know what Daoud wanted him to say. Was he really asking about Porachis, or was this something else?

«If I knew I could do what I wanted,» said Jinadh. «Be who I wanted, and still have all the things I loved . . . I would be there between this heartbeat and the next. But some paths cannot be pursued without appalling compromise.»

«What if *all* paths lead to compromise?»

«Inevitable.» Jinadh looked past him to Lillian and smiled. «Life is a series of compromises. But a wise man will make his own, instead of accepting other people's.»

«Semantics,» said Daoud.

Jinadh shrugged and straightened his hat. «If they get you through the day.»

The neon sign over Lyle's wasn't on. Lillian parked awkwardly at the curb and checked the street. An old woman sweeping the footpath. A shopkeep rolling up her grate. In the doorway on the other side of the street, a rag lady stirred beneath her blankets and her cardboard.

Daoud got out of the passenger's side. «Glamorous.»

«We have not put her in the Cliff House yet. You cannot ask for a red carpet and a limousine.» Lillian scanned the street again, to make sure they had shed every reporter who chased after the car, and any other nasty thing they might have picked up on the way. «Down the stairs.»

Daoud trotted to the subterranean door and knocked. Lillian followed, stepping down just as the door came open on six feet of sinister-looking muscle.

"We're here to see Opal," she said, standing her ground. In heels she was nearly as tall.

The bruiser cased her, then Daoud, then shut the door on them.

«A lot of fuss for nothing,» said Daoud. But before he could get much else out, the door opened again on the same man, now nodding his head.

"Come on in," he said.

Only a few of the lights were on. Saeger was embedded at the same table where Lillian had met with her before, a thousand years ago. No beer this time. She sat with her arms crossed, staring nakedly.

"Good morning," Lillian said. "May I introduce Daoud Qassan?"

"A pleasure to meet you," said Daoud, extending a hand to shake.

Saeger took it—her hand was bigger than his, but he didn't flinch. Lillian wondered if her grip was gentle, or his mask was on.

"I'm getting the strangest visitors lately," Saeger said, and looked at Lillian like they shared some kind of joke. Lillian experienced an emotion that only usually arose in her nightmares. She had no idea what she was supposed to say or do, or why.

"Eli," said Saeger. "Watch the door? From the outside, if you don't mind."

The heavy made himself scarce. Saeger sighed and settled back into her chair. "So. You know who blew the warehouse."

"I do," said Lillian. She and Daoud took the seats opposite. All the other chairs in the place were up on tables, legs in the air.

Saeger opened her hands, inviting the rest of it. Lillian remembered she had been a gaffer in the theatres before the Ospies, and imagined her turning a spotlight to catch someone at center stage.

"Frye's people." Lillian eschewed elegance for brevity. "She did it herself."

That elicited a grunt and half a smile. "You got proof?"

Lillian looked to Daoud.

"Not precisely," he said, and Saeger's face closed up. "Not in the manner that police will ask for. But testimony is evidence, and there is my word as an employee of Cross-Costa, as well as boxes and boxes of paperwork that tells the truth of what was in Frye's warehouse. Or rather, that tells a lie, which becomes apparent if one knows how to read it. To be plain: poppy tar. A great deal of it."

"And she lit it all up because?"

"Wouldn't you?" asked Lillian. "If you wanted to eliminate two problems at a stroke?"

"She wanted me out of the race, all right. But nobody was sniffing around about a drug deal. And anyway—" Saeger inclined her head toward Daoud, "—I'm asking him."

Pausing before he answered, Daoud put one finger on the edge of the table in a splintered chip some more restless person would have picked at. "My direct supervisor at Cross-Costa is—was— Aristide Makricosta. Who had some personal stake in the tribunals Frye proposed. He used the leverage he had, and she was not pleased."

"That poxy rotten sculler." Saeger's laugh sounded like a blow to the gut. "I ought to ring up Horkova right now, tell her to scratch him at the border and toss him back to the hounds."

"What?" asked Lillian. "What border? Who's Horkova?"

Saeger raised an eyebrow. "You really didn't know?" Then, to Daoud, "She didn't know?"

Lillian turned to him, beseeching.

"Magnusson told me where to find Ms. Saeger," said Daoud. "Aristide wanted to speak with her. About . . . you know."

She hadn't, but it was coming together. Saeger had been Catwalk, an ally to Tatien separatists. If one needed to get out of Gedda, it was the closest international border. Battlefield chaos made it easy to disappear.

"I almost told you," said Daoud. "But you said you didn't—"

"Want to know. I don't." She closed her eyes briefly, swallowed past the tightness of her throat. "It's safer for everyone if we don't mention it again."

"So let's talk about what you came to say, instead." Saeger crossed her arms. "I think it's flimsy."

"It's sensational," said Lillian, clawing her way back to the line. "And more importantly, it's the best thing you've got. With Cyril gone, Frye is scrambling for something to sell to voters. This is your chance to slip in and steal the show."

"You told anyone else?" This was aimed at both of them. "Anybody else know anything about it? Your husband, maybe? Ain't he a pen-fencer?"

Guilt made sweat prickle on her palms. "My husband is an arts and culture editor. It isn't exactly his beat."

"There is a journalist," said Daoud, words dropping like stones, one at a time. "A radio anchor, with FWAC. Aristide spoke to him, but then the explosion happened, and . . . things changed."

"He never ran it. Because, like I said, it's flimsy."

"Never ran it as a bulletin," said Lillian, unfurling her strategy now that all the pieces were in place. "There's not enough evidence for that. But might he run it as an exclusive interview with a former employee of Cross-Costa? Someone who could read those papers and tell us what kind of lies they tell? Someone who could turn those papers over to the police, upon request, and cooperate with any resulting investigation?"

The irritation on Saeger's face faltered, and then crumbled into curiosity. Lillian had lined up this shot and sunk the ball, neat as billiards.

She should have felt victorious. Instead she felt only gratitude and terror.

THIRTY-ONE

By the time he dragged into the dusty waiting room, sometime after a breakfast he hadn't eaten, Cyril was inclined to be uncharitable. But even in a good mood he'd have said it: rural little Tarbycliff Station wasn't exactly Bythesea.

So why did he feel like his heart was being squeezed for oil? Like he'd jammed his finger in a socket? Like he was sitting on a pipe bomb waiting for the fuse to run down?

False papers. Early morning train. It wasn't as if he hadn't done this before.

He wished he had never done this before.

Aristide was loitering down the road. He had booked his ticket in advance, for Erikh Prosser, and now Cyril had to do the same for Ambrose Adam Wallis. Their ostensible final destination was in Ibet—a through-trip, with only a stop at the Tatien border for customs and document checks. No visas necessary in advance, as long as they didn't leave the train.

As Cyril understood it, they would be leaving the train at some point, though Aristide had been hazy about details.

Now he faced the ticket counter on his own and had to swallow past a dry mouth and aching throat, heartbeat hammering against his sternum.

Calm down. Nothing gives a lie away like fear.

He had to *be* the man in his altered passport. Just as he'd been Ambrose van Weill on the way over, so he had to be Ambrose Adam Wallis on his way out. And Adam—he went by Adam, yes—wasn't worried about being waylaid on his way out of the country.

Sweat made the handle of his suitcase slippery.

Space and time telescoped as he approached the ticket booth. He forced air into his lungs like a bellows. He had traversed minefields in Liso's monsoon season, crawled belly-down through flooded trenches, laid spike traps for the encroaching republican army. For Queen's sake, he had killed the regionalist government. Or at least plunged a knife in. This was just one train ticket.

Just one ticket, on which hung a thousand hopes that had already been thwarted once, twice, three times.

"Good morning," said the clerk, stifling a yawn.

"Morning." He searched for his Enselmese accent: a flattening of the vowels, a dizzy tip between the back of the throat and the tongue on the teeth. Not unlike the way northern Tatiens spoke Geddan. He thought briefly of Vasily Memmediv, and let the immediacy of that anger anchor him in the present time and place. "The six forty-three to West Ballye. Just third class, please."

"Of course," she said. "I'll need to see your passport."

His hand would not shake. It *couldn't*. He smiled and reached into his jacket, producing the rippled mess of Adam's official identification.

She remained unfazed until she opened it, revealing smeary ink, illegible.

"Sir," she said.

"I know. I was drinking, on the train down from—" shits on shits, some Enselmese town, let it come to him before the pause grew obvious, "—Angbrouk, and it got a little rowdy. It's been causing me problems ever since. I'll apply for a new one as soon as I'm home."

"And that'll be when?"

Holy stones, this would never end. He wished great ill on Aristide and his unsteady hands, and recanted in the next instant. Neither of them could afford ill-wishes now. "Perhaps a week or so?" He shrugged. "I'm visiting friends."

"In Ibet?"

"Yes."

"And what were you doing in Gedda, before?"

"A wedding," he said. "My sister's."

Suspicion colored her expression and he felt one foot sink into the grave. "Seems a little late to be planning an international trip, especially given the terrain you'll be traveling through."

"I heard the Tatien border isn't such a fuss," he said. "Just a quick checkpoint."

She raised her eyebrows eloquently at that.

"My friends came down all right for the wedding," he said, settling deeper into his character's tale. "They told me I wouldn't have any trouble getting through."

"If you're lucky," she said, glancing down at his illegible passport.

He could feel the few people in the waiting room beginning to stir, to stare and make whispered commentary. He had hoped to do this without causing a scene.

"Ma'am," he said, injecting it with an icy courtesy that would have made his sister proud. "I hardly think it's your concern."

The words didn't even shake on their way out. He was beyond that, floating just over his own right shoulder watching a stranger's drama play out.

Inside the ticket booth, suspicion became anger on the woman's face. And then, finally, it sank into irritated resignation. She stamped something illegible across his ticket and shoved it through the window with his passport. "As long as you're not my problem anymore."

He barely made it to a seat—his knees had turned to gelatin and his bowels to water. Cold sweat soaked his shirt beneath his sweater. In warmer weather he would have been scratched.

After a bare few minutes of reprieve, the bell above the station door rang. Cyril looked up and saw Aristide approaching the ticket counter, rucksack over one shoulder. He had to look down again before his face gave them both away.

The train ground to a stop in the midst of razor wire, sandbags, and corrugated metal. Palpable tension crept through the cars. Aristide looked up from his battered paperback—*Return to Wolf's Neck*, which someone had left lying in the waiting room at Tarbycliff—and caught Cyril glancing in his direction.

He returned to his book without acknowledging the eye contact. Julian and Maurice had just met for the first time since university. He was trying to remember who they were, and why he should care, when the door at one end of the car slid open to reveal a pair of Tatien border guards, the collars of their sheepskin coats turned up against the cold. One held a submachine gun low across her stomach. The other led her down the row, confronting each passenger with an ominous, "Papers, please."

Aristide produced his passport and ticket when asked, setting his book over one knee. The guard who'd asked for his papers scanned the photograph and information in his passport, considered Aristide's face, and then handed the passport to his colleague. She squinted at it and then nodded.

"Step outside," said Papers, Please. A rustle of apprehension passed through the car. Aristide rose, put his book into his coat pocket, and shouldered his rucksack. Pointedly, he did not meet Cyril's eyes. He hoped that Cyril wasn't staring. Nobody else was—they didn't want to get involved.

Outside the train the wind across the plains hit him like a wall. Machine Gun and Papers, Please marched him toward a tin-roofed shack that didn't look like it ought to be standing against the onslaught. Barbed wire coiled around it like malevolent briars.

Saeger had made the call for him. They had been watching for him and waiting; this was just the next phase of the plan. That didn't stop his nerves from stretching taut, sizzling with electricity. Things in Tatié changed depending on the wind, the time of day, the whims of heavily armed and splintering factions. Who knew what he'd really meet, despite what he'd been promised.

Inside the shack, with the door shut, the wind became an icy thread against the back of his neck and a constant high-pitched whistle. The place was crammed with maps, a ticker-tape machine, several wireless sets, and a boxy desk at which sat a middle-aged woman, olive-skinned and silver-haired, in the same uniform as the guards who had brought Aristide from the train. A straight smoldered in the ashtray at her elbow.

"Sergeant," said one of the guards.

She looked up over the steel rims of her spectacles and cased Aristide with a gaze like a strigil. He was surprised he didn't lose any skin.

"Thanks," she told his minders, then picked up her straight and took a long drag. "You're the peacock's man, right?" Smoke plumed toward the ceiling. "Satri's friend? Next time you see her tell her thanks. Those chain guns kept the Teezees off our asses down in Marjenek."

"Of course," said Aristide, trying to fight off a coughing fit and failing. The cold had woken up the tickle in his chest, and the second-hand smoke wasn't doing him any favors.

"Sorry there's not another chair," said the sergeant. She didn't sound it.

He waved her off and cleared his throat, eyes streaming. "That's quite all right. I'll stand."

"Aren't you supposed to have somebody with you? Gaffer told me two; Erikh Prosser and companion. Didn't give a name."

"Ambrose Adam Wallis."

"Bet that's not his real one. You two! Go and get him."

The guards' salutes and heel clicks came in tandem, echoing. Aristide looked down and saw soil through a gap in the floorboards.

An uncomfortable several minutes passed. Or, uncomfortable for Aristide. The sergeant seemed perfectly happy to ignore him. When the door opened again, the temperature in the room dropped ten degrees.

Between Machine Gun and Papers, Please, Cyril looked small and wilting. Sweat shone on his face despite the bitter cold. He stumbled on the threshold.

"Thank you, Ereni, Milosz," said the sergeant. "That's all."

Another double salute. Another ring of boots on boards. Cyril flinched. Aristide did not reach out to him, though without the guards supporting him on either side he looked liable to drop into a dead faint.

"Welcome to Tatié, Mr. Wallis," said the sergeant.

Cyril glared at Aristide. "You could have rotten *warned* me. I thought I was going to be arrested."

"I told you I had it sorted. But I'll admit I wasn't sure how it would play out."

"Friends all up and down the ladder, still." Cyril shook his head, wiped grit from his eyes. The skin of his face looked delicate with exhaustion, liable to tear.

"Not really my friends," said Aristide. "More friends of Vasily Memmediv. And, in a way, Cordelia."

"Do I want to know how that story goes?"

"Perhaps at a later date."

"I hope you two weren't going to take a train to Dastya, too," said the sergeant. "The tracks turn into twisted metal about fifty miles outside Kareniv."

"Damnation," said Aristide. "I don't suppose it's safe to lift a thumb?"

She laughed. "That depends on who picks you up." Then, checking her watch, "I'll tell you what. There's a supply convoy leaving Eré this evening for the front, and I've got a couple of messengers who are supposed to catch it. They're due to leave town in half an hour, and I'm sure there's some room in the back of a jeep for friends of friends."

"And once we get to the front?"

The sergeant shrugged. "You seem like a man who knows how to improvise."

At nine o'clock in the evening, Lillian and Daoud sat outside the Icepick in her car, watching the door. She daren't go into a building packed with so many hungry paperfolk and radio personalities, but in the dark, between the streetlamps, she could stay anonymous while waiting for the particular anchor she required.

It also gave her a private moment to ask, "Do you think they're all right?"

Daoud shrugged, staring out the windshield. "How can I guess? They made it out of the city, I assume. And by now . . ." He looked at his watch and she saw him consider several ends to his sentence before discarding them and lapsing into silence.

Kostos came out of the tower at a quarter past nine, coat open and scarf crooked. The evening was unseasonably warm. Lillian stepped out of the car and intercepted him as he crossed the street.

"Laurie Kostos?" she asked, extending her hand as she approached. He eyed her suspiciously, but she forced the issue without letting her smile falter, and he shook.

"I'm Lillian DePaul," she said, once she had a grip on him. "And my associate and I—" she tilted her head back toward Daoud behind the windshield, "would like to speak with you."

She saw him about to ask a question, then think better of it, before he followed her back to the car.

"Good evening, Mr. Kostos," said Daoud, when the radio host climbed in. "I am Daoud Qassan." They shook hands over the seat. "I work for Cross-Costa Imports, and I have a lead you may find interesting."

"Cross-Costa," said Kostos. "Why is that familiar?"

"You spoke with my . . . erstwhile employer, several weeks ago. Aristide Makricosta."

"Yeah," said Kostos. "He wanted me to get in on some scheme of his. WCRC was moving drugs, he said. But the Catwalk blew the proof and my editor wouldn't let me touch it."

Lillian turned the key in the ignition. "I thought we'd chat on the move."

In the rearview mirror, Kostos caught her gaze. "Nervous," he said. "I don't blame you. I'll wager your doorstep is three feet deep in scullers. And you come to me."

She half-smiled, and kept her eyes on the road. Let him think this was an offer, if it kept him listening.

"WCRC *was* moving drugs," said Daoud. "Ours. Cross-Costa's. Lisoan poppy tar, to be exact. Frye blew the warehouse after Makricosta approached her with a mix of blackmail and bribery—there is evidence of a sizable campaign donation, you will find."

"But not much else," said Kostos. "I already turned this story down."

"There is me," said Daoud. "I am evidence. I am offering to go on air with you and discuss it."

Leather creaked. Lillian risked a glance in the rearview and saw Kostos vehemently shaking his head.

"News," he said. "I told Makricosta I report *news*, not half-cooked rumors still raw in the middle. That's *asking* to get sacked."

"Nonsense." Lillian flicked up the stalk to indicate and took them onto a side street that led away from the Keller Tower and its neighbors, toward the harbor, under the warmly lit windows of tenement buildings. Few people were out, despite the mild weather—winter habits, perhaps, keeping them inside.

"Nonsense?" Kostos asked. "Who works in the wireless, here?"

"Exactly. People like a story." Guilt pinged off of her like hail, leaving dents. She should talk to Rinko. She *would* talk to Rinko. Once she had this business sorted out. "They don't care if it's true— this one is, by the way—they just want something to chat about on the trolley."

"I'm not some gossiping grandmother," he protested. "I'm in the market for facts."

"But you've got sponsors to keep, and your current model isn't cutting it. Marlowe Flanders has already filled the fast-talking, no-nonsense news anchor slot. You need another angle."

Silence told her she'd struck her mark with Flanders.

"What about interviews?" she said. "Exclusive interviews. The kind no one else can get. People will spew all kinds of swineshit—lies, slander, rumors, libel—and all you've done is given them space to say it. If the story turns out to be false, nobody's going to pin you. You're just the platform."

More silence. Then, "I'd have to talk to the desk."

"And how long will that take?" she asked.

"Department meeting's early next week."

"What if you aired your conversation with Daoud tomorrow, and used it as proof of concept? It would give you some numbers to go on."

"Won't hurt you none, either," Kostos said, "eating up the airwaves with this shock and awe. It'll put lesser concerns—like escaped convicts—out of people's heads."

"I'd be lying if I said that wasn't a consideration." Lillian brought them around the end of the block. Black water spread out below. A distant buoy blinked, and the lighthouse at the end of the spits spun slowly, casting its beacon into the dark.

The pop of a match filled the car with sulfur stink, and Kostos lit a cigarette. "It ain't a bad idea for a show."

"So you'll do it?" asked Daoud.

"I might. But that's just one interview. What about the night after that, and the next one, and the next? Who am I supposed to talk to then?"

Lillian made the mistake of looking into the mirror again, and found him staring straight at her, eyes lit by the ember of his straight.

"Give-and-take," said Kostos. "I'll put him on air if you come after him. And, get your brother's lawyer on to talk."

"That's not quite fair," she said. "Two for one?"

"I don't know," said Kostos. "That's supply and demand, ain't it? How badly do you want me to air this interview?"

This was why she hated to show her hand. People were never kind about it; they played to win the kitty. "All right, fine. You can put me on the air."

"And Higata?"

She willed down the part of her that wanted to cry, to slam the heel of her hand hard on the steering wheel. "I'll do my best, but I can't promise anything. I'm not sure what sort of terms we're on, at present." When Kostos didn't reply, she said, "Does that suit you?"

He exhaled a thread of smoke and shrugged. "Ain't like a tailor, but it'll do for now."

They barely made the convoy, scrambling into a truck bed sometime after the sun had set. Engines coughed and rumbled. Diesel smoke made the cold air noxious.

If Cyril had stopped to think about it, touching Aristide would have felt strange. But the cold and the late hour and the tight space meant that Cyril found himself curled against the other man, wedged between crates of ammunition and barely sheltered from the wind. He halfway slept, and halfway woke with dawn.

Shell craters and barbed-wire barricades across the road took him back to his first days in the Foxhole. Bombing sales in stores with shattered windows, smoky bars where contractors and correspondents drank their way through nights full of gunfire.

The convoy came to a halt as the sun hauled itself over the horizon. Aristide blinked and cursed and unfolded from their knot. Not so far away, mortars began to fall.

"Morning," said one of the soldiers, unlatching the gate at the back of the truck. The jolt of jumping down resonated through every one of Cyril's bones. He felt a thousand years old.

Aristide looked like he felt worse, and Cyril remembered the difference in their ages, remembered the wet and hacking cough that had been on occasional display during Solstice.

"You're all right," he said. He couldn't bear to make it a question.

Aristide nodded, cleared his throat, scrubbed sleep from his eyes.

"Any thoughts on . . . improvisation? Thank you." This last to a spotty enlisted man, barely over sixteen, who offered him a steaming paper cup of coffee. Scorched, but warm. The heat made his hands prickle.

Aristide took the second cup the boy offered up, and then stopped him leaving. "How far is it to Dastya from the front?" It ended in a cough. Coffee sloshed across his knuckles.

"Too far to walk," said the boy.

Cyril saw Aristide bite back a sharp retort, but sarcasm still larded his "Thank you."

"How could we get there?" Cyril asked, speaking across the top of his cup. Steam collected on his nose and cooled in the wind.

"Can't," said the soldier.

Cyril swallowed frustration and the accompanying irrational tears. "You can't sell me that. I've been in worse than this, and there's always a way. Aid convoys. Ambulances. Someone selling drugs or skin, or moving spies. And everybody knows, but nobody will say out loud."

The soldier hesitated for a moment, nose dripping, and then sighed and leaned in closer. "Henson."

"I need a little more than that."

"Contractor. Works for the Teezees on paper. She can get you what you want. Markup's mean, but if you need something bad enough, you'll pay. She's usually through once a day, on a little detour from her route, but no guarantee when. She might have already gone."

"Thank you," said Cyril, less caustically than Ari had. "Where do we find her?"

The scrawny private sighed, then said, "I'll draw you a map."

By the time they reached the bend in the road marked on the hastily scrawled directions, Cyril had grown and obliterated a series of blisters. Aristide looked strangely gray. It was daytime, fully, though the sun hid behind a low pall of leaden clouds. A rocky outcropping kept off the worst of the wind, but it certainly wasn't warm.

Aristide lowered himself onto a lichen-covered boulder and produced a matchbook and a pack of straights from one pocket. He lit up and inhaled, then burst into painful hacking.

Cyril took the straight from him and smoked it, standing close without touching. Aristide's breath came unevenly for a while, and then began to grow steadier.

"Thank you," said Cyril, flicking ash into the scrub at his feet.

"Pardon?" Ari's voice was another man's, raw and crackling with phlegm.

"For all this." Cyril gestured with the butt of his straight, then took one last drag and pitched it. "Thank you."

"Save your gratitude until we're out of the elements, or you might be thanking me for hypothermia."

"Well, I'll die free at least," said Cyril. Then, not letting himself think, "With you."

Aristide paused. Just as he turned on the rock, about to speak, a truck came around the bend. Then another, and a third, and suddenly Ari was standing in the middle of the road, one arm thrown up to halt the oncoming caravan. Then it was haggling and hustling and the distribution of cash. Aristide hopped into the back of a van. Cyril climbed into the cab of the rear truck. He spent the ride squeezed between the driver and a woman holding an E4 Hoare submachine gun, the same model the border guards and soldiers had carried. Vintage, but kept in fine trim. The sort of thing Gedda had used in the Spice War, in his grandmother's time. The stock banged him in the ribs every time they hit a pothole.

An hour outside Dastya the convoy nearly took a mortar—the western suburbs of the city were fortified with artillery against Tatien incursion.

"Jumpy," remarked the gunner, and that was the only comment anyone made.

After that, adrenaline ate the time up, and suddenly they were at the checkpoint outside the city. Adam Wallis presented himself looking suitably battered for a man who had just made his way through an insurgency, and told them he was a war correspondent with Siebenthal's. He had no luggage to speak of—the cardboard suitcase had disappeared somewhere along the way, he hoped with nothing valuable inside of it.

"Lost my bag somewhere between Eré and Kareniv," he said. "Along with my driver. They wanted the car, and he went along. Setup. Should have known. They took my press credentials, too, and my letter of transit. Managed to keep my passport, though it's in a bit of a state."

Henson's convoy had arrived in the middle of some kind of dust-up with a group of refugees, and the document's streaky illegibility seemed low on the list of the soldier's concerns. She gave it a cursory glance. "You're lucky you didn't lose your head along with the rest of it. Luckier still you ran into Henson. She's a treasure. Staying long?"

"Only long enough to book passage. No offense meant, but I think I've had enough of this bit of the world for a while."

She snapped his passport shut so hard the pages slapped, and told him, "Have a swift trip," rather than a pleasant one.

It was late by the time Lillian got home. She had offered to drop Kostos at his flat, and then Daoud at his hotel. Magnusson was there to let her in, and offered to pour a whiskey. Remembering the empty decanter from the other night, she declined until he assured her there was half a case in the pantry. Money, or lack thereof, was never mentioned. He was simply smart enough to know her mind.

"I've got to make a call," she said. "But you can go on to bed. I won't need you anymore tonight."

"Thank you, ma'am," he said, and left her alone.

She twisted the dial, picking out Rinko's home exchange. It was past any kind of polite time to call, but time was another thing she was short on. She didn't want Kostos changing his mind, deciding she hadn't held up her end of the bargain. She wanted insurance. And she wanted to talk to a friend.

"Hello?" Disembodied, without the distraction of her immaculate presence, Rinko's voice sounded tired. Lillian glanced at the clock on her desk and cringed.

"Rinko," said Lillian. "It's me. I—"

"Lillian?" She was angry. Of course she was.

"I'm so sorry I haven't called. Or sent a check. I've been—"

"Busy of course, but you're all right?"

"Sorry?" She kept her voice low, conscious of Jinadh and Stephen asleep upstairs.

"I hadn't heard from you. And I was worried you'd been . . . oh, who knows. I don't know what I thought."

That she had disappeared into a cell, warrantless. Or something along those lines. "I'm fine. Or, not fine, but . . . I'm making my way." She picked at a loose upholstery tack on the seat of her chair. "I thought you might be cross with me."

The laughter on the other end of the line was more a sigh. "You didn't jump out the back of a prison transport and leave me standing like a fool in front of the judge."

"No, but I did put you in the situation to begin with. And I should have been in the courtroom with you." The first part was the truth; the second part was not. She had been glad not to stand there, waiting for Aristide to succeed or fail.

"I am a grown woman with a license to practice law. I agreed to take this case. And now I will tackle the consequences."

"Will you be all right? I mean, with the federal investigators, and the police, and whoever else?"

"Will you? It's a game of wait and see now, I think. They look into it, and then they come around."

"My favorite thing." Lillian put her face into her free hand. "Waiting on other people."

"Yes," said Rinko. "You are more the type to implement a plan, not to be caught up in someone else's."

A sharp edge on the sentence told Lillian it was an unasked question, something Rinko didn't want to say over the telephone. That was wise; Lillian certainly didn't trust her own line. And if she didn't want to say it, Lillian knew what it was and was equally unable to answer.

"Less and less these days," she said, instead of pleading innocence. "Lately I seem to find myself caught in the cross fire of other people's machinations more than I would like."

"Really?" Rinko didn't sound like she believed it.

"Well, I suppose I agreed to go on Laurie Kostos's *After Dinner Hour* of my own volition."

"What?" From the surprise in Rinko's voice, Lillian's tactic had worked—a distraction to move them away from a dangerous conversation toward one that might yield results.

"He asked me on to talk about recent events and I said yes. And then he . . . he asked if I might extend an invitation to you."

A long pause took years from whatever life she had left. She could almost hear the click of abacus beads as Rinko made calculations on the other end of the line. Finally, Rinko said, "You're really going to do this?"

"I have . . . significant stock invested in the interview." Lillian picked her way around the facts like they were bear traps. "Doing it of my own volition doesn't mean I'm doing it out of altruism."

"You didn't *promise* me to him, did you?"

"I said I'd do my best."

"You still owe me for those consultation fees."

Heat spread across Lillian's cheeks. "I know. I'm sorry. But this is . . . it's about . . ." She hated what she was about to say, and said it anyway. "Justice. Of a sort. The future of Gedda, if you want to be dramatic."

"Playing to my convictions?"

"No. Just telling the truth."

"I know what kind of truths you tell, Lillian. Exactly the same kind I do."

"The kind that require a convincing argument?"

Now Rinko's laugh made a real appearance, loud enough the line distorted it. "Why don't we have lunch tomorrow and you can talk me around in person? Come to mine. That way perhaps we can avoid the cameras. I look awful in candid photographs."

"I can help you with that," said Lillian.

"You'll be helping me with a lot of things until your fortunes change. I'm flexible about payment, but I don't forgive a debt. Even for a friend."

"Nor should you," said Lillian. Then, timidly, "We are, still? Friends?"

"I should hope so," said Rinko. "You're in dire need of them."

When Lillian rang off, it took her a moment to realize she wasn't alone. When she did, it took her another moment to parse the man lurking in the shadows of the doorway as her husband.

"Mother and sons," she said, hand over her pounding heart. "Jinadh, you scared me."

"And you woke me up." He came into her office and looked around for a lamp to light, which there wasn't. The overhead sconce would have been too bright, so he left them in the gloaming of distant streetlights and the city glare reflected from the clouds.

"Sorry." She swept fly-aways out of her face, wondering when her hair had begun to escape from its pins.

«I heard the last half,» he told her, settling on a corner of the desk. "Justice? The future of Gedda? And you are going on the wireless with Laurie Kostos." He grew more accusatory as he spoke. «Lillian, what are you up to? And when were you going to tell *me* about all this? Before or after you went on the radio?»

"I'm *sorry*," she said. "Really. Things are just happening so fast . . ."

«Daoud was here *yesterday*, Lillian. And you and I sleep in the same bed. You had time. I'm not a fool; I know that wasn't a social visit. And I've begun to think you left me in that courtroom knowing what would happen. What's going on?»

She sighed and put her face into her hands, unable to look at him. «You are not going to like it.»

«I didn't think I would. But I still want to know.»

Before she spoke, she made herself lift her head. «I had some idea what they were planning. Aristide and Cyril. But I was not involved. I only did not want to be here, when . . . »

«I see,» he said. «And the wireless?»

«We're breaking the story about Frye. And the tar, and the bomb at the warehouse. On Kostos's show. Tomorrow night.»

Closing his eyes, Jinadh took a deep breath and swallowed whatever he had been going to say. After a moment, he composed himself and asked, «We?»

«Qassan, really. My interview—and Rinko's, if she'll do it—that's just Kostos getting what he wants from me, because he knows how much *I* want *this*.»

«Why do you?» asked Jinadh. «Want it? Just revenge? Or has Saeger promised you something?»

«No promises. Her consideration, at most.»

Jinadh's smile finally made an appearance, only slightly tinged with rue. «Don't tell me my wife has suddenly developed a conscience.»

"If Saeger is elected," said Lillian, "maybe it will come in handy. A conscience, I mean."

Fondly, Jinadh tucked a bit of hair behind her ear. "You had some mail today."

"Magnusson didn't mention it."

"I said I would give it to you. From the look of the envelope . . . I thought it would be something we should discuss together."

Apprehension crept up the back of her neck. "The look of the envelope?"

"It looks . . . financial." He reached into the inner pocket of his dressing gown and produced a creamy envelope with an elegant gold stamp over the seal. "Or possibly legal."

She looked at it, then looked at him, and considered that it had been in his pocket all this time. "I didn't wake you. You were waiting up for me."

He shrugged. «It's hard for me to fall asleep when you aren't here. Especially when I know you're up to mischief. Open it.»

There had been a pearl-handled letter opener in this office once, but that was long gone, so she tore the envelope open with one finger and withdrew a folded sheaf of paper.

The letterhead gave her no clue—no bank or lawyer she had ever worked with. And the packet of papers was thicker than a simple invoice or angry letter would have been. She barely skimmed the body, turning instead to the next page: a table of figures.

"Securities," she said. "Apparently we now own significant shares in Lisoan real estate."

"I assume you have not been playing the markets without telling me."

"I didn't do this," she said, staring at the ledger of quarterly interest statements. The numbers wouldn't stay steady on the page. "I didn't."

"Then who?"

She knew before he finished the question. "Makricosta. Who else?" Blood money, reparations, some strange kind of dowry? What was this supposed to be?

"Your expression worries me. May I see it?"

She handed it over, feeling dizzy. "He's done this out of guilt."

Jinadh stared at the balance, face blank. "And perhaps it made him feel better. I really do not care. This money will send Stephen to school. It will make us . . . hm."

"Solvent?"

"At the least."

"Well, I suppose he *is* a sort of uncle to Stephen now. Though Queen save us if he decides to act . . . avuncular, in any way." Her hands were shaking.

Jinadh took them in his own. «Moon-eyes, I'm not sure we'll be hearing from either of them very soon.»

If ever, she thought, and began to cry.

CHAPTER

THIRTY-TWO

Cyril dropped the Adam Wallis persona with gratitude once the door to his boardinghouse room closed behind him, though he couldn't shed the exhaustion so easily. Or the chill. He couldn't remember ever being so cold, for so long. His bones felt brittle, and every muscle ached. He was starving, too; there'd been very little food or sleep over the last three days to blunt the stress and hardship.

His window looked down on a sooty, salt-crusted street, the gutter filled with butts and garbage. Beyond that the sea wall, and beyond that, fishing boats at their moorings in the oily water.

So this was the harbor Memmediv had betrayed him for. The sound of mournful bells came through the glass. Long blue evening shadows made the vista grim. Still, he supposed people had held stranger things dear.

Someone knocked on his door. "Coming," he said, and pushed back from the sill.

Aristide stood in the doorway, posture stiff and face drawn into a frown. Cyril wondered if this was Erikh Prosser's worry, which would fall away when he crossed the threshold, or if he was truly as nervous as he looked. In one fist, he held a greasy paper sack. Cyril smelled fry oil, pork fat, and cabbage.

"Come in," he said, already reaching for the food.

Ari left Prosser in the corridor, yes, but the frown came along. Once he was in the room he seemed not to know what to do with himself. The windowsills weren't deep enough to sit in, and the room had only a bed and a washstand, no chair. He hesitated in the middle of the floor, boots shifting on the bare boards. At least he looked less drawn, less bloodless. Maybe he'd already eaten. Maybe he'd just gotten drunk.

Springs squealed as Cyril sat on the edge of the bed. The open sack revealed potato dumplings, burnt at the edges and speckled with brown where they'd touched the grill. He bit into one: ground pork, cooked to gray paste with cabbage and onions. A thread of grease slid down his chin. "Your luggage came in all right?"

That settled Ari. He didn't relax, but his weight at least stopped shifting. "Delivered from one ship to the next, as promised. It will be in the cabin when we board."

"Only one cabin?"

He'd hit a tender spot, and saw Ari flinch. "There's room enough for a cot, and if you're uncomfortable with that, I'm sure we can arrange . . . it only seemed less suspicious to . . ." He trailed off, and began to shift his feet again, eyes searching for something to fix on that wasn't Cyril.

Unfortunately for him, they strayed across the surface of the washstand mirror, where Cyril snared his gaze and held it. "I don't remember that you were ever this stuck for a line, before."

To see Aristide so unsure of himself was more frightening than mortars or freezing or border control. It was more painful to see him like this than it had been to see him in full glamour, rouged and vicious, imperiously putting the prison guards into their place. His lips moved, abortive, and then he abruptly looked away. "I don't know what my cue's supposed to be."

At which point Cyril realized he had never needed one before. Aristide had always been assured of Cyril's desire. Of *everyone's* desire. He had wanted his lovers desperate, begging, at his mercy, and Cyril had obliged him on all counts.

Perhaps he didn't know how to ask, when something hadn't been offered already. Perhaps his pride made him afraid to. But any less prideful and he wouldn't be Ari.

If Cyril wanted this, then he would have to make the first move. Which meant he was faced with a decision: Did he want this? Now?

It wasn't as though he'd kept it down, in Lișo. Put people in mortal peril and what else did they do but rut? That was different, though; mechanical.

Which made him think of Lillian's first embrace, the instinct he'd quashed that said to block a strike and flip her on her back. The surge of adrenaline when anything moved at the edge of his line of sight. All his reactions were compromised by the memory of violence.

But he remembered, too—and vividly—the scratch of wool against his wrists, bound with his own necktie, one end a leash in Ari's fist. The ease there was in letting him lead, and the power there as well: He did not do as he was told because he *had* to, but because he chose to. A welcome change, in those days. And enough now, maybe, to keep him from remembering the jungle, and everything that he had done there. That had been done to him.

He raised his hand to the top button of his shirt, feeling the thickness of the looped thread, the raised edges of the horn.

"It can't be how it was," he said. "Not . . . not now, anyway. You can't hit me."

Aristide nodded, once, worried lines crimping the corners of his eyes.

The button slid stiffly out of its hole, and Cyril felt cool air on his throat. "I'm not the man I used to be, Aristide."

"Darling, you never were. Neither was I." Ari came to sit on the bed. The tortured springs objected. With a weighted elegance that spoke less of caution than of reverence, he lifted his hands to Cyril's second button. "Here. May I?"

And Cyril, breathless, let him.

It was nothing like it had been. It was . . . not better, or worse. It moved slowly, like a puzzle, or a game of chess.

Aristide undressed Cyril as he had the first night they saw so much of each other's skin: patiently, savoring. The wrapping had been more beautiful then—platinum shirt studs through starched white piqué, rather than plain horn and cotton. More layers, loops, hooks, and catches. But he took longer now, lingering, unsure of what he was allowed.

First he uncovered the familiar scar: the shining line that bisected Cyril's stomach. The one he had never asked about. He traced it with a finger, and wondered if he would dare, someday.

"You do that for all of them, we won't sail with our ship."

"Hush," said Aristide. The first command he'd ventured. He laid it down lightly, almost teasing. Cyril rewarded him with a small smile and silence.

Aristide peeled him like an apple from which he meant to carve one single, spiral ribbon. Steady, delicate, slow: teasing himself as much as anything. Cyril should have been keening by the end of it, sweat at his temples. He would have been, then. Now he had his eyes shut tight, brows furrowed, his lower lip pinned between his teeth. Half-hard, yes, but only that. And his expression belied his arousal.

Aristide paused, fingertips just touching the bare skin of Cyril's thigh. "We don't have to—"

"No," he said, curling his fingers into Aristide's waistband and pulling at the button fly. "I want you to make me forget."

So entreated, Aristide vowed to put the whores of the Prince and Temple to shame.

All those perfunctory afternoons with Daoud, all that time he had spent wishing for someone who would plead, someone who would play the power games that pleased the capricious, predatory part of him . . . it fell away and he lost himself in the taste of Cyril's skin, the smell of him, the flex of his calves as he put his heels to the mattress. Need twisted into a knot at the base of Aristide's spine, making his whole body clench and ache.

But Cyril turned his face into the pillow and said, eyes shut again, "I'm sorry. I can't . . . I just—"

"Your *hands* then," said Aristide, strangling on the words. "Queen's cunt, *please.*"

Shame vanished from Cyril's expression, swept away by shock at hearing Aristide beg. He'd surprised himself as much, and wasn't ready when Cyril sat up fast, throwing him off-balance so he fell back in turn.

Aristide had forgotten how, when Cyril's pupils widened with desire, they left only a fine ring of frosted blue like creeping ice at the edge of a black pond. Or, as they hung above him now, with the reflection of the bedside lamp bright in their center: like the white ring around the moon on a cold night before snow.

One of Cyril's hands pressed into the center of his chest, weight pinning him to the complaining mattress. He wet two fingers of the other with his mouth and then—

Aristide made a sound he might have been embarrassed of, under any other circumstance. After that, it was all over rather quickly. And that, too, might have embarrassed him. But not tonight.

Sated now, but remembering the sudden bloom of lust in those bright blue eyes, Aristide reached between Cyril's legs. Nothing, still.

Rolling over, Cyril put his arm across his face, looking as ashamed as Aristide should feel. "I'm sorry," he said again, less desperately this time.

"Shh." Aristide stretched out beside him, luxuriating in his own nakedness against someone else's skin. Against, miraculously, *this* skin. With as much wonder as he now traced the ridge of Cyril's hipbone, he said, "There will be other times. Plenty of them."

Cyril glared from the crook of his elbow. "If you don't drop dead first, old man."

"I'm not even sixty," he protested.

"With the lives we've led, that's quite an age."

"Well then," said Aristide, and leaned in to kiss him. Deeply, as he had not kissed anyone for years. "We'd best rick our hay before the rains."

The wind picked up, past midnight. Something in Cyril's deep memory of the place said *rain*, though still a long way off. Nights like this in late winter and early spring, he remembered the smell of damp sweeping across the plains from the sea. But despite the draft, tucked beneath the blankets Cyril finally felt warm.

They laid in silence for a time, listening to the loose panes of glass rattle in their frame. Aristide, beside the wall, lifted one hand to scratch at a chip in the paint.

"Small lies," he said. "Do you promise?"

Cyril tucked his chin. "Mm-hm." Even without a segue, it didn't catch him off guard. The hour was right for confessions, skin pressed on skin in the dark.

There was a pause in which it seemed Ari had chosen not to speak. Then, after too long, he said, "You got the letter. Why didn't you come?"

"I tried to. But . . . I was afraid of Lourdes. I thought he would lead them to you."

"So you killed him." Aristide said it so reasonably, made it sound as simple as it had been in that moment: a hard decision made in haste, the only possible outcome. "I read it in the paper. I . . . stopped reading papers, shortly thereafter."

"It wasn't my first choice," said Cyril. "I didn't go there to shoot him."

"Then why did you?"

His own stupidity was so much harder to bear in retrospect. He imagined it would grow harder every year, until it or he passed some critical point that made the whole thing seem humorous. A critical point he would never have reached, if not for the man whose elbow was currently pressed into his ribs.

"I was going to send him after you," said Cyril. "I even took a bottle of peroxide for his hair, so he would match the papers."

"What went wrong?"

"Me."

Aristide waited for him to go on, fingers making a cage over the hem of the blanket.

"I—I had seen the name on the visa and I didn't trust myself to keep my teeth shut."

"Cordelia used to say it just like that."

Her name conjured a warmth in Cyril's chest that had lain dormant too long. But like blood returning to a senseless limb, it was agony. "Can you imagine? I told her she ought to pitch in with the Ospies. Said she'd make a good fox."

"She would have." Ari laughed, or almost. "Rather say, she did. You propped up the Ospies, in your way. But she tripped them and they stumbled down."

"You said you saw her. After you left. Before she died."

"Long story," said Aristide, and when Cyril began to protest he put one hand up and said, "which I'll be happy to tell, sometime. But the last I saw of *you*, you were waving a snubby around her dressing room and looking like someone had peeled you off their shoe. How in perdition did you get from there to an Orriba slum?"

"Who told you it was Orriba?"

"Asiyah. Said the hounds brought you in on a drunk and disorderly, and you gave them a false name. Paul—"

"Darling," said Cyril. "A stupid work name. Sentimental. That's the kind of thing that gets you caught."

"I know." He stared into dead space. "I couldn't help it."

"You could have," said Cyril. "You just like being clever. It'll get you into trouble."

"Orriba, Cyril. How—?"

"A friend of yours, actually." Not that he had known it at the time. Not like she knew him. How she'd recognized him, busted like an overripe fruit, and only from the description on a set of false papers . . . "Same friend who let you put that stupid name on my visa."

"Zelda Peronides? How—?"

"I stowed away," said Cyril. It wasn't the whole truth. He'd hauled himself onto the first boat with a ladder in the bay and let the world go black around him. He'd woken hours later in the grip of a thug, to the sound of a motor and water breaking on the hull. But he was allowed small lies. "She was turning tail. Got out of the city with the skin on her bones and not a lot besides. Had some bruiser named Marto with her. After the swelling went down, she clocked me. Said I was a roto print of some actor named Solomon Flyte, if he'd taken a few good slugs to the face."

Ari looked like he was trying not to be sick, but Cyril pressed on. "We were halfway to Agrakoti by then. And I was in no shape to hunt after you. By the time we made landfall and I caught up on the news, I . . . I didn't really want to."

"I wish you had."

"No you don't. I was a midden heap walking."

"You still are."

"Stroll off."

When Aristide's arms tightened around him his first instinct was panic—he was trapped and strangling, snared—but then Aristide spoke into his ear.

"Never again."

The sound of that familiar purr, crackling now with smoke and age, told him he was safe, and brought him home.

Aristide woke up in the early morning to the grumble of thunder. It was not the first time he had woken—Cyril had never been an easy bedfellow, and was less so now. Still, every time a cry or jerk tore Aristide from sleep, he remembered where he was and with whom and felt amazed all over again. And so he didn't mind.

This time, it was not one of Cyril's nightmares that woke him. Dawn had crept, indistinct, into the sky. An early spring storm battered the window with sheets of rain. Cyril was gone from beside him and sitting half naked on the foot of the bed, twisting the tuning dial on the radio.

Quietly, without moving, Aristide watched his reflection in the sideboard mirror: his concentration and economy of movement. The shift of small muscles beneath scarred skin. He did not fidget, didn't pause when he came across a station playing an old song by Marcel Langhorn. He looked grave and focused, brows drawn down over his newly crooked nose. Everything about him had changed, it seemed, except that livid scar across his stomach.

Then a piece of shaggy hair fell across his forehead and he jerked his chin, tossing it out of his eyes.

No knife had ever plunged so deep.

"What are you looking for?" asked Aristide, and saw him jump but clamp down on the reflex. A shudder of skin like a horse scaring flies.

"The news," he said, voice so even that his tic might have been a figment of Aristide's imagination. "From Gedda."

"Good luck finding a signal." Aristide sat up, dragging the blankets with him. Despite himself, he was interested. They were nearly out of any kind of danger now, but it might be good to know what kind of silt they had kicked up behind them.

"You can usually get it," said Cyril, "or at least, you used to be able to. And transmitters are better now. Though the weather—ah, wait. That was it."

Silence as he moved the dial by millimeters. The static and the rain became one sound. Then, out of the white noise, a garbled, shushing voice. It grew stronger as Cyril fine-tuned the dial.

"—claims are still unsubstantiated. But Qassan's close association with the company adds credence to his story. Here he is speaking to FWAC's Laurie Kostos on last night's *After Dinner Hour.*"

"Well," said Cyril. "It's not what I was—"

"Hush." Aristide sat forward, bare feet on the cold floor.

"You're saying Makricosta tried to blackmail Emmeline Frye to save DePaul from the tribunals she'd proposed?" Laurie Kostos might not think he had a radio voice, but it was certainly unmistakable, even with a weak signal. "And this is why she blew her own warehouse and blamed it on the Catwalk."

Cyril, face still close to the radio, slid his eyes in Aristide's direction. Aristide feigned intense concentration on the broadcast.

"I am." In contrast to Kostos, Aristide almost didn't recognize Daoud. If they hadn't introduced him by his surname, if the story wasn't so familiar . . . his voice sounded deeper, and Aristide wasn't sure if it was the airwaves or an affectation. Resignation no longer colored his words, nor spite. He sounded sure of himself, unburdened by misgivings. "In addition to acting as Mr. Makricosta's secretary, we were engaged in a . . . personal relationship, and so I was privy to information beyond the scope of Cross-Costa's business. That warehouse exploded shortly after Aristide approached Frye, and it held large quantities of Lisoan poppy tar that Cross-Costa had entrusted to WCRC, our primary Geddan shipping partner. That was not a terrorist attack. That was retribution."

Cyril switched the set off and stared at him. Digging deep, Aristide summoned a trace of the man Malcolm Sailer had put behind a microphone. It powered one saucy shrug, and a "Don't say I never did anything sweet for you, spicecake."

It didn't make Cyril smile, but it melted some of the ice out of his expression.

"I'm almost proud of him," said Aristide, swaddling himself more tightly in the displaced bedclothes. "I wouldn't have thought he'd have the nerve."

"Perhaps he finally lost patience with you," Cyril said. "You can be unbearably vexing."

"Yes, but usually he just puts up with it." Aristide paused. "Put up. Past tense."

"Well." Cyril stood and stretched, checked the clock. "You can be damned sure I won't. Get dressed. We've got a ship to catch."

CHAPTER

THIRTY-THREE

Kostos walked Lillian out of the Icepick and flagged down a cab. He even tried to pay her fare.

"Please," she said. "It's not necessary."

He waved her off. "Company funds. Let the boss slather on a little, will you? This whole interview racket is bringing in bread and cheese and he couldn't be happier."

"In that case, thank you." She could still be gracious, even if she felt like she'd been peeled raw.

"No, thank you. That was a rotten aria in there. An eleven o'clock song and it's only just gone nine."

It felt long past midnight, and her patience with Kostos had been worn thin by an hour of invasive questions: Her childhood with Cyril; had they gotten along? What about their parents? Why did she think he had done what he did? How had she felt when she thought he was dead? When she learned he had survived? What were her thoughts on the proposed tribunals? Who had she supported before Frye put forward the idea? After? What about now, given the allegations against Frye? Had she known Aristide Makricosta well? What about Lehane?

She had answered, mostly, with honesty. It would do Cyril no harm now, and might even help. She had tried to keep the focus on the upcoming election—Sacred arches, only three weeks away!—subtly underlining Saeger's suitability as a candidate without explicitly giving her support. The official endorsement of a DePaul wasn't a burden Saeger needed to bear right now, even with her numbers ticking steadily up. An independent federal commission had begun to unearth some unsavory facts about the bombing at Frye's warehouse, and the police response to it, and with every new revelation, Saeger gained in the polls.

Kostos caught Lillian at her tactics each time. He brought the questions back around to her brother, her family, and the sticky strings that tied them to the Ospies, the Catwalk, civil war. It was an hour of parry and failed riposte, fighting not to give ground and failing. She felt exhausted, as if she had really been on the strip.

"Who's your next victim?" she asked.

"We're gonna fill a couple slots with university folk and expert commentators while we work on this," he said. "Any news from Higata?"

"She may come around to it," said Lillian. "But she's busy setting up a practice. I'm not sure when she'll have the time."

"She tell you to say that? Or you come up with it on your own?"

"I'm afraid it's the truth," said Lillian. "I seem to be telling a lot of that tonight."

The cabby, still idling at the curb, cleared her throat.

"Sorry," said Lillian, dropping into the seat. Kostos tipped his hat and shut the door on her.

Spring had made faint inroads in the city. Rain had melted most of the snow, except where it had been shoveled into truly giant heaps. Forsythia bloomed along the fencerows of Loendler Park. Some optimistic crocuses were creeping from the earth: feathery green leaves, and here and there a blossom baiting the frost.

In front of number twenty-four on Coral Street, there was still a bevy of reporters. Now that she'd let one draw first blood, she wondered if the others would tear in harder or perhaps back off.

This time she was prepared to meet them and didn't steer the cabbie around the back. But she wasn't prepared to take any more questions tonight, so she sorted through her masks and chose the one that made her unapproachable while still inviting empathy. A proud angle to the chin, but soft around the mouth and eyes.

Outside the cab, the street was chaos. If the neighbors didn't already despise her, the flashbulbs would certainly do it. She walked through it like the Wandering Queen through a mountain gale, toward the front door, which opened for her. Magnusson stood framed at the top of the steps, in his impeccable necktie and tails. He'd been waiting by the front window, no doubt. Probably with a pulpy novel on his knee.

Maybe that was why he stayed on with her—never a dull moment in the DePaul household. It was near as he could come to living like Rita Ryder.

"Thank you," she said, as he closed the door against the crowd outside. Their questions faded into a disappointed murmur beyond the stained-glass panels of the vestibule.

"Not at all."

"Dinner?"

"There's a plate kept warm for you. And, ma'am, if you have time tomorrow, I received several notices of interest from qualified cooks. With excellent references."

"Of course," she said. "I would be delighted to speak with them."

The staff wouldn't grow much beyond that, for now, but thanks to Makricosta's largesse she could at least take the burden of feed-ing the family off Magnusson's back. If she or Jinadh had ever tried, they'd have set number twenty-four on fire. Like talking about money, she had not been raised to feel at home in the kitchen.

Magnusson took her coat and scarf. "Mr. Addas is in the library with Stephen. I regret that I cannot attend to drinks, but—"

She flapped a hand. "You have plenty to do. I can pour a tum-bler of whiskey myself."

"Of course, ma'am." And then he was gone, and she was off to find her family.

The radio was turned to a station conspicuously different from the one she had just spoken on, playing a bit of—oh, she'd always been bad at composers, but it sounded like Innevin. Soft piano music in three-four time.

"Good evening, gentlemen," she said, collapsing onto the sofa be-side Jinadh. He put his arm around her shoulders and squeezed her, briefly. Enough that she knew the change of station had only occurred after she spoke. He had heard every word of it.

"Any good news?" she asked. "I don't want to hear the other stuff."

"Beastie?" Jinadh stretched out one leg to jostle Stephen's foot. He was sprawled across the rug, reading a comic book. Now that his exams were over he'd returned to less academic fare.

"Oh, yeah." He sat up and snatched something from the end table. "This came."

Lillian took the envelope from him—torn hastily at the top, which meant Jinadh had let him open it. The Cantrell seal at the flap told her what it was, and if it was good news . . .

Dear Ms. DePaul and Mr. Addas,

    We are pleased to inform you that your son, Stephen DePaul, has, after due consideration, been readmitted to The Youth Academy at Cantrell.

It went on in the same vein, with instructions for payment, registration, and the beginning of classes. Payment she could make, again thanks to Makricosta. All she had traded him was her only brother.

Cyril had always been a hassle. A nightmare. A mess in need of sweeping, mopping, tidying up. But in that, he had been dependable. A constant. A foil she could always count on. Guilt made her chest ache. Was that really all she had used him for? Was that the only reason she would miss him? Because without him she had no way to downplay her own flaws?

No. But it was the reason that occurred to her first, because of what their parents had made them. And what she had made herself.

But their parents had not prepared them for this Gedda—the Ospies, the war, the chaos in its wake. Their lessons and their expectations had to be set aside. Maybe now, Lillian could simply miss Cyril as a sister missed a brother she would never see again.

Under the guise of a headache, she pressed the heels of her palms to her eyes. If she used the motion to wipe away tears, she was practiced at hiding it. When she blinked her vision clear, she saw Stephen flopped back onto the floor, nose buried in the three-color adventures of—

"What's that you're reading?" she asked, proud that her voice didn't quaver.

Stephen rolled his eyes at her and said, "Mind your own."

Her first instinct was a sharp rebuke, but she caught it before it flew. He reminded her of Cyril, yes. But she wouldn't treat him the way Cyril had been treated. He wasn't her legacy; he was her son.

She poked his belly with her toe, and when he scowled and rolled away she said, "Believe me, I am."

The *Ao Hinso* was not what Cyril had expected. The passageways smelled of mold and fermented cabbage, and the cramped cabin would never have fit a cot. At least there was a porthole, which they kept open when the weather held. Brine and diesel blew in on the breeze. Cyril thought of the Alain de Nils perfume he'd streaked across Cordelia's wrist so long ago, and the glittering party where they'd encountered Aristide, his eyes done up in kohl.

The memory contrasted sharply with their current circumstances.

They'd been on the *Ao Hinso* nearly a week now, and its shabbiness had grown familiar, almost comforting. Besides, Cyril had lived with much worse.

But Aristide had chosen this. So when Cyril was first confronted with their second-rate surroundings, he'd observed them in surprise and said, "It doesn't seem very . . ." then waved a hand rather than find a word.

"Chic?" asked Ari. "No. But it's what we can afford and still avoid fleas."

"Afford? Aren't you some kind of criminal tycoon?"

Ari opened a piece of his luggage, which occupied most of the room, and located his cigarette case and lighter. Purple enamel, golden braid. Cyril remembered wanting to lick the gleaming lighter in his stuffy Lisoan safe house, amazed something so beautiful could still exist.

The memory recalled a more recent one: the taste of the tender skin beneath Ari's jaw. The metallic tang of his sweat.

Ari lit a straight and savored it, eyes closed. "Not anymore."

Cyril took a straight from the case, too, and plucked the lighter from Aristide's fingertips, startling him from his contemplation.

"I wasn't being facetious when I said you'd bankrupt your sister. And me, too. A lot of it went to Frye's campaign; I was trying to set her up as a sort of puppet, I suppose. Lillian will get a little bit of it, and the rest went to pay our way out of that wreck." He gestured eloquently with his cigarette, indicating Gedda, though by Cyril's reckoning he was actually pointing northeast. "There's enough to get us where we're going, and a house to live in once we're there. And what I do have will go further than it might elsewhere."

"Mother and sons, we aren't going back to Liso, are we? I know they owe me a pension but I'd rather—"

"No, no." Aristide waved smoke from his face. "After Daoud's little sojourn into radio journalism, my manger there is well and truly shat-upon. Cross would probably hire a hit man the moment she heard I was back in the country. Perhaps you can collect that living from abroad?"

"Really," said Cyril. "Where are we going?"

Ari took another drag and his eyes lost their cynical squint. A little of that old emcee's lyricism came into his voice: Central City cream poured over stagefolk charm.

"There's a bungalow," he said. "On a red sand beach in Ishin Sao. I should have sold it years ago, but . . . It's just outside a village, on a road that will take you to Oizhan if you've got bus fare or a motorbike."

"You've been there?"

"No," he admitted, smiling ruefully. "But the letting agent told me it was quiet, lovely, close enough to the city for comfort, but far enough there won't be tourists wandering the streets. A few folk from around the world, but largely locals."

"It could be a midden heap."

"It's not," said Aristide, with the peaceful conviction of a martyr.

"Still, I wager we won't be lighting up absinthe at any mirrored bars." Not that he was particularly eager to reenter that world. Only that it was the one he knew; the one he could place Aristide within. Beyond the confines of the Foxhole and the Bee, he didn't know who they were to one another.

Aristide snorted. "I only ever drank it on fire because it made a good show for the punters. And besides, Malcolm served cheap absinthe. You shouldn't light up something good. Shouldn't even add a sugar cube." The sibilance of the Central City lingered on his palate, and his wrist beneath the cigarette grew languid.

Perhaps it wasn't all gone, after all. "Will you do it now?" asked Cyril.

Aristide raised an eyebrow. They were thicker now, and had started to get ragged at the edges during the trek across Tatié. But the angle was familiar. Cyril, filled with sudden daring, kissed the apex of its arch.

"The stutter," he said, his lips close to Ari's skin.

"D-D-Darling." Aristide pulled back and stared him in the eyes. "I'm sure I d-d-don't know what you mean."

ABOUT THE AUTHOR

LARA ELENA DONNELLY is a graduate of the Clarion Writers' Workshop, as well as the Alpha SF/F/H Workshop for Young Writers, where she is now a volunteer staff member. She is the author of the Amberlough Dossier, beginning with the Nebula and Lambda Award–nominated *Amberlough*. At present she resides in Harlem, with a cheesemonger-slash-filmmaker. Her neighbors are Alexander Hamilton and the Royal Tenenbaums.

laradonnelly.com
@larazontally